THE TRUTH WE HIDE

THE TRUTH WE HIDE

A Homefront Mystery

Liz Milliron

Level Best Books

Historia

First published by Level Best Books/Historia 2023

Copyright © 2023 by Liz Milliron

All rights reserved. No part of this publication may be reproduced, stored or transmitted in any form or by any means, electronic, mechanical, photocopying, recording, scanning, or otherwise without written permission from the publisher. It is illegal to copy this book, post it to a website, or distribute it by any other means without permission.

This novel is entirely a work of fiction. The names, characters and incidents portrayed in it are the work of the author's imagination. Any resemblance to actual persons, living or dead, events or localities is entirely coincidental.

Liz Milliron asserts the moral right to be identified as the author of this work.

First edition

ISBN: 978-1-68512-313-0

Cover art by Level Best Designs

This book was professionally typeset on Reedsy. Find out more at reedsy.com

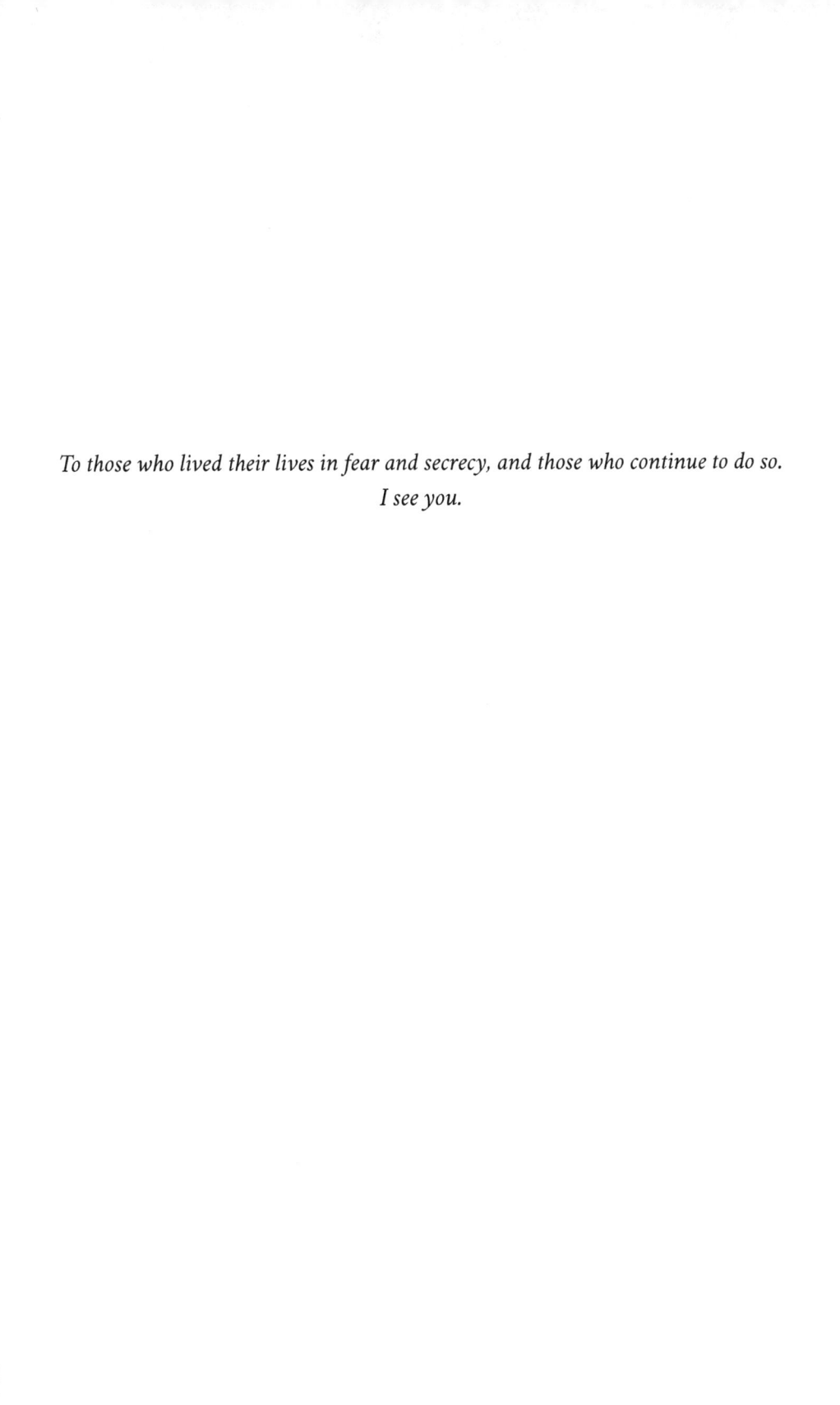

*To those who lived their lives in fear and secrecy, and those who continue to do so.
I see you.*

Praise for The Truth We Hide

"Budding private investigator Betty Ahern takes on a new case that has her questioning her own belief system and prejudices in this charming, thought-provoking, and impeccably researched historical mystery set in World War II era Buffalo. This superbly crafted mystery provides the perfect entry point to Milliron's Home Front Mysteries."—Edwin Hill, author of *The Secrets We Share*

"In *The Truth We Hide*, Milliron captures the snappy pace of 1940s P. I. thrillers with sharp dialogue and delicious period detail. Unlike most detective fiction of the time, she explores the homophobia embedded in the period and in her layered protagonist, Betty Ahern. Will Betty see past her upbringing to acceptance? It's the mystery underneath the mystery of this engaging novel."—John Copenhaver, award-winning author of *The Savage Kind*

Chapter One

May 1943

Truth is a funny thing. People make a big deal about it. When folks are in court, they swear to tell the truth, the whole truth, and nothing but the truth. The Bible tells us "the truth will set you free." Even Superman came to fight for truth, justice, and the American way. Yet with all that, people seem to go out of their way to avoid the truth, 'specially if it's inconvenient, uncomfortable, or downright dangerous. Unfortunately for them, the truth will out, as my grandma used to say. And when it does, well, you'd better know how to duck and cover.

I sat in a booth at Teddy's Diner, facing the door so I could watch people come and go. It wasn't quite noon on a Monday. The remains of my lunch—a fried baloney sandwich on white bread—sat in front of me, along with a thick white diner mug of black coffee and a slice of apple pie. I glanced out the window, my subconscious telling me I should be somewhere else. I hadn't yet gotten used to not being at Bell Aircraft on a weekday, where I'd worked building P-39s. It had been hard turning in my resignation at Bell. But Pop convinced me that if I was serious about becoming a private detective, I needed to devote all my time to finishing the PI correspondence course to get my license.

The diner was my office. My best friend, Lee Tillotson, talked to me a couple of days ago. We agreed to meet so he could introduce a potential client, but they hadn't shown yet. Now that spring had arrived for good, folks had shed winter coats and scarves, but I wouldn't have a problem spotting Lee. His trademark newsboy cap and limp, courtesy of a childhood tire swing dare gone wrong, made him stand out no matter the weather. The bells over the door jingled, and I looked up. Still no Lee.

The waitress came by to refresh my joe. I pulled the plate of pie closer. As I did, I turned the diamond on my left hand so it caught the light. But it refused to sparkle the way it normally did. I ate a few mouthfuls of pie. Despite the cinnamon-flavored goodness, it sat like a lump in my stomach.

I'd eaten the last bite and licked the juice from the fork when the bells chimed again. This time, it was Lee and an older man. Lee took off his cap and ran his hand through his sandy hair. He spotted me and nudged his companion. Lee led him to my table. "What's shakin' Betty? This is Edward Kettle. He's the client I told you about."

Mr. Kettle frowned. A shock of dirty blond hair flopped over piercing blue eyes. He was prob'ly in his early forties, face lined from a lifetime of squinting and he stood just a smidge taller than Lee. His working man's clothes covered a body that was neither fat nor thin. He brushed his hair aside with a well-callused hand. The rough skin, dirt embedded in his cuticles, and the clothes said this was a man who'd done manual labor for most of his adult life. He turned to Lee. "I thought you were taking me to see a private detective who could help me."

Lee pointed to the seat. "It's all jake. Edward, this is Betty Ahern. She's a friend of mine."

Edward held out a hand. "Miss Ahern. I'm sorry. I was under the impression you were a professional. I don't mean any offense. But I don't think you're the right person for me to talk to."

I grasped his mitt, feeling the sandpaper-like skin. "None taken." *A little taken.* "Please sit down, Mr. Kettle." I closed my textbook and put it beside me.

"Call me Edward."

I pointed at the seat opposite. "Sure thing. Take a load off." He didn't budge, and I added, "Maybe I can help you, maybe I can't. But I won't know until you tell me what your problem is."

CHAPTER ONE

Lee bumped him again. "Edward, I told you. Betty is square. Don't be fooled by the textbook. She may not have a license yet, but I'd take her over any private dick in the city. She saved my bacon last March."

Edward arched an eyebrow. "This is the girl who found your dad's killer?"

"Yep. She's pals with a homicide detective, too." Lee gave up on making his buddy sit and slid into the booth. "Coffee, milk and sugar, and a slice of cherry pie if it's fresh," he said to the waitress who appeared at the table.

I'd worked with Detective Sam MacKinnon of the Buffalo police to solve the murder of Lee's father last March. My success there had kept Lee, who only let his mother call him by his Christian name of Liam, outta prison. After that, he threw his name into the group of people who supported my career change. 'Course he'd directly benefitted from my inability to mind my own business, so it wasn't surprising.

"Baked this morning." The waitress jotted Lee's order and turned to Edward. "What about you, honey? You gonna sit and order or not? If not, you gotta move. You're in the way."

He hesitated, then slid in next to Lee. "Just coffee, thanks. Black." He barely smiled at her.

"Be right back." She winked and left.

I took out a notepad and pencil, flipped to a clean sheet, and looked at my prospective client. "It's true I don't have my PI license yet. That doesn't mean I don't have experience and I can't help you. Tell you what. You describe the problem you've got, and I'll let you know if it's too big for me. Deal?"

The waitress returned with two mugs of coffee and a slice of cherry pie that oozed syrup. She set the joe in front of the men and handed Lee the plate. "Anything else, you just holler."

Lee splashed some milk and sugar into his mug and lifted a forkful of pie. "Go on. Tell her. You said it yourself. It's not like anybody else is gonna help."

"That much is true." Edward blew on his coffee and added some milk. "All right. I work for American Shipbuilding Company. How much do you know about the project currently happening down on the lakeshore, just south of Buffalo?"

"About as much as anybody else in the city." I leaned back. The anthill of activity over the past months had made it clear *something* big was going on. But the armed Coast Guardsmen had done a good job of keeping the nosey Parkers away. All anybody knew was that American Shipbuilding had a big project. While I waited for a response, I lit a cigarette and took a drag.

Edward nodded. "Then not much." He paused. "The fact is, we've been working on a big job for the government to support the war."

I held up a hand. "Stop right there. I don't wanna hear any official secrets. I don't do that kind of work."

"I wasn't going to say anything specific. It's enough that you know the project is big and for Uncle Sam. Although everybody will know in a few days at most." He took a sip. "I've worked on it since the beginning, which was last year. A couple of weeks ago, they caught a reporter from the local press sniffing around. He wasn't from the *Courier-Express*. It's some paper named *The Daily*. A real rag, from what I hear. Nazis next door, mobsters downtown, a lot of sensationalism, not a lot of facts."

I twiddled my pencil. "Tabloid press."

"You got it." Edward took another sip. "The Coast Guard ran him off, and nobody said anything about it. Two days ago, he ran a story about our project. It wasn't very factual, but it did contain a couple of nuggets that were true and not things the general public could have figured out."

"Such as?" I didn't read the tabloid papers. Pop, a dedicated *Courier-Express* man, would have skinned me alive for bringing trash like that into the house.

"They said the ships we're building were going to be used in the Pacific, as weapons against the Japanese. The story also said the ships were equipped with a new feature that would put American vessels way ahead of the enemy." He paused. "The first statement is only sort of true. But the second, well, let's just say it's closer to the truth than the company bigwigs want it to be. Naturally, they started looking for the leak."

I'd said I didn't want to know any government secrets and I meant it, so I ignored that part of the story. "Let me guess. They landed on you and you were fired."

He exhaled, peepers fixed on his java. "I protested, of course, but the head

CHAPTER ONE

office needed a scapegoat. I'm it."

Lee polished off the last of his pie. "Why would they fix on you?"

"The way I heard it, someone said he saw me talking to the reporter as I was leaving the shipyard a couple of days before the story broke." Edward picked up his mug, then set it down.

"Did you?" I asked.

He nodded. "The guy waylaid me as I was coming out. He asked a ton of questions, and all I told him was no comment."

"Did the story quote you?"

"No. Inside sources, no names…you know the drill."

I did. On the surface, it sounded like Edward got a bum rap. But why? Being seen with a tabloid reporter struck me as flimsy. "That doesn't answer Lee's question. Why accuse you? Why not some other guy?"

He squirmed in his seat. "What do you mean?"

Maybe it was my imagination, but Edward got a shifty look in his eyes. I glanced at Lee, who gave me the teeniest frown. "A tabloid writer wouldn't corner one joe out of what, dozens who work at the shipyard? Hundreds? He'd talk to as many as he could, 'specially if he was an eager beaver, and I bet most of 'em are." I tilted my head. "But the brass specifically fingered you. Who doesn't like you, and what's the reason?"

There was no imagining it. Edward refused to meet my gaze. "I don't know what you're talking about. I've been at American Shipbuilding for a couple of years. No one has ever complained about my…my work." His foot beat a rapid tattoo against the floor, and he clammed up quick.

I stared at him. Sam told me once that silence was a great tool in an interrogation. People didn't like being quiet. The chapter in my private investigator course about questioning suspects gave me the same advice. I waited.

Sure enough, before more than a minute had gone by, he broke. "Aren't you going to ask any more questions?"

"No, I think I've got enough dope to know the situation."

He turned to Lee. "I'm supposed to take her seriously?"

Lee stayed calm. "I've seen Betty solve cases with less info than you gave her."

Edward shook his head. "I'm trusting you, Lee. Don't make me regret it." He returned his gaze to me. "We've talked. I don't think I said much, but it's up to you. Do you want to take my case or not?"

I was pretty certain Edward wasn't being completely truthful. Normally, I'd tell him to pound salt for lying, but something about him intrigued me. He didn't wear a wedding band, but he'd not given the waitress, a cutie who gave Judy Garland a run for her money, more than a tentative smile despite the fact the girl beamed right at him. He felt gentle, his language precise and educated, even though I was pretty sure a guy working as a manual laborer at a shipyard hadn't gone to college. I'd take his case just 'cause he was a little bit of a puzzle. "I'll look into it."

"How much?"

This was the part I hadn't looked forward to. Talking money. The correspondence course hadn't been much help. I couldn't charge ordinary folks what I'd asked Lee's lawyer to pay last March, nor could I afford to charge peanuts, not if I hoped to make a living. "Fifty bucks for the week, plus expenses. If the case takes longer than that, it's fifteen dollars a day, again, plus expenses. Does that sound fair?"

Edward thought a moment. "Deal." He took two twenties and a ten out of his wallet and handed them over. Then he reached across the table, took my pad and pencil, and scribbled a phone number. "That's the number at my boarding house. If you need to reach me. I'd prefer it if you don't just drop by. Call, and I'll meet you. This diner is convenient."

I shot a covert look at Lee, who didn't look surprised. I'd expected Edward to have to go to the bank first. The bills were not crisp, but they'd still spend. Who carried that kind of cabbage around with him? "Where do you live?"

"I'd rather not say."

He was either an intensely private person, or he was hiding something. I'd talk to Sam and see if he'd give me the skinny on my client. I didn't object to working for a convict, but it'd be nice to know. I held out my hand. "Well then, Mr. Kettle. You've got yourself a deal."

Chapter Two

Edward left. Another waitress, not the Judy Garland look-alike, came and topped off our coffee mugs. "How do you know Edward Kettle?" I asked Lee.

Again, he added milk and a spoonful of sugar into his mug, turning the contents a dark caramel color. "He's a friend of a friend."

"From GM?" Lee worked at General Motors. I wasn't that surprised one of his pals would know a guy from the shipyard. Heck, for all I knew, American Shipbuilding bought Allison engines from GM, same as Bell Aircraft for their planes.

Lee tried to take a drink, but the coffee must have been extra hot 'cause he set it down before he got more than a teeny sip. "Harvey, that's my friend from work, introduced us a couple of weeks ago. I saw him again the other night. I'd gone out for a beer with the guys, and Edward was at the bar. They got to talking about whatever happened at the shipyard and how Edward had really gotten the short end of the stick. He mentioned how he'd have to hire someone to make it square, and that's when your name came up. I said I'd make the introduction, but it'd be your call. What did you think of him?"

Steam curled off my java and I wrapped my hands around the thick ceramic, enjoying the warmth. Spring wasn't so far along in Buffalo, and there was a definite nip in the air, even if the mercury said it was over forty degrees. "He's...interesting."

Lee appeared puzzled. "What do you mean?"

"There's something he isn't telling me. Oh, not about his situation. I think he came clean about that." I took a drink.

"What do you mean?" Lee tested his coffee.

"Did you see his expression when I asked why someone would frame him? He wouldn't look at me." I tapped my diner mug. "Just like when I asked Michael if he'd left the milk on the counter overnight. It's not a good sign when your client lies to you right from the off." Michael was one of my younger brothers and a terrible liar. My other brother, Jimmy, wasn't much better. They overdid the act. And they wondered why our mother never bought their protestations of innocence.

"But you took his case."

"He interests me. I didn't get the impression he's a crook or anything like that. But he didn't tell me everything. Could be it has nothing to do with his situation." I took a gulp of coffee. "It'll come out."

Lee shrugged. "He seems like a good guy to me. Lousy at darts, good at pool. Harvey vouched for him, and Harve's a straight-arrow if there ever was one. He wouldn't get mixed up with someone shady."

"At least Mr. Kettle didn't haggle about the cabbage." I checked the wall clock. It was only one-thirty. There was plenty of time to stop at police headquarters and talk to Sam. "I gotta wonder where he got it though, since he's outta work. Does he come from a family with dough?" Eddie was a working man's name. Edward, that was refined.

"I don't know, but he paid for a whole round of drinks the night we met. I mean, that was before he got canned, but even afterward, he didn't have any trouble payin' his tab at the bar. If his family is one of the swells, it might explain why he had all the cash on him." Lee shot me a look out of the corner of his eye. "Have you heard from Tom lately?"

I thought of the diamond that refused to sparkle. "Nah. It's too soon." I'd written my fiancé, Tom Flannery, a letter telling him about my switch in careers. I hadn't heard anything from him. Realistically, I knew I couldn't possibly get an answer yet. Tom was with the 1st Armored Division, currently somewhere in North Africa, or so I gathered from the newspapers. It had not even been six weeks since I'd sent my note. Logic played no part in my imagination, though. The longer I went without Tom's answer, the more I feared he would tell me a young lady had no place bein' a private

CHAPTER TWO

detective, 'specially his wife, and I'd best get my butt back out to Wheatfield where I belonged. At least for the duration of the war.

I shook my head. *Stop bein' silly. Tom loves you, and he'd never stand in the way of your dreams.*

I hoped. *Keep tellin' yourself that.*

"He might have sent you a letter before that." Lee smoothed out a napkin. "You told him about studying for your private detective license, didn't you?"

"I did." I fixed Lee with a stare. "Did you get V-mail from him?"

"Nope." His coffee had cooled, and he took a gulp. "I promise, Betty, we aren't talking behind your back. I was curious, that's all."

The idea of Tom and his best friend exchanging letters shouldn't make me nervous. After all, Lee knew how important detective work was to me, and he supported my decision to get a license one hundred percent. How could he do anything less after I'd bailed him out over his dad? Yet I was antsy. I shook myself. *Stop borrowing trouble. Deal with it when, and if, it comes.*

"What are you gonna do now?"

I startled. But then I realized Lee wasn't asking about Tom. "I figured I'd go see Sam. I want to know if Edward is hiding a criminal record or anything. If he is, that could explain why he's so skittish. And why they'd pin this leak at the shipyard on him."

* * *

From Teddy's, I took a bus downtown to the corner of Franklin and Church Streets. Once there, I stood and stared at the spire of Saint Joseph's Cathedral. Behind me, the Erie County Courthouse loomed, gray and sedate in the early afternoon sunshine. The grass in front of it was the fresh, light green of new growth, and the trees were finally showing tiny buds. April snowstorms were not uncommon in Buffalo, but it seemed as though spring was digging in to stay. The breeze off the lake had switched from biting cold to slightly crisp, and I could see birds pecking the grass. I wasn't close enough to tell if they were robins, those harbingers of warm weather, but they weren't seagulls either.

I turned and went inside. The desk sergeant was one I'd seen before. I went to him. "Good afternoon, I'm here to see—"

He held up a hand. "Detective MacKinnon, I know. Hold on a moment." He lifted a phone and spoke, then set the blower down and pointed to a bench. "He'll be right down. Have a seat over there."

I moseyed over and sat. While I waited, I flipped through the meager notes I'd taken at my meeting with Edward. He hadn't given me a lot to go on. I tapped out a Lucky Strike Green and lit it. Sam bought the correspondence course I was taking to get my PI license. That fact and the knowledge he was a professional investigator who thought I'd make a darn good private dick was another reason why I didn't give up and go back to work at Bell.

It wasn't too long before Sam appeared, his jacket off, shirt sleeves rolled to the elbow, and his own cigarette dangling from his lips. "I didn't expect to see you today. You need something?"

"Yeah." I stood. "I met with a client earlier. His name is Edward Kettle." I ran down Edward's description and what I knew of his background. "I want to know if he has a criminal history. Can you look into that?"

"I can tell you if he's been arrested and convicted in the city. You think he has a rap sheet?"

"I don't know. He's awfully squirrelly about his background. It makes me wonder if he's covering something up."

Sam drew on his smoke and exhaled. "What's his story?"

I told Sam what I'd learned at the diner.

"If he's working that project at the shipyard, I can't see them hiring an ex-con." Smoke leaked from his mouth while he talked.

"Could be they didn't know when they hired him. If his boss, or one of the higher ups, found out, they might look for a way to get rid of him." I flipped my notebook shut and dropped it in my purse. "Do you know what all the hubbub is down there?"

"Beyond the fact it's big, and it has to do with ships, not a clue." He ashed his gasper. "Those Coast Guard boys are pretty good at keeping the public at arm's length."

"Edward said it's a project for the government. I know, I know." I held up

CHAPTER TWO

my hands. "He shouldn't have told me, but he also said it will be over soon. That's all he said, though. I s'pose I'll go down there and take a gander. See if anything jumps out at me."

Sam laughed. "I have a great deal of respect for your ability to ferret out information. However, if you can get an armed Coast Guardsman to talk, you aren't merely a good interrogator. You're a magician."

Chapter Three

I left Sam and took a bus to the waterfront. The American Shipbuilding Company was a massive operation. I knew it owned yards in a lot of cities along the Great Lakes. I also knew the company had wrapped up a huge project the previous summer under top-security conditions. They'd done a good job of keeping the details secret, but anybody walking along the lake had seen the old paddle-wheel ship being worked on.

I looked around. The shipyard was fenced off, and the Coast Guard substation they'd built last year guarded the only entrance in sight. It had to be the only entrance, period. I knew I didn't have a chance of talking myself inside the yard and I wasn't gonna try. But that didn't mean the men at the gate couldn't, or wouldn't, provide any dope.

I checked for traffic, crossed the street, and strode up to the guard house. As expected, a member of the Coast Guard holding a rifle met me when I was still a good twenty feet from the fence.

"Sorry, miss. No civilians allowed." His voice was polite, but firm.

"No worries. I don't wanna get inside."

His mouth twitched, like he was fighting a grin. "You also can't stand on the sidewalk and take pictures."

"I don't wanna do that either." I debated telling him who I was. "My name is Betty Ahern, and I'm a private detective."

That did make him smile, but he stayed polite. "You aren't convincing me to let you stick around."

"No, I s'pose I'm not. Look, I'm not interested in what's going on over there." I waved to the shipyard. I was, but he didn't have to know that. "Were

CHAPTER THREE

you on duty the day they ran a reporter outta here? Not anyone from the *Courier-Express*, but a newshound from one of the local rags." I squinted at his name tag. It read Barnhard. The patch on his sleeve had two diagonal stripes. "Surely you can tell me that, Private Barnhard."

"Seaman." He looked around and leaned toward me. "I guess there's no harm. No, I wasn't here. I heard about the guy, though. All I know is that it took four of them to convince him to beat it."

The reporter was stubborn, then. Big surprise. "Do you know if he was seen with anyone? An employee from the yard?"

Seaman Barnhard frowned. "I didn't hear anything about that. Doesn't mean he wasn't, though. At least not one person in particular. From what I gather, he pestered just about anyone coming in or out, even the men on duty here in the substation."

"You know what is goin' on over there?"

His face stayed solemn. "That's on a need to know basis, and I don't need to know. But I can't see how this one's gonna float with all the steel that's come in." He blushed. "I shouldn't have said that."

"Consider it forgotten." A gust of wind from the lake blew hair across my face and I tucked it behind my ears. "You can't be the only one on duty today. Any chance of you asking your buddies if they saw him?"

Seaman Barnhard studied me for a long second, then pointed at the sidewalk. "Wait here." He disappeared inside the guard house and came back a couple of minutes later. "None of the guys have any more information than I do. But the name of the paper is *The Daily*. You might get more details from them." He hefted his rifle. "Is that all?"

I decided not to press my luck. I might need to talk to Seaman Barnhard again, and I didn't want to be remembered as the nosy dame who couldn't take a hint. "That's all. Thanks for your time. You've been very helpful, Seaman."

"I aim to serve." He paused, then winked. "Speaking of that, I bet a girl like you could use a pal. Especially if you are a private investigator. I get off duty at sixteen hundred. That's four o'clock in the afternoon to you civilians."

I waggled my left hand at him. "Thanks for the compliment, but I'm

13

engaged."

He snapped his fingers. "Just my luck."

* * *

A quick check of the phone book, which Seaman Barnhard brought out before I left and allowed me to use, said *The Daily* offices were on Main Street at the corner of East Tupper. It turned out to be a small place, not dingy, but not swanky, either. Just a plain space smushed in between two other businesses with a simple black and white sign in the window. It was about what I expected of a rag newspaper. When I walked in, bells chimed, and a young Lana Turner look-alike, right down to the wavy blond hair that couldn't be her natural color, smiled at me from the front desk. There were two telephones on it, both of which were ringing. She ignored them. "Welcome to *The Daily*. Can I help you?"

This rag needs two phones? "I'm looking for one of your reporters. He would have been assigned to snoop around the operations for American Shipbuilding Company, looking into their hush-hush project." I could hear a faint clatter coming from the back where they printed the paper.

"Are you here to give a tip?"

I put my hands on her desk. "I'm a private detective." I gave her my name and wished, for about the hundredth time, that I had a badge or identification to go with it. Maybe I should invest in business cards.

Her forehead puckered as she frowned. "I don't think I should give you that information."

"Is your editor-in-chief here?"

"I don't think I should call him, either."

"Look." I pulled over a chair, set it close to her desk, and sat. I leaned in and used my best conspiratorial voice. "I'm not tryin' to get anyone in trouble. I just want to ask some questions. I promise, they won't even interfere with any story you may be planning to print here."

She paused. Then her platinum curls swung as she shook her head. "No, sorry."

CHAPTER THREE

A man came from the back. He was thin. His black hair was slicked back and ended in a sharp widow's peak high on his forehead. He wore a blue-striped button down, open at the collar. Red suspenders held up wrinkled brown trousers. His fingers were stained black. "Emma, I—" He stopped short. "Who is this dazzling young lady?" He swaggered toward me.

Dazzling? Not even Tom had called me that. Not ever. Dot Kilbride, my other best friend, and Lee's sweetheart, was the curvy pinup model type that prompted stares. I was a stick in comparison. But I smiled and introduced myself. "Pleased to meet you. Are you the editor-in-chief?" I stood and held out my hand.

His deep brown eyes were thoughtful as he shook and looked me up and down. Twice. "Private dick, huh?" A leer made a brief appearance on his puss before he wiped it off. "What are you doing here?"

"She's looking for Melvin." Emma blushed.

The reporter's first name. Thanks for the slip. "I'm working a case and I have a few questions about his activities down at American Shipbuilding." I put the chair back. "I'd be much obliged if you could help me, mister…?"

"Carmichael. George Carmichael. I'm not only the editor-in-chief, I own this paper." His fingers twitched as if he wanted to reach out and touch me. "What's in it for us?"

Of course a newshound would want something in return. "I'm not paying you, if that's what you're after."

Emma returned to her typewriter, but the slowness of the clacking meant she was more engrossed in the conversation than her work. That or she was a lousy typist.

Mr. Carmichael barked a laugh. "Money is always appreciated, doll. But there are other types of payment." He rubbed his hands together.

I made to push by him, but he stopped me.

"I don't mean *that*. You said you're a private investigator. Working a big case? Newsworthy?"

I crossed my arms. "Are you after a scoop?"

"Always." He tilted his head. "Tell you what, honey. You give me an exclusive, and I'll see about helping you out."

I shouldered my purse. "I don't think this is a newspaper-worthy story. Thanks for your time." I turned.

He hurried around to block me. He brushed my shoulders and squeezed my upper arms. "Now, now. Let's not make snap decisions, sweetheart. You can't expect me to give you my reporter's name, and you give me nothing. That's not how it works. I'm sure we can hash something out, though."

Honey? Sweetheart? *Who does this joe think he is?* "How do you know what I'm working on is worth the paper and ink?"

He gave a sly smile and rubbed his hands together. "Melvin was following a story about the shipyard. Big secret, real hush-hush stuff. If you're looking for him, chances are good whatever you're investigating is related. We could help each other out." He gave me an exaggerated wink and nudge with his elbow.

I stepped a pace away from him. It was the most space I could make in the tiny area. "My understanding is the job at the yard is for the war effort. You wouldn't want to get in the way, would you? Loose lips sink ships and all that." I pulled my deck of Luckys out of my pocket and tapped one out.

Mr. Carmichael took a lighter from his pocket, flicked it, and held it toward me. "Of course not, sweetheart. I wouldn't torpedo anything critical. But we don't know the real dirt until we ask questions, right? Melvin's doing what you're doing. Digging around. Not much difference between us, you get my drift?" He put away the lighter and stuffed his hands in his pockets. He leaned toward me and put his hand on my arm. "This is more of an 'I scratch your back, you scratch mine' situation. If whatever you're working on turns into a story, well, you give us first dibs. Nothing wrong with that. I wouldn't expect you to do anything unpatriotic or illegal."

Between this guy's smile, oily voice, and inability to keep his mitts off me, I had a powerful urge to shower. "I'd have to consult my client on that, and I have the feeling his answer will be no." My gaze swept the tiny office. Now that I paid attention, I could see the scuffed linoleum, faded wall paint, and the leaves at the bottom of the plant on Emma's desk that were tinged brown. "Are you gonna give me Melvin's surname or not?" I could get it from a copy of the paper, of course. I asked as more of a test to see just how cooperative

CHAPTER THREE

Mr. Carmichael was. I mean, if he wouldn't give up a name I could get in a snap, chances were he wasn't gonna be as friendly as he pretended. No matter how much information I gave him.

"Not." Mr. Carmichael favored me with what I'm sure he thought was a rueful expression.

"Okay." I stepped around him and headed for the door.

"That's it?" His voice held a note of disbelief.

I paused, hand on the door, and looked back. "Yes. Frankly, I've got better things to do with my time than yap with a schmoe like you."

Chapter Four

Lee and Dot might have thought my trip to *The Daily* offices was a waste. I, however, knew different. Sure, neither Emma nor Mr. Carmichael had coughed up Melvin's full name. But they had given me *a* name. It meant spending money on a paper I didn't particularly want to buy, but I could find the rest on my own.

I bought a copy of *The Daily* from the corner newsboy and flipped the pages. It didn't take long for me to conclude the paper was junk. *The Daily* was light on facts about anything, but it went in big for speculation. Bell Aircraft was not secretly supplying the French resistance with planes. I highly doubted Mayor Kelly's wife was passing intelligence about Buffalo's manufacturing scene to the Germans via the neutral, but German-leaning, Irish. The headlines were bold, slanted, and designed to catch the eye, but the stories that went with them were fluff and nonsense. The *Courier-Express* didn't need to worry about competition from these fat heads.

But I didn't buy the paper for its content. I skimmed, looking at the by-lines, and soon found what I was looking for. Melvin's last name was Schlingmann. Betting there weren't very many of those in Buffalo, I went inside a soda shop and grabbed the phone book from the payphone. There were two entries for M Schlingmann, both of the addresses in the Polonia neighborhood. I dropped a nickel and called the first one, but the elderly woman told me her husband, the M of the listing, died last fall. I thanked her and called the other number. It rang at least a dozen times before a sour-sounding woman answered.

"I'm looking for Melvin," I said. "Is he in?"

CHAPTER FOUR

"No, he ain't. And if you find him, tell him his rent is due." She slammed down the phone.

I hung up the blower. Melvin must be a real charmer. I made a note of the number and address, which was on Girard Place over by Fillmore Avenue. I replaced the book and checked the clock on the wall. It was quarter after three. By the time I got to Polonia and found the address, it would be well after four, or so I figured. If the woman on the phone had been Melvin's landlady, she didn't sound as though she'd appreciate a stranger busting in at the dinner hour. And that assumed he'd return. If he owned her dough, he wouldn't announce his arrival.

It appeared some kind of stakeout was in order, since it was too early to go home and I doubted Sam would have any dope on Edward Kettle for me yet. I had two options, the offices of *The Daily* or Melvin's house. The problem was I didn't know what he looked like. His name conjured the image of a hack. I didn't have the feeling a man who worked for a tabloid paper would look distinguished, like Gregory Peck, but that didn't mean anything. He very well could be.

I returned to *The Daily* office. I didn't see Mr. Carmichael through the plate glass window, just Emma, sitting and filing her nails. It was almost definitely not what she was s'posed to be doin'. Maybe I could use that. I went in.

She looked up, blue eyes wide. "I'm sorry, Mr. Carmichael is out."

"I'm not here to see him." I pulled out my purse and got a couple of dollar bills from my wallet. Fortunately, I'd held on to at least half of what I'd earned on Lee's case for a rainy day, so I had some payoff money. I held it out. "This is for you—"

She snatched at it.

I held it out of reach. "Not so fast. If you do me a favor."

"What kind?" Greed showed plainly in her expression.

"Do you expect Melvin to come back here?"

"Who knows? He comes and goes on his own schedule."

I waggled the bills. "C'mon. Take a guess."

She paused. "I think so. He has a story to file before five for tomorrow's edition. The one he's been working on about the shipyard. He has to get something in or else Mr. Carmichael won't be happy."

"Will you be here?"

She nodded, expression pouty. "I work until five-thirty, Monday through Friday. Mr. Carmichael never lets me off early."

"Then here's what I need you to do." I pointed through the window at the drugstore across the street. "I'm gonna be sitting over there, right at the table in the front. When Melvin comes in, you give me the high sign." From my chosen spot, I'd have a clear line of sight into the office.

"Why would I do that? You're going to get him in trouble."

"I just wanna talk to him."

She narrowed her peepers. "Promise?"

I drew an X over my chest. "Cross my heart and hope to die."

She mulled that over. "Okay. What should I do?"

"When he comes in, run your fingers through your hair, like this." I demonstrated.

Her jaw dropped. "I'll ruin my curls!"

"No sweat. I guess you don't want the cash." I turned.

"Wait!"

I smothered a grin. The dough would buy a lot of niceties at the drug store, things like nail polish or perfume. I was betting Emma spent a lot of her paycheck on them and would jump at the chance to make a little extra.

"I'll do it. But you better not be lying to me." She held out her hand.

"Tell you what. Here's a dollar." I gave it to her. "You finger Melvin. I'll come by right after and pay the other buck. Call it a sign of good faith. Deal?"

She scowled. "Do I have a choice?"

"Not really. Take it or leave it."

She tossed her curls. "You'd better not wander off and stiff me."

I replaced the second dollar in my purse. "I wouldn't dream of it."

* * *

CHAPTER FOUR

I parked myself at the counter of the drugstore, choosing my seat so that I had a clear view of Emma, who'd gone back to filing her nails as soon as I left. I bought a bottle of Coca-Cola and a box of Cracker Jack to munch and settled in. I'd also brought the book for my PI course to study. This way, if Melvin never showed, at least I would accomplish something.

No one approached *The Daily* offices until a few minutes after four. *If this guy isn't a Melvin Schlingmann, I don't know who is.* The joe across the street was scrawny and short. His light brown suit hung on him, and the tie was crooked. Even at a distance, his face seemed thin, and his features a little on the sharp side, with a thick shock of brown hair that clearly hadn't seen a barber in weeks. There was a white spot on his chin, maybe toilet paper blotting a nick from his morning shave. He held a notepad in his hand. I thought I saw a dark spot on the coat pocket, maybe from a leaking pen? From what I could see at a distance, his overall impression said *shifty reporter*. He paused outside the door, and looked up and down the street at least four times before he went in.

Through the plate glass window, I saw him pause at Emma's desk. She ran her hand through her hair, our prearranged signal. Bingo. Did I want to corner him now or wait? I decided to follow him from the newspaper office to his next stop. The man did have a story to file by five. I'd be polite and stay outta his way until then. No sense interfering with the mark's job. Gettin' in the way of his making some lettuce wouldn't make him want to talk to me.

Melvin was a fast typist, he had writer's block, or he didn't care about quality, 'cause he reappeared in the front of the office not even thirty minutes later. Based on what I'd read of the paper, my money was on the last one. He stopped at Emma's desk to jaw. I saw her toss her head with a coy expression and wiggle her fingers. He blew her a kiss and left.

I threw away my empty bottle, slipped my book back into my bag, and prepared to follow. But first, I nipped into the office and gave Emma her reward. She didn't even say thanks, just snatched the bill from my hand.

Fortunately, there were enough people on the street that I was able to stay back and not be noticed. Melvin walked down Main Street toward East

Chippewa, where he was just in time to catch the bus from the corner stop. I jumped on through the back door and picked a seat where I could keep him in sight. We rode through the neighborhoods until we reached Polonia. I tailed him from the corner of Broadway and Fillmore to a boarding house on Girard Place. He entered, and I waited five minutes before I knocked on the front door.

A narrow-faced woman in her fifties answered. "What do you want?"

The woman from the phone. "Good afternoon." I introduced myself. I really needed those business cards. "I'm looking for Melvin Schlingmann."

"He ain't here." She started to close the door.

I put out my hand, having learned the hard way about stopping doors with my feet. "Ma'am, I saw Mr. Schlingmann enter this house just a few minutes ago. I haven't seen him come out. Unless you have a back door, that means he's still here."

She looked me up and down. "What are you? An ex-girlfriend? That can't be it. You're too good-looking for Melvin to be your guy."

"I told you, I'm a private detective. I need to ask Mr. Schlingmann some questions."

"You're telling the truth, huh? Good for you." She ran her tongue over her lips. "He's late on his rent. Again. If I call him to the door, what do I get in return?"

The handbook hadn't mentioned how people constantly wanted to be paid for the smallest thing. Good thing I had saved that cash. I pulled out my purse. "Two dollars." I had told Edward there would be expenses.

She held out a hand. Once she stuffed the bills into a pocket of her apron, she turned and yelled. "Melvin! There's a girl here to see you. Get your skinny bum down here." No answer. "Melvin! I know you're here, you crummy, no-good, lazy, yuck. Why a girl this nice wants to talk to you, I have no idea, but come here!"

It wasn't the most enticing speech, but it worked. Melvin appeared. I'd been right. His features were on the sharp side, his nose a bit long. His coat was off, and his shirt needed a serious ironing. His black suspenders were the only thing keeping his pants up. The shirt was off-color, like it had gone

CHAPTER FOUR

through a lot of washing. The fabric of his trousers had an inexpensive shine and I could see frayed threads at the hems. His whole frame was thin, as though he'd missed a few dozen meals. But there was a mischievous sparkle in his brown eyes. If he wore better clothes, put on a few pounds, and smiled, he wouldn't be half bad lookin'. "Keep your shirt on." He rubbed his chin. "I don't know this dame. What the heck does she want?"

The landlady threw up her hands and stalked off. "Don't forget your rent, you bum."

"Crazy broad." He focused on me. "Do I know you?"

"No." Again, I introduced myself. "I need to ask you some questions about your activities at American Shipbuilding Company not that long ago."

"Who said I was over at the shipyard?"

"I read your article." I dropped my voice. "I think you might be on to somethin', and I may be in a position to help you."

He narrowed his peepers. "You read the story?"

"Yeah."

"Quite an accomplishment since I only filed it today, and the paper ain't been printed yet."

Busted. I put up my hands. "Okay, I exaggerated. Emma, the secretary at your office, hinted that you had a big fish on the line. I still think I could be of service. If the price was right, you know. I don't work for free."

His gaze darted behind him, and he stepped outside. "Activities is an overstatement. I haven't done much except hang around." His fingers beat a rapid staccato on his leg. "Are you here to give me the skinny on what's going on?"

"It depends on what's in it for me." I wondered if the guy was on something, 'cause he couldn't seem to keep still. He reminded me of the boys all sugared up on soft drinks. "Did you ever speak to a man named Edward Kettle?"

"I might have. I talked to a lot of people down there." His answering look was coy. "What's it worth to you?"

"Seems you're not getting the drift here. You answer my questions, and I *might* be able to lend you a hand. I'm not here to pay for information." Did people think I was stupid? I didn't want an answer to that. "Have you talked to Mr. Kettle or not?"

"Who's he?"

"He works at the shipyard." No reason to let Melvin know the truth about Edward's employment.

He rubbed his fingers together while he thought, then shook his head. "Name doesn't ring a bell. What does he look like?"

I described Edward.

"Nah, he don't sound familiar. Why?"

"Allegedly, he met up with you to give you the dope on what was happening at the yard." I tilted my head.

Melvin snorted and cussed. "If I'd had an inside source, I wouldn't have wasted the last three days trying to get past the guard at the gate, or waylaying guys coming out, would I? I take it you know this Kettle guy? Can you introduce me?"

"I do. But you haven't given me much of a reason to help you out." I studied him. "The girl at the paper, she said you had to file a story by five. What about?"

"The yard."

"But you just said you don't know anything."

He grinned. "That doesn't mean I can't write a story, sweetheart. Something big is going on. You don't post armed guards, with a brand-new station, for no reason. If they won't come clean, well, it ain't my fault if I get some of the facts twisted, is it?"

Considering what I'd read of *The Daily*, the editor didn't care much, either. "But you definitely never talked to Edward Kettle?"

"Like I said, never heard of him. What kind of help are you talkin' about?"

"Sorry. I'm not gonna do something for nothing and it seems to me you got a whole lotta nothing on your hands." I turned. Melvin didn't know squat, and it sure didn't seem like he'd talked to anyone at the shipyard, much less my client.

Melvin stuck his tongue in his cheek. Then he asked, "Say, how about an interview? A female private dick is a new one. You can give me all the details. Might be good for business. I'll even pay you. Five bucks, we go for

CHAPTER FOUR

coffee, and you spill your guts. Sound good?"

I didn't even turn around. "I'll pass, thanks." Melvin could certainly give me some publicity, but something told me it was a kind I didn't want.

Chapter Five

When I arrived home around six, Mom and my sister, Mary Kate, were finishing up the dishes. Mom rinsed a plate and handed it to Mary Kate to dry. "I left your dinner in the oven to stay warm."

I leaned over and kissed her cheek. "You're the best." I grabbed my food and a fork. Meatloaf, mashed potatoes with thin gravy, and green beans, which had to be left over from last summer's canning. It wasn't my favorite, but I didn't care. It was food, and it was hot. Well, sort of. It wasn't stone-cold.

Fact is, Mom had almost completely changed her tune about me bein' a private detective. She didn't say much, but I knew she was proud of me. My success must've won her over. When I started last October, she wouldn't have kept dinner warm for me while I was out on a job.

Mary Kate stacked the clean plates, put them away, and sat down. "Didja get a new case?" She rested her chin on her fist.

I wiped some gravy from the corner of my mouth. "I don't know how exciting it is, but I did get a new client. Lee referred him to me."

Pop entered the kitchen. "You're getting referrals already? That's my darling girl."

"I don't know if Lee counts." I dragged a forkful of potatoes through the gravy.

He patted my shoulder. "It all counts."

Mary Kate's eyes shone with anticipation. "Can you talk about it?"

"I don't see why not." I told them Edward's story, most of it, anyway. "Mary

CHAPTER FIVE

Kate, I know you've talked about being a reporter someday. If you go to work for a tabloid, I'll find you and beat you like a rug."

She giggled.

I ate for a bit, then put my fork down. "Pop, I have a question."

He packed his pipe with tobacco and lit it. The sweet scent of the smoke filled the kitchen. "What about?"

"If I can believe the reporter at *The Daily*, and I'm not saying I do, he never spoke to Edward Kettle. Other men, yes, but not him. But Mr. Kettle swears that was why he was fired."

"You think your client is lying to you?"

"He's not telling the whole truth, that's for sure." I pushed my plate aside. The beans were soggy and cold, but Mom would skin me if I threw out food. Too bad I'd spoiled Cat, my adopted stray, so badly he didn't eat vegetables. "Is it possible that management at the shipyard was looking for an excuse to get rid of Mr. Kettle? I don't understand why they wouldn't just fire him, though."

Pop sat and puffed his pipe. "It's entirely possible. If the shipyard is unionized, and I'm sure they are, the union heads would put up quite a stink if one of their members was thrown out for no reason. By accusing Kettle of talking to someone he shouldn't have, it gives management an out."

I eyed my plate. I'd wait until Mom left the kitchen to dump the beans. "Lee told me Mr. Kettle is a good guy, a hard worker. I believe Lee, no question. But if that's the case, why would American Shipbuilding want to fire Mr. Kettle? There'd have to be something wrong with his work."

"Or him personally."

I hadn't thought of that. "Like he's a secret Nazi sympathizer?"

Pop puffed again. "That or something like it."

"Lee wouldn't fraternize with a traitor."

"No, I agree. But that's assuming he knows."

Mom had left the kitchen. Mary Kate, clearly bored by the conversation, followed her.

I crossed my arms. Pop was right. If Edward really did support the Germans, or the Japanese, it's not something he'd advertise. He'd be sneaky

27

about it. But it felt wrong. If management at the yard had found out, why hide the fact? They'd be more likely to call those armed Coast Guard sentries in and have him escorted out under guard. They might even turn him over to the government to be tried for treason. He wouldn't be fired and left out on the street, would he?

"What are you thinking?" Pop asked. "And don't tell me nothing, because I can see you are."

I shook my head. Pop always knew. I told him my thoughts.

"I tend to agree with you. Which means they might have wanted him gone for entirely different reasons. Something that had nothing to do with the war."

"Like what?"

He stood. "You're the one who wants to be a detective. You'll have to find out." He took a step toward the door and turned. "I'll keep your mother occupied. But if you don't want her to know you threw those beans out, I recommend burying them in the garden."

Like I said. Pop always knew what I was thinking.

* * *

I took Pop's advice and disposed of my unwanted vegetables by digging a hole in the back corner of our Victory garden and dropping them in. I covered it, then scattered dry dirt on it to disguise the fact the patch was freshly turned over. We weren't gonna start planting for a few weeks. Hopefully the beans would have mostly rotted away by then.

I stood and brushed dirt from my knees and heard an accusatory *meow* from behind me. Cat was perched on the back step, swishing his tail, green eyes fixing me with a stern feline stare. "Okay, okay. I didn't eat them. You wouldn't eat beans from last summer, either. Heck, you don't eat them at all."

Meow.

I picked him up and nuzzled his soft gray head. He was lean and sleek, nothing like the mangy stray I'd encountered last fall. "Promise me you

CHAPTER FIVE

won't tell, and I'll give you extra milk in the morning."

He wriggled and leapt down. With a flick of his tail, he disappeared behind the garbage can. *Typical feline.*

I went inside, got a light coat, and headed down the street to the Tillotson house. The front yard was cleaned of winter debris, and the flower boxes freshened in anticipation of spring. Someone, prob'ly Lee, had also painted the shutters on the front windows. Ever since Mr. Tillotson had died, Lee had stepped into the role of the man of the house with determination and fixed all the shabby exterior details. The place looked better than it had in a long time.

I found my friend in the garage working on a girl's bike. Dot sat on an overturned crate next to the toolbox. "Hiya Betty!" Even though she was still in her work clothes, heavy blue trousers and a button-down shirt with the sleeves rolled up, her curly hair held back by a bandanna, she looked pinup girl perky. The slight chill in the air now that the sun had gone down made her cheeks rosy. Of course, being next to Lee helped. They'd become an item in March, and I rarely saw one without the other these days.

Not that I minded. My friends were obviously in love, and that made me happy. It also made me miss Tom more than ever, but he'd be home soon enough. I waved. "What's buzzin', cousin?"

"Not much. Bell is still Bell. All the girls miss you. You should have heard Florence this morning." She proceeded to tell me the latest antics from the factory. "The best part was Mr. Satterwaite never did figure out what had happened!" Dot wiped tears of laughter from her eyes.

I snorted. Mr. Satterwaite, the shift manager, was a real knucklehead if there ever was one. "That man couldn't match his shirt to his trousers. I bet his wife tells him what clothes to wear every day."

Lee squirted oil on the bike chain, a cigarette clamped between his lips. "Hand me that three-eighths wrench, Dot."

She grabbed the tool. "Three-eighths, you got it."

He grinned at her. "There are definitely benefits to having your girl work in manufacturing." He tightened a nut on the bike. "What did you find out about Edward's problem so far, Betty?"

Dot swiveled to look at me. "You got a new case?"

"Yep." I looked around, but there was nowhere to sit, not unless I parked my butt on the concrete and it was too chilly for that. "I ran down the reporter Edward talked about, but I have some more questions for you, Lee."

He spun the bike's rear tire and tested the pedals. "Now all Anna has to do is learn to ride the thing." He wiped oil off of his hands with a rag. "Shoot."

"First, you said Harvey at GM vouched for him. Edward Kettle, I mean. But how well do you personally know him?"

"I don't know him much at all." Lee exhaled, sending up a cloud of smoke. "Aside from those two times at the bar, I've not spoken to him. Harve knows him from his neighborhood."

"Where's that?"

"Allentown. Edward wouldn't tell you, but Harve said he lives at the boardinghouse across the street." Lee put the tools away. "Anyway, that night at the bar we got talking shop, you know, comparing stuff about work. Edward said he couldn't talk specifics about his latest job, but it was a real pain in the neck. I saw him again at the same bar a few nights ago, and he told us he'd been fired, and it was a bum rap. He said he wished he could hire a private detective to help set the record straight, and I mentioned you."

"I thank you for that." I flicked ash from my cigarette. "He didn't give you any more information the second time?"

Lee wheeled the bike to a corner of the garage and came back. "No. Just that the company was working on a big project for Uncle Sam, and they'd fingered the wrong guy." He wiped his hands on a rag.

It would have been swell if Edward had let something slip, but even losing his job hadn't made him run his yap. If that was the case, why did the muckety-mucks at American Shipbuilding think he'd talk to the press? I planned to corner him tomorrow, but I didn't hold out a lot of hope he'd give me any more to work with. "What do you think of him?"

Lee took a drag off his cigarette and exhaled. "He seemed like an okay guy. He can sound a little like a professor, all proper English and stuff. It makes me think he went to private school, maybe even spent some time at college. But that's crazy. A guy with a degree isn't gonna work at a shipyard."

CHAPTER FIVE

Dot picked up a few more of the tools on the ground and put them back in the box. "You sound iffy on that. Not the education, the first part."

"I dunno." Lee ground out his gasper. "I can't put my finger on it. At least two of the waitresses flirted with him, and he never batted an eye or did more than thank them for his beer. I asked Harve about it later, and he said Edward was deeply in love when he was younger. He got engaged, but before they could get married, he went overseas in the Great War. After he returned, he was all set to get hitched. Harve said the girl jilted Edward a day before the wedding. He took it hard, but eventually found himself another girl. That one broke it off a month after the engagement. The next girl eloped to Niagara Falls with some other joe. After that, Edward swore off women. Said his heart couldn't take it."

"Talk about unlucky in love," I said.

"I know." Lee brushed off his hands. "Anyway, Edward is jake. I mean, sometimes it seems like he's trying too hard to fit in, but it's like I said. Someone who went to a private school and college, and whose family has money, isn't exactly the same as a guy like me, someone who graduated from a public high school and went straight to work at General Motors, right? We come from different worlds."

I thought. "Do you think that's why he acted so standoffish when I first met him? He grew up with the swells, and I'm from the First Ward?"

Lee shut the toolbox and snapped the clasps. "Could be." He turned and waggled his eyebrows. "Maybe you can use your feminine wiles to get him to 'fess up."

Dot and I both threw greasy rags at him. Feminine wiles my foot.

Chapter Six

The next morning, I ate breakfast and read the morning *Courier-Express*. The Japanese had taken to bombing Australia. I didn't know much about the Aussies, but the Japanese aggression felt misplaced. Then again, they'd lost one of their most important military leaders, Admiral Yamamoto, not long ago when his plane was shot down by our boys over a place called Bougainvillea. That was a big story. Meanwhile, the American tank corps were still harrying the Germans in North Africa. That had to be what was keeping Tom from answering my letter. Heck, with all the fuss, it was possible he hadn't gotten any mail in weeks. Yeah, that was it.

Edward had refused to give me more than his phone number, but Lee had given me Harvey's address, so it'd be a piece of cake to find the boarding house. I was gonna visit Edward today, whatever he'd said about calling and arranging to meet.

The guy was hiding *something* from me. If I got him by surprise, it'd be harder for him to keep it under wraps. If he'd really given inside information to Melvin Schlingmann, I had a feeling the reporter would have bragged to me about having an "inside contact" at American Shipbuilding. He came across as that type of guy.

I'd been raised to believe it was impolite to visit or call a person before nine in the morning or after eight at night, even if I was trying to gain an element of surprise, so I didn't leave for Edward's boarding house until well after I'd eaten and cleaned up the dishes. I also fed Cat and slipped him a bit of the sausage I'd had. I wasn't an expert on feline emotions, but from

CHAPTER SIX

the way he gobbled it down, licked his whiskers, and gave a hopeful *meow*, I think he appreciated the treat.

The boarding house was up in Allentown, over on North Pearl. I took a bus to the nearest stop, which was at the foot of Main Street and Virginia Avenue. From there, I hoofed it to my destination. On the way, I thought about the best tactic for getting my client to pry open his jaws and confide in me.

I turned onto the street and slowed. Up ahead was a Buffalo city cop car and a white car that had to be a meat wagon from the county coroner. A few local residents, at least I assumed that was who they were, clustered on the sidewalk. My path would take me right through the crowd. I didn't want to interrupt, so I crossed to the other side of the street.

I halted when I realized the crowd wasn't only in between me and my destination, they were standing almost directly in front of it. From my post across the street, I could see where the cops had strung a line to keep the people out. At least one of the women, an older lady with her graying black hair pulled back from her face and dressed in a housecoat, appeared agitated by the action.

I hustled across the street and approached a middle-aged man wearing work clothes that identified him as a worker in one of Buffalo's industrial companies. "Excuse me, sir. What's going on?"

The man turned to me. His face was a funny color, almost like the ashes Pop shoveled out of the fireplace every week. "There's been a murder. It's almost like someone gutted a cow in there." He swallowed hard.

"I'm sorry." I didn't know this guy from Adam, but it seemed like the right thing to say. I glanced at the faces in the small knot of people. No Edward. "Are all these folks residents?"

The man nodded.

"I'm looking for Edward Kettle. I don't see him here. Do you know where I can find him? He and I need to talk."

The man's jaw dropped. He looked a little like a landed fish. "Edward ain't gonna be doing no talking. Not anymore."

I turned to the patrol car. I didn't see anyone in the backseat. "Is he with the cops?"

"Sort of." The man gulped. "Edward's the one who got his throat slit."

* * *

This case had sped up. I'd gone from the simple job of figuring out who was spreading lies to murder. Again. Nothing Edward had said to me yesterday made me think someone wanted him dead. If he really had blabbed about what was goin' on at American Shipbuilding, I could see someone beating on him. But killing him? Heck, even if I thought—no, I *knew*—he'd not told me the whole truth, I couldn't believe it was enough to get him killed. Why did I always find myself hip-deep in death?

At least he paid me in advance. I bit my lip. That was mean. A man was dead. I barely knew him, but that didn't matter. Now was no time to be thinking of money. Then again, I'd been hired to clear his name. Not find a killer. Was this even my job? I couldn't know until I talked to someone in charge.

After I said a Hail Mary and crossed myself, I approached the young patrol officer standing guard at the door. "Excuse me."

He didn't respond. He didn't even move.

I waved my hand in front of his face. "I said, excuse me."

He shot me a dirty look. "This is a crime scene...miss." The last was hesitantly tacked on. "You have to leave."

"I'm not asking to go inside." I craned my neck, but I couldn't see anything. "I'd like to speak to the detective. Assuming there is one. A joe on the sidewalk said there's been a murder. That means you must have called someone from homicide."

"The detective's got better things to do than talk to you."

"You haven't even asked who I am. I might have important information."

His mouth twitched, like he was gonna sneer and decided not to. "Do you live here?"

"No. But I know the man who died." I was gonna buy business cards, no matter what they cost. "I'm a private detective, and the victim was a client of mine."

CHAPTER SIX

This time, the young cop did curl his lip. "Yeah, right. Listen, I have better things to do than crack wise with you. Now scram."

A man in a suit came out of the house. "Is there a problem, Officer?" It was my buddy from the Buffalo police homicide division, Detective Sam MacKinnon.

The younger man straightened. "No, sir. This br...lady is trying to gain entry. She claims she's a detective. I've told her she has to leave."

Sam lit a cigarette. He used the Zippo I'd given him last Christmas, the one with the shamrock on it. "How do you know she's not telling the truth?"

The officer gaped.

"Word of advice, son." Sam clapped a hand on his shoulder. "Keep a civil tongue in your mouth when dealing with the public, no matter what you think. Do that, and you'll have a long career. Ignore me, and I'll personally make sure you're still pounding a beat when you're fifty."

I tried to keep a straight face, but it was hard, 'specially when Sam glanced at me and winked. "Thank you, Detective. I'd like to talk to you, if you have a minute."

"Let's go over here." He led me to a spot in the yard, away from the front door and the group of onlookers, which had increased in the short time since I'd spoken to the neighbor. He turned so he faced the front door, forcing me to put my back to the house to look at him. "I should have known I'd see you, Miss Ahern."

Had we been in private, I might have swatted his shoulder. But I didn't think it was a good idea to be seen hitting a police detective, even in jest. "I thought we agreed to use our Christian names."

"We're in public." He blew out a cloud of smoke. "Why are you here?"

"Edward Kettle hired me yesterday. I came to talk to him and learned from that guy over there someone had cut his throat." I jerked my thumb toward the source of my information.

"Correct."

"What happened? Can I see the body?"

"No." Sam inhaled. "One, this is an official crime scene, and I'll never hear the end of it if I let a civilian trample all over the place—no matter how

35

careful she is." He held up a hand to forestall my objections. "Two, you don't want to see this one."

"I've seen dead guys before."

"Not like this." He glanced over at the uniform at the door. "I don't even want to see it. This is vicious. When I say his throat was cut, I don't mean a little gash. Somebody sliced him all the way through his windpipe. The room looks like an abattoir."

I couldn't help it. I shuddered. If Edward's place could have passed for a slaughterhouse, that was bad. "Any leads?"

"None. What did he come to you for?"

I gave Sam the highlights of Edward's case. "I don't think he lied to me, but he didn't tell me the whole truth. That's why I'm here." I tapped my fingernail against my teeth.

"Do you think he was killed over whatever he was hiding?"

"No clue. Do you know this Melvin Schlingmann or anything about *The Daily*?"

"Only that it's a fine example of the adage, 'if it bleeds, it leads.'" Sam tapped ash from his smoke. "Schlingmann denied talking to Kettle?"

"That's his story."

Sam furrowed his forehead. "Easy enough to prove it didn't happen. Even Schlingmann denies it. I wonder why management used that as a reason to fire Kettle?"

"That's my question." Noise at the front of the house made me turn around. Two men in white coats brought a black bag out of the house, one that had to contain the body. I swallowed and faced Sam. "Did you find anything inside?"

Sam threw away the smoldering butt. "His rooms are very sparse. No pictures, not a lot of items beyond clothes and toiletries."

"What about next of kin?" I could find out myself, but I knew that would be one of the first things Sam looked at.

"I don't know yet. But I'm going to interview the landlady. She might give me some contacts." He took a step toward the house. "I suppose you want to join me."

CHAPTER SIX

I covered my surprise. I knew Sam had a high opinion of my skills, but I hadn't expected him to ask me to tag along. Then again, there was nothing stopping me from coming back to talk to the woman, and he had to know that. Maybe he figured it was better to keep an eye on me. "If I won't be in your way."

His mouth twitched. "I think you know enough by now not to interfere. At least too much. Besides, you'll only talk to Mrs. Finch after I leave. This way, she only has to tell her story once. But no way I'm letting you in Kettle's rooms until we're done. Understand?"

There were times I'd cajoled Sam into letting me do what I wanted. But I could tell from his tone of voice this wasn't gonna be one of them. I waved toward the front door. "After you, Detective."

Chapter Seven

I'd built up an image of boarding house landladies based on the movies. They were older women who looked like they could have been grandmothers. Edward's did not disappoint me.

"Miss Ahern, this is Mrs. Ida Finch. Mrs. Finch, Miss Ahern is a colleague of mine and a very fine private detective," Sam said.

I held out my hand. "Pleased to meet you."

Mrs. Finch was a mess. Even sitting down, I could tell she was short, maybe Dot's height or even shorter. The lines on her face were those of an older woman, and the hair held back in a net was a beautiful silver gray, bordering on white. Her eyes were a bold shade of blue, even if they were red-rimmed. The ashy color of her face highlighted them. She'd never have been called a beauty, even in her youth, but there was a striking quality about her I couldn't miss. In fact, she reminded me of Bette Davis if the actress was twenty years older and thirty pounds heavier.

Sam pulled out a chair and nodded for me to take the one across from him. "Once again, I'm sorry this morning has been so hard. I understand you found Mr. Kettle's body. It must have been a terrible shock."

Mrs. Finch pressed a handkerchief to her mouth and nodded. "He's usually up so early to go to work. I knew he'd lost his job, so when he didn't appear for breakfast as usual, I thought nothing of it. But when I hadn't seen him by nine, I was worried. That's when Mr. Carter, he's another tenant, said he'd smelled this awful scent from Mr. Kettle's room. I went in and…oh…I still can't bear it." Her voice rose, and she squeezed her eyes shut.

Based on Sam's description of the room, I couldn't blame her. Nice elderly

CHAPTER SEVEN

landladies didn't deal with slaughterhouse scenes. "Did you know Mr. Kettle well?" I asked.

She took a deep breath. "Are you a relative? He never mentioned your name."

I shook my head. "He was a client of mine."

She mouthed the word client, and if anything, her expression grew more horrified. "You're not...one of *those* girls, are you?"

It took a moment for me to process her meaning. "No, ma'am. I'm not a prostitute, if that's what you mean. Detective MacKinnon already told you, I'm a private detective."

She looked at him. "I...I didn't think you were serious." She shook her head and murmured.

I caught the words "indecent" and "not in my day." I figured Mrs. Finch was one of the older generation who believed women belonged in the home and nowhere else. I didn't bother to tell her I used to work in a factory. That shock, on top of the way her morning had gone so far, might've sent her for the smelling salts.

Sam pretended he hadn't heard a thing. "How long had Mr. Kettle rented from you?"

Mrs. Finch blinked her eyes. "Not all that long," she said. "No more than a year. That nice Mr. Brickett across the street vouched for him. I think they are friends. Or were friends. Oh dear."

"What kind of tenant was he?" he asked.

"The best kind." She blew her nose, which sounded a little like the horn of a ship on Lake Erie. Not very ladylike. "He was single, quiet, clean, polite, and paid his rent on time. Sometimes he worked nights, and he was always very conscientious about keeping quiet when he left. And I think he had a lot of schooling."

It matched my impression of him. "What makes you say that?"

"His speech. It was very polished, and his grammar was perfect. He corrected me on occasion. It was our little joke. And he read, oh my, so many books. The library was his favorite place on his days off, and he had at least a dozen volumes in his room. He lent me one, but it was too sophisticated for me. Some kind of novel, I think, by a man named James. But I did like the Emily Dickinson poetry he read to me. So sweet." She dabbed her eyes. "I'm going to miss him."

"Let's go back to this morning," Sam said. "Did you see anyone enter the house and go to Mr. Kettle's rooms? Or maybe you heard him talking to someone?"

"I'm afraid I was out early this morning," she said. "Mrs. Neilson, she lives at the end of the street, her littlest one has croup. I took over some homemade soup and an ointment my mother used to put on me when I was little. I returned around seven-thirty and served breakfast. Mr. Kettle's door was closed. I asked about him, but no one else had seen him that morning. Around nine..." She gulped.

"No need to tell us again." Sam paused in his note-taking. "Did he ever bring any lady friends to the house?"

"Never." Mrs. Finch folded her hands. "I told you, he was a quiet, nice person. Not that I object to my gentlemen having visitors, but I make it quite clear to all of them that women should be entertained in the front room. Mr. Kettle never had a lady over in all the time he stayed with me. Not even for a glass of sherry."

"What about other friends? Did they visit?" he asked.

"No one. He didn't talk about his personal life."

Edward sounded exactly like Lee described him. A guy who kept to himself and had maybe given up on women. It didn't surprise me too much that he'd never brought any friends from work to the boarding house. This wasn't a place for the guys to hang out. Mrs. Finch wouldn't have appreciated drunk men in her front room. "How about family?" I asked. "Did he ever mention a brother, sister? Parents maybe?"

"Not parents." She frowned. "I do seem to remember there was a sister. Younger, I think he told me. She's married and has her own family. I don't know where she lives, though. Mr. Kettle simply didn't talk about himself much."

"That's quite all right." Sam read over the notes he'd written. "Did Mr. Kettle ever mention a former lover or an enemy? Maybe you saw him

CHAPTER SEVEN

arguing with someone on the street outside?"

She frowned in thought. "Last Valentine's Day was the closest he got. Some of the men were talking about how to get gifts for their sweethearts. With the war, it's so expensive to buy even the smallest thing. One of them asked Mr. Kettle if he had anyone special. He said something about a person named Sydney, how she'd been the love of his life." She sniffed. "Sounds like a very vulgar name to me, Sydney. But there's no accounting for some people's taste."

I couldn't see this as a crime of a jilted lover. A woman didn't usually slit a man's throat, and surely not as deeply as Sam had described. Then again, if she was tryin' to shift the blame away from herself, maybe she'd do exactly that. I'd have to ask Sam what he thought. Once we were away from Mrs. Finch, of course.

Sam rubbed his chin. "Did you see anyone at the house last night who you didn't recognize? Or maybe someone who shouldn't have been here?"

She hesitated, then gave a shake of her head. "Not a soul. All the men were here for dinner, at least the ones who usually are."

"What do you mean?" I asked.

"Some of them work the night shift. Mr. Townes, for example. They eat earlier so they can get some sleep before they leave."

That made sense. Pop didn't work nights often, but when he did he kept much the same schedule. "No strangers came to visit later?"

"No one." She spread her hands. "I'm sorry. It was a very quiet night. Although…"

"Yes?" Sam prompted her.

"I did think I saw Mr. Townes. This would have been around nine o'clock. I put out the milk bottles, like I always do, and I spotted him in the hallway."

"I don't s'pose you saw anything off about his clothes, did you?" I asked. "Was he running or anything?"

She fussed with her skirt and avoided lookin' at me. "Oh no, it was much too dark. I got the impression he was leaving." She folded her hands in her lap.

That meant Mr. Townes had been there. It was possible he'd seen something. I made a note to follow up with him.

Sam gave me a questioning glance. "Thank you for your time, ma'am," I said as I rose from my chair. "Once again, I'm so sorry you had to see this."

He followed suit, adding his condolences. He handed her a card. "If you think of anything else, please call me."

We left the kitchen. "Can I see his bedroom?" I asked.

Sam hesitated. "They've taken the body away, and I think they've cleared the scene by now, but are you sure you want to? I'm willing to bend the rules and let you know what I find just to spare you the experience."

I considered his offer and shook my head. "No. I can't be relying on the cops for information. What if the next time it's not you on the spot? I'll be up a creek."

"Suit yourself. This way." He headed down a hallway.

"I do have a question, though."

"What's that?"

"Where do you get your business cards?"

Chapter Eight

Despite Sam's warning and my determination to stay cool while viewing the murder scene, I froze at the door to Edward's room. Sam had described the place as a slaughterhouse and that wasn't far off. The blood seemed to be everywhere, on the floor, the walls, the bedding, and even a little splattered on the ceiling. The heavy metallic scent made me cover my nose with my hand. *Breathe through your mouth and keep calm.* I'd been sure I was ready for anything.

I wasn't.

Sam wasn't fooled. "You don't have to go in, you know."

I swallowed the lump in my throat. "Unless I'm gonna limit my career to finding lost cats, cheatin' spouses, and petty theft, I do." I glanced at the floor. Most of the blood had pooled around the bed, but there were a few clear spots. I inched inside, making sure to stay clear of any red. "Are you gonna get in trouble lettin' me in?"

"They've taken everything they want from this room." He sidled up next to me. Whether he was tryin' to avoid the stains himself or he wanted to be close enough to catch me if I fainted, I didn't much care. "Truth be told, aside from the body, there wasn't much to find. As you can see, Mr. Kettle wasn't big on possessions." He swept his arm around.

"I don't see any footprints."

"We didn't find any."

"How is that possible? The killer had to have tracked blood all over the place." And why hadn't someone noticed a person covered in gore leave the house?

"Not if he did the act from behind." Sam positioned himself behind me. "The coroner thinks our guy was behind the victim. He slashed his throat." Sam mimed the cut against my neck. "Then he pushed the body forward and escaped out the door. You can see most of the blood is on the bed and the surrounding carpet. Because such a cut would sever the carotid artery, there would have been a fair amount of spray outward. That's what you see on the curtains, the wall, and even a bit on the ceiling."

I could see what Sam was describing. "And if the murderer was wearing a coat or something, he might be able to cover up anything that splattered on him."

"Possibly. Or he skedaddled before anyone could see him." Sam let go of me.

I scanned the room. There weren't any photos on the bureau, and the top of the desk was bare. Plain curtains, no doubt provided by Mrs. Finch, hung at the windows. One of 'em, the one closest to the bed, had a few flecks of red on it. The closet door was open, showing off one suit, a pair of scuffed wingtips, one pair of galoshes, and a heavy winter coat. The bureau drawers were askew. A few books graced the top. "Did you find anything in the desk or elsewhere?"

"There wasn't anything except clothes in the bureau. His work attire, from the look of it." Sam stuffed his hands in his pocket. "Aside from one letter and a well-read Bible, the desk was empty."

"Who was the letter from?"

"A woman named Genevieve Zellwig. We think that might be the victim's sister. I can't show it to you, but she begged him to come home and make things right. The most interesting bit was 'No matter what you've done or what you are, you're still family. I know you can come to see your error. I enclose this Bible for you to read and pray on. It was Grandfather's, and I know he'd want you to make things right.' I am going to assume that's where the book came from."

"*What* you are not *who*. Hm." I picked my way over to the desk. "Does she live in Buffalo?"

Sam watched me. "No, Hamburg."

CHAPTER EIGHT

If she lived in the Southtowns, she had money. Or she'd married it. "I wonder what he did to need reconciliation."

"We won't know until we talk to Mrs. Zellwig."

I swept my gaze around the room. A small wooden cross with a silver figure hung above the bed. "What version of the Bible?"

"Come again?"

I pointed. "That's a crucifix. Protestants don't display the crucified Christ, not usually. At least, that's my understanding. I'm wondering if he was Catholic. What version of the Bible did he have?"

"King James." Sam's faint smile carried the stamp of approval. "Good catch. The crucifix could belong to Mrs. Finch. Do you think his faith is important?"

"I don't know, but it's a fact about him no one's mentioned." I eased to another clear spot on the floor. "Where's the book?"

"I took it as evidence." Sam watched me, although what he was on the alert for was anyone's guess. "The name on the inside flap was Jeremiah Kettle, and it was dated in the late 1800s, so that is presumably the aforementioned grandfather."

The bedspread was soaked in red, but unrumpled. "Where was his body?"

"There." Sam pointed to a spot at the foot of the bed. The place was dark, almost black. "On his stomach, surrounded by what was probably most of the blood in his body. The coroner thinks that's where he fell after he was killed. Oh, he was wearing a shirt and slacks, not pajamas."

"He'd gotten up, dressed, and made his bed. I wonder where he was going. He'd lost his job."

"He might have been going out to look for work. With the lack of men in the city, I'm sure he would have found something." Sam rubbed his chin. "Mrs. Finch didn't mention a visitor this morning."

"He coulda been killed by another boarder. Or someone slipped in without her knowing." I turned on the spot and tugged at my ear. "Or he never got a chance to get undressed last night."

"What's bothering you?" Sam asked.

"This." I waved my hand around the room. "It's too empty. Except for a

45

crucifix, which I don't think was his. How long did Mrs. Finch say he lived here?"

He consulted his notes. "A year, more or less."

"A person doesn't go that long in one space and only accumulate a bunch of books." I strained to see the cover of the top column. "*Ulysses* by someone named James Joyce. How much you wanna bet those are library books?"

"I don't have to place a wager. They are. I saw the stamp inside the covers. We didn't take them as they didn't seem relevant." He shrugged. "Nothing was hidden inside, no notes or anything else. The man liked old authors, I guess. The others are *A Portrait of the Artist as a Young Man* and a play by Oscar Wilde, *The Importance of Being Earnest*. There are some volumes of poetry over there, but those belong to him. Not quite a dozen, but more than your typical working man owns and certainly more literate."

Highbrow stuff. My high school English classes hadn't included either of those novels or the play. I had a dim recollection of Wilde being called "inappropriate" by my teacher. I'd have to ask Lee. He knew that kind of thing. Bringing my mind back to the current situation, I reviewed what I'd read so far in my detective's handbook. "What about fingerprints?"

Sam chuckled. "I wondered when you'd ask that. Yes, we took a bunch of prints. Some are the victim's. I'm pretty sure some will turn out to belong to Mrs. Finch. As for the rest, who knows? The landlady said Kettle didn't have visitors, but that doesn't mean none of the other boarders ever came into this room." He paused. "Are you done?"

"Yeah." I picked my way back to the door. "Not exactly a gold mine, is it?"

"Nope." He glanced at his watch. "I have to get back to the office."

"You aren't gonna interview the other residents?" I left the room and inhaled a deep breath of fresh air.

Sam followed. Once we were outside, he took out his cigarettes, tapped one out, and flicked his lighter. "I have people for that. That's why I'm going back, to review what they learned. You are free to talk to them. Some are standing right over there." He pointed to the sidewalk. Most of the people had wandered away, but a couple men stuck around, all of them dressed in working man's clothes. "Anything else I can do for you?"

CHAPTER EIGHT

I almost said no, but changed my mind. "What's the address for Mrs. Zellwig? You said she lives in Hamburg."

"I should make you research it, just to hone your skills." He noted my expression and took half a step back. "She lives on Highland Avenue, number 384. I don't know how you'll get out there, though. I can't give you a ride."

I gave a short laugh. "The same way I get everywhere, Sam. The bus. Having a car has made you soft."

He pointed a finger at me. "We'll be talking to her. But if you find out anything you think is important—"

"I promise. I'll call you. Thanks, Sam."

He went to his car, got in, and left. I'd looked at the clock in the front room before I'd left the boarding house, and it was right around eleven in the morning. I wanted to talk to Lee, but he wouldn't be home until at least four that afternoon. Plenty of time to take a trip to the Southtowns. After I talked with the men on the sidewalk.

* * *

I didn't learn anything useful from the onlookers at the boarding house. They were boarders, but all of 'em repeated what I'd learned from Mrs. Finch. Edward didn't bring people to the house. He was quiet. "He hung out with us around the dinner table," one man said, "but he always felt a little like an outsider to me. He mentioned once that his family had money. He tried, but he didn't really fit in with us working stiffs."

The bus didn't go to Hamburg, so I took the trolley. It deposited me at the corner of Union Street and Hawkins, which was surrounded by nice looking houses and trees. The lawns were green and neat. Life appeared to be good in the suburbs.

The address Sam had given me was 384 Highland Avenue. I had no idea what direction I should go from where I stood, but I was sure I could get someone to tell me. All I had to do was find a corner store.

I'd never been there, but Hamburg was a nice place, easy to walk. I passed a school, Union Elementary, an impressive building of yellow stone with broad steps leading up to the front door. I paused on the sidewalk and could see kids in classrooms through the big windows at the front of the building. A boy was staring outside, plainly wishing he was anywhere else. I waved at him, and he waved back.

Down the street, I saw a decent-sized park with a covered pavilion and lots of large trees. A path wandered through the park. An older gentleman smoking a pipe walked a bulldog. A young woman watched over two kids, who were too young to be in school, play with a ball. Their mother or a governess? The houses I passed were all tall and elegant, nothing like the small squares of the First Ward. Every place had a yard and a separate building in the back. Through one open door, I saw a dark-colored car. I didn't know much about cars, but it looked swanky. *These people have houses for their automobiles.* Yes, life in Hamburg was definitely on a different level than my neighborhood.

My wandering took me all the way down Main Street, where I could see the white-topped spire of a Catholic church. Curious, I strolled down, and the sign in front of the red-brick building told me the church was called Saints Peter and Paul. I opened the front door and walked through the narthex into the nave.

The inside was beautiful, almost like a cathedral. Stately wood pews marched up to the chancel, where a massive wood altar stood in front of the tabernacle. Along the way, towering stained glass windows depicted various saints. Behind the altar, another huge stained glass window of the crucifixion was lit with the incoming sunlight.

I genuflected and crossed myself. *This is where they go to daily Mass?* A few elderly women who knelt in the pews, rosaries in their hands, glanced at me, but returned to their prayers and devotions without speaking. I offered up a quick prayer for Tom, Sean, and the soul of Edward Kettle. My client might not have been Catholic, but I figured God was okay with that.

I don't know how long I stood there, lost in thought, but eventually, I made my way back outside. I wasn't in Hamburg to gawk at churches or houses. I was there on business and I better get cracking.

I walked back up Main Street, which held a variety of stores, including a

CHAPTER EIGHT

soda shop. Inside, I asked for and got directions to Highland Avenue. Just my luck, it was in the opposite direction I'd taken from the trolley stop. Normally, I'd resent the lost time, but the sun was out, the sky was blue, and the birdsong lifted my spirits. I bought a Good Humor ice cream bar to eat while I walked.

If I'd thought the houses I'd seen so far were swell, the ones on Highland were even fancier. I'd finished my ice cream well before I arrived at my destination, but I couldn't throw the stick away. This place was too clean to litter.

Mrs. Zellwig's house was another tall one painted a dark blue with white trim. The front porch had gleaming white pillars and fancy wood trim cut in swirly shapes. The shutters next to the windows, which gleamed in the sunlight, were also white. I didn't see any stars in the windows. The whole place looked like a gingerbread house.

I climbed the stairs and used the heavy brass knocker to announce my presence. I didn't wait long before a woman opened the door. She wore a green dress with a collar and two large shiny buttons with a brown leather belt at her waist. It wasn't unlike one I'd wear to a dance, but I could tell the fabric was much softer and finer. The swingy skirt's hem was a little lower than I'd like, but she was also older than me by a good twenty years. Her face was made up, and her light brown hair was pinned back at the temple to fall in curls to her shoulders. She even wore earrings, pearls that matched the strand at her throat. I couldn't see her shoes, but I was sure they were shiny and heeled.

A puzzled expression on her face, she said, "I've already given at my church for charity, bought enough war bonds, and taken my paper and cans to our local collection point. I'm not interested in buying anything, and if you're from the Jehovah's Witnesses, I'm Anglican."

What this lady thought of a strange young woman dressed in pants showing up at her house in the middle of the day, I couldn't guess. Of course, I didn't have to. She'd just read off a whole list of reasons a stranger would knock on her door. "None of the above." I identified myself. "Are you Genevieve Zellwig?"

She laughed. "Is this a practical joke? I've heard of girls going to work in the factories, but not being detectives. Isn't that a man's job?"

"I'm not pulling your leg. I'm a real detective." I wished I had identification. "I used to work for Bell Aircraft. If you're Mrs. Zellwig, your brother, Edward, was my client."

Her laughter died. "You know Edward? No, I don't believe it. Why would he need a detective?"

Mrs. Zellwig was gonna need some convincing. I described her brother to her, right down to the grease in his fingernails from working at the shipyard. "He hired me to help prove the American Shipbuilding Company made a mistake in firing him."

She gripped the door. "He lost his job? I don't understand." A tiny line appeared between her perfectly shaped eyebrows. "Wait, you said he *was* your client. It sounds like he isn't any longer. If he let you go, why are you here?"

I'd beaten the cops to Hamburg. *Oh boy.* Sam should have been here and gone by now. After all, I had to take the trolley.

A familiar car pulled into the driveway and parked. Sam got out and hustled to the front door. "You came straight here?" he asked me.

"I told you I was gonna. Why are you surprised? I expected you to beat me."

"I had things to take care of first."

Mrs. Zellwig looked from me to Sam. "Who are you?"

He showed her his badge. "Detective Sam MacKinnon, Buffalo police. May we come in?"

Her face paled, but she stood her ground. "What's going on? Why do I have a police detective and a private investigator on my porch in the middle of a Tuesday afternoon?"

I looked at Sam. *This one is all yours*, I hoped my expression said. I didn't fancy bein' the person to tell Mrs. Zellwig her brother had been murdered, even if he was an estranged brother.

Sam shot me a quizzical look. Mind-reading only existed in science fiction movies, but his message was clear.

CHAPTER EIGHT

I stepped back.

He turned to her. "Mrs. Genevieve Zellwig?"

"Yes?" She strung out the word.

"I think we should go inside to talk."

Chapter Nine

Sam and I followed Mrs. Zellwig down a corridor lined with a fancy length of carpet. Pictures with gilded frames hung on the wall. Most of 'em were of old men with sour expressions. There was one mirror, also in a heavy frame, that hung over a small dark wood table with curving legs. A lamp with a painted glass shade cast a soft light, and the table wood gleamed as though someone had finished polishing it just a minute before we entered.

She led us through an arch to a sitting room full of formal furniture, all chintz fabrics, and more shiny wood. An Oriental carpet with the colors red, blue, and green covered the hardwood floor. Two end tables flanked the couch, each with a lace doily and an oil lamp, the bases a heavy cut glass and clean as a whistle. No one lit those, that was sure. A clock with Roman numerals and an aged ivory face took center stage on the mantel, the hearth a gleaming marble over a fire laid and ready for lighting. Heavy bookcases took up the wall on either side of the fireplace.

The house reeked of money.

Mrs. Zellwig gestured at the couch. "Please sit down."

I did and took a moment to study my hostess. In addition to the jewelry and clothes, her makeup was perfect. Up close, I could tell the material of her dress was not simple cotton. Maybe silk or a shiny satin. As I suspected, her black heeled shoes were polished so highly they reflected the light. I caught the light scent of her perfume. I didn't recognize it, but it smelled pricey.

Sam settled next to me and took off his fedora. "Mrs. Zellwig, I'm sorry

CHAPTER NINE

to have to tell you this, but your brother Edward was murdered."

She gasped. Her eyes welled with tears, and she fumbled a lace handkerchief out of her pocket. "Are you...are you sure?"

"Quite sure, ma'am." He studied her.

I noticed he didn't go into details. Of course, she didn't need to know he'd been slaughtered like a pig.

"I don't...no, it can't...oh my." She clutched the hanky to her mouth and took great shuddery breaths. Her face became pale ivory, like the lined paper the boys used to practice their letters.

I hoped she wouldn't faint. I didn't have smelling salts on me. Of course, in a house like this, there might be a maid who could bring some if needed.

Mrs. Zellwig didn't swoon. After dabbing at her eyes, she asked, "Who did it?"

"That's what we're trying to find out." Sam took out his notebook. "When was the last time you saw your brother?"

"Oh, um, it's been quite a long time." She pressed her hands together. "Years, in fact. We...we weren't close, you see."

"But you knew he was working for American Shipbuilding?" I asked.

She nodded. "That was one of the reasons for our continued separation. His insistence on working as a mere dockyard hand drove the wedge in our family even deeper. My father grew particularly angry, on top of everything else."

I wondered what *everything else* was. But before I could ask, Sam spoke up. "Do you know if he argued with anyone recently? Anyone who wished him harm?"

"No." Her voice was low and shook with emotion. "Edward was a very gentle man. He was like that as a boy, too. I always wondered if I should have known earlier."

Known what? "Mrs. Zellwig," I said. "What do you know about Edward's job? Did you know he'd been fired and why?"

"I didn't know anything. We heard he'd gotten the job through a friend." She gave me a quizzical look. "Who are you again?"

"I'm a private investigator. Edward hired me to clear his name. Whatever

53

he was working on at the shipyard was secret, something related to the war effort." I paused. "He was fired for talkin' to a reporter about it."

She shook her head, brown curls swinging. "No. Edward would never have done that. Whatever other faults he had, Edward was a patriot. He would not have talked to anyone about his work if it would have compromised the war effort."

Sam leaned his elbows on his knees. "In his room, we found a Bible, one you gave him, I think. Inside was a note. It spoke of forgiveness for the error of Edward's ways. What was that about?"

She averted her eyes.

"Mrs. Zellwig?"

The silence stretched. Eventually, she got up and went to a sideboard, where an old-time picture of a man with a long white beard stared out of the silver frame from deep-set eyes. "This is my grandfather, Jeremiah Kettle. He was a very religious man."

Sam and I exchanged a look. "You mentioned you were Anglican," I said.

She ran a finger over the top edge of the picture. "Yes, high church. I believe Grandfather's grandfather was a bishop in the Church of England. He was a boy when they immigrated to this country. His father began as a worker in a textile mill. When Grandfather was thirty years old, he bought that mill."

"That's where he made his money," I said. "What does this have to do with Edward's need for forgiveness?"

She stared at the picture. "Grandfather was very insistent that all the boys go to private schools. The girls, my mother, and aunts, had private tutors. Education was very important. Edward was his pride and joy. After high school, he went to Canisius College. Grandfather wasn't pleased that it was run by Catholics, but it did give Edward a chance at a very prestigious education."

Why won't she answer the question? From what she said, Edward was the apple of his grandpap's eye. What could have caused the rift? "Did he fail or something? Is that what Edward needed forgiveness for?"

She refused to meet my eye. "When he was at Canisius, Edward made

CHAPTER NINE

some...friends. They made him do things. Oh, I don't think the college had anything to do with it, nor the Jesuits. Neither did Grandfather, for all he disliked Catholics. But he disapproved of Edward's habits. The books he was reading. He brought home dirty things, like plays from English playwrights who were known to be renegades and worse. People like Oscar Wilde."

I remembered seeing Wilde's play in Edward's room along with the books by James Joyce. I couldn't understand the rancor in her voice when she said the name. Who was he, anyway?

She continued. "Edward and another boy were caught at the end of his junior year in a situation that would have been quite the scandal if the details had become known. The school expelled them both. Grandfather made a large donation to the college, and Edward came home. After that, we didn't speak. I couldn't believe that of my brother. As I said, he'd been very gentle as a boy. He looked after me, read to me. I was heartbroken."

I snuck a look at Sam, whose lips were pressed together. He wouldn't look at me. What could be so awful that a boy would be thrown outta college and estranged from his family? My brothers were no saints, but I couldn't imagine Pop turning any of them out just for making a mistake.

"Mrs. Zellwig." Sam cleared his throat. "This is all very interesting, but it doesn't tell us anything. Why would your brother need forgiveness? What did he do?"

"It wasn't just what he'd done, but what he was." She closed her eyes, took a deep breath, and touched the picture. "You see, Edward was a homosexual."

* * *

Mrs. Zellwig didn't have much to say after that. She hadn't seen her brother in over ten years, so she didn't know anything about his friends, or lovers, or life. Sam and I gave her our sympathy again, he left a card, I wrote down my telephone number, and we headed out.

Nothing had changed outside. The sky was a brilliant blue, with just a few clouds. Birds hopped across perfectly cut green grass. The street was quiet. I slung my coat over my arm. "Well, how do you like them apples?"

Sam tugged on his fedora. "Which ones?"

I gave him a look.

His face flushed. He had to know what I meant. "Yeah. Right."

All those busted relationships. Edward wasn't unlucky in love, he was loving the wrong people. The girls must have found out and broken things off, quietly, of course. No one would want it known she'd dated, much less been about to marry, a queer. And the love of his life couldn't be *Sydney*, it was *Sidney*. "What are you gonna do now?"

Sam shrugged. "Go back to the office and try again to track down any connections to the victim. What did you say that reporter's name was?"

"Melvin Schlingmann, but wait." I got to the end of the driveway and faced him. "You're gonna keep investigating?"

"Of course." His expression turned puzzled. "Betty, a man has been murdered. Pretty violently. I can't let that slide."

"Even if he's, you know…."

He took a moment to process my words. "Yes." His voice was firm. "The law is pretty clear. So are the Ten Commandments. Thou shalt not kill. There aren't any loopholes in that one." He paused. "You're too young, but I remember my grandfather talking about the days of 'No Irish need apply' signs. If you deny justice to one group because of who they are, don't be surprised if you're the next group getting the same treatment."

I studied my toes. He was right. Of course, he was. I'd grown up having those Commandments drilled into me, along with "love thy neighbor." But it still made me uncomfortable. No, that wasn't the right word. I was right on the edge of horrified. What Edward had been, it went against everything I'd ever been taught. If I'd known this fact before he died, I'd never have taken his case. In my whole life, I'd never met anyone who was homosexual. Well, not that I'd known. It put Lee's comment about Edward trying too hard to fit in with the guys in a different light. It wasn't just 'cause he had money. He'd have been desperate to keep the truth about his private life a secret.

Sam tossed his keys from hand to hand. "What are you going to do?"

The question startled me. "I'm not sure. On the one hand, he's dead. What

CHAPTER NINE

can I do? On the other, he did pay me for the week. I s'pose I should at least complete that. Although no one would know if I quit. I just...I gotta think about it." *I gotta pray about it, too.* If any situation called for divine instruction, this was it.

"You would know."

Sam's voice made me look up. Yes, I would. It didn't sit right, not finishing a job I'd been paid for. But wouldn't everyone understand if they knew about my client? "Will your new captain play ball on that? You sticking with it?"

"I think so. He doesn't want an open case staining his record. Oh, some of the guys will undoubtedly tell me to sandbag the investigation or let it go cold, especially when they learn about Edward's life, but I intend to see it through." He looked around the quiet neighborhood. "You want a ride back into the city?"

Before I could answer, the door opened. Mrs. Zellwig hurried down the walk. "Oh, thank goodness you haven't left yet. Miss Ahern, right? May I ask you a favor?"

I figured she wanted me to keep my yap shut about her brother. "I'm not gonna say anything. About Edward, that is. His secret is safe with me."

She waved a hand. "Not that. He hired you to clear his name, you said. Did he pay you?"

"Yes, ma'am. For the week."

She bit her underlip. "I'd like you to complete the job. Whatever else Edward might have done, he loved his country. He wouldn't have betrayed the men in uniform. If that's why American Shipbuilding fired him, they thought he spoke out of turn about whatever project they are working on, they are wrong." She glanced at Sam. "I suppose everybody will learn the truth about him now."

His shoulders twitched. "Maybe. Maybe not."

She wrinkled her nose. "Well, I may not be able to keep people from knowing what he was, but I can make sure he isn't remembered as a traitor. What did you charge?"

I told her my rates. "I don't know if I'll be able to wrap it up in a week

57

now that he's dead."

She brushed away my concerns. "Don't worry. I'll pay it." She hesitated. "And if the police have to…well, I want his murder solved. Can you do that, too? Find his killer?"

Now, I'd done just that on a couple of occasions, but aside from Lee's dad back in March, I hadn't ever been *hired* to find a murderer. Not by a stranger, at least. "Ma'am, I'm not the police. Detective MacKinnon here, he's one of the best. I don't think I can add much." I didn't want to tell her I wasn't sure I wanted to help her brother.

"The police are subject to politics." She held up a hand. "Don't bother to argue with me, Detective. I know it's true. But you, young lady." She held my gaze. "You aren't bound by someone else's agenda. I want to hire you. I'll double your rate."

Double. I wanted to whistle, but figured that was the mark of an amateur. I definitely could use the scratch, and it seemed Mrs. Zellwig had it to spend. I glanced at Sam, who gave the tiniest of shrugs, then turned back to her. "Let me think about it."

"Here's my telephone number." She held out a sheet of thick notepaper. "Call me tonight and let me know what you decide."

Chapter Ten

I asked Sam to drive me back to Edward's boarding house on North Pearl. We didn't say much on the way there. I guess he'd already said what he felt he needed to.

He parked at the curb, and I opened my door. "Thanks for the lift." I put my foot on the pavement.

"You're going to accept Mrs. Zellwig's offer."

"I haven't decided yet."

He tapped the steering wheel. "Then why didn't you tell me to take you to the First Ward?"

Why hadn't I? "The day is half over. I might as well poke around some more. This way I haven't lost any time if I do tell Mrs. Zellwig yes." I got out of the car.

"Betty."

The serious tone of his voice made me turn around. "What is it?"

"This was a particularly brutal murder, one of the worst—if not *the* worst—one I've seen in my years of police work." He paused. "You've worked some tough cases. Whoever killed Edward Kettle sent a message. You don't slice a human throat like that without a lot of underlying anger. Please be careful on this one."

That was Sam. He didn't tell me to drop it or stay away, and he didn't tell me how to do anything. That didn't stop him from being concerned. "I will. See ya round."

I watched as he drove down the street and turned a corner. Then I considered my options. No one I'd talked to so far knew anything about

Edward's life or friends. But someone had to. A joe didn't often go through life with no one being aware of him. He must have what the cops called "known associates," even if they were only casual drinking buddies. To my mind, the best starting points were this Harvey person and Mrs. Finch. This morning she'd claimed to know nothing, but maybe I could jog her memory. Luckily, I could talk to 'em both now, since they lived across the street from each other. I checked my watch. It was a little after two in the afternoon. If Harvey was at work, he wouldn't be home until four, maybe four-thirty if Lee's schedule was any guide.

The cops were gone, and the crowd from earlier had dispersed. Except for flattened patches of grass from multiple pairs of feet, the front of the boarding house held no evidence there'd been a grisly murder. I walked to the door and knocked.

Mrs. Finch answered. "Go away, you vulture. I've got nothing—" She stopped when the door was half-open. "Oh, I'm sorry. I thought you were someone else."

Clearly. "Who were you expecting?"

"Some reporter. He was a skinny man with a cheap suit. He said he writes for a local paper, but it's not one I've ever heard of." She sniffed.

It had to be Melvin Schlingmann. I made a mental note to go back to *The Daily* offices to talk to him again. If he'd never spoken to Edward Kettle, why'd Melvin been on the scene? And how had he gotten Edward's address?

"Weren't you here earlier? I'm sorry, I don't remember your name."

Mrs. Finch's voice brought me back to the moment. "Yes, ma'am. Betty Ahern. I was here with Detective MacKinnon after they took Mr. Kettle's body away."

She squinted at me. "You're a private detective, he said. If you don't mind my saying so, it's not a very nice occupation for a young lady. Girls in my day wouldn't do such a thing. Of course, when I was young, a lady wouldn't wear trousers, either." She looked at my slacks and sniffed.

"Times have changed, 'specially with the war and all. We have to change with it."

Mrs. Finch didn't say anything, but her expression said volumes about

CHAPTER TEN

her thoughts on the matter.

At least she didn't say anything more or give me a long lecture. She looked a little haggard, which wasn't surprising considerin' the morning she'd had. But she didn't tell me to scram. "Do you mind if I come in? I'd like to ask a couple more questions."

"I don't have anything to add."

"It'll only be for a few minutes. I've learned a bit since this morning and I'm following up."

"Very well." She held the door for me and shut it as soon as I was inside. "We can talk in the kitchen. I'm preparing dinner for my residents. Would you like a cup of tea? I have coffee left over from this morning, but I'm not sure I'd drink it at this point."

"Tea will be fine." I followed her to the same room we'd talked in earlier. The only difference was the smell of cooking, some type of beef stew from the scent, along with placemats and settings on the table. I sat in the same chair.

Mrs. Finch filled the kettle and put it on the stove to heat. She pulled out a teacup patterned with blue flowers and added a teabag. "Do you want milk or sugar?"

"I'll take it black, thank you." Sugar was a precious commodity. No sense dipping into the boarders' allotments if I didn't need to.

"Let me give the meat a stir and finish these biscuits, and I'll be with you." She bustled about the stove and brushed a little melted butter on the tops of the dough circles. She set the tray aside and sat down, smoothing silver hair from her face. "What is it you want to ask? I can't imagine I'll have any more information for you."

I took out a notepad and pencil. "When we talked earlier, you said Mr. Kettle was a fairly private person, quiet, polite, and paid his rent on time. He didn't bring over any women, and you didn't ever see his friends." I wondered if she knew why Edward didn't bring home a girl.

"That's right. A very nice gentleman. He wouldn't hurt a fly. I can't imagine anybody disliking him."

Except the person who slit his throat like a butchered hog. "Are you sure about that? It's just...I find it odd a man would live somewhere for a year and never mention a friend or co-worker or a girl."

The kettle whistled, and she jumped up to grab it off the stove. "To tell you the truth, I did think it was strange," she said as she poured water into my teacup. "He was a good-looking man, even if he was over forty. The only girl he ever mentioned was Sydney."

"The love of his life." Steam rose from my tea, and I blew on it. "He never told you a last name?"

She put the kettle back. "Mason. Manson. Masson. Something like that." She lowered her bulk back into her chair.

I jotted down the names. "Based on what you said earlier, you liked Mr. Kettle a lot."

"Oh, he was the nicest one here." She gave me a smile. "I never could understand why he was single. He told me once he had no luck with women. But he was the most helpful of all the men. No matter what I needed, I could ask Mr. Kettle. Carrying the groceries, fixing things around the house, mowing the yard, anything. When the water pipes under the sink leaked, he took care of it. And he never asked for a dime. He did so much handiwork I offered to reduce his rent, but he wouldn't hear of it. 'Happy to help, Mrs. Finch,' that's what he said. Just the sweetest man."

"Did Mr. Brickett ever come over? Harvey Brickett from across the street?"

"Oh, once or twice. They'd have coffee in the front room, sometimes a whiskey after dinner. They'd talk about politics, the war, books. But never sports. Funny. I thought all men talked about sports."

Sean, Tom, and Lee liked to gab about baseball, especially the Buffalo Bisons, our International League team. They had some pretty intense discussions about the Yankees, Dodgers, and Red Sox, too. Pop didn't talk much about sports, though. I thought maybe it was an age thing. "He never brought anybody else to the house?"

"Just Mr. Brickett."

"What about outside? Maybe he talked to someone on the street? I know I'm askin' a lot, but I can't believe the guy never talked to anybody. Was he

CHAPTER TEN

friends with your other boarders?"

"Oh, he was friendly with everybody here. Except Mr. Townes." She sighed. "They definitely did not get along. If one was in the dining room, the other would take his meal in his room or go elsewhere."

I scribbled the name. "Why didn't they like each other?"

"I'm sure I couldn't say." Except the expression on Mrs. Finch's face said she'd very much like to say.

I waited.

After a moment, she leaned in. "I wouldn't want to dirty anybody's reputation, you understand."

"My lips are sealed." Unless what she was gonna tell me directly related to the murder, in which case they were not sealed at all.

"Mr. Kettle came in late one evening. Well after the dinner hour. Mr. Townes was in the front room, listening to the radio with some of my other gentlemen. They were listening to a serial or something. It might have been The Pepsodent Show, you know, with Bob Hope. One of the other men asked Mr. Kettle to join them, and he declined. He said he was tired and going to his room to read."

I couldn't imagine anybody passing on listening to Bob Hope, but to each his own. "I guess that didn't go over well with Mr. Townes."

"He started making fun of Mr. Kettle, and he said, well, I don't even like to repeat it." She folded her hands.

I could tell Mrs. Finch was just burstin' to do just that. "I understand your not wanting to gossip, but it could be important."

That was all the landlady needed. "Mr. Townes used the most awful language. He said maybe a"—her voice dropped to a whisper—"faggot"—her voice returned to a normal volume—"like Mr. Kettle didn't appreciate good old American humor. It was disgusting." She gave a sharp nod. "I told Mr. Townes later that if I ever heard such language out of him again, he could find himself another place to live. I won't tolerate that sort of low-brow behavior in my house. No sir, I won't. Calling nice Mr. Kettle names like that. It's indecent."

Interesting. I was dead certain Mr. Kettle had done everything in his

63

power to look like a regular joe. It sounded like Mr. Townes wasn't fooled. "Is Mr. Townes here so I could talk to him?"

"No, he works at Bethlehem Steel. I mentioned before that he's working the night shift this week, so he's out running errands. I expect him home no later than six for dinner. Maybe earlier."

I glanced at the clock. It was going on two-thirty. I could come back. "And you're sure you never saw Mr. Kettle with anyone else?"

"No. Well, there was that young man."

I beat back the urge to scream. Is this what Sam had to deal with? "Who was he?"

"I don't know. He stopped Mr. Kettle on the sidewalk one day. He must have been passing out pamphlets or something because he was dressed like one of those door-to-door salesmen, but he didn't have any samples with him. He was a good-looking young man, too. You'd have liked him." She patted my knee. "Very Cary Grant, if you know what I mean."

I did, but she must have missed the engagement ring on my hand. That or she didn't care. "Is that all?"

Mrs. Finch thought a moment. "Yes. At least, I'm pretty sure."

I tore off a page in my notebook and wrote my name and phone number. "I shoulda given this to you before. You can call me at that number if you think of anything else. Thank you very much for your time."

I let myself out. It hadn't been a bad visit. I had three more people to talk to, four if you counted Melvin: Mr. Brickett, Mr. Townes, and this mysterious young man. If I could find him.

Chapter Eleven

Since I had time to kill before I could catch Mr. Brickett or Mr. Townes, I decided to try and track down Melvin again. The bum had lied to me. He may not have talked to Edward at the shipyard, but if Mrs. Finch could be believed, and I thought she could, Melvin had visited Edward's home. Was he followin' up on the murder story or was there another reason he was so hot to talk to the victim's landlady? 'Cept he couldn't know about Edward's death. That wouldn't make the news until the evening edition. Something else had brought him there.

The first thing I did was call *The Daily* office. I used a fake name and asked for Melvin. "I have a tip for him. It's a big story, so I'm sure he'll be eager to hear what I have to say."

"He's not in right now. Can I take a message?" Emma asked, sounding like she'd heard the same line a hundred times a day.

"No. But it's real juicy. Do you know where I could find him? I wouldn't want him to get scooped by another paper."

Emma huffed, and her breath sounded like a gust of wind. "He's working a story now. When he's out pounding the pavement like this, he likes to eat and drink coffee to keep going."

"Does he have a favorite joint?"

Emma's voice took on an annoyed tone. "He said something this morning about going downtown to hassle the police, so check around there. I have to get back to work, sorry." She hung up.

She had to get back to her nails was more like. Emma said he'd gone to corner the cops, and Moe's Diner was right across the street from police headquarters. It was mid-afternoon and I didn't think it was very likely Melvin would be there. I decided to go downtown and try my luck.

When I arrived at Moe's, the joint was nearly empty. A few men in suits were drinking java in a booth in the back corner, and a man who I figured was either just gettin' off work or about to start was gobbling a blue plate special. Other than that, I didn't recognize a soul. I plucked the sleeve of a passing waitress. "Excuse me."

She snapped her gum. "Take any table in the place, and I'll be right with ya."

"I'm not here to eat. I'm looking for someone. I'm s'posed to meet him, but I'm running late." I described Melvin. "Have you seen anyone who looks like that in here this afternoon?"

"Sounds like Mel. He comes in when he's haunting the halls at police HQ. You a friend of his?"

"I'm meeting him for an interview."

She eyed me. "You just missed him. Sorry." She turned away.

Drat. "Wait. You said he comes here a lot?"

"I wouldn't say that. But he always makes a stop when he visits the cops. I think he's sweet on the other waitress." She smirked. "I'll see him three days in a row, but if she's on the morning shift, he doesn't darken the door."

"Would you give him a message? I'll pay you."

She pulled away, but the mention of dough brought her back. "How much?"

"A buck." I took a dollar out of my purse. "All you have to do is tell him the girl from the shipyard is looking for him and has some dirt he would be interested in. If he is, he should meet me here tomorrow at eight in the morning. Would you do that?" I realized that by setting the appointment, I had decided to go on with Edward's case. Except I hadn't. I needed to talk to Pop. I could always meet Melvin tomorrow and tell him the deal was off if I had to. Or blow him off. I'd be out the buck, but that was the cost of doing business in this job.

"Girl from the shipyard, dirt, eight tomorrow right here. I don't know if I'll see him again today, though."

CHAPTER ELEVEN

"That's okay." I gave her the money, and she tucked it into her shirt pocket. Then she whirled away without another word.

* * *

I left Moe's and went over to Arlington Park in Allentown, where I thought about what I'd learned, which wasn't much. Who was the unknown man who'd accosted Edward outside his boarding house? Mrs. Finch had described him as young, handsome, and wearing a suit or something very much like one. Someone with money? Not too many guys of draft age weren't overseas serving in some fashion. Even in a city the size of Buffalo, a joe who should be in a uniform stuck out like a sore thumb. He might even go back, 'specially if he didn't know Edward was dead. I made a mental note to ask Mrs. Finch to keep her eyes peeled.

I sat on a park bench, basking in the sun. The winter had not been a particularly hard one, at least weather-wise, not by Buffalo standards. But the return of warmth and green was always welcome, no matter what. There'd been snow in small amounts through April. Sixty degrees felt like the middle of summer.

I stared at a couple of robins pecking the ground. As I did, I twisted the engagement ring on my finger. *Tom, I wish you'd hurry and write back.* What would I do if he told me to give up detective work? Would Lee be able to talk his best friend around?

What would Tom think of me taking on a client who was a homosexual? Even if he was dead?

One of the birds looked right at me, beady black eyes unblinking, just as if it knew what I was thinking. It cocked its head, waiting for my response. Only problem was I didn't have one. "What would you do? Huh?"

The robin didn't have an answer. After a couple more quick pecks at the ground, it flew off. "Thanks a lot." Clearly, I wasn't gonna get any advice from the local wildlife.

A glance at my watch told me I still had plenty of time, so I pulled out my textbook and studied the chapter on questioning a witness again. It seemed simple. I needed to know the facts: who, what, where, when, why, and how. As a stranger, I'd need to make Mr. Brickett and Mr. Townes trust me and want to talk. Sam told me once I had a gift for getting people to open up. *Be friendly. Mr. Brickett is Edward's pal, he'll want to find the killer. You gotta convince him you're on his side.* Mr. Townes would be a different story. I might get an idea once I met him.

Did Mr. Brickett know about Edward's homosexuality? Maybe yes, but if Edward was any good at hiding it, maybe not. I debated telling Mr. Brickett, but decided not to talk about it unless he brought it up. I hoped he wouldn't. Things would be so much easier if I could pretend Edward's secret life had nothing to do with his death. If only that life didn't make a swell motive for murder.

I checked my watch again. Only five minutes had gone by. "C'mon, Betty. You coulda had Sam drive you home, but you didn't. Get on a bus or get going."

* * *

I made my way back to Edward's boarding house and asked Mrs. Finch to keep an eye peeled for the young guy. "Is Mr. Townes home?"

"No. One of the others said he was pulling a double shift tonight."

Rats. "Have you seen Mr. Brickett this afternoon?"

She wiped her hands on her apron. "I spied him walking down the street when I went out to get the post."

I thanked her and crossed North Pearl. The Brickett house looked like every other one on the street, plain but neat. There weren't any stars in the window. There also weren't any toys or bikes in the yard. It made me wonder if they had kids. I knocked on the front door.

A man dressed in heavy work pants and suspenders over a white undershirt answered. "May I help you?"

"Are you Harvey Brickett?"

"I am. Who are you?"

He hadn't opened the outer door, so I couldn't hold out my hand. "I'm a

CHAPTER ELEVEN

friend of Lee Tillotson's and a private investigator."

Mr. Brickett stepped outside. "You're the young lady who was helping Edward."

"That's me." I gave him the once over. He was about five-foot-ten, dark hair that was running away from his forehead, and dark eyes that squinted a lot. I wondered if after working in a factory, he'd become unused to sunshine. His face was lined, and I suspected he smiled frequently. His fingernails were torn and dirty, the skin of his hands callused and beaten up from manual labor. He looked like an average joe trying to make an honest wage. "Have you heard about Mr. Kettle and what happened this morning?"

He nodded. "My wife told me when I got home. Shocking. I can't believe that would happen to someone like…to Edward."

"I'd like to ask you a few questions. Can we go inside to talk?"

He took my arm and guided me away from the house. "I'd rather do this outside. My wife is the nervous sort. This conversation would upset her. But she's also nosy. There's no way she'd keep herself out of it, and I'd rather she not learn any more than necessary."

Taking notes standing would be a pain, but I'd manage. I took out my pad and pencil. "How long have you known Mr. Kettle?"

He threw a quick look at the house. "Edward and I have been friends for quite a while. We served in the same unit during the Great War, at least for a short time. We entered the service together, almost too late to do anything."

"You came from different kinds of families, I think. How'd you become friends?"

His shoulders twitched. "Two young men from Buffalo, of course, we stayed close. We may have grown up differently, but we found we had a lot in common."

"Like what?" I could not imagine Harvey Brickett, who seemed like he'd have more in common with Lee, having a lot of similarities with college-educated Edward Kettle,

He fidgeted. "I don't want to talk about it. It's very personal. A topic best left in the foxhole."

A seed of suspicion took root in my mind. If they'd liked the same baseball team, why not say that? "You said you served together briefly. Did one of you transfer out of your unit or somethin'?"

"Not exactly." He stuffed his hands in his pants pockets. "Edward...left the service rather abruptly. There was talk, of course, but the brass didn't share a ton of details with the enlisted men. I missed him. I was friends with the others, but there was no one quite like Edward."

The seed grew. "I'm surprised Mr. Kettle didn't become an officer somehow. He went to college, didn't he? Don't college boys get to be officers? My fiancée is in the Army, and that's what he told me."

"Edward attended Canisius, but he didn't finish his degree." He stared at his shoes.

"Because of the war?"

"Not exactly, but I don't believe leaving school was his decision." He focused on a passing milk truck. "This is all terribly awkward to talk about. I shouldn't say anything more. A lot gets said when you're under fire that wouldn't be mentioned in other situations."

Mr. Brickett seemed unable to meet my gaze, which fed my idea. "Did you know his family?"

"Edward wasn't on speaking terms with them, not since he left college. They had a falling out, as I understand it."

"Do you know what it was about?"

He dragged his fingers through his hair. "He didn't like to discuss it. He didn't have to. It as one of those things I simply understood."

It was an answer, but not to the question I'd asked. I plowed on. "Did Mr. Kettle ever mention a newspaperman named Melvin Schlingmann to you?"

"Once or twice." He relaxed. "He works for some tabloid rag. Edward said Schlingmann was trying to get him to spill the beans about the project at American Shipbuilding."

"Do you know about it? The project?"

Mr. Brickett spread his hands. "Only what the general public knows. Edward told me the rag was after a story, and Schlingmann had approached him a couple of times. The last time, it got a little nasty, as I understand it."

"Nasty how?" I held my pencil over the paper.

CHAPTER ELEVEN

But Mr. Brickett's hunted look returned. "It wasn't a good conversation." Another non-answer answer. "I see." I paused. "I spoke to his sister, Genevieve Zellwig."

"Genny talked to you?"

"Yes." I tilted my head. Genny? Mr. Brickett knew the family better than he let on. Or Edward had told him his sister's nickname. "There was a letter from her in Mr. Kettle's bedroom. It was tucked into a Bible that had been owned by their grandfather and mentioned past sins and forgiveness. Do you know anything about that?"

A sheen of sweat glistened on his forehead. It wasn't hot enough to cause that. "It's really not my place to say. I think I hear my wife calling me." He turned.

He knew. I looked around the yard. "Mrs. Zellwig said Edward was a homosexual. Did you know that?"

"I can't believe it. She must be mistaken. I knew Edward had a checkered past with women, but I never dreamed of anything like that. He was a gentle man. We were good friends." He clenched his fists and stared at them. "He understood me like no one else did."

I rolled the dice. "You don't have children, I take it. Mr. Brickett, is that 'cause of what you and Edward had in common?"

He looked up. "What? I don't have children, so I must be homosexual myself, is that it? I'll have you know my wife and I were never lucky in that regard. It's as simple as that."

I waited a beat. "Mr. Brickett, be honest with me." I steeled myself for the answer. Did I want him to confirm my idea or not?

His hand clamped around my arm, and he dragged me to the sidewalk. "Keep your voice down." His words came in a hiss. "How dare you...I'll have you know I've been married for twenty years. If my wife heard...what a preposterous...."

I looked around, but there was no sign of another person. "You're one yourself, aren't you?" I asked, voice so low as to be practically a whisper. It was all I could do not to pull away.

He didn't say the words. He didn't have to. His expression said it all.

I removed his hand from my arm. "Why did Mr. Kettle leave the army?"

"It was a blue discharge," he whispered. "He told me before he left. None of the officers said anything. It was very hush-hush. They just said he left for personal reasons. I always thought they believed it would be bad for morale or...something if they told the truth."

"Were you lovers?" My stomach turned at the idea.

His eyes went wide. "No, not us. But we'd talk sometimes, late at night, especially if we were on patrol together. You wouldn't understand, but it was such a relief to find someone who knew, who was like me." He rubbed his chin. "I think that's how he was discovered. Someone overheard our conversation. Whoever it was, he couldn't identify me, but he knew Edward. He wouldn't tell them my name. He took his discharge and went home. After Armistice Day, when I got back to Buffalo, I tracked him down. His father disowned him. He'd taken a job as a janitor. We talked about his failures with women. He simply couldn't pretend enough with them, I guess. I knew American Shipbuilding was hiring, and I told him to apply. I taught him how to keep his head down. A year ago, he got thrown out of his living space, and I found him a room with Mrs. Finch across the street." He half-laughed, a derisive sound. "She's always had a soft spot for Ernestine and me, what with us not having kids and all. She was glad to take a friend of 'that nice Mr. Brickett.'"

I didn't know what to feel. His expression and voice begged for sympathy, but he was another person whose lifestyle went against everything I'd been taught. I shoved that aside. "Does your wife know? About you or Mr. Kettle?" I had to ask, but I already knew the answer.

"Heavens, no." He shook his head. "The doctor said after her third miscarriage that she's just not fit to have children. It shattered her, and we haven't been intimate in years. Everyone knows, all our friends and family. Because of that, no suspicion was ever raised about me. I never introduced her to Edward. Unfortunately, he was as bad at fitting in with other men as he was with women."

"But it's why he never finished college."

"Yes." His face took on a defeated look. "The priests found out. Canisius

CHAPTER ELEVEN

is a Catholic school. There was no way they'd let him stay. His family made a large donation, and the whole thing was glossed over."

I gazed around the street. "Did Mr. Schlingmann know? Is that why he was harassing Mr. Kettle for the scoop on what was going on at the yard?"

"I think so, yes. Edward told me that no matter what that awful man wrote, he'd never betray his country. 'Who would believe anything he printed in that rag of his anyway?' he said. Besides, anyone who knew Edward well knew he was a patriot. I think getting tossed out of the Army was more hurtful to him than college. Part of the reason he took the shipyard job was because he'd be contributing to the war effort." He paused. "But I also know Schlingmann was persistent. He was going to get his story, no matter what."

Maybe Melvin had tried a bit of blackmail to get what he wanted, but it didn't make sense for him to kill his target. Unless something had happened to sour the deal. "One last question. Did Mr. Kettle ever mention a young man? Nicely dressed, handsome, I don't know much more about him than that. But did he?"

"Not to me. I think I saw someone who might be who you're talking about, though. He stopped Edward one night after he left here. But I don't know who he is. I asked Edward, but he didn't tell me. It was one of the few times he wouldn't."

At least someone else had mentioned him. I wasn't chasing a ghost. "Did Mr. Kettle ever talk about a person named Sidney?"

"Not that I remember."

It was a cagey answer that didn't tell me anything. But I let it go. "Thank you for your time." I turned to leave.

"Wait." Mr. Brickett grabbed my arm. "Are you going to tell anyone? About Edward or me?"

I removed his hand. "I don't intend to."

"Will you need to talk to me again?"

Mr. Brickett looked like I'd kicked his puppy. "I honestly don't know. Good-bye." I walked away. I didn't want to think about his sad life. But I couldn't help it. He was living a lie to his wife, to society, almost everyone he knew. He most likely went through every day afraid someone would find out and blab about him. Did he even love his wife? Could he? As for her, she couldn't have a clue. I couldn't imagine a woman stayin' with a man she knew was queer. I also couldn't wrap my brain around having to pretend to be someone I wasn't every day of my life.

    I thumbed my engagement ring. What if Tom forbade me from bein' a detective after we were married? Would I end up living a lie, too?

Chapter Twelve

I made it home for dinner just in time to sit down with the family for grace. I knew Mom wouldn't be all that keen about me talking about dead people over the table, so I kept my trap shut about my day. At least I tried.

Mom ladled some stew into a bowl and passed it to me. "Elizabeth Anne." It was never a good sign when she trotted out my full name. "Yes, ma'am?"

"I do not appreciate you using this house and our phone for your messages. I understand you want to become a private detective, but you need to find another means of communication."

"Eventually, I'll pay for an answering service, but I'm not making enough dough yet." I aimed for meek and hoped she'd take pity on me. "Please, Mom. It's just for a little while. I'd be very grateful. And I'll only give out our telephone number when it's really important. I'm not gonna spread it all over the city."

She *tsked*. "That's what you say now, but what happens when you have more clients? I won't have this house disrupted with endless phone calls from strangers."

I did not miss her assumption that I'd be successful and have lots of people hiring me. Mom might say she didn't like the interruptions, but her confidence in me shone through clear as crystal.

Pop helped himself to bread and spread a thin layer of margarine on it. "Be reasonable, Mary. Betty can't run a business without some way for people to reach her."

"Be that as it may, I don't think—"

"I'm sure she won't have our telephone ringing off the hook, will you my darling girl? And it's not like she'll be interfering with our daily life. We don't get that many calls a day."

Good ol' Pop. "No, sir. I'll only give it to the people who really need it."

"Then it's settled. Besides, it will give Mary Kate some experience with taking messages. Who knows, that might come in handy someday." His eyes twinkled. Mary Kate was fourteen, almost fifteen, and loved being given extra responsibility.

Mom knew when she was beaten and didn't continue to argue. She switched her focus to my younger brothers. Michael, eleven, and Jimmy, twelve, were barely a year apart in age. Irish twins, people called them. "Boys, you have homework. I want it done before you turn on that radio. Mary Kate and Betty, you will clean up the kitchen."

"Hey, Pop, would you mind helping me instead of Mary Kate?" I asked. "I, uh, need to talk to you."

He stood. "Don't worry. I'll be in the living room when you're done. We can speak then."

"I want to talk privately, if you don't mind."

He stared at me. "Mary Kate, it seems like you get some extra sewing or reading time tonight."

My sister scrambled out of the kitchen before he could change his mind.

The boys and Mom left, and I filled the sink with hot water. I wasn't sure how to start this conversation.

Pop brought over the scraped plates. As usual, he saved me the trouble. "Is this about your new case?"

"Yes." As I washed the dishes, I told him about Edward, his being fired, and the murder. "All that would be jake, but I learned today that Edward is, I guess I should say was"—I lowered my voice—"a queer."

He dried the plates. "Say homosexual, Betty. I will not have vulgar language used in my house."

"Yes, sir." I swallowed. "But—"

"You're not sure you should continue to investigate. Is that it?"

"Sort of." I told him what Sam had said about the need to apply the law

CHAPTER TWELVE

equally. "It all makes sense, I guess. But...homosexuality's a sin, isn't it?" I tried to keep my voice normal, but from Pop's expression, I wasn't successful. "It's wrong. That's what the Church says. If I do this, am I sinning, too?"

"How so?"

"I don't know. Someone might think I approve of Edward's choice or something. I don't. Approve of homosexuality, that is. At least, I don't think I do. But he paid me. I didn't do the job. His sister wants to see it finished. Part of me says I have an obligation to see it through."

He set down a dish. "First, let's address the easy part. Detective MacKinnon is right. We can't selectively apply the law. Not if we want a just, peaceful society."

I remember what Sam said. *What if I'm in the next group someone says doesn't deserve justice?* "I get it. But I'm not a cop. Me deciding I don't want...this type of client isn't gonna throw things to the dogs."

"No, it won't." He hung up the towel and took out his pipe. "Which is why the second half of your question isn't as easy. What does your heart say?"

I hugged myself. I'd wanted a simple answer, but it didn't look like I was gonna get it. "Well, what Edward was is wrong, I s'pose. At least that's what the Church says. 'Cept...Jesus ate with all kinds of people his faith said were sinners, didn't he? Tax collectors, and adulterers, and what-not."

"And?"

"He treated 'em like normal people worthy of his time and attention. So I'm thinkin'...if it's good enough for him, it oughta be good enough for me, right?" I looked at my father.

He patted me on the shoulder and took out his pipe. "If that's what you believe, then you know what you have to do." He thumbed tobacco into the pipe bowl. "Remember, Betty, you aren't responsible for what this man did or didn't do. You're only responsible for your own actions. If you walk away, will you be able to look at yourself in the mirror? I believe you know the answer to that." He lit the pipe, puffed, and left the kitchen.

* * *

I hoofed it down to the Tillotson house. Lee was in the backyard, tinkering with the lawn mower. Dot stood beside him, the grease on her pants evidence that she'd helped with the repairs. "Hey, Betty," he said. "I didn't expect to see you tonight." He lubed up the blades, set the wheels on the ground, and gave it a push.

"I need to interview you," I said.

"About what?" He gave the handle to Dot. "Would you mind pushing this inside the garage while I carry the toolbox?"

"Give it to me. I can handle it."

"I am a lucky guy."

She kissed him. "As long as you remember that." She trundled off, pushing the mower with one hand and carrying Lee's toolbox in the other.

They were such a cute couple. Almost as sweet as Tom and me. *Why hasn't he written?* I pushed the thought aside. "Let's sit down over here." I waved to the back step.

"You sound awfully formal. What's wrong?"

"Nothing, well, nothing with you personally. I need to ask you about Edward Kettle as if you're a witness. Because you are."

Dot returned. "A witness to what? To a crime? Oh, should I leave you two alone?"

"No, it's nothing secret. I want to ask Lee some questions about Mr. Kettle's character." I sat on the concrete and took out my notepad. "How many times did you go out drinking with Mr. Kettle?"

Lee frowned. "Two? No more than three. But I'm almost positive it was just two. There was the night I met him, and then the night I told him about you."

"The first night. You said Harvey introduced you. That's Harvey Brickett, right?"

"Yes. I told you, I know Harve from GM. We went out for a beer, the two of us and a couple of others from the plant, and Edward was there. Harve said the two of 'em were friends from way back."

Exactly what Mr. Brickett had told me. "At that time, did Mr. Kettle say anything about his job?"

CHAPTER TWELVE

Lee ran a hand through his hair, messing it up even more than it had been. "No, well, not aside from where he worked. Someone asked what was going on at the shipyard, and Edward said he couldn't talk about it. He also said we'd prob'ly find out in a week or so."

"Did he mention a reporter?"

Dot piped up. "What does this have to do with anything? You sound like you already know this."

I held up my hand. "Other people have told me a story. I want to hear it from multiple sources before I believe it. Lee? Did he?"

He tapped out a smoke, but didn't light it. "Harve asked if things were goin' okay. Edward said yes, but there'd been some joe claiming to work for a local paper hanging around, pestering him. He, Edward, had blown the reporter off, but it hadn't worked. At least that was the general idea I got from him."

"Did he say why?" Watching him made me want my own cigarette, but I couldn't hold pencil, pad, and gasper all at the same time. At least not comfortably. I could wait. "And did he tell anyone?"

"Why what?"

"Why the newspaper guy wouldn't take a hint?"

Lee twirled his unlit Chesterfield. "I don't think so, not exactly. I seem to remember Harve asking, and Edward just said, 'He says he knows about people like me.' Or something like that. Frankly, it didn't make any sense." He lit his smoke. "I don't know if he talked to anyone at the yard. I would think he would. Some random citizen, snooping around what is clearly war activities, that'd be treason or espionage or something, right?"

I figured that was Edward's way of telling his buddy that Melvin knew about his homosexuality. " I guess it depends on how much he learned. The second night, what did Edward say about losing his job?"

Lee exhaled a cloud of smoke. "He told us he'd been fired, supposedly for talkin' to this reporter, said it wasn't true, and he wished he could set the record straight. That's why I told him about you, that you'd help him get to the truth." He ashed his gasper. "Why don't you talk to Edward again?"

"I can't. He's dead." I told them about the murder. "I'm surprised you haven't heard about it." At least Lee woulda. Dot didn't read or listen to the news, not more than she had to. She said the war depressed her.

"I didn't bother with the evening paper, and I didn't turn the radio on when I got home. I wanted to get started on the mower repairs." Lee's expression was bleak.

Dot clapped her hands to her mouth. "That's awful! That poor man. Somebody musta hated him to do that."

I stretched my legs. "Lee, who is Oscar Wilde?"

As Lee spoke, smoke leaked out of his mouth. "He was a playwright in England at the end of the 1800s. He wrote a bunch of stuff, like *The Picture of Dorian Gray*, and *The Importance of Being Earnest*. Don't you remember from school?"

"I musta missed that day."

He gave me a flat look. "Sometimes I think you missed everything. Anyway, Wilde had a bit of a reputation."

"For what? His work?"

"That and a bit more." Lee took another drag. "See, he was married, but he got arrested for foolin' around with another man. It made quite a stir. Because of that, a lot of folks don't think he's all that appropriate to read. They make assumptions about the people who do, too."

Spots of red appeared on Dot's cheeks. "I should think not! I don't remember readin' any of his stuff."

"We didn't." Lee tossed aside his butt. "Our teacher mentioned him, and I was curious, so I checked him out at the library downtown. *The Importance of Being Earnest* is funny."

She pushed him. "Lee! You did not read that, did you?"

"It's just a play, Dot. Be cool." He tilted his head. "Why do you ask, Betty?"

"Edward Kettle had a couple of books by Wilde in his room." I tapped my pencil on the pad. "Did he…make a pass at you or say anything like that?"

Lee choked and coughed.

Dot glared at me. "Betty! That's not funny. Lee wouldn't hang out with that sort of guy."

How much should I tell them? What if he didn't know Edward was that

CHAPTER TWELVE

way?

Her peepers widened. "Are you saying…"

Lee held up his hands. "No way. I mean, he was odd, but not like that."

I said nothing.

His face paled. "You mean…he was? I had drinks with a…I don't even want to say it." When he didn't get a response, he uttered words I knew Mrs. Tillotson wouldn't approve of.

Dot stood up and put her fists on her hips. "If this is a joke, Betty, it's a terrible one."

I let out a slow breath. "It's not a joke."

Her jaw dropped.

I turned back to Lee, whose face had gone all stony but at least he didn't look like a landed bass. "That answers my next question. You didn't know. When Edward talked, did he mention anyone at all he was having issues with? Besides the job stuff."

Lee took out another cigarette with shaking fingers. "Not a single name. I really thought…I figured he was just a regular guy, a little out of his place. That's all."

I stood and brushed the dust from my rear end. "He was. Like they say in the movies, if you think of anything, let me know." I took out my pack of Luckys, slid one out, and lit it.

"You're not gonna keep at it, are you?" Dot asked. She couldn't sound more horrified if I'd asked her to go skinny dipping at Woodlawn Beach. "Not now you know what he was."

I exhaled a cloud of smoke. "The man paid me, Dot. His sister wants to hire me to finish the job."

"Why should you care? You don't want a client who's like *that*, do you?"

"Because a man died." I faced her. "I saw his room, and Detective MacKinnon told me what happened. Whatever he was or did, he didn't deserve to be killed in cold blood. And in such a horrible way. His sister seems a bit snooty, but a nice lady. If I can help her, I will. I understand if you two need to sit this one out."

I turned and walked away. Neither Lee nor Dot tried to stop me.

Chapter Thirteen

I arrived at Moe's bright and early the next day. The waitress I'd talked to the previous afternoon was working again. I snagged her. "Is Melvin Schlingmann here?" I glanced at her name tag. "Or didn't you get a chance to pass on the message, Gert?"

She pulled away. "I did. He didn't say nothing. But he ain't here, not yet." She flounced off.

I sat at the counter and ordered coffee, two eggs over easy, and a side of ham. While I waited, I grabbed a copy of the *Courier-Express* from the counter and skimmed the headlines. The big story continued to be horrors leaked from Japanese prisoner of war camps, including what they were calling the Bataan Death March. The Japanese were not kind to their captives, from what I read. The other big story was the fallout from what the paper called the Palm Sunday Massacre, when dozens of German aircraft were shot down before they could rescue their countrymen stranded in Tunisia.

The story of Edward's murder rated a couple of inches below the fold in the local section.

Murder was ugly. The war was uglier.

I'd finished my eggs and almost given up on my quarry when Melvin plopped down on the stool next to me. "Morning. Gert says you wanted to talk to me. Is this foreplay or are you in need of friends?"

I stared at him. "What happened to you?" He had a doozy of a shiner under his right eye, and the right side of his lip was cut and swollen.

"It's nothin'. You didn't answer my question."

CHAPTER THIRTEEN

Someone roughed him up, but I doubted I'd get the details from him. Not yet. "Neither. I'm engaged, and I have plenty of pals."

"Shame." He pulled over a menu. "I assume this is on you. Since you're the one who wanted to flap her gums and all."

I shoulda brought more money with me. "Try not to bankrupt me over one meal."

He whistled for a waitress. "Stack of hotcakes, two eggs scrambled, hash browns, and coffee, doll. Put it on her tab." He hoisted his thumb toward me.

The waitress looked at me for confirmation. At my nod, she wrote down the order, walked off, and brought a mug. She poured Melvin's joe and offered to warm mine up. I waved her off and lit a cigarette.

He dumped sugar in his coffee and added enough milk that the liquid turned light brown. "What's the scoop?"

"I got a bone to pick with you."

He slurped. "Get in line."

"Behind who?" From the condition of his face, clearly, at least one person wasn't happy with the reporter.

"My editor." He called his boss a couple of names I'd heard some girls use to describe Mr. Satterwaite when they thought no one was listening. "Carmichael hasn't been on the street in ages. He doesn't know bupkis. I can't keep spinning something from nothing forever." His breakfast came. He dumped syrup over everything, loaded his fork with eggs and pancakes, and shoveled food into his mouth.

His table manners were awful. "You lied to me." I took a slug of java, tapped ash from my Lucky, and watched for a reaction.

His lip curled. "Prove it." He talked with his mouth full.

Mom would have delivered a lecture. I merely inched away so he wouldn't spray chewed food on me. "You told me you'd never spoken to Edward Kettle. But I have it on good authority you went looking for him at his boarding house, and you were there again yesterday after the cops left. Which means you know he's dead."

He washed down some hash browns with coffee and smacked his lips.

"Yeah, who told you that? A little birdie? Birds sing funny songs."

"This one's name is Ida Finch, and she runs the place." I swirled the contents of my cup. "I think she knows the tune pretty well."

He muttered another dirty word. "Finch, bird, cute."

"I oughta wash your mouth out with soap." I set down my mug. His attitude didn't put me in the mood to be polite. "Maybe after we're done. And don't talk with your mouth full. Hasn't anyone ever taught you how to eat like a human?" If Emma thought he was a catch, she'd never seen him with food.

He snorted and kept gobbling his breakfast. The way he ate, it was the best meal he'd ever had. Maybe it was.

"You told me you'd never talked to Edward. Yet you know where he lived. Do you often have the addresses of total strangers?"

He dragged a bite of pancake through a puddle of syrup. "All right, all right. I talked to him at the shipyard, okay? I got his name, too. That's how I found him, in the phone book. For all the good it did me. The stinkin' queer wouldn't tell me anything I didn't already know."

I noted the word. "That's a heck of a thing to say about a guy."

"You call yourself a detective, and you didn't even know he liked men?" He chuckled.

"I knew. I'm wondering who told you he was a homosexual." I rested my head on my fist. "I know it wasn't Edward."

A cocky smile appeared on Melvin's puss. "I'm a reporter. I know things."

"Oh, don't give me that baloney. Who gabbed?"

"A reporter never gives up his sources." He finished his potatoes, pushed the empty plate away, and took a gulp of coffee.

Sean and Lee had both taught me how to throw a good right hook, but as much as it would help me blow off steam, I figured it wouldn't loosen Melvin's lips. While I didn't think I could do any more damage to him, I wasn't in the mood to try. Also, considering the number of uniformed cops currently in the joint, it might also get me arrested. "Go ahead, clam up. I have a good friend in the Buffalo PD. I'm sure he knows someone in the Coast Guard who'd love to hear that a tabloid reporter has been snooping

CHAPTER THIRTEEN

around where he's not supposed to be. I figure you'll get a visit from the military police in a couple of hours."

"Who do you think did this?" He pointed at his cheek. "Couple of the Coast Guardsmen on shore patrol *encouraged* me to scram when I showed up last night. I'm done with that."

"Oh. Well, in that case, I'll be going. See ya." I ground out my smoke and moved as though I was gonna slide off my stool.

"Wait." He grabbed my hand.

I eyed it. "Let go of me." I kept my voice low, but filled it with as much menace as I could.

He snatched his paw away like he'd touched a hot stove. "You can't call the cops."

"Who'd you talk to about Edward?"

Melvin ran his tongue over his lips. "What's in it for me?"

"I won't sock you in the jaw?" I held up my hands. "Fine. How'd you like to report on a murder? You talk to me, I'll give you dibs on the story about Edward's death and my investigation. A first-hand account, you could say."

He paused. "Deal." He waved at the waitress and asked for coffee. "It's like this. Last fall, we got wind of a big project at American Shipbuilding. A bunch of folks saw a paddlewheel steamboat sail into the harbor. The Coast Guard built a special station and set up a few of their men for security. You must have seen all the activity."

Most of the city had. "Yeah. And?"

"A few months later, there's a hush-hush ceremony, and the ship leaves. But it sure wasn't the same boat."

He fell silent while the waitress set down his mug. She left, and he doused it again. "No one would say where it went, but Carmichael put me on the story. All I could find out was it was a job for the Navy. Then another paddlewheel sailed into Buffalo. They're still working on this one. Scuttlebutt has it there's some kind of new feature."

"So what?"

He gave me a withering look. "Where'd the first boat go? What're they doing, and why so hush-hush? It's gotta be something big. I started talkin' up guys as they were leaving, shipyard workers. None of 'em would say boo. But one guy, he acts real canny. He tells me to look for a man named Edward Kettle. He'd set the record straight." Melvin leaned in. "He also told me if Edward gave me any lip, I was to tell him I knew his secret and I wasn't afraid to go to the bosses."

"Didn't you wonder why he'd do that?" I asked. "He wouldn't talk to you, but he'd send you to another guy to get the dope? That didn't make you suspicious?"

"Hey, I don't look a gift horse in the mouth."

"Did this joe have a name?"

Melvin shrugged. "Arthur, Albert…something that started with A and sounded like it ought to belong to some stuffy old king. He made it sound like Edward would be happy to squeal, but he blew me off, same as everyone else."

I rolled that around in my head. Melvin knew from his secret source that Edward was homosexual. Melvin had to believe Edward would do anything to keep that detail quiet. But from what everyone told me of Edward, how dedicated he was to his country, I could believe he'd stay mum, even if it cost him. "Next question. When you went to Edward's house, did you ever see a young guy there? One you might think should be enlisted?"

"I wasn't exactly payin' attention to the scenery. Wait." He shook a finger. "I remember. There was someone. Movie-star handsome, bet he gets all the girls. I was going to Edward's, he was walking down the street coming toward me. I wouldn't have even paid attention to him 'cept I knew a fella that young oughta be in a uniform. At least a different one than he was wearing."

Every time I'd heard about this mystery man, he'd been in slacks and a shirt. "What kind of uniform?"

"Like they wear in hospitals. You know, the orderlies. I accidentally-on-purpose bumped into him. You never know, he might be a draft dodger. There could be a story there." He finished his joe.

"Then you talked to him."

"We didn't say much." Melvin burped. "I said sorry, he said don't worry

CHAPTER THIRTEEN

about it, and that was that. But I scribbled down his name, just in case." He gave me a side-eyed glance.

"He gave you his name?"

"Don't be dense, sweetheart. It was on his name tag. Bet you'd love to know what it is. What's it worth to you?"

"I already promised you a scoop on the murder. What more do you want?" What a stinker.

"An interview with you. Over dinner. Betty Ahern, girl detective. The full story." He leaned over. "What d'ya say?"

He smelled of cheap aftershave and syrup. I leaned back. "Yes to the interview, no to dinner."

There was a pause. "Fair enough. There wasn't a last name, but the tag said Frank. He works at Buffalo State Hospital."

That was the old Buffalo State Asylum for mental patients. It didn't explain why Frank wasn't in the armed services, but how many young men with that name could be working there? I would visit this afternoon. Maybe. "Okay. Last question."

"You sure are nosy."

"I'm a detective. It's part of the job description. As a reporter, I'm sure you know the drill."

He mumbled under his breath.

"What did Edward say when you threatened him? I mean, when you said he'd better talk to you, or you were gonna rat him out to his bosses?"

"He told me before I could do that, he'd turn me in to the authorities. Attempted espionage." He lifted his eyebrows. "What? You think I killed him?"

"Did you?"

"You're a pretty stupid broad if you believe that." Melvin slid off his stool. "Why would I ice him before he gave me the scoop?" He shrugged into his jacket. "I'll be in touch, Miss Ahern. You owe me a story. Two of them. Thanks for a swell breakfast." He winked and strolled out of the diner.

The waitress came by, but I declined her offer of a refill. Melvin was the stupid one. Sure, a newsman wouldn't kill someone who could give him the goods. But if the same person threatened him with who knows how many years in Fort Leavenworth for spying?

That sounded like one heck of a motive to me.

Chapter Fourteen

I left Moe's and took the trolley back to Hamburg. The cheerful spring day mocked my somber mood. I'd made my decision, but my friends thought I was crazy. I hadn't felt this alone last month, when I vowed to clear Lee's name. Back then, I'd had Dot, even if she'd been more on the sidelines than she usually was.

This time I knew where I was goin' so I lit a smoke and set off at a brisk pace down Hawkins toward Highland Avenue. As I walked, a tendril of doubt wormed its way into my thoughts. These houses were so pretty with their flower beds and perfect lawns. If I married Tom, maybe we'd end up living out here, like Mom always hoped. Would it really be so bad, bein' a housewife in the Southtowns? I could be part of the local women's group. My kids would go to a nice school, and I could volunteer there. There might be a garden club or somethin'.

The idea didn't fill me with joy.

It seemed like very little time passed before I was going up the steps to the porch of Mrs. Zellwig's home and knocking on the door. I'd finished my cigarette and thrown it away before I arrived. Good thing. I doubted she'd want me to litter up her flower beds. As I waited, I thought maybe I should have called first. For all I knew, she was a member of those women's associations I'd thought about and spent little of her time at home.

She opened the door. She wore a dress much like the one she'd had on yesterday, only this one was deep red. The same pearls hung around her throat and dangled from her ears. "Miss Ahern. Can I help you?"

"It's me who might be doin' the helping. Yesterday, you said you wanted me to clear your brother's name. Maybe even find his killer. Is that still the situation?"

She didn't hesitate. "Yes. Edward and I...we had our differences. But he was not a bad person except for his proclivities. I want him to get justice."

My vocabulary didn't include the word "proclivities," but from how she said the word, I gathered she meant his preference for men. "Then I'll take the case. Edward already paid through Saturday."

"What if it took you longer?"

"He was gonna pay me fifteen dollars a day. Plus expenses."

She pressed her lips together for a moment, then said, "That sounds fair. What will you do first?"

"I'd like to talk to you some more, if you aren't busy."

She stepped back. "Not at all. Please come in."

I followed her to the same sitting room we'd been in yesterday and took a seat on the chintz-covered chair near the window. It had doilies on the arms and a nice view of the street and the park across the way. I unbuttoned my spring coat and fished my notebook and pencil out of my purse. I'd worn my Sunday clothes, but my surroundings still made me feel underdressed.

She held out her hand. "May I take your coat and get you something to drink? Coffee, water, or tea?"

I stood and gave her the coat. "Coffee is good. Black."

"Just a moment."

Instead of taking my seat, I walked around the room. I thought about lighting up, but I didn't see an ashtray. Maybe the Zellwigs weren't smokers. There was the picture of old Jeremiah Kettle. Another lithograph showed a man and a woman in formal attire, him in a coat with tails, her in a lacy dress with ruffles at the cuffs and hem. It could be Edward's parents. There were also a few pictures of children, from babies to toddlers. A boy with chubby cheeks in a sailor outfit sat with his arm around a little girl in a frilly dress. I picked it up.

"That's Edward and me when we were children," said Mrs. Zellwig from behind me. "We were very close. He couldn't say Genevieve, so he gave me my nickname, Genny. It stuck with me."

CHAPTER FOURTEEN

I set it down. "How many years apart were you?"

"Three." She set down a silver tray that held two delicate china cups on matching saucers, white with a band of silver on the edge, filled with black liquid. There was also a sugar bowl, a tiny milk pitcher, and two silver teaspoons. The scent from the cups was the same as home, though. Living in Hamburg still only got you chicory coffee. But if she had milk and sugar to offer, she was good with her coupons. I couldn't see Genevieve Zellwig as a black-market shopper. She came over to me. "Unlike most older brothers, Edward was very kind to me. We did everything together, and he always included me in his games. He bandaged my scrapes and read me stories before bed. Sometimes I thought he enjoyed playing with me more than the neighborhood boys. Except for Sidney."

I latched onto the name. "Who was he?"

"Sidney Madison. He was Edward's best friend. His family lived three doors down from us. Our home was in Buffalo back then. Here." She moved to another table and picked up a picture. "This is Edward and Sidney when they were in high school." She handed it to me.

This must be the infamous love of Edward's life. I wondered if Mrs. Zellwig knew that. Sidney was handsome, in a Rudolph Valentino sort of way. He was slim, with a narrow face and dark hair. He and Edward wore suits, their arms around each other's shoulders, laughter on their faces. "Where is Sidney now?"

"He died." Mrs. Zellwig took the picture back and set it on the table. She returned to the tray. "He caught the Spanish flu in early 1918. He'd been drafted and sent to Fort Riley in Kansas. He died before he could be deployed." She waved toward my chair.

I took a cup and sat. "How did Edward take it?"

"He was devastated. They were like brothers. Edward was in college, but he entered the Army about a year later. I think he found it a relief, not to have to be around Sidney's family any longer."

"Sidney didn't go to Canisius?"

She sipped. "No. I believe he said he'd go to school after the war."

How to put my next question? "Did you or your father ever suspect Sidney and Edward were more than friends?"

Her mouth made a perfect O. "Oh, no. It was nothing like that. Sidney did not have Edward's abnormality."

Apparently, Sidney had been a better actor. There was no point in telling her the truth. "But you knew about Edward. I've been told he got kicked out of Canisius because he got caught with another boy." I wondered if this was before or after Sidney died. I wasn't gonna ask, but it was prob'ly after.

"He did." She fiddled with a doily. "That's why he enlisted."

"He wasn't drafted? Another friend of his told me he was."

"No, although he might have let it be believed that is what happened. Our father gave him a choice when Canisius dismissed him. Father would get him a job in the family business, or Edward could enlist. He chose the Army." She stirred her coffee even though I hadn't seen her put anything in it.

"And then he got thrown outta the service, just like college." I watched her over the rim of my cup.

"Yes. I believe they called it a blue discharge." Abruptly she laid down her spoon. "Instead of coming home, he took a job as a menial laborer in the city. Father disowned him on the spot. He said he could gloss over his son being a deviant, but not a common workman."

"That doesn't make any sense."

She lifted her hands and let them drop. "You had to know our father. He could hide Edward's private life, but not his choice of employment. Father was so proud when Edward was accepted at Canisius. The first Kettle to get a college degree. Father built his own business. Edward could follow him or better himself. But ending up as a manual laborer was simply not acceptable. Father saw it as a step down in life. I begged Edward to come home, but he wouldn't." She set down her cup. "Father and Edward didn't have a lot in common, but they were both as stubborn as mules."

"He loved you enough to keep that letter. And the Bible. When did you send them?"

She played with her pearls. "A year ago, probably more. Father's health was bad. I thought if Edward apologized, he could make peace between them before it was too late. I was wrong."

CHAPTER FOURTEEN

I sipped. "Do you know a man named Harvey Brickett? Or William Townes?"

"Neither of those names is familiar to me. Edward was very close-mouthed about his job at the shipyard. And about his life in general. Which is why I can't believe he'd talk to a reporter."

Her words snagged in my mind. "Edward only started working at the yard last summer. You said you haven't spoken to him in over a year." I put down my coffee. "How would you know he was working at American Shipbuilding if you haven't seen him?"

She looked through the window and bit her lip so hard there should have been blood visible against her lipstick.

"Mrs. Zellwig? I need an answer."

She clasped her hands, knuckles white.

"Look, you hired me to help get justice for your brother. I can't do that if you won't tell me the truth." I paused, stood, and brushed my skirt. "Since you won't be honest, I'm afraid I can't do anything for you. Have a nice afternoon."

"I used to meet him at the park near his house," she said in a near whisper. The morning sun shone on her unshed tears.

I resumed my seat. "Arlington Park?"

"I believe that's the name of it." She closed her eyes. "You must understand, Miss Ahern. I knew what my brother was. Father forbade me to speak to him. My husband would be disgusted if he knew. But I loved Edward in spite of it all." She looked at me. The blue of her eyes was slightly darker than Edward's. Tears overflowed and ran down her rouged cheeks, but a fierce light shone from her peepers. "Whatever he was, whatever he'd done, he was still the one who protected me, who fixed my dollhouse when it broke, who bandaged my knees when I skinned them. My parents didn't have time for me, but Edward always did. I couldn't walk away from him."

I thought about my own family. What if Sean or Michael or Jimmy turned out to be homosexual? What about Mary Kate? I wouldn't just walk away from any of them, no matter what they did or turned out to be. "Of course not." I almost reached out, but she didn't look like she wanted to be touched.

"When would you meet?"

She dabbed at her eyes with a lace handkerchief she took from her sleeve. "Sunday afternoons. My husband thought I was at a women's prayer group. Edward and I would meet in the park and talk."

"Did he ever mention any…special friends?"

"You mean, did he have a lover?" She gave me a wry look.

It was exactly what I meant, and if it'd been a normal relationship, I woulda said that. Why couldn't I bring myself to say the words for Edward? I waved my hand, prompting her.

"I think so. He said he'd met someone, but he didn't give me details. No names or how it had happened, I mean. I did manage to figure out that this man is married and lives in the city."

I wondered if Harvey Brickett knew anything. He hadn't said, but he could have been holding back. "When you'd talk to your brother, what did you flap your gums about?"

She blinked at me, maybe tryin' to figure out what I meant. Finally, she said, "We'd talk about the war, my children, politics, a little about his job, but no specifics, mind you. This last time, he told me…he told me it was possible, probable even, that everyone would find out about him, but he'd do his best to shield me from any gossip."

I sat back. "Why would he say that?"

"He said some people at work had found out about his homosexuality. They were threatening to expose him. He also said something very strange." She twisted the fabric of the hankie.

"What was it?"

"He said if a man named Albert Riker ever came to the door, I was not to talk to him. That sometimes, your personal wants had to come second to the greater good. Or something like that." She picked up her cup and drank half of the coffee, even though it had to be lukewarm at best.

Albert. Melvin Shlingmann had mentioned a joe with a name like a "stuffy old king." Albert sounded like he fit the bill. I jotted down the name. "One final question." I looked up. "Some people have mentioned seeing a young man, movie-star handsome, around Edward's boarding house. In one case,

CHAPTER FOURTEEN

they talked to each other. Sometimes this joe was in a suit, other times in clothes like he worked in a hospital. I think his first name is Frank. Do you know him?"

She twisted her wedding ring. "It could be Frank Hicks. His father owned a business near Philadelphia, I think. They live in Orchard Park, where they have a furniture store. That's where I saw Frank. I'm surprised Edward would speak to him after everything that Edward said about them."

I leaned forward. "What?"

"Edward told me the Hicks family, particularly Frank, wasn't as respectable as they wanted the world to believe. 'Everyone's out to make a buck, Genny,' he said once. 'They'll sell out their family, their religion, their country, everything if it means lining their pockets.' He wouldn't say anything more." She straightened the things on the tray, which was completely unnecessary since we'd barely touched them. "After Edward left college, Father sent him briefly to Buffalo State Hospital for a treatment. I'm fairly certain that's where he came across the Hicks family for the first time, through Frank. Edward didn't like to talk about that time. Perhaps you should speak to Frank directly."

Unless he has shipped out by now. "I don't know if I can. I mean, how would I find him?"

Mrs. Zellwig looked up. "It would be easy. I saw him at his family's store recently, and he said he still works at the hospital."

Chapter Fifteen

I spent the trolley ride back to Buffalo makin' notes for myself and thinkin'. I had three more names on my list. Well, three more people. I didn't have a moniker for Edward's nameless lover, but he, Frank Hicks, and Albert Riker joined Melvin and Mr. Townes as suspects.

I rubbed my forehead. I wanted Edward's secret life to have nothing to do with his murder. It would simplify things. Make the whole situation about politics and espionage, not abnormal behavior. 'Cept I knew that was impossible. I hadn't been at this long, but previous cases told me a spurned lover or an affair of the heart gone bad was just as strong a motive as money. If this nameless man was married, he'd have even more incentive to keep his relationship with Edward off the books. What if Edward was frustrated, wanted more, and this man worried his secret would be uncovered, costing him everything? How far would a man go to protect the life he'd built, even if it meant hiding the truth?

I'd learned that answer when I investigated the death of my friend Emmie Brewka's grandmother. Pretty far.

I got off in Allentown and ran down my list. Who should I tackle first? Frank Hicks, I had to find. Same with Albert Riker. I not only had to find the lover, I had to put a name to him. I decided to start with the easiest target.

I knocked on the door to the boarding house, and Mrs. Finch answered. "You're back again?" she asked. "I've told you everything I know."

"I'm looking for William Townes."

"He's not here. Go away." She waved her hands at me.

CHAPTER FIFTEEN

A tall bull of a man came out of the sitting room. "Who's looking for me?" Mrs. Finch scowled.

I sized up William Townes. He towered over his landlady, but I put him at an equal height with Lee and a couple of inches shorter than Sam. He easily had either of them by at least twenty pounds. I bet most of it was muscle from workin' in a factory. His face was square, his jaw covered in stubble. His brown eyes were flat and held no warmth or expression under a head of wavy brown hair. "You're William Townes?"

"That's me." He watched Mrs. Finch as she threw up her hands and scurried away. "Who're you?"

I told him my name. "I'd like to speak to you about Edward Kettle."

"The faggot? Why would I want to talk about him?"

My own feelings about Edward might be muddled, but Mr. Townes's certainly weren't. From his dismissive tone of voice, he didn't have a very good opinion of his boardinghouse neighbor.

"Whoever killed him did the world a favor," he continued. "We don't need his kind walkin' around, thinkin' they're just as good as everyone else."

"Would you like to go somewhere and sit?"

He settled into a stance with his legs slightly apart and arms crossed. "We can talk right here."

"Okay. I take it you didn't like Mr. Kettle much."

"It don't take a private dick to figure that out." He smirked. "I don't got any use for his kind."

"Was that the only reason you disliked him?"

"Isn't that enough?"

I looked at my notes from talkin' to Mrs. Finch. "Monday night, where did you go?"

"I went for a drink at Chauncey's. That's my local joint."

"How long were you there?"

He frowned. "How should I know? Late."

He wore a watch. Didn't he use it? "It couldn't have been that late. You were seen here by Mrs. Finch around nine o'clock."

"The old lady is crazy. It wasn't me. I was out with a couple of friends.

That's all I'm gonna tell you."

This wasn't going anywhere. I tried another tack. "How did you find out? That Mr. Kettle was a homosexual, I mean. He kept pretty quiet about it, from what I understand."

"He oughta. Disgusting is what it is. But he got sloppy." Mr. Townes bared his teeth in what he might have thought was a smile, but looked more like a snarl. "I overheard him on the horn in the kitchen. We only got the one, and everybody uses it. From the way he was talking, I knew he was on the phone with a lover."

"It might have been a woman."

"Before he saw me, I heard him use a name. Ray. Does that sound like a broad's name to you?"

It wasn't much, but I wrote it down. "When Mr. Kettle saw you, what did he do?"

"He hung up the blower real quick. Tried to make it seem like he'd been talkin' to a friend. I wasn't having any of that garbage." Mr. Townes rubbed his jaw. "I told him he had two choices. Get out, or I'd tell everybody in the house about him. I'm pretty sure old lady Finch don't want one of his type as a boarder. She'd have thrown him out before he could blink."

I didn't doubt it. "Then what?"

"He tried to threaten me. He said he knew I'd been having women in my room, and all he had to do was tell Finch. We could have a race to see who was tossed out on the pavement first. I'll give him credit. He had balls. If he hadn't been a faggot, I mighta liked him."

Until now, I'd wished Dot was along for company. She'd faint dead away from this kind of language. "I bet you didn't take kindly to him sayin' that."

"Nope." He pulled himself up straighter. "Told him he'd better watch out. Otherwise, I'd make him squeal like a pig at the slaughterhouse. And yeah. I know exactly how that makes me look." He stalked off without another word.

* * *

CHAPTER FIFTEEN

While I'd been talking to Mr. Townes, Mrs. Finch had left the house. None of the few tenants could tell me where she was or when she'd return. "She just better be back in time to fix dinner," one man said after reopening the door.

"You could warm up something," I said. "I bet it's not hard."

He stared at me as if I'd started speaking a foreign language. "I don't pay rent to cook for myself." He moved to shut the door.

"Wait."

He paused. "Yeah?"

"What do you know about William Townes?"

His forehead puckered. "Will? Ornery cuss. He's got an opinion on everything, and unless you agree with him, he'll show you the rough side of his tongue, as my ma used to say."

"Did he do that to Mr. Kettle a lot?"

He gave a short laugh. "They butted heads every time they were in the same room. Will didn't like Ed's type, if you catch my meaning."

I did. "You knew then. About Mr. Kettle."

"That he was a queer? I knew. You'd have to be blind to miss it."

His attitude was too casual. "It didn't bother you?"

He came back. "Look, missy." He wagged a finger at me. "I don't hold with 'em. Unnatural, that's what it is. Ed kept himself to himself. We both liked it that way. He didn't like it when I called him Ed, but what was he gonna do about it? Will liked to rile him up. I pretended he didn't exist. End of story." This time, he did close the door.

Nothing he'd said made me any less interested in finding out more about Mr. Townes. But I'd have to come up with a plan first.

Buffalo State Hospital, with its collection of red brick buildings, certainly didn't look like one. The pristine grounds had been designed by Frederick Olmstead, the same joe who designed the park down by the art museum. The administration building looked like a miniature castle, with green-roofed towers and everything. It had been a big deal when the place was built and the newspaper stories talked all about how it was gonna use a "more enlightened" method of treating crazy people. But whatever it looked like, it was still a joint for the insane.

I went straight to the main office. An elderly secretary typed away. I waited. When she didn't look up, I cleared my throat. "Excuse me."

She paused her clacking. "May I help you? Admissions is down the hall. If you're looking for a patient in residence, you should speak to the head nurse."

"I'm not looking for anyone like that, and I don't need help becoming a patient. Do you have an orderly here named Frank Hicks? He's a young man, dark hair, really handsome."

She sniffed. "I don't associate with the staff." She returned to her task.

"Who would know? What about the head nurse you talked about?"

She didn't look up. "Young lady, we are exceedingly busy. No one has time to help you solve your personal problems. If you want to speak to your beau, wait for him to get home."

"That's not why I'm looking for Mr. Hicks. I'm not his girl." I crossed my arms. "I'm a private detective, and he could be a witness in my current case. I need to talk to him."

That got her attention. "Telling outlandish tales isn't going to get you any further with me."

"It's not a story."

She glared at me. "By all means, go talk to the matron. Woe to you if you're wasting her time. First floor, next building over. Good day." She was done talkin' to me. She increased the speed of her typing, as if to reinforce the message.

I left the main building and walked the path through the grounds. I saw lots of people wandering around, some mutterin' to themselves, others tendin' the flower beds. One man was havin' a lively conversation with an elderly oak tree about how fast the new leaves were appearing.

"Don't you agree?" he asked as I passed.

I slowed, not sure what I should do. "Um, I don't know. I s'pose it's workin' as fast as it can. It's only a tree."

"Only a tree?" His face reddened. "This mighty oak has been on the grounds for decades, or so they tell me. Wouldn't you think a tree that old

CHAPTER FIFTEEN

would know how to put forth leaves by now?"

I glanced around, hoping to see a staff member, but no one appeared to be paying attention. "Well, yes, but I'm pretty sure it knows its business better than we do."

He grabbed my arm. He looked like a scarecrow with spindly limbs and disheveled hair, but he had me in a grip as strong as any vise I'd used back when I worked at Bell. "We are man, young lady. Human beings! Our knowledge is vastly superior to a tree."

I pulled a bit. "Whatever you say, sir."

"A benevolent God has gifted us with knowledge vaster than that of mere plants or anything in the animal kingdom. To imply otherwise, that a mere tree could know more than God's ultimate creation, is sacrilege." Spit flew from his mouth, and his eyes shone with a wild light.

Where is someone when you need him? If this was the "kinder, gentler" way of dealing with crazy people, letting them wander around and grab innocent bystanders, I didn't think much of it. "Sir, you're crushing my arm. Please let go." I tugged again, but although he looked like I could snap him like a twig, he had a wiry strength. I didn't want to hurt him, but I didn't want him breaking my arm, either.

"Mr. Stiles, you need to let go of the young lady." A stocky middle-aged man in an orderly's uniform appeared. Mr. Stiles whipped around, hand still wrapped around my arm. The orderly grabbed him in a bear hug and pried his hand away finger by finger. Mr. Stiles yelled and cursed, Latin phrases peppering his speech. He writhed like a fish on a line in the orderly's arms and tried to kick him. But the orderly knew his business. "Miss, I think it's best you leave."

I blinked. "I'm off to see the matron, but actually, I'm looking for an orderly named Frank Hicks. Do you know him?"

The man tilted his head down the path. "Frank is over there, in the vegetable gardens. Or he was ten minutes ago. If he's not there, you can find the matron in that building. Now you really should move on."

I thanked him, but his full attention was on Mr. Stiles, who was now shoutin' in some foreign language, maybe French. I hurried away. I'd always thought of mental patients as harmless. They were people who mumbled to themselves off in corners. The violent ones only appeared in movies. Apparently not always.

I wandered down the path. The grounds were very peaceful and lovely. Mr. Olmstead had put as much thought into the hospital as the art gallery. Eventually, I saw a few people who were watering plants and pulling weeds under the watchful eye of a young man dressed like my rescuer. It had to be the vegetable garden. If the orderly wasn't Frank, hopefully, he'd know where I should go next.

"Excuse me," I called as I crossed the lawn. "I'm lookin' for someone. Can you help me?"

He turned and smiled. "Perhaps. Who are you looking for?"

Words failed me. The person in front of me should have been dressed in a tuxedo with a glamorous actress on his arm. His hair was dark and wavy, his eyes a deep brown I could've drowned in. They had Jimmy Stewart's boy-next-door twinkle, although their owner was a bit broader than the beanpole actor. He had an adorable dimple in his right cheek. His teeth were perfectly straight and whiter than any I'd ever seen. My heart did a pitter-pat. It had no right to. I was engaged to a wonderful joe who had his own killer smile.

But not like this one.

He waited. "Miss, is there something I can help you with?"

It was silly, gaping like I'd just met a Hollywood heartthrob. *Get a grip, Betty.* "Yes. I'm looking for a man named Frank Hicks." I told him who I was.

"I'm Frank Hicks." His puzzled expression wiped away the dimple. "I'm not sure why you'd be looking for me, though. I haven't done anything that would involve a private investigator. Well, not intentionally. At least, I don't think so."

The question came out before I could think. "Is there something wrong with you?" He looked perfect, from the waves in his hair to his well-trimmed fingernails. I couldn't see his feet in the heavy shoes he wore, but were they the problem?

CHAPTER FIFTEEN

He stepped back. "I beg your pardon?"

Good job, Betty. What a great way to start a conversation. It was not a tactic the detective course recommended. Insulting your subject, that is. I fumbled to recover. "I'm sorry, I shouldn't have said that. It's just...most men your age are in the service." Maybe he had asthma or a heart condition. "Are you a 4F? One of my best friends has a bum leg that kept him out. What's your deal? If you don't mind my askin', of course. Feel free to tell me to mind my own beeswax." I could hear my mother's voice tellin' me not to be rude, but I couldn't help my babbling. Even if he couldn't fight, he was easily handsome enough to be in the short films supporting the war effort. Unless he didn't know anybody who could get him a job like that.

After a moment, he relaxed and again showed his dimple. "I'm a conscientious objector. I'm a Quaker. My faith doesn't support the violence of war."

His words poured icy water over my heart, which immediately stilled. He was a conchie. "Then you're okay with Hitler stampeding across Europe?" My brother and fiancé, thousands of American boys were laying down their lives for freedom, and this guy wouldn't fight 'cause of his religion? Maybe he wasn't that good-looking after all.

"I didn't say that." He didn't sound insulted. Maybe he got this reaction all the time. I sure hoped so. "What Hitler and Mussolini, and Hirohito, are doing is terrible. But there is a better way of stopping them than war."

"Like what?"

"Negotiation would be a start."

"Neville Chamberlain tried that. It didn't work too well."

"That wasn't negotiation, that was appeasement."

I opened my mouth, then closed it. I wasn't here to debate the war. "Do you know a man named Edward Kettle?"

The shift in topics must've caught him by surprise 'cause he paused. "I... that's none of your business."

"So you do know him."

He looked over his shoulder at the people tending the garden. "I have to watch the patients." He took a step back, then turned. "You seem like a nice girl. I noticed the ring on your finger. Edward Kettle is not as kind as you've been told. If you know what's good for you, you'll stay away from him. I wish I had." He walked back to the garden, leaving me speechless.

Chapter Sixteen

I stood on the sidewalk, gaping after Frank. What kind of business had he had with Edward? Whatever it was, I didn't think it had ended on friendly terms, if it had ended at all. 'Course, Edward's death meant it was over, but maybe Frank didn't know that. Or was pretending he didn't. He hadn't denied knowing my client. Did he know about Edward's secret life? Was that why I was s'posed to stay away from him?

My stomach growled, reminding me I hadn't eaten lunch. The grounds of the hospital bordered Forest Avenue and Elmwood. There had to be a diner or someplace nearby. I thought about goin' back to the secretary to ask, but I decided to walk around. I needed to clear my head.

The block of Elmwood with the hospital was all houses, not quite as fancy as the mansions in Delaware Park, but bigger than the ones in the First Ward. Most of 'em were brick with front porches and small front yards. Some of 'em had blue stars in the windows. Here and there, I saw flowering bushes, the yellow of forsythia and the light purple of lilacs. The yards looked a bit raggedy after the winter, but once spring got into full swing, I s'posed they'd be neat and green. Except for the fact they were across the street from the insane asylum, it seemed a nice place to live.

I found a small diner on the corner and grabbed a booth. The waitress came over. "Are you alone?"

"Yes. I'll have coffee and whatever the special is today."

"Roast chicken with boiled potatoes and carrots. Gravy on the chicken?"

"Please."

She walked off. I took out my notepad to review what I'd written and add to it. My list of suspects was not long, but enough to keep me busy. Albert Riker was an unknown, aside from the fact he also worked at American Shipbuilding. I needed to find out more about William Townes and Frank Hicks. I s'posed I could use a bit more background on Melvin as well. Was there anything in his history besides stickin' his nose where it didn't belong? The hardest would be trackin' down Edward's lover. Two men would not have advertised and all I had was the name Ray. I assumed that was short for Raymond. Maybe Mr. Brickett could help with that. If I assured him I wouldn't spill the beans on the secret, that is.

A shadow fell over the table. "Is this chair taken?"

I looked up. "Sam! What are you doin' here?"

"I was on my way to the hospital, saw you through the window, and thought I'd stop. May I?"

I waved at the seat. "Of course. I bet we're here for the same person."

"Almost certainly." He looked up at the waitress, who'd hurried over as soon as she saw him, a bright smile on her lips that looked a little redder than they'd been when I arrived. "Coffee, please."

"Sure thing, honey." She gave him a smile and fluffed her hair. She didn't even look at me. "I'll bring that right out."

"I think she's tryin' to flirt with you, Sam." I watched her walk away with a little wiggle in her hips. "I ordered my coffee minutes ago, and it hasn't come yet. And if she didn't take a sec to swipe on a fresh coat of lipstick before she came over, I'm a monkey's uncle."

Sam took off his fedora and set it next to him. "Don't be ridiculous. I have to be at least fifteen years older than her."

"That may be, but there's a war on, you know. You're a decent lookin' guy. An older man is better than none at all."

He snorted.

She returned with two cups of joe. She set mine in front of me almost as an afterthought. She leaned toward Sam, exposing a little of her bosom, and said, "You let me know if there's anything I can get you. Anything at all." She giggled and smoothed her finger curls before leaving.

I smothered a laugh at Sam's expression. In his suit, he cut a good figure.

CHAPTER SIXTEEN

He must know that. "Don't you have a woman in your life? I know you aren't married 'cause you don't have a ring on your finger. Unless there's some police rule against wearing it."

"I'm not married." He blew on his java. "I had a girlfriend once. I was even going to propose. But she made it clear she wanted a house in the suburbs, and for me to quit police work, so we parted ways. I haven't found anyone since. I'm a little busy. Besides, it gives my mother something to nag me about at holiday meals. You should always make your mother happy, and mine is the sort who's happiest when she's complaining."

My food arrived. The smell set off another round of rumbling from my tummy. "I hope you don't mind, but I'm starving."

"Go right ahead." He set aside his mug. "Have you talked to Frank Hicks yet?"

My mouth was full, so I nodded and swallowed. "He's a handsome one, I'll give you that much."

"You have a guy."

"I'm engaged, not dead, Sam." I cut another piece of chicken. "I kept my head, though. Not only because he's a murder suspect. It turns out he's also a conscientious objector. Can you believe that?"

"I haven't spoken to him yet, but I'm not surprised. I knew he was a Quaker."

I paused. "I don't know much about them. Quakers, I mean. Frank said somethin' about how he thinks Hitler is wrong, but violence isn't the answer. Has he paid attention to the news? How else are you s'posed to stop a guy who rolls his tanks over everything? Hitler has said outright he wants to rule the world, him and his stupid Third Reich. Do Quakers think they can reason with someone like that?"

"I guess so. They have a long tradition of non-violence."

"Do you think they're right?"

"Not my place to say. I think some of them genuinely believe in what they preach. As for others…." He shrugged.

"They're shirking their duty to their country, that's what I think. All of 'em. My brother, and Tom, and thousands of other men are ready to die for freedom, and guys like Frank Hicks sit on the sidelines. Heck, even the Pope says this is a just war." I attacked my chicken, and gravy slopped over the plate. "I don't care how handsome he is. He could be doin' *something*. He could be helpin' at a field hospital."

"He thinks he is. He's caring for the mentally ill. If you've already been to the hospital, you might have seen it isn't easy."

I thought of Mr. Stiles and his near attack on me. "It's not enough."

Sam merely shook his head and drank.

I slammed my silverware down. "You disagree? You think he's right? What about you? Did you serve in the Great War?"

He mopped up a bit of gravy from the table. "Don't be ridiculous, Betty. I'm not that old. I was too young to be drafted back then. I tried to enlist this time, but I have a slight heart murmur. So here I am." He tossed aside the napkin. "I don't personally agree with conscientious objectors, even if I may understand them. There comes a time when talking simply isn't enough. As many people have pointed out, Mr. Chamberlain tried appeasement, and where did it get him? Out of a job. And some COs do serve in non-combat roles, like in hospitals. Some don't want anything to do with the war. Frank Hicks seems like one of the latter."

Heat crept up the back of my neck. "Sorry. I didn't mean to shout at you."

Sam waved his hand. "Did you learn anything from Hicks?"

"Not really." I stabbed my chicken. "He didn't deny knowing Edward Kettle, but he said flat out it was none of my business and I should stay away from Edward. He walked off before I could ask anything else."

"Did he know Mr. Kettle was dead?"

"He didn't talk like he did. 'Course, if he's smart, he'd act like he was ignorant, wouldn't he?"

"This is true." Sam took his notebook out of his pocket.

"You know a bit more about him, don't you?"

Sam thumbed the pages. "Francis Hicks, Junior, age twenty-two. He grew up in Orchard Park, which is where his parents still live. He graduated from the local public high school with honors and attended St. Bonaventure College, where he majored in history. His father owns a furniture store

CHAPTER SIXTEEN

there and does pretty well for himself. The family came from Philadelphia."

"He sounds awfully boring."

"Except for the fact the elder Mr. Hicks was accused of war-profiteering in the Great War, he is."

I whistled. "What was he doing?"

"Nothing was ever proved, but the story was the elder Mr. Hicks was involved in a scheme to sell materials to the War Department at higher than market cost. Or something like that. I haven't spent too much time investigating beyond knowing that it happened. It's why the family left Philadelphia and relocated to Buffalo."

"Interesting. But why would Edward and Frank talk to each other?"

Sam flipped a page. "I don't know if you know this, but rationing was voluntary during the first war. Not so this time. Officials are constantly on the lookout for black marketeering or related activities. Orchard Park is the latest target."

The facts clicked in my head. "The cops there think Mr. Hicks is involved."

Sam set the notebook down. "His history makes him suspect, but they've not seen a hint of illegal activity around the store. Mr. Hicks has been questioned. He was very polite and helpful. A search came up empty. However, his son has definitely been seen in the company of, shall we say, less than savory individuals who have loose ties to the black market."

"A furniture store would be a good front for a distribution center. I bet they have trucks comin' and goin' all the time."

"Indeed." Sam swirled his coffee and drained the cup. "As I said, officials haven't turned up a trace of illegal activity. To date, it's a lot of speculation, and no one can prove anything yet. But it's noteworthy."

"I guess, but I don't see where Edward comes in."

"You don't?" Sam stared at me. "Where did he work?"

"At the shipyard...on the lake." He could have seen boat traffic, maybe even where they docked and unloaded. Perhaps even who picked up the goods. "You're thinking he could have wised up to the scheme, even seen Frank's father—or Frank himself—take delivery of the goods. Edward was threatenin' to turn them in."

"Or he wanted a cut. Remember, Edward's family had cut him off. The extra money would have been helpful."

"But that doesn't square up with things people have told me about Edward bein' a patriot." I poked at the chicken, which had gone cold while I talked. I pushed the plate away. "There are two other names that have come up. One is Albert Riker. He works at the shipyard with Edward. Or worked with him, I should say. Supposedly, he's the canary who told Melvin to talk to Edward. He said Edward had a secret Melvin could use to get information. Based on what you told me, it could have been the black-market deal, but that's not Melvin's story."

Sam tapped his pencil on the table. "But Riker definitely knew about Kettle's homosexuality and was holding it over him, huh?" He glanced around and leaned in. "By the way," he said, voice soft enough that only I could hear. "We've learned there was a leak at the shipyard involving this second boat. When we informed officials at the yard of Kettle's death, they said he'd gone to his supervisor with information. He wanted a meeting with senior officials at the company. He claimed he had details of a mole, but didn't want to say anything to anyone outside the executive level."

"When was the meeting s'posed to happen?"

"Later this week." Sam sat back. "Convenient, huh?"

"Very." How was I gonna follow up on that? "One more thing. Have you learned about any, um, personal relationships Edward may have had?"

Sam's gaze was knowing. "Personal as in sexual?"

I gulped. "Yes. Another man at the boarding house, William Townes, overheard Edward on the telephone with someone named Ray. Mr. Townes thought it sounded like a...a lover." I swallowed again. "I don't have a last name."

"No one named Ray has come up, but I'll look around."

"I don't know if Mr. Townes can be trusted, though. He hated Edward 'cause he was, you know, homosexual. He even told me he threatened to make Edward squeal like a pig 'cause Edward threatened to tell their landlady Mr. Townes had entertained women in his room."

Sam drummed his fingers on the table. "Interesting choice of words,

CHAPTER SIXTEEN

considering how Kettle died." He gave an approving nod. "Nice to see you haven't been wasting the effort you've put into that correspondence course. I need to go. But let me know if you find more on this Ray person. I'll do the same." He threw down some money and left.

I stared into my coffee cup. There were two categories of motive. Someone hated Edward 'cause of what he was, or I was once again staring at a case of espionage or maybe more war-profiteering. I swallowed the rest of the coffee, even though it was stone-cold and bitter.

The waitress returned, her disappointment written on her face. "Aw, where'd the cutie go?"

"He had to scram." I noticed he'd left a five-dollar bill, more than enough to cover my lunch and his coffee. One of these days, I'd get to the tab first. I nodded at the money. "Keep the change."

Chapter Seventeen

After I left the diner, I thought about what to do next. I could hang out and tail Frank Hicks home from work. Dot would recommend following a dreamboat over almost anything else. If I knew where he lived, I could stake out his home. I'd see who visited him and maybe be able to "accidentally" bump into him on the street. We would go for coffee, and I'd get him to spill about his father and Edward. Then we might go for a walk, through a nearby park or down at the lake. The day was nice and the weather warm. Perfect for a stroll.

I shook myself. *You. Are. Engaged.* Not only that, Frank was a suspect. An incredibly handsome one and he prob'ly knew how to treat a girl to a good time, but nevertheless. He could be a murderer. I had no business admiring the man's eyes or his dimple when he might've killed my client.

However, it was only two-thirty. I'd have to waste hours waiting for him to leave the hospital. If his family owned a business in Orchard Park, he'd be easy enough to find when I wanted him.

What about Albert Riker? I needed a telephone book. A quick scan of the businesses around the diner turned up a drug store. They had to have a pay phone, which meant there'd be a book. I went inside. "Do you have a telephone?"

The counter clerk pointed toward the back. "In the corner near the pharmacy."

I thanked her and headed in that direction. I grabbed the thick book and flipped to the R's in the white pages. I ran my finger down the column of names. There was one A Riker, with an address over near Kaisertown, and

CHAPTER SEVENTEEN

an Albert Riker who lived on the West Side. I dropped a coin in the phone and dialed the first number. A woman answered.

"Yes, this is Miss Jones from American Shipbuilding. I'm calling with a message for Mr. Riker. May I speak to him?"

"You'll have a doozy of a time with that, my dear," said the woman, who had a harried note in her voice. In the background, I could hear a screaming infant. "He's currently somewhere in the South Pacific, and I don't think he can accept your call."

"Sorry, I must have the wrong number." I dialed again. This time the telephone rang for well over a dozen times before I hung up. I scribbled the phone number and the address on Fargo Avenue into my notebook. It was more likely to be the man I was looking for. Given the time, I figured he was at work. I returned to the counter. "If I needed to get to the West Side, what's the fastest route?"

The girl scowled. "How would I know? I don't work for International Railway."

Even though she hadn't been helpful, I thanked her and left. I knew the city and the International Railway Company, which ran the city's streetcars, had agreed to replace the cars with buses 'cause of the poor condition of the rails. I studied the area. The next block of Elmwood also looked residential, but there had to be a trolley or bus stop around here, somewhere close to the hospital. I took off down Forest and was rewarded when I saw a stop for both on the corner where it met Grant Street. I checked the schedule. I had options. I could go talk to Mr. Riker, but I'd have to waste time waiting for him to come home. Same with going to see Mr. Brickett. But at least if I struck out with him, I'd be positioned to take the line to Orchard Park and move on to the Hicks family. A retail store had to be open on weekdays.

I consulted the schedule again and took the next bus, which dropped me within walking distance of Mr. Brickett's place. As I approached, I saw Mr. Townes coming from the other direction. *Perfect, I can kill two birds with one stone.* "Good afternoon, Mr. Townes. I hope you remember me."

"The girl detective," he said in an amused voice. "Have you found the faggot's killer yet? I want to send him a thank-you note."

"I'm kinda surprised you're so...vocal. Aren't you afraid someone might start suspectin' you? After all, you lived with Mr. Kettle. You're perfectly placed to have done it. No one would find it odd to see you here in the house, and you'd have known how to get in and out of his room without being noticed."

"Nope." He stuffed his hands in his pockets. "I told you, if he hadn't been what he was, he'd have been a good guy. I knew he came from money, but he didn't look down on people like me, who didn't have his fancy education. He seemed honest. He did his part for the country, workin' down at the shipyard and supporting the war. But none of that makes up for what he was. We can't say we're a moral, Christian, God-fearing country and put up with the likes of him and his kind. I made no secret of the fact I hated him because of it. If I'd offed him, don't you think I'd act like we were buddies?"

Mr. Townes was so blunt, I didn't expect such crafty thinking from him. "But he was a human being, a person. That's gotta count for something, right? It's one thing to think he was sinful for being a homosexual and another to think killing him was okay. How is that Christian?" I didn't know why I was arguing with him. It struck me I was fumbling my way through my own feelings. My faith told me homosexuality was wrong. But murder was worse. Wasn't it? It had to be. It was right there in the Ten Commandments. None of those said anything about men loving men.

Mr. Townes's face didn't move. "You believe someone like that is still human?"

His words slapped me. I knew in my bones I could never think that way. The worst criminals were still people. The Bible was full of awful men and women who had committed terrible sins, but it never denied they were people, just like the ones who stood by God. "Where were you Monday night?"

"I told you. Chauncey's."

"But you won't tell me when. You coulda killed Mr. Kettle, changed your clothes, and gone out."

His answering grin was sly. "Aren't you a clever broad? Have it your way. I was out with some pals. Chauncey's isn't far from here. I arrived at seven

CHAPTER SEVENTEEN

and didn't leave until closing."

"Can anyone confirm that?"

He smirked. "Only my friends, the barman, and the waitress. We went back to her place to have a bit of fun. You know, what real men do."

I schooled my face. "The Bible says intercourse outside of marriage is sinful. How is what you did any different from Mr. Kettle?"

"In one very important way, sweetheart." He leaned in so close I could smell his sour breath. "I did it with a woman."

I coulda been remembering my catechism wrong, but I was pretty sure that didn't make it better. "This Ray you claim to have heard Mr. Kettle talkin' to."

"Not claim, I did hear him."

"I don't s'pose you have any details. Such as a last name?"

"No last names." He rubbed his chin. "But right before he noticed me, he said somethin' like 'I'll see you at Cosmo's this weekend, right?' At least, I think that was what I heard."

"Is that a man's name, a restaurant, a bar, what?"

"Don't know. If Kettle wanted to go there, I most definitely did not. Now outta my way. I got things to do." He moved past me, deliberately bumping my shoulder with his.

It hurt, but I waited until he went inside to rub it. I wasn't gonna let an oaf like William Townes know anything he'd done had made me the least bit uncomfortable.

And I would stop at Chauncey's on the way out to Orchard Park.

* * *

Mr. Brickett was not home. His wife eyed me when I asked. I don't think she was convinced that I was a private detective. The way she talked, it was exactly as if she thought I was a floozy out to corner her man. "I won't give him a message," she said. "Stay away from my husband."

"Ma'am, it's about the murder across the street, honest. If I was tryin' to move in on your marriage, would I leave a note with you?"

"You might if you thought a cockamamie story would confuse me, but I'm on to you, young lady. Harvey has nothing for you." She slammed the door.

At least not in the way you think.

Chauncey's was a typical neighborhood watering hole in Allentown, located on Delaware Avenue. The decor leaned heavily on polished wood, leather that was showin' signs of age but was obviously well-oiled, and stained glass in the windows. The bar took up a corner, curving like a horseshoe that had been pulled wide. Bottles of all sizes lined up in front of a mirror that had Chauncey's painted on it in fancy letters and stools in front of the counter. A man wearing a dark green apron dried glasses before placing them on the shelves that lined the wall.

"Excuse me," I said. "I'm—"

"Buy something or get out."

I didn't want booze, especially not in the middle of the afternoon. "Uh, got any Coca-Cola?"

"Does this look like a soda shop, sweetheart?"

What could I possibly order? "How about a glass of tonic water with a twist of lemon?" Pop drank that sometimes. Surely Chauncey's had the drink.

The man shook his head, but he poured a glass of the clear liquid and squeezed in the juice from a wedge of lemon. "Ten cents."

I pushed a dime across the bar and took my drink. "Can I ask my questions?"

"What about?"

"Were you working on Monday evening this week?"

He wiped another glass and placed it. "I'm the owner. I work every night." He flipped his towel over his shoulder. "Why?"

"Did you see a man named William Townes in here?"

"Bill? Sure. He's one of my regulars."

Rats. "When?"

"Why do you care?"

"I'm a private detective." I sipped. "I'm investigating a murder. Mr. Townes is using your place as his alibi, and I'd like to know if he's shamming or telling

CHAPTER SEVENTEEN

the truth."

"A private dick, huh? You girls are doin' everything these days, aren't you?"

The handbook said to keep it simple when stating your purpose and not to let your witness drag you off the main topic. I waited.

He leaned on the bar. "Bill got here around seven-thirty. No, maybe closer to seven. He came in with a bunch of friends, who are also regulars. They opened a tab and sat in that corner." He pointed.

"When did he leave?"

"Not until I closed around four in the morning."

"Did he leave with his friends?" The tonic was bitter, and the lemon didn't make it better. How did Pop drink this stuff?

"Nope." The barman draped his towel over his shoulder. "He left with one of my waitresses. They'd been flirtin' all night. I'm pretty sure they went back to her place for a nightcap, if you know what I mean."

I did, and I thought it was tacky, but I didn't want to sound like a prude. Of bigger concern to me was that Mr. Townes's alibi was solid. "You're sure he was here all night."

"Yes. Although, I lost track of him around nine or so." The bartender swiped his towel over the shining wood.

I almost set my glass down, but it would leave a mark. "How do you lose track of someone in a joint this small?"

"I looked up, and he wasn't there. One of the other guys came to buy another round. I asked if Bill had gone home, he said no. Bill'd stepped out but would be right back. Sure enough, I looked over about thirty minutes later, and he was here."

Thirty minutes was plenty of time to go back to the boarding house, kill Mr. Kettle, and return. As long as Mr. Townes hadn't dawdled around while he was there. "Did he look odd? Like were there any stains on his clothing or anything like that?"

"Not that I could tell. His face was red, but it was hot in here. Say." He frowned. "You aren't lookin' to finger Bill for this, are you? I won't help you with that. He's a little rough around the edges, but he's good people."

"If you say so." I looked at my drink. I'd barely made a dent in it, but I couldn't bring myself to have more. I set it down, not caring if it left a mark. "One last question. Have you ever seen a man named Edward Kettle?" I described him.

The bartender shook his head. "Doesn't ring any bells. He a friend of Bill's?"

"They know each other." I stood. "Thanks for your time."

He picked up my glass and wiped away the water on the wood. "Word of advice."

I expected more protests that Mr. Townes couldn't be a criminal. "Yeah?"

"If you're gonna come into a bar askin' questions, learn to drink what they serve."

I'd have to ask Pop how to make tonic water taste good. I knew for sure he wasn't gonna teach me to drink whiskey.

Chapter Eighteen

It was nearly three by the time I made it out to Orchard Park. The downtown area had a little more hustle and bustle than Hamburg, since Orchard Park was not a cozy village, but a larger town. I could tell there was money here, though. The women were all dressed in what I'd consider church clothes, nice dresses with light coats, heels, and jewelry. The stores were a little more high-end, if not quite up there with the downtown Buffalo department stores. I strolled down the sidewalk, looking at the window displays of fancy clothes and things. I'd had a hard time picturing myself as a housewife in Hamburg. I couldn't imagine livin' in Orchard Park.

Hicks Furniture was near the corner of Buffalo, and Quaker Streets, and I went inside. The display models had lots of polished wood and rich fabrics. They were beautiful, but I couldn't even think of having them in your house to sit on, 'specially if you had little kids. My younger brothers, Michael and Jimmy, would destroy these things in no time. And they weren't even really little kids. What would you do if you had babies?

I ran my hand over a queen-sized brass bed, complete with knobs and a plush bedspread. I pushed on the mattress. It was firm, but springy. The pillows were plump and filled with goose feathers, according to the tag. I tried to picture the setup in our bedroom after Tom and I got married. We wouldn't have space for anything else in the room.

A woman's voice sounded at my elbow. "Can I help you with something, miss? Would you like to lie down and try it?"

I spun and saw an older lady with dark eyes and immaculate silver hair.

"Um, no, thank you. I'm looking for Mr. or Mrs. Hicks, if they are available."

"May I ask why?"

I introduced myself and explained the reason for my visit. "I met their son, Frank, up at the Buffalo State Hospital. He wasn't willing to talk and I wanted to see if they could help me out."

"I'm Eliza Hicks, Frank's mother." She tilted her head, a bird-like movement. Her brown eyes sparkled. "You said you were a private investigator?"

"Yes, ma'am." I steeled myself for a lecture. I was sure Mrs. Hicks was another one of those elderly women who had definite ideas about appropriate jobs for young ladies.

"How fascinating." She clasped her hands. "If you don't mind my asking, what drew you to the profession?"

The words I'd prepared died on my tongue. Fascinating? I'd never gotten that reaction before, 'specially not from someone who looked like she could be my grandmother. "I like helping people. And solving puzzles. You know, figuring things out. It turns out people have a lot of secrets, things they'd rather not talk about. Sometimes that hurts others, the folks who come to me for help."

She nodded.

"I've always liked detective movies, the ones with Sam Spade or Philip Marlowe. But the pictures always have men in the starring roles. The women are always the sidekick, sometimes a girlfriend or maybe a reporter. Why can't a woman do the same job as a man? Well, aside from the fistfights. I try to avoid those. And I'm not big on the drinking."

"I should think not. Shall we sit?" She gestured at a handsome dark wood dining room set. The edge of the table and the backs of the chairs were covered in elegant scrollwork. "You like the challenge of finding the hidden truth. But have you considered that sometimes the truth is better off staying in the dark? I don't believe people should lie all the time, mind you, but there are things that would be more hurtful if they were commonly known."

I figured the chair would be hard and uncomfortable, but for a wooden seat, it was surprisingly welcoming. "Sometimes." I thought of Edward

CHAPTER EIGHTEEN

Kettle and Harvey Brickett. They were definitely better off with nobody knowing what they really were. "Although generally, I believe the old saying. You know, the truth shall set you free."

She took the seat next to me. "From the Bible. It's one very good place of wisdom. You go to a church or a meeting?"

"I'm Catholic. I go to Mass every week. I don't know what you mean by a meeting."

"It's what we Quakers call our services. We sit quietly in contemplation. We may speak if we feel the call, but oftentimes it is complete silence."

"No music or preaching?"

"Nothing."

What an odd way to worship. I couldn't imagine Mass without the hymns and chanted prayer. "So you're a Quaker as well? Frank mentioned he was."

"Oh yes. My husband and I still practice." She folded her hands.

"Does Frank?"

"He goes with us every week."

He'd told the truth about being a Quaker. "Mrs. Hicks, do you know what your son is? Why he didn't enlist?"

Her smile was gentle. "A conscientious objector? Of course. We supported his decision. We believe in the Peace Testimony."

"That's part of your beliefs?"

"It's more of a description of our actions than a belief as you think of it," she said. "Frank is helping those in need by working with those poor people. This particular hospital tries to do better, but in general, the mentally ill are treated dreadfully. Don't you think working there does more good than killing people?"

The conversation was drifting somewhere I didn't want to go. "Do you or your husband know a man named Edward Kettle?"

A man walked up behind Mrs. Hicks. It had to be her husband. He was as handsome as his son, with a full head of wavy silver hair, the same lively brown eyes, and gorgeous dimple when he smiled. His teeth were also movie-star white and even. If Frank looked like his dad in thirty years, the woman he married would be very lucky. Mr. Hicks put a hand on his wife's shoulder. "My dear, who is this charming young lady?"

Mrs. Hicks introduced me. "She's a private investigator, Francis. Isn't that interesting?"

"Pleased to meet you." I held out my hand.

"Delighted. But why are you asking about Edward Kettle?" His grip was firm.

"He was a client of mine."

"Was?" asked Mrs. Hicks.

"He's dead. Murdered." I watched their reactions.

Mrs. Hicks gasped and put her hand to her mouth. Mr. Hicks said nothing, but his face was too calm. "Who did it?"

"That's what I'm here to find out."

She pressed a hand to her cheek. "Surely you don't think our Frank had anything to do with it? The Quaker stance against violence isn't only regarding war. We abhor *any* violence, and that most certainly includes murder."

Her outrage was obvious, but human beings were all the same in my book. Push 'em far enough, and they were capable of anything. Even those who belonged to a peace-loving religion. "I'm not accusing anybody of anything, Mrs. Hicks. But Frank was seen with my client before he died. I want to know about that. Frank wouldn't tell me. I hoped you would. If not, I'm wastin' my time and yours. Tell me so, and I'll leave."

They exchanged a look. "Mr. Kettle and I had a disagreement," Mr. Hicks said.

From the way he spoke, I was sure it was more than a simple argument. "Over what?"

"Some time ago, he came into the store. He'd learned his sister had visited with the intention of purchasing a bedroom set." Mr. Hicks's eyes grew solemn. "Mr. Kettle had heard we were connected to the black market. I assured him that was not the case. Yes, the Orchard Park police and federal authorities have been here, but they've found nothing. He then said that might be true of us, but could we be sure of our son? Mr. Kettle said he'd heard Frank had been seen with people out of Buffalo who were rumored to

CHAPTER EIGHTEEN

have ties to illegal activities. I assured him Frank would never do that, he's a good person. He accepted my words at first, but came back later insisting I was not being honest."

He was talkin' around the facts, but if he thought I'd buy it and drop my question, he was wrong. "Did he offer you any proof?"

"Only his word that he'd seen Frank firsthand. I didn't doubt he'd observed my son with a person who may have looked like a criminal, but I am absolutely certain Frank would not fraternize with such a person. I've lived through the effects of rumor and innuendo once. I don't care to do it again, and I will not have people slandering my son, either. I told Mr. Kettle the police had cleared me, and Frank, and told him to leave." He looked at his wife, then back to me. "Are you shopping for a bedroom set?"

"Someday, but not right now and not one this big. If you won't talk to me about Edward Kettle, at least not more than you've already said, I'll stop taking up your time. Have a nice afternoon." I left. They had a lot of nice things. No wonder they'd chosen to market it in the Southtowns. No one I knew could afford it. I'd never been to Philadelphia, but I knew there were lots of families with old money there, people who had whole houses of furniture like Mr. Hicks sold. Why had he relocated all the way to Buffalo? Had the accusations spread so far outside of Philadelphia the family had to go to another state?

Once outside, it had cooled off, so I buttoned my coat. I figured I'd head home for dinner. I didn't have the dough for a restaurant out here. I hoped I didn't have to wait too long for a trolley back to the city.

"Miss Ahern? Miss Ahern, wait a moment," said a woman behind me.

It was Mrs. Hicks. She walked forward and stopped a foot or so away. "Oh, thank goodness I caught you."

"What can I do for you?"

"It's more what I can help you with." She paused and glanced back at the store. "Is Frank truly a suspect in this man's murder?"

"I can't speak for the police, but he's on my list. He was seen arguing with Mr. Kettle not long before he died. Until I know more about that, I can't ignore him."

She wrung her hands. "Oh dear."

I waited. Motherly concern might get me what I was after if I was patient enough.

"It was a big misunderstanding," she finally said. "During the last war, Francis—my husband, not my son—agreed to take delivery of some boxes for an acquaintance of his. The man had lost the lease on his own warehouse. He told us it was a short-term arrangement, and all we had to do was store the shipments for a couple of months. Francis even gave this man keys to our warehouse, so he could have access to his goods."

This story didn't have a happy ending. I'd seen too many setups like this in the pictures. "Let me guess. The merchandise wasn't on the level."

She shook her head, hands still writhing. "Francis kept me out of the details, but it had something to do with the military. There were federal agents at the store all the time. They searched us, but didn't find anything. We hired an attorney. He had to go to court. In the end, they couldn't prove the charges, but the scandal forced us out of our home. Frank was only a child, but he has very clear memories. His classmates called him the most awful names and said his father had betrayed the country. We relocated here because Francis had friends who worked in the steel industry, and they told us Buffalo was a growing city. Now there's another war, and the old rumors are being brought out again. This time it's worse, because of Frank."

"Did Edward Kettle visit you more than once?" I took out my notepad and pencil.

"He was here at least twice that I know of. The last time I saw him was early April. When Mr. Kettle came into the store the second time, Francis took him into his office. They spoke for at least half an hour. When Mr. Kettle left, I remember him speaking to my husband and saying 'I won't let him get away with it.' I'm pretty sure those were his words. Francis looked quite upset."

I said nothing.

She seemed to realize what she'd done, because she hurried on. "Oh, don't think I believe Francis, my husband that is, would have anything to do with this man's death. I told you, it's against everything we believe in. Mr. Kettle's

CHAPTER EIGHTEEN

visit upset him terribly. He wouldn't drink the tea I made for him, and we closed early."

I didn't suspect her husband. But her son was another matter. "Frank knew about this?"

"He was here the day Mr. Kettle visited the second time. I didn't know about him going to see Mr. Kettle at his house. I wish Frank had stayed away and let his father handle it." Her eyes, so like her son's, were big with worry. "But you must believe me, Miss Ahern. Frank wouldn't hurt a mouse. It's against everything we've taught him."

'Cept I'd seen before how far sons would go to protect their family name. "Did you see or talk to Frank on Monday night of this week?"

"No. We pay for him to have a small apartment in the city. It's easier for him to walk to the hospital. He usually only visits on the weekends." She paused. "You believe me, don't you?"

"You've been very helpful, ma'am. Thank you for talkin' to me." I wished her good evening and left.

I caught the trolley in the nick of time. On the way home, I thought again about how Mr. Kettle had been killed. Slitting a man's throat the way Sam described was brutal. I couldn't see Frank Hicks doin' that, not with his education and movie-star looks. He didn't seem the type.

But looks could be deceiving.

Chapter Nineteen

I had a visitor when I got home. Melvin sat on the couch, an untouched cup of tea in front of him. "Hiya, Toots. Your mom's a doll. We've been talking while we waited. The way she tells it, you're quite a character."

Mom grabbed his cup. "Betty, before you and Mr. Schlingmann have your talk, I want to discuss dinner plans for tonight."

I followed her to the kitchen. There were no dinner plans. At least none that needed a private conversation between Mom and I. "I didn't know he would come here. If I did, I woulda told him to stay away."

She waved her hand. "I'm not mad at you. The man wants something, Betty. He claimed he needed information for a story he's writing, but his questions were hardly appropriate. You're not a public figure. He has no right to know about your childhood. Or your marriage plans."

"He told me he was gonna do a piece 'cause I'm a woman detective. I also told him I'd give him first dibs on the story about Edward Kettle's death."

"That may well be the case, but you watch your step with him. He gives me the willies."

"You're not the only one." Melvin didn't rouse a warm feeling in me, either.

I returned to the living room. "What are you doin' here?"

He looked up from the notebook he'd been writing in. "Is that any way to speak to a pal?"

"You aren't my friend." I perched on the chair opposite him and crossed my legs at the ankles. I knew instinctively he wanted to be complimented on his craftiness in finding me. I would not give him the satisfaction.

"After what we've been through?"

CHAPTER NINETEEN

"I hardly think two conversations counts as friendship. I haven't even crossed you off my suspect list."

He sat up straight. "You seriously think I killed Kettle? Whatever for?"

"The one thing I never took you for was a fat head." I crossed my arms. "You tried to bust into a secure facility, one guarded by the U.S. Coast Guard. You tried to blackmail an employee of the shipyard to get insider information. I don't think you wanna make Fort Leavenworth your permanent address. If Edward Kettle threatened to turn you in, that seems like a good motive to me."

"Come on." He ran a hand through his hair. "Yes, I walked around the fence line. So did dozens of other people. If they arrested every person who tried to get a peep, they'd run out of jail cells. And I never threatened Kettle."

"You said you knew what he was hidin'. Why do that unless you were gonna expose his secret if he didn't play ball?"

He tossed down his pencil. "This is outrageous."

I kept my mouth shut and stared at him.

"They found Kettle on Tuesday morning, right? I have an alibi. All Monday, I was at the paper. I met a source for dinner and went back to the office to finish my story. I stayed late and then went home."

"Anyone with you at home? What about the office?"

"One of the typesetters was at the paper. I was by myself at home. But I was there."

"I'll need a name of who you ate with so I can check your story."

"No way. A reporter never gives up his sources."

I eyeballed him. "Even when not doing it could land the reporter in the pokey?"

His knee jiggled. "I spent half of Tuesday running down leads. Do the cops think he was killed on Monday night or early Tuesday morning?"

Either he didn't want to share, or he didn't have a name to give. I hadn't asked Sam about time of death. When we'd talked at the crime scene, I'd figured he thought Monday evening, but I could be wrong. I coulda kicked myself for the rookie mistake, but I kept still.

"You haven't asked?" He smirked. "Not much of a detective, are you?"

"I said I'd give you the scoop when the case was closed. It's not over yet so I'm not gonna talk to you about every little thing I know." It wasn't much of a comeback, but it would have to do.

"Right, sweetheart." He gave me an exaggerated wink.

"Don't call me that. Let's get down to brass tacks." I leaned forward. "Why are you in my living room?"

He waited a good long minute before answering. "Edward Kettle had a lover."

"I know."

"His name is Raymond Lovelace."

On one hand, he'd beaten me to the name. On the other, he'd offered it up without much of a fuss. Why? What did he think I could give him that the police wouldn't or couldn't? "How d'you find that out?"

"I have my methods, which seem to be better than yours."

"I hadn't put a last name to him yet." I raised my hand to nibble my thumbnail, but I didn't want him thinking I was nervous, so I scratched my nose instead. "You talked to this guy?"

"His wife blew me off." Melvin tapped his pencil. "I like you, Toots. Here's the deal. I'll give up Lovelace's address, and you give me daily updates."

I scoffed. "No way. I can get the info from the white pages, you sap."

"But can you get his work address?" Melvin tore off the top sheet of his pad and waved it at me.

It was a deal with the devil. Melvin would squeeze me for every drop, and hound me day and night. If he knew where I lived, he'd know our phone number. His alibi was weak.

But this would save me time. A lot of it. I stared at the sheet of yellow, waving lazily in front of my eyes. *I'll have to be smarter than Melvin. How hard can that be?* I snatched the paper from his hand. "Deal. Oh, and one other thing."

"What's that?"

"Don't come near my house again, or all bets are off. 'Cause you'll be cooling your heels at the county jail, explaining why you shouldn't be arrested for treason."

CHAPTER NINETEEN

* * *

I soothed Mom's mood by cooking dinner. After, I sent her to the living room with a cup of tea while Mary Kate and I cleaned up. Now that Melvin knew where I lived, how was I gonna keep him from showin' up unannounced? I didn't quite trust him to stick to our bargain.

"Was the man who was here earlier visitin' about your case?" Mary Kate asked as she dried a plate.

"He was."

"I didn't like him. He looked sneaky."

Even my teenage sister had a bead on Melvin. "I told him to get lost and not come back. Do me a favor?"

She perked up. "Sure! What do you need?"

"Let me know if he comes around again. You know, if I'm not home or anything."

Her forehead wrinkled. "How'm I s'posed to let you know if you're not here?"

"When I get back, silly. Or if I call for messages."

"Oh." Her face cleared. "Sure thing. I'll let Jimmy and Michael know, too. Maybe we can follow him."

They could be pests, but I loved my siblings. "All you need to do is tell me if he comes back. I don't want you three gettin' hurt." My mother would kill me.

Once we finished, Mary Kate went off to finish her homework. I grabbed the telephone and sat on the floor in the hallway. I pulled out the paper with Albert Riker's number and picked up the handset.

"You would not believe what she tried to serve for dinner," a familiar woman's voice said.

"Mrs. Grady, this is Betty Ahern. I gotta make an important phone call. Can you get off the line?"

She sounded waspish. "Young people these days. What makes you think your call is more important than mine?"

"Mine has to do with findin' a murderer." *Top that.*

"Oh really? Do tell."

In my haste to retort, I'd forgotten what a gossip she was. "Please, ma'am. This'll only take a minute. I'll tell you all about it next Sunday after church."

She *tsked* her disapproval, but hung up.

I dialed the number. "May I please speak to Mr. Riker?" I asked when a man answered.

"Yeah? Who are you, and what do you want?"

I identified myself. "I'm investigating the murder of Edward Kettle. I understand you knew him."

He chuckled. "Isn't that a job for the police, girlie?"

A key trait in a successful investigator is confidence. That's what the handbook said. "Mr. Kettle hired me before he died to look into why he was fired."

"That's easy. They canned him 'cause he yapped to a two-bit reporter. I gotta go."

"Wait." I heard breathing, so I knew he hadn't cut me off. "That was the reason, but Mr. Kettle swears he didn't do it. I've spoken to the reporter in question, and that's when your name came up."

There was a pause. "Why the hell should it?"

"The reporter said you told him to hit up Mr. Kettle for some inside dirt on American Shipbuilding's activities. If Mr. Kettle wouldn't play ball, the reporter should threaten to expose a secret."

"Look, sister." Mr. Riker's voice was sharp. If we were face to face, he'd be jabbing a finger at me. "I don't know nothing about Kettle and his so-called friends. And whatever Schlingmann is peddling, you're a dummy if you buy it."

The *thunk* of him slamming down the phone nearly busted my eardrum. I stared at the blower and put it back in the cradle. As I mulled over the conversation, one thing stood out.

I'd never mentioned Melvin's name.

Chapter Twenty

I gobbled my breakfast the next morning. I'd gone from having no leads to having my hands full. According to the dope Melvin had given me, Raymond Lovelace worked at a bank on the East Side. On the one hand, crashing his job and asking if he was in a homosexual relationship might not be the best approach. I could easily get thrown out on my keister. On the other, cornering him at work might be the ticket. I could catch him at lunch or when he left for the day. I wanted to get to him when he was unaware and not give him time to cook up a story. He also wouldn't want his wife and kids overhearing our conversation. I called the bank. "Good morning. I'm looking for Mr. Lovelace. Is he in?"

"He's in a meeting. May I take a message?"

"I'll call back. Thank you." He was at work. I mulled my choices. I could show up, but he sounded like a man who you needed an appointment to talk to. Barging into the bank would not be successful. But he must eat lunch. Even if he brown-bagged it, was he the type to take advantage of a nice spring day and eat outside? The sky right now was a little cloudy, promising some rain, but it could clear up by noon. I didn't want to threaten him or anything, but I had to try and convince him to give me five minutes to talk about his old friend Mr. Kettle.

Mrs. Hicks had given me a little info but not much about Frank. All of it was through a mother's eye, so 'course it was rosy. I had the low-down on him from Sam, but those were just facts. I needed dirt, and my meeting with him yesterday didn't make it seem like he was gonna take me out to dinner and tell his life's story. A candlelit dinner, of course. I'd wear my best dress.

He would look smashing in a suit, maybe a tuxedo.

Snap out of it. He's a suspect and a conscientious object, nothing more.

I could ask Sam if he knew anything about Albert Riker. But I wanted to have some independence and be able to do it on my own. Mr. Riker had dropped Melvin's name last night, which meant they'd talked. Reporters were creatures of habit. Melvin liked breakfast at Moe's. I'd start there.

The diner was hoppin' when I arrived. I craned my neck to scan the crowd.

Gert met me at the door. "You need a table, hon? Or are you lookin' for someone?" she asked as she grabbed a menu.

"I dropped by to see if Melvin was here. You seen him?"

She nodded toward the counter. "Third stool from the end. Be careful, or you'll end up with the tab."

I thanked her and threaded my way over. The seat next to him was free. "Hiya, Melvin. Long time no see, huh?" I sat and waved to a waitress. "Coffee, black. Please and thank you."

He didn't look at me. "Now, what do you want? Don't tell me you've made a breakthrough since last night." He slid a fried egg onto a piece of toast and crammed it in his mouth.

"I see your manners haven't gotten any better."

He mumbled a response.

I couldn't make out the words, but I didn't want to. "Why don't you tell me about Albert Riker? I heard you've been talking to him."

"Who?"

"Don't play dumb. He's the guy who put you on to Edward Kettle. And don't bother to deny it, 'cause he knows your name." My coffee arrived, hot and strong. I loved this part of the job. Meeting witnesses and suspects in diners where I could get real java.

"You talked to him?" Melvin asked around half a mouthful of egg and toast.

"Last night."

"What did he tell you?"

"Wouldn't you like to know?" Instinct and the correspondence course told me not to let Melvin know I'd gotten absolutely nothing useful from Mr.

CHAPTER TWENTY

Riker. Sam had taught me that, too. Let the person think you knew more than you did, and you'd be a lot more successful. "He doesn't think much of you, though."

Melvin stared at me. "Oh yeah?"

"He said I was a fool if I believed a word you said."

"That crummy, no good...." His words trailed off into a string of curses.

"Now, now. Language. Or is that as bad as your table manners?" I sipped my coffee. "Just tell me what your connection to Albert Riker is."

Melvin swallowed. "It's not much, to be honest. I told you I wanted to be the first to break the story about American Shipbuilding, and I got this for my efforts." He pointed at his puss.

"Because it would give that rag you work for some credibility."

"More than that." He wiped his mouth and pushed away the plate. "You don't think I'm much of a reporter 'cause of who I work for. Got it. I want to move up. I want to write for the *Courier-Express*. To do that, I need a big story to my name."

I didn't know much about the newspaper business, but I could see what he meant. He needed to prove himself. "And you thought reporting war secrets was it?" He was dumber than I thought.

"It was a work in progress. Who knew what I'd write? It coulda been a story on disloyal workers. Anyway, after I first visited and struck out, Riker found me. He told me he could give me a scoop on a great angle, but I couldn't afford his price."

I nearly dropped my coffee cup. "He said *what?*"

"Didn't know that, didja?" Melvin smirked. "True fact, Toots. And he was right. He quoted the dough he wanted, and it was way beyond my means. Then he told me that since he liked me, he'd do me a favor. There was another guy who'd give me the dope and it would cost pennies. Heck, it might be free. That's when he gave me Kettle's name and told me all I had to do was threaten to expose Kettle to unlock the story of my dreams." He slurped his coffee.

Albert Riker had fed Edward to the sharks. Because he knew Edward was a homosexual? Why would that be so newsworthy? "You're sure Mr. Riker didn't get more specific about what this magic information was?"

"No. I figured out it had to be something to do with the shipyard. The details were fuzzy. Based on what he told me about Kettle, it could've been an exposé of immorality in American industry. Or maybe something illegal was going on, like defrauding the government while appearing to help the war effort. I was attracted to the secrecy, and who knows where it could've gone?"

I'd assumed Melvin wanted to uncover the nature of the work at American Shipbuilding. Maybe Mr. Riker knew about some double-dealing? No, that still didn't make sense. If he wanted money for squealing, why send Melvin elsewhere?

"Anyway, it doesn't matter. I've ditched any idea that has to do with that place. Too much physical risk. The murder story is a better deal. Based on what I've learned about the victim, it could be a real juicy one, too. Edward Kettle's secret life. That sort of thing."

"I told you not to write about that."

"No, you didn't. Besides, you can't tell me what to write. Free press and all that. It's right there in the Constitution."

Darn it. He was right. At least it explained his following me around like a puppy. The cops weren't gonna give him insider dope, but he thought he might be able to milk an amateur.

The tale Melvin told was logical, but it rubbed me the wrong way. If Mr. Riker hated homosexuals so much, he coulda sold that story to Melvin, no problem. The bit about saying Edward'd sing about some dealings at the shipyard in exchange for Melvin keeping quiet felt complicated. No, somethin' else was there, but I couldn't put my finger on it.

Melvin tapped his finger on the counter. "You're thinking of something. What?"

"None of your beeswax." I made some notes on my pad. "What do you know about a joe named Frank Hicks?"

"Nu-uh, sweetheart. I gave you Riker, now it's your turn to talk. Is Kettle's death related to his work at American Shipbuilding?"

I didn't want to say anythin', but I had promised to give the guy some

CHAPTER TWENTY

information. "I don't know, not yet."

"You're holdin' out on me."

"I'm not." I drank, buyin' time. "It could be connected. But there are some other things in Edward's personal life that are also good motives."

"The homosexuality? Or something else?" His eyes gleamed, and he pulled out a stubby pencil and notebook.

"I don't know yet. I'll tell you when I do, you got my word. Stop hassling me." He knew how to play hardball. But so did I. "My turn. Tell me what you know about Frank Hicks."

"No way. You haven't given me a single fact I can work with."

"I don't have anything. Look, if you need a story to sell, do you want facts or speculation? I promised you could have the scoop on Edward's murder, but I gotta solve it first." I shrugged. "But if you don't wanna talk about Frank Hicks, fine. You'll just have to wait longer for the payoff." I swirled my coffee.

Melvin appeared to chew over my words. Eventually, he caved. "Dames think he's a dreamboat, but he's a conchie, and that tends to turn 'em off. He works at the loony bin, but I've spied him talking to Kettle a couple of times. Hicks's family is from Philly, left there under a cloud. I asked him about it."

Since most girls had sweethearts or families on the front line, either in Europe or in the Pacific, I could see where opting to be a conscientious objector wouldn't go over well. "What did he say?"

"Told me to get lost. I'll say this, he may be a Quaker and a pacifist, but he ain't no chicken. He told me he'd give me a fat lip if I didn't stay away from him. Come to think of it—" he took another gulp of coffee—"he ain't much of a pacifist if he'd threaten to hit me, now is he?"

Another interesting tidbit. Yeah, it would be a big step from fighting to murder, but it meant Frank wasn't as peaceful as he said.

"You're quite a cookie, you know that?" A cocky grin spread over his puss. "I got another offer for you."

"I'm listening."

"Let me tag along." He tapped his finger on the counter. "I got a few connections. You need sources. I'll share if you let me follow and write my story. A good private dick needs friends who can give her the inside scoop. I can do that. We both win. I get my story, you get the information you need to crack the case. If it works out, I'm open to making it a long-term partnership."

Ugh. "I've already got a friend in the police department."

"But he may not always be able or want to share. Plus I can talk to people who won't give the cops a second look. Trust me, Toots, this is good for both of us."

It was tempting. I didn't have much of a network outside Sam. "I can't bring you along."

"Give me a reason why not."

"'Cause you're a suspect, you numbskull!"

He scoffed. "I didn't kill the guy. Why would I?"

"You're poking around in secret, war-related business. Places you aren't s'posed to be. At least that's what it looked like to anyone on the outside lookin' in. I told you. How do I know Edward didn't threaten to have you arrested?"

"What will it take to convince you I didn't do it?"

I thought. "An iron-clad alibi."

"Which I don't have."

I stood up. "Then we're done."

Melvin grabbed my wrist. "Not so fast, sweetheart. Okay, I get it. You don't trust me. Let me help, and I'll prove I didn't kill him. Fair deal?"

I eyed his hand as though it was a snake. I didn't like it, not one bit. But he had me on one point. He *could* help. If he helped himself right into handcuffs, well, so be it. What was that saying? Keep your friends close and your enemies closer? "Fine, But I have one condition and a promise."

"What's the condition?"

"You can't write *anything* until the case is over."

He scowled. "That ain't square."

"Hey, a big story will be worth more to the *Courier* than a handful of little ones."

He tilted his head. "Okay, deal. What's the promise?"

CHAPTER TWENTY

I pulled my arm away. "You call me sweetheart one more time, and I'll give you a knuckle sandwich."

I didn't believe him, not completely. Just like I didn't believe my brothers when they swore they had nothin' to do with Mrs. O'Keefe's disappearing pie. I'd have to keep a tight leash on him. I managed two little boys. I could handle Melvin Schlingmann.

Chapter Twenty-One

Melvin and I walked out of Moe's into a fine misty rain. He hunched his shoulders in a tan overcoat that had seen better days. I tied a scarf over my head. I'd get damp, but I'd been wetter.

"First thing is to find Albert Riker," he said.

I waved my hand. "I already did that."

"Huh?"

I resisted the urge to rub my knowledge in Melvin's face. "He lives over on Fargo Avenue. But this time of day, he'll be at work. I have a different target."

He flipped up the collar of his coat. "Who?"

"Do you know a place called Cosmo's? Or have you run across anyone with that name?" I walked for several paces before I realized he'd stopped. I turned.

Melvin was rooted to the ground, an expression of disbelief on his puss. "Are you pulling my leg?"

"No. Why?"

"Who told you about Cosmo's?"

His tone made me consider my response. "A witness said he heard Edward mention it." I'd been wondering if Cosmo was the name of a person or a bar. Melvin's response told me. It had to be a bar. And knowing Edward's personal life, it was a bar for men of a certain type.

Melvin took a couple of steps forward and whistled. "He really was a faggot, wasn't he?"

CHAPTER TWENTY-ONE

I was at his side in a split second. "Not so loud. And don't use that word."

"Why not?"

"I don't like it."

"You're the boss." He rubbed his hands together. "Hot diggity. I thought Riker mighta been pulling the wool over my eyes. This is gold."

"You promised. Nothing written until the case is over."

"Are you gonna make me swear not to write about Kettle's personal life? I won't do that. It's part of the story."

I knew it was. I was also pretty sure I'd never be able to keep an eager beaver like Melvin, who could think of nothing except juicy headlines, from tellin' the world. "No. I'm also not gonna expect you to develop a sense of dignity and spare Edward or his family. But I *do* expect you to wait until we've got his killer. Even if that's you. That was the deal."

"How many times do I have to tell you? I'm not your guy. Besides, if I'm the killer, how am I gonna write the story?"

"Do it from prison. Now." I crossed my arms. "Do you know about Cosmo's or not?"

He wiped water from his face. "It's over on West Chippewa." He paused, uncharacteristically sober. "I'm not sure it's a place for girls like you."

"Because I like men?"

"Because you're an innocent."

What did he know about me? I'd done stakeouts for black market vendors. I'd investigated murders. Industrial sabotage. Not only that, I'd interviewed prostitutes. I wasn't totally ignorant. "I am not."

He held up his hands. "Look, Toots. No offense. If you think about it, I'm givin' you a compliment. I'm sure you've done all sorts of things as a budding private dick you think have made you tough. But this is different. These people, they aren't like you and me."

I fixed him with my best Mom stare. "Would you go there for a story?"

"I already have. But I'm not you, okay? I have a bit more familiarity with the…dirtier side of the city."

I brushed him off. "My last case involved gangsters and police corruption. How much worse can it get?" I waited, but he didn't answer. "You know what bus to take?"

"I do." He blew out his breath.

"Then lead on." Maybe I should have been touched. Frankly, I suspected he might have another motive. Maybe he *wanted* to keep me away from Cosmo's 'cause he was afraid of what I'd learn.

If that was the case, he didn't know me very well at all.

We didn't speak on the ride, and we sat in different places on the bus. I watched him out of the corner of my eye. He twirled his pencil, lips moving in silent speech, eyes fixed on the seatback in front of him.

The bus deposited us at the corner of Chippewa and Elmwood, a quiet strip of small restaurants and mom-and-pop stores. Cosmo's was shoved in between a drugstore and what looked like an office. Heavy black drapes hung over the window, and the door was solid, the wood interrupted by a small brass slot at eye level. The name wasn't painted on the window, and no sign hung anywhere.

"Are you sure this is the place?" I asked Melvin. "It's only eight-thirty in the morning. I don't think anyone is gonna be here."

"Positive. Look." He squared his shoulders. "It's not a nightclub. They're open at all hours as kind of a refuge, you know? A place where everybody knows who they are and no one cares." He shot me a look. "You really want to go in here?"

"Are you gonna open the door, or am I?"

He pushed in front of me. "You don't just open the door. Hold on." He knocked, an odd pattern of rapid beats broken by pauses.

After a minute, the cover to the slot opened to reveal a pair of medium-brown eyes. "Yeah?"

"Melvin Schlingmann. Mr. Cosmo knows me. I'm here with an acquaintance."

The eyes cut over to me. "Who is she?"

I stepped forward. "My name is Betty Ahern, and I'm a private detective. I'm investigating the death of my client, Edward Kettle."

The eyes didn't blink. "We heard about Edward."

"I'm particularly interested in a man named Raymond Lovelace. Do you

CHAPTER TWENTY-ONE

know him?"

Silence.

I waited, but he said nothing more. I couldn't tell much from a pair of eyes, but the skin around them was wrinkled, and the voice didn't belong to a young man. Finally, I asked, "Are you gonna let us in? If you're tryin' to keep a low profile, this isn't the best way to do it. I swear I'm only tryin' to do right by Edward. I'm not interested in anything else."

Still no blink. "For Edward's sake, you can come in. But don't be surprised if no one here wants to say anything. A lot of these men have public lives, and they don't want to mess them up. Got it?"

"Got it."

"And you." The eyes shifted to look at Melvin. "None of your smarmy tabloid stories based on what you see or hear. Understand?"

Melvin drew his fingers across his mouth. "My lips are zipped."

The answer shocked me. Melvin had never made any pretense about being above selling out his mother for a good headline. What made these people so different?

The little slot cover snapped back.

He looked at me and must've read my expression. "I told you, Toots. You don't sell out a source. I may write for a rag, but I got some ethics."

I heard locks being undone, and the door opened. Melvin and I entered. Despite what he said, I'd expected a smoky atmosphere. But the interior of Cosmo's was more like the upscale social clubs I'd seen in films than anything else. A few men sat around tables. Some of 'em had plates heaped with breakfast food. A few lounged in the leather armchairs, smoking and reading the morning paper. Here and there, I spotted men holding hands like they were couples. Where else could they openly show affection? I guessed not too many other places in town.

I hugged myself and shifted. The men ranged in age from a little older than Lee to Pop's age or more. The low hum of conversation stopped when they saw me, but the couples did not break apart. If anything, they seemed a little hostile.

Well, I'm not s'posed to be here. I bet they know I'm not like them. If they've

141

gone to such lengths to stay hidden, no wonder they aren't happy.

Melvin turned to the guy who'd let us in. "Which one is Raymond Lovelace?"

"I didn't say I'd let you talk to him. Mr. Cosmo is over here. Follow me." The doorman, who was dressed in a plain white shirt and dark slacks, without a tie, led us to the corner.

The man sitting there could have doubled for Orson Welles. He was heavyset with a head of wavy dark hair, but he didn't have a mustache, like the one the actor'd had in *The Magnificent Ambersons*. Mr. Cosmo's eyes were a dark blue. His face was soft, not quite babyish, but not what I'd expect from the owner of a club. He had to be at least forty-five or fifty, but he might have been mistaken for younger. "Mr. Schlingmann." His voice sounded mild. "The last time we spoke, I was under the impression you weren't going to come back here."

"I'm doin' a favor for a friend." Melvin waved at me. "Cosmo, meet Betty Ahern. She's a private detective."

Mr. Cosmo shifted his gaze to me. "You brought an investigator here?"

"Don't worry, she's jake." Melvin waited, then said, "You gonna talk, Toots, or have I wasted my time?"

I startled a bit. I'd been examining the man in front of me, tryin' to ignore the rest of the men who'd gone back to their previous activities. Mostly, that is. Every once in a while, I caught one of 'em staring, whispering behind raised hands. It was enough to make anyone jumpy.

"Miss Ahern? Why are you here?" Mr. Cosmo asked.

I refocused. "Yes. Mr. Cosmo…uh, is that what I should call you? Or is that your first name?"

He chuckled. "Calling me mister is perfectly fine."

"Right, well." I squared my shoulders. "I had a client named Edward Kettle. The man at the door seemed to know him."

"He was a regular. We're a small community, Miss Ahern. Most of us know everyone else. The news of Edward's death was quite upsetting." Mr. Cosmo pushed a chair toward me. "Please sit. Looking up at you is straining my neck."

CHAPTER TWENTY-ONE

"Yes, sir." My reply was automatic, and I sat. After all, he was not much younger than Pop, and I'd been taught to respect my elders. I'd have done the same if I didn't know the man was homosexual. Why not take a load off? I took a notepad out of my purse.

He held up a hand. "No notes, please. I'll talk to you out of respect for Edward, but I don't want a record of this conversation."

Reluctantly, I put it away. I'd have to rely on memory until I could make some notes. "Edward hired me to look into why he lost his job at American Shipbuilding. 'Cept he was murdered the very next day."

Behind me, I heard the scrape of a chair and figured it was Melvin. I ignored him.

Mr. Cosmo clasped his hands. "Admirable dedication to a dead man."

"Sort of. He paid me for a week. Plus, now his sister hired me to investigate his death."

"Genevieve? Edward loved her very much."

"You know her?"

His answering smile was faint. "I know *of* her. Edward mentioned her during our talks. He'd broken from most of his family, but he said his sister kept in touch."

"Gotcha." I swallowed. *It's just like any other witness, Betty. Ask the questions and keep your cool.* "I'm tryin' to get a better picture of Edward. Did he ever meet a man called Raymond Lovelace when he was here?"

"I won't discuss our members's private affairs. I aim to create a space where men feel they can be themselves without judgment. That includes not talking about their relationships."

Okay, that was a strike. "Did Edward talk to you about his job at the shipyard?"

"Occasionally. Not in detail, you understand. Only that what he was working on was for the war effort, and he hoped it would benefit our boys." Mr. Cosmo opened a silver cigarette case and removed one. A Camel, I thought. "Do you smoke, Miss Ahern?"

"Yes, uh, thanks." I didn't like Camels, but holding the stick would occupy my hands. And maybe help me relax. I put it between my lips, and Mr.

Cosmo lit it with an elegant silver lighter.

"You mentioned Edward's dismissal from American Shipbuilding. He was fairly sure it was because of his being gay, but of course, there was no way to prove that. Not without admitting he was, which would have been unthinkable."

"They got rid of him because he was happy?" That made no sense at all.

Mr. Cosmo gave me a real smile this time. "Gay is a term we use to describe ourselves."

It sounded odd, but it struck me as a nicer word than *queer* and definitely better than *faggot*. Who wouldn't want to be happy?

I took a drag and exhaled off to the side. "Why would he believe that? I mean, I'm sure he was careful about not lettin' people know about his private life." It was all I could do not to choke on the taste of the Camel. I laid it in the metal ashtray on the table.

"He was." Mr. Cosmo ashed his gasper. "But sometimes, no matter what we do, word leaks out. Unfortunately, it's often the worst people who learn the truth."

I thought of Albert Riker and William Townes. They'd made it pretty clear how they felt about homosexuals. "Did Edward ever mention a name? You know, who he thought might have blabbed?"

"There was a man he talked about. Albert Riker. As I understand it, he and Edward did not get along. Not even before this Riker fellow learned about Edward. Edward didn't trust him."

I leaned forward. "Why not?"

"It started as little things. Edward would find Riker in parts of the shipyard where he had no business being. He inspected areas where he didn't work. At one point, Edward swore he saw Riker making notes, but when Edward confronted him, Riker denied it and said Edward had been seeing things. Shortly after that was when Riker let Edward know he'd found out about this place. He told Edward to mind his own business or things could get ugly."

"What did Edward say?"

"That Riker should watch his step lest he be accused of treason."

CHAPTER TWENTY-ONE

I'd wondered why Mr. Riker set Melvin on Edward's tail. He could kill two birds with one stone. Edward would be disgraced and shamed, and Mr. Riker would be free to continue whatever it was he was doin'. If he was, in fact, tryin' to sell secrets about the business at American Shipbuilding. "Did Edward ever talk about anyone at his boarding house? What about a man named William Townes?"

"Very little." Mr. Cosmo puffed on his cigarette. "I gather Edward kept to himself, mostly. He certainly wasn't friends with anyone there. I don't remember the name Townes."

Now came the delicate question. "I, uh, understand Edward had a, um, lover." I could feel the heat in my cheeks and figured my face was flaming red. But Mr. Cosmo gave no sign he noticed. "Are you sure you won't talk to me about Raymond Lovelace? It would really help my investigation."

He tapped ash from his Camel. "I'm sorry, Miss Ahern. You seem like a delightful young woman. But I can tell you also have some of the attitudes of general society." He leaned back. "I'm afraid you'll not learn anything from me on that front."

I glanced at Melvin, who shrugged. I stood. "Thank you for your time, Mr. Cosmo."

He held out a hand. The skin was smooth and unmarked. Not the hands of a working man. "I hope this helps you find Edward's killer. I truly do. But please, do not come back here again."

Chapter Twenty-Two

Melvin and I left Cosmo's. The rain had turned into to a drizzle, so we scampered to the drugstore across the street to stand under an awning. I tapped out a Lucky and lit it. Mr. Cosmo's refusal to give me any more information on Raymond Lovelace did not surprise me, not completely, at least. I hoped his concern for another member of his group would mean cooperation. It had, after a fashion, but not as much as I needed. I puffed and stared at the little building across the street, sandwiched between its showy neighbors. It hid in plain sight. Much like the men who went there.

"What now, Toots?" Melvin asked as he shook his head, sending droplets of water everywhere.

I stepped back to avoid the spray. "I told you not to call me that."

He wagged a finger. "You told me not to call you sweetheart. And I didn't. How're we gonna work together if I can't give you a nickname?"

I could add the word to the list of things not to call me, but I decided not to. I wasn't sure Melvin would actually listen, and I guess I preferred *Toots* to *sweetheart*. "You're a pain in the butt, you know that?"

"But you need me."

I didn't want to admit it, but I did. At least until I had more contacts of my own. I vented my frustration with a muttered oath.

He cupped his ear. "Sorry, but I didn't quite catch that."

"Shut your yap and let me think." I blew out smoke. "Mr. Cosmo as much as admitted Mr. Lovelace comes here, and he's been with Edward."

"How do you figure?"

CHAPTER TWENTY-TWO

"His answer. He didn't give me a flat *no*, just said he didn't discuss members. Plural." Speaking the words still struck me as wrong, but the more I did it, the less awkward I felt. *Edward was a joe who just wanted to be loved. Focus on that.*

Melvin rubbed his chin. "Nice catch. But he didn't give up any information, did he." He paused. "He did talk about Riker, though. He definitely had it out for your client."

I glanced at Melvin. "You're sure you don't know anything else about the Hicks family?"

"Nothing you don't already know." He cocked his head. "You want to hit up the son again, see if he'll talk?"

I did, but not with Melvin in tow. One suspect should not be around when I questioned another. Plus, I wanted Frank to myself. It was irrational, I knew that. He wasn't any different from my other targets. On the other hand, he was a lot better looking, and as much as I didn't want to admit it, that was a factor. I didn't expect an invitation to dinner or anything, but I didn't want an audience when we talked.

Melvin waved his hand in front of my puss. "Hello? Are we gonna interview Frank Hicks?"

"I'll do that on my own." I jabbed my smoke at his chest. "Your task is to find more about Raymond Lovelace."

He growled.

"We know Mr. Lovelace is a bank manager, but I don't wanna confront him at work or home. We won't get any answers there. Mr. Cosmo told us not to come back, so where else can we talk that he'll open up? That's your job."

"That could take all day."

"But it won't. You want a story, you gotta do some legwork. I'm not gonna let you tail after me, get in my way, and be rewarded with a fat, juicy scoop." I held my cigarette between my lips and buttoned up my coat. All that was true. Plus, having Melvin off doing homework would give me some freedom to check his background and learn if he was keepin' something from me.

He still wasn't satisfied. "You know where Hicks lives? Or are you planning

147

to hit him at work?"

I lied. "Of course I do." I knew where he worked. His mother had said they paid for his apartment so he could walk to the hospital. How many apartments could there be within walking distance? "Last time we talked, he wasn't very helpful. Maybe getting him in a more relaxed setting, like his home, will get him to open up."

Melvin still seemed doubtful, but he said, "All right. Meet me for lunch?"

"Where?"

"I know a diner not far from Riker's place, near the D'Youville campus. How about we meet at noon?" He gave me the name and address.

I jotted it down. "You'd better have some results."

"I will." He took a few steps and turned. "And Toots?"

"Yeah?"

"You're buyin.'"

* * *

The answer to "how many apartments could there be?" was more than I expected. Or wanted. There were no fewer than two boarding houses and three apartment buildings all within six blocks of Buffalo State Hospital. I figured if he lived farther away, he'd take a bus or trolley to work, and Mrs. Hicks had specifically said he walked.

I came up empty at both boarding houses. After the building supers at the two stops told me to get lost, and not in very nice terms, I quit talking to people and instead scanned the mailbox names.

My dogs were barking when I finally hit the jackpot. An F. Hicks lived in Apartment 4C at a place on Claremont Avenue. Now the big question. Should I go knock on his door? I didn't need my textbook to tell me that was a dumb idea. As handsome as Frank might be, he could be a murderer. And it hadn't been a nice, neat killing either. I had no desire to get my throat slit in some apartment where no one would think to look for me. I remembered the last time I'd unwisely followed Sam into a suspect's home. Not good.

But before I picked a spot where I could watch, I knocked on the door of

CHAPTER TWENTY-TWO

1A. An elderly man answered. "May I help you? We bought our war bonds, and we don't have any metal or paper to collect, although seeing a pretty young face brightens my day."

What a sweetie. Dot was the cutie, not me. I wasn't a dogface, by any stretch of the imagination, but I had a firm grasp on my own attractions. "I'm not selling anything or collecting for the war effort, sir. I'm looking for a friend of mine, Frank Hicks. I believe he lives up on the fourth floor. I've lost his telephone number. I'm supposed to meet him, but I'm running late and just walked from the bus stop. If he already left, I don't want to walk all the way up there. Have you seen him today?"

"Oh yes." A smile broke out on the wizened face. "Not surprised a fella like Frank has such a nice young lady asking after him. He took his trash out this morning. Took mine, too. With my arthritis, my hands hurt something fierce when it rains. On the one hand, I don't hold with conchies like Frank, but on the other, having a young man around sure does come in handy."

"I bet it does." A thought came to me. "Do you know Frank well? I mean, we've only become friends recently. He doesn't talk much about himself. What is he like?"

"He's nice enough. My wife says he's a handsome devil and very helpful, whatever he's chosen to do with the war. She blushes whenever she talks about him, and all he's ever done is change a lightbulb, so I'd say he's got a way with women. He's a Quaker, I think. That's why he's a conscientious objector. I lost my son in the Great War. Young people have a duty to their country, that's what I say." His faded green eyes glistened. "But despite that, Frank is a good young man. Very polite, quiet, always has a friendly word and a helping hand when I see him. I believe he works down the asylum with the crazy folks. At least if he isn't off fighting, he's doing something useful. Not lying around writing novels or some such nonsense."

His tone clearly said what he thought of novelists, and I shoved back my amusement. "Then you like him? Never had an argument with him or seen him fight with anyone?"

"I won't say he doesn't have a temper." The older man nodded as though taking me into his confidence. "I understand Quakers are pacifists, but

Frank, he can get riled up. Why, he came home just a couple of nights ago all red-faced and very upset. I asked if anything was wrong, but he told me it was nothing. Closest I've ever seen that boy come to being rude."

A couple of nights. That might have been when Edward was killed. "Do you know when that was?"

The old gent rubbed his chin. "Tuesday? No, Monday. Heck maybe it was Tuesday. I'm sorry, I can't keep the days straight anymore. Is it important?"

"Not really. I was only curious." Killing a man would definitely make one upset. "Since Frank is here, I'll pop up and let him know I arrived. Thanks for your time."

"My pleasure." He closed the door.

I didn't go up the stairs. Instead, I jogged across the street where I could stand behind a large maple and watch the front door. Then I settled in to wait.

Chapter Twenty-Three

I waited nearly half an hour before Frank Hicks came out of his building. He wasn't wearing his uniform this time. I figured it was his day off. He had on a white shirt, unbuttoned at the collar, dark slacks and shoes, and a jacket. He didn't carry any protection against the rain, which had thankfully stopped for the moment. I could have rushed over to speak with him, but he'd already blown me off at the hospital. I didn't expect better treatment if I ambushed him at home. Besides, I didn't want him to think I couldn't stay away. I decided to tail him for a bit.

He strolled down Claremont and exchanged greetings with the paper seller at the corner. Then he went left onto Forest. Foot traffic was not heavy, but there were enough people that I was able to keep a good distance behind him while not losing sight of my target.

Frank kept this up for several blocks, and I was beginning to think he was wandering aimlessly when he stopped to talk to a heavyset man. More accurately, the other man stopped Frank. The stranger stepped out from between two buildings and planted his considerable bulk in the middle of the sidewalk.

"Frankie. Nice to see you," the man said. He had one of those booming voices that coulda been heard anywhere, even over the air guns we used for riveting fuselages at Bell.

Frank stopped more than a pace away. "Hello, Lester. I asked you not to call me that."

I darted forward and ducked behind the sidewalk display in front of a mom-and-pop grocery store. Neither man would be able to see me, but I could hear better and see exactly what was goin' on. I sized up Lester. His dungarees were faded at the knees and stained black. Oil maybe? He wore an old tweed jacket over a button-down shirt that strained across his gut. His hands were thick with fingers like small sausages. His crooked nose and cauliflower ears told me he was a bruiser. A battered black porkpie hat covered dark hair and sat forward on a broad forehead. I couldn't see the color of his eyes, but they were small in his fleshy face. A gold signet ring was on his left pinkie, and when he smiled, I could see a gap where one of his front teeth should have been.

"Sorry," Lester said, not sounding sorry at all. "I been meaning to come see you."

"You don't need to do that."

"Yeah, but I ain't heard from you in a few days. I wanted to check up. See how things are going."

"It's fine. I told you I'd have it resolved by the end of this week."

"How's that goin' for you?"

Frank paused. "Just a few details to wrap up. The major obstacle is out of the way. As I've told you numerous times before, I'll be in touch when the arrangements are complete."

The enforcer stepped forward. "I'm gettin' impatient, Frankie."

This time, Frank held his ground. He was overmatched physically, but you wouldn't have known it from his expression. His face was as still as pond water. "I'll have it all sorted out by Monday. You need to be patient because something like this takes time. I'm a man of my word."

The goon poked a thick finger in Frank's chest. "You better be." He brushed past and sauntered down the street. He didn't give me a second glance.

Despite my reservations about Frank, I was impressed by his casual attitude. What had he promised to deliver? Lester didn't make it sound like anything good. Was the major obstacle Edward? I inched around the display so I could watch Frank's next move, but kept my face averted, pretending to be interested in the display of vegetables.

Frank stared after the other man for a moment then entered the store, some kind of soda shop. I counted to twenty, real slow, then went in after

CHAPTER TWENTY-THREE

him.

He was sittin' at the counter, and the waitress poured a cup of joe while he studied a menu. "Blue plate special, as usual, Darla. Please."

"Coming right up," said the waitress, a brunette maybe twice my age.

"Frank Hicks, right?" I said as I took the stool next to him. "What a coincidence. Do you live around here?"

Darla came over, and I ordered coffee and a slice of apple pie.

Frank's answering smile was teasing, but the dimple made it adorable. "I have to say, after our last encounter, I didn't expect to see you again so soon. But I am happy that you found me."

"I was in the neighborhood, following up on some leads, and decided to stop for a mid-morning bite." I unbuttoned my coat. "Lousy weather, isn't it? I hate this misty stuff. Either rain or don't. Right?"

His brows went higher over brown eyes so dark a girl could fall in and drown in them. "Do you honestly expect me to believe this was an accident?"

"What do you mean?"

He leaned in. "Before you met me, how many times have you been in this neighborhood?"

I gave him my best stare.

"I thought so. Yet you've visited twice since you learned about me. Therefore, logic says you're looking for me. Not just wandering around and stumbling into this meeting by chance." He beamed, as though he'd answered the question of the month.

"Believe what you want, but don't flatter yourself too much. You may be a looker, but I'm not some khaki-wacky teenager." Who was I kidding? Two girls around my age, who were sitting further down the counter, had looked at Frank the whole time I spoke and shot dark looks at me. My coffee and pie arrived, and I dug in, pretending a nonchalance I didn't feel.

Darla put down his plate and java.

"Then you admit you're attracted to me." He held up a hand. "Or at least you think I'm a good-looking man. I'll have you know the feeling is mutual. Quite honestly, I don't meet too many girls like you."

"We've only talked once before. How do you know what kind of girl I am?"

"I'm good at reading people." The dimple showed in his cheek again. "How is your investigation coming, anyway?"

The pie was pretty good, the apples browned, juicy, and with a hint of cinnamon. The crust could have been a little flakier. "I'm not gonna discuss my case with a suspect."

"Me? I barely knew Edward Kettle."

I paused. "But you did. Know him, I mean."

Frank shifted. "He came into my father's store spewing some absurd notions."

"You went to his boarding house."

He pushed his food, a slice of meatloaf in gravy with mashed potatoes, around on his plate. "Yes."

I waited. "Why?"

"The second time he came to the store, he had questions for me, personally. He said he'd heard some disturbing rumors about my work at the hospital, and he wanted to set the record straight. I told him whatever he'd heard was absolutely false." He took a bite of meatloaf.

He'd not met my eyes when he spoke. "What kind of rumors?"

"The kind that don't bear repeating."

Frank might be good-looking, but I didn't think his pretty face covered an empty head. He had to know it was exactly the kind of answer that would make me keep digging. "What did Edward say to that?"

"He thanked me for seeking him out and trying to set the record straight, but he had a few more things he was looking into. To settle the issue in his own mind." He dabbed some potatoes in a puddle of gravy.

"And you left it at that."

"I did."

Baloney. My witness told me in no uncertain terms Frank and Edward had argued. But I sensed Frank wouldn't change his story if I continued to hammer him. "On the way over, you stopped to talk to a guy, a real thug. What are you fixing for him?"

"None of your concern. And it's impolite to eavesdrop. I wouldn't have

CHAPTER TWENTY-THREE

thought a girl like you would have such bad habits."

"How do you know what kind of girl I am?"

He smiled, breaking out the dimple. "You're intelligent. I can tell that from the way you investigate. And you're attractive, too. You pretend to be tough, but I can tell you have a kind heart. Is that close enough? You interest me, Miss Ahern. Not many people do these days."

We'd talked twice. I was smart and pretty with a good heart? Was he puttin' me on or butterin' me up so I'd stop thinkin' of him as a killer? I took another bite, chewed, and swallowed while I thought of a response. "Your mom told me you went to Saint Bonaventure College. Why would a Quaker go to a Catholic school?"

"There aren't a lot of Quaker universities around. Besides, I admire the community at Bonaventure."

"What did you study?"

"History."

I drank some coffee and stared at his profile. Even when he wasn't smiling, I could see the bare hint of a dimple. He was well-spoken and obviously educated and intelligent. I realized that not once had he expressed surprise at a woman detective. "Why did you do it?"

That made him look up. "I thought I just explained why. Saint Bonaventure is a good school, and I respect the Franciscans."

"No, not that. Why'd you become a conscientious objector? You said you studied history, so you must know why men like Hitler and Mussolini have to be stopped."

"I do. What I do not believe is that war and violence is the right way or even the only way." He was serious. I could see it on his face. His gaze was earnest, and I could tell by his tone of voice he wanted me to understand.

I held my fork in midair. Juice from the apples dripped on my plate. "What other way is there? Did you miss the whole Pearl Harbor attack? If someone bloodies your nose, you don't shake his hand and ask him to sit down over tea and cookies. You hit him back."

Frank shook his head. "Saint Francis of Assisi didn't believe that. He preached against violence whenever he could. You're Catholic. Why do you not understand this?"

"How do you know what religion I follow? I have an Irish last name, so I must be Catholic?"

The dimple came out in full force. "You're wearing a crucifix, a very nice one. Who else besides a Catholic would wear such a thing?"

I fingered the small gold cross that my parents had given me last month for my birthday. Smart, handsome, caring, and observant. Why did he have to be a conchie? And a murder suspect?

Not to mention the fact I was taken.

"To be honest, Miss Ahern, I cannot answer your question. But I do not believe war is the answer. I follow my conscience and instead work for those less fortunate than I who live in mental hospitals under less-than-ideal circumstances. The Buffalo hospital is better than some, but being mentally ill is still dreadful."

"You're tellin' me it's okay if you make dough while other boys die, is that it?"

"I do not get a paycheck from the hospital. As a CO, I am prohibited from drawing a salary. My parents give me a small allowance and pay my rent."

He worked with people like the guy who attacked me for free? I didn't know that.

"I see you're speechless. I suspect that doesn't happen often." He stood and put some money on the counter. "I've enjoyed talking to you, Betty. This should cover your pie."

"You don't have to do that. I got the dough."

"Consider it a gift to a woman I admire." This time he held my gaze, fixing me with his soulful brown eyes. "I'm not a murderer. I wish I could convince you, but I guess that's something you have to learn for yourself. When you do, look me up. Next time, don't pretend it's accidental. Playing dumb doesn't suit you." He leaned on the counter, his face inches from mine. The light in his eyes danced. "Perhaps next time we can make it dinner as well."

I watched him walk away. Frank had gotten the upper hand this time. And what was that guff about bein' a woman he admired?

I'd be talkin' to him again, no doubt about it. When I did, I'd spend less

CHAPTER TWENTY-THREE

time being dazzled by his smile and more on outwitting him.

Chapter Twenty-Four

I arrived at the D'Youville College campus a little before eleven, more than an hour before I was to meet Melvin. I spotted the diner he mentioned immediately, but I didn't go in. I doubted he was there, which meant I had an hour to myself. I wanted to learn more about my supposed partner. I headed for the campus library.

The D'Youville library was not as grand as the main branch of the Erie County one, but it looked decent enough. I wandered around until I found the magazine and newspaper stacks, where a young woman with round glasses sat behind a counter and read a thick book while she took notes. I read the title upside down at the top of the page, *Advanced Nursing*. Her white blouse was crisp and looked like it had been ironed that morning. Every once in a while, she pushed her glasses up on the bridge of her nose.

"Excuse me," I said.

She didn't budge.

I repeated myself three more times, getting a bit louder with every mention.

She finally looked up. "Shh. This is a college library." Her voice was thin, her tone superior.

"I was quiet the first time. Perhaps you oughta listen better."

She eyed my clothes. "You're not a student here."

"No. I'm a private detective, and I'm doin' some research."

"I have very important work to do." She sneered. "I don't have time to waste with a girl who has pretensions of her own importance and who most likely didn't even finish high school. D'Youville is for serious students, not

CHAPTER TWENTY-FOUR

those who are taking advantage of current social and political events to further their own ambitions."

I wasn't quite sure what *pretensions* were, but it sounded awfully close to *pretend*. I took a deep breath and stayed cool. "For your information, I did graduate from high school. After that, I went to work at Bell Aircraft to help the war effort makin' P-39 airplanes. I see you're studying nursing, so good for you for doin' your part. But I don't have *pretensions* of anything."

She opened her mouth to speak.

I didn't let her. "I am, in fact, a private detective. I thought a school such as D'Youville would have the resources to help me out. Seems I was wrong. Have a nice day." I turned and took two steps.

"Wait," she said.

I took a second to smile before settling my face into a serious expression. Then I faced her again. "Yes?"

"I might be able to help you. What are you looking for?"

Sure as anything, this girl wasn't impressed by me. Why would she be? Only a lucky few had the cabbage and time to go to college. I wasn't one of 'em. But whatever she thought of me, I got the feeling she didn't want me thinkin' badly of her school. "I'm looking for copies of a newspaper."

"We have an extensive collection of past issues of the *Courier-Express*."

"Not that kind of paper. This one is barely worthy of the name. It's called *The Daily*."

She thought a moment. "I've never heard of it."

"It's what they call a tabloid."

"I'll have to look. Stay there." She disappeared.

I took the time to take stock of the students. All were women. Then I remembered that D'Youville was an all-girl Catholic school. I'd never thought of goin' to college, even before the war. That was for people who didn't have families to feed or who came from dough. A working-class girl like me would never fit in. Seein' those students in their prim skirts and blouses told me I'd made the right call.

The nursing student manning the stacks returned, her arms full of papers. "We have a few copies. I spoke to the librarian. She thinks the journalism professors keep them as examples of bad writing. Are you sure this is what you want?"

"Positive. Thanks." I took the pile from her. "Another question. I'm interested in information on a reporter for this rag, a joe named Melvin Schlingmann. Do you have anything that could help me?"

"Hmm. He wouldn't be an alumna, obviously."

"Huh?"

Her superior tone returned. "Someone who graduated from D'Youville. Was he perhaps a professor?"

"Oh. I don't know, prob'ly not." Melvin wasn't that old, less than thirty for sure. But he didn't strike me as the college type and definitely not a teacher.

"Then I don't think I can help you. We're an institution of higher learning, not the police department." She nodded at the papers in my arms. "Don't write in those and don't try to smuggle them out of the library."

The police department. "I'll remember that. Do you have a pay phone?"

"In the front lobby. Is there anything else you want?" She pulled her textbook toward her.

I could tell from her tone she'd lost any interest in helping me. "No, this is swell. Thank you." I hustled to the front of the library, found the payphone, and dropped my coin. "Sam, I need a favor."

"What now?" he asked.

"Did you ever find out anything on Melvin Schlingmann, the reporter?"

"No, I can't help you." His voice dropped. "Not over the phone. The guys in the office don't have a great opinion of me at the moment. My new captain watches me like a hawk."

"Why?"

"Captain Finney."

Sam and I, well Sam mostly, had been behind his old captain's ouster. "Why would they blame you for that? You followed the law."

"In their eyes, I broke the blue wall. I'm a snitch. Why are you asking about Schlingmann?"

I told Sam about my agreement and Melvin's run-in with the Coast Guard. "I haven't crossed him off my list yet. I'm hopin' he'll either be useful or

CHAPTER TWENTY-FOUR

make a mistake and I'll nab him."

"Betty, I don't need to tell you what you're doing is dangerous. If Schlingmann killed Kettle, he'll not hesitate to attack you if he feels threatened."

"It's jake, Sam. I'm not goin' anywhere with him that isn't public. I know better than that." I glanced at the clock on the wall. "I'm at the D'Youville College library. I'm s'posed to meet him at noon, but can you come talk to me?"

"No, I'm heading out to do some interviews. But." He lowered his voice some more. "Schlingmann claims he has an alibi for the night Kettle was murdered."

"Yeah, he told me."

"I haven't been able to find anyone who can confirm that."

"I know the secretary at *The Daily*. I'll talk to her again."

"Watch your back," he said.

"I will." I thanked Sam and hung up the telephone. I found an empty table and read the papers I'd borrowed. It didn't take me long to figure out that Melvin wasn't gonna win any prizes for his work at *The Daily*. As with the stories I'd seen in more recent editions, the pieces were long on guesses and short on facts.

I stacked the papers and returned to the desk. "I'm done with these."

"Find what you were looking for?" the same young woman asked in the exact bored tone she'd used earlier.

"No."

"Too bad."

The insincere response put my teeth on edge. "If I wanted to find out more about this Schlingmann, is there somewhere you'd suggest looking?"

"Not unless you think he's written for another paper in town." She put the newspapers aside.

Based on my previous talks with Melvin, I doubted it. "Next question."

"You have more?" She made sure I saw her look at the clock and then at her pile of texts.

"It's what I do. Do you have a phone book? Or a directory of businesses in the city?"

She sighed and left her desk. A minute later, she returned and banged a thick telephone directory on the counter. "Don't you dare ask me for anything else. I'm busy."

I grabbed the book. "Wouldn't dream of it."

Back at my table, I flipped to the section that listed newspapers in the city. There were a couple more little ones. I considered the section of magazine publishers, but was it likely Melvin would be workin' for a tabloid if he'd had a job at a magazine? *Maybe he got canned.* I wrote the names and numbers of a few likely candidates. I wasn't gonna have time to call all of 'em before I had to meet him, but I would make time later, maybe when I swung by to speak to Emma again.

* * *

Melvin was waiting for me when I entered the diner. "You're late," he said.

"I'm five minutes early," I retorted, taking the seat across from him. "Just 'cause I arrived after you doesn't mean I'm late."

"Relax, Toots." He slid over a menu. "I recommend the fried chicken."

Maybe it was silly, but I was determined not to take his advice. "Coffee and a fried baloney sandwich, please," I asked the waitress. "Hold the onions."

He wrinkled his nose. "You eat that slop?"

"I like it." I rested my arms on the tabletop. "What did you learn?"

He pulled a notebook out of his jacket pocket. "First, Lovelace was easier to track down than Riker. I hit up a source in the Society section of the *Courier.*" He thumbed a few pages and read. "Raymond Lovelace, age forty-nine, married, three kids. Wife's name is Nancy, and they've been married for twenty-six years. They live on Vanderbilt. He's a bank manager. I found a couple of references to them from a charity gig last winter, along with a picture. They look like a perfectly nice couple. If he's a faggot, he's a good actor."

I shot him a look. "I told you, don't use that word in front of me."

"It's what they're called."

CHAPTER TWENTY-FOUR

"I don't like it. Do you want me to call off our deal?"

He gave me an irritated glance. "Fine. If he's *homosexual,* you can't tell from the society pages. He and his wife look lovey-dovey in all the snaps. So I called the bank."

My coffee arrived. "How'd you get them to talk to you?"

"Told 'em I was a reporter doing a profile on the leading citizens of Buffalo, neighborhood by neighborhood." Melvin puffed up a little.

I had to admit to myself it was a good story, but I wasn't gonna tell him that. "And?"

"The woman I spoke to, a secretary named Edna Mayes, said Mr. Lovelace was a wonderful man, very attached to his family, active in the community, a good boss, and an all-around great guy."

Not very helpful.

"However." He held up a finger. "She said Lovelace goes out to lunch every day, like clockwork. Leaves at noon, back at one. Never varies his routine."

I tapped my fingers. "That's not suspicious, really. Maybe he meets his wife for lunch."

"Nope." Melvin read from his notes. "Edna said one of the loan officers invited him to eat one day, and Lovelace said he had plans. When the guy asked if he could join them, Lovelace brushed him off. The guy questioned why so exclusive, and Lovelace got snippy. 'What I do on my time is my business. I don't need anyone tagging along. This is a private matter.' That's an exact quote."

My sandwich arrived, and I sat back. When the waitress left, I dumped ketchup on the baloney. "Kind of a harsh response. If he was meetin' a friend, or his wife, why didn't he just say so?"

"That was my thought. What if he was meeting Kettle? Of course, Kettle would have been working at the shipyard. We'd have to find out if he left regularly at midday. And it's not a short hop from the lake shore to the East Side."

Was he meeting Edward? Or was Mr. Lovelace cheating on him? If they met halfway, maybe it could work. "Swell job. What about Albert Riker?" I took a bite of my sandwich and looked at the bones in front of Melvin, which were picked clean. I shoulda ordered the chicken.

"He was harder." Melvin turned a couple of pages in his notebook. "I called the shipyard, pretending to be a loan collections officer. They weren't that helpful. Aside from confirming he was an employee and how long he's been there, they didn't say much."

"It may not be all that important, but how long *has* he worked at American Shipbuilding?"

"Ten years, mostly as a welder. The one interesting bit the woman in the office did say is that he's been working on the current project since the start. He got it because one of the men originally assigned was injured pretty badly. Riker was the replacement."

"Welding is rough work."

"Maybe, but she said it was a shame the first guy was hurt. 'He's worked for us for twenty years and never had an accident.' A joe with a perfect, or near perfect, record gets hurt just in time for Riker to be assigned to a big project with implications for the war?" Melvin's voice sounded skeptical. "Fishy, very fishy."

I took a moment to be impressed with his creativity. Melvin hadn't broken any laws, and he'd managed to get more dirt on both men than I could have. I made mental notes on his techniques. "Not bad."

"That's it?" He gave me a sly look. "What would you say if I told you I almost talked to Riker?"

I nearly dropped my sandwich. "What?"

"I went to his apartment and told the super I was taking a survey of opinions about the war, how well it had been managed, that sort of thing." Melvin's grin was so smug it oughta been fined. "I told him my employer was particularly interested in talking to people who worked for the war effort, either through manufacturing or government jobs. Stuff like that."

I stopped eating. Hot grease dribbled down my fingers, so I set down the sandwich and grabbed a napkin. "What did he say to that?"

"He told me I definitely wanted to talk to Mr. Riker in 2B. The super said he had a very important job high up in defense manufacturing, and he would be home later this afternoon, so I should come back."

CHAPTER TWENTY-FOUR

I wiped my hands on a napkin. "Did you ask him about Mr. Riker?"

"It'd look pretty suspicious if a man who was doing surveys started asking specific questions, wouldn't it?" Melvin held up a hand. "I know what you're gonna say, Toots. We already knew Riker worked at the shipyard. But what's this very important job nonsense? Riker is a welder."

Melvin was right. I knew from my work at Bell that welders were needed in manufacturing planes or ships, but the job wasn't management-level or anything. What made the building super convinced Mr. Riker was high on the ladder?

"Looks like I should go over there and talk to him again," I said.

"I can't. If I say I lied, the guy might tell Riker, and we're blown."

I waved to the waitress. "Who said you were goin' with me?"

Chapter Twenty-Five

I left Melvin coolin' his heels across the street from Mr. Riker's apartment building. "Hey, you said it yourself. You've already been there with a story."

His stormy expression left no doubt as to his feelings on the matter. "You better not hold out on me, Toots."

"Yeah, yeah. Stay here, and don't go anywhere." I jogged over to the building and found the super's apartment.

A man around Pop's age with a chrome dome and a fringe of wispy gray hair around it answered the knock. "Can I help you? If you're looking for an apartment, young lady, I don't think this is the right place for you." He wore dungarees held up by black suspenders over a white T-shirt streaked with oil. It gleamed a little in the light, so it was fresh. Either he hadn't shaved that morning, or his beard grew like weeds, because a noticeable shadow, flecked with gray, covered his blunt chin.

I gave him my name and job. "I don't want an apartment. I'm looking for information on one of your residents."

He raised eyebrows that resembled fuzzy gray caterpillars. "A woman private dick? What will they think of next. Who're you lookin' for?"

"Albert Riker. I've been told he lives in 2B." I paused. "I'm sorry, I didn't ask for your name."

"Bill Toye. I'd shake your hand, but I just finished a boiler repair and I got grease all over me. Wouldn't want to get you dirty, miss."

"I used to work for Bell Aircraft making P-39s. I'm not afraid of a little dirt, but I appreciate your thoughtfulness."

CHAPTER TWENTY-FIVE

His whistled. "You sure got a colorful background, Miss Ahern."

"That's what they tell me." I smiled. "Would you answer a few questions about Mr. Riker?"

"Well, I don't know." The words came slowly. "The police would be one thing, but I'm not sure I should talk to a private dick."

"I'm not lookin' to get him into trouble or anything." Not more than he had gotten himself into, that is, if he had killed a man. "Just a little background. It might help my current client. I won't take more than a few minutes of your time, and you can tell me to scram whenever you want."

"That sounds fair to me. Wouldn't want a man, even a stranger, to get into trouble if I could help him out. What do you need to know?"

Edward Kettle was beyond trouble, but I wasn't gonna say that. I took out my notepad. "How long has Mr. Riker been a tenant?"

"Let me see. I've been the building super for ten years, and he didn't live here before I got the job. Had to have been a couple of years after that, at least. At least five, no more than seven?"

"What kind of tenant is he? Is he quiet? Does he have company? Does he pay his rent on time?"

"Albert's a good 'un." Mr. Toye took a bandanna from his pocket and wiped his hands. "Rent's paid every month like clockwork. He don't have loud guests, and since he's worked as a welder at the shipyard, he does some of his own repairs. Fixin' pipes, light metalwork, stuff like that. He's helped me around the building a couple of times."

I jotted down what he said. "He doesn't have company?"

"Didn't say that. Only that they weren't loud."

"You ever seen them? Men, women?"

"No women, I don't think Albert's into dames." He sputtered. "Not like that. He's no queer. I just don't think he's got the time or temperament for a woman, if you catch my meaning. Likes things the way he likes 'em, Albert does. I don't think he'd be flexible enough for a wife. You know women. Once they get an idea in their heads, a man has a hard time getting 'em to change it. No offense."

I swallowed my retort. Why did men always peg women as the stubborn sex? I'd known plenty of times when Lee, Sean, Tom, or even Pop got fixed on something and wouldn't budge. I'd seen Mom handle her husband with a touch softer than I could imagine. And Pop always came out the other end of the argument thinkin' the solution was his idea. "Did you ever see any of these guests?"

"Lemme think." His forehead wrinkled. "Not usually. Like I said, Albert's quiet. I did see a guy a couple of months ago. I only remember him 'cause he looked out of place."

"How do you mean?"

"He was wearin' a suit. I think. At least he wasn't dressed like a guy who gets his hands dirty, like Albert and me. I only saw him leave. Albert walked him out, but didn't introduce us or nothin'. I asked who he was, and Albert said it was a cousin or some such, in from Cleveland." Mr. Toye's cheeks reddened. "He asked me not to mention it, now that I remember. Somethin' about the cousin bein' on the outs with people in Buffalo. I'd appreciate it if you didn't say nothing."

"Not a peep, I promise." A man in a suit? "Just curious. Was this an old man, younger? What did he look like?"

Mr. Toye's expression took on a suspicious cast. "Why do you care?"

"Never mind, it's nothing." The man was talking. I didn't want to arouse his suspicion. "You said Mr. Riker works at the shipyard. Does he ever talk about the work down there?"

"Nope. I know it's a Navy job, same as the rest of the city, but Albert never says a word. He takes his work seriously he does. 'Course he oughta, seein' how he's a bigwig down there."

"What makes you say that?"

"Always goin' to meetings about it. Least that's what he tells me. He comes home, eats supper, and goes out. I asked him once, kidding him, if he had a dame. Told me he was on important business for the yard." He blushed again. "I wasn't s'posed to say anything about that either. You sure are an easy one to talk to, Miss Ahern. With that sweet face of yours, all innocent like, I bet you get people to spill their guts all the time."

"Again, I won't say anything, Mr. Toye. You've been really helpful." I

CHAPTER TWENTY-FIVE

checked my watch. "You said Mr. Riker gets home around dinner time? Would that be five o'clock? I'd like to talk to him directly about my client, you see."

"He works the seven-to-three shift six days a week. Gets here around four. At least that's when I usually see him." Mr. Toye tilted his head. "You want I should tell him you're looking for him?"

"No need. I'll come back." I held out my hand. "Again, you've been swell, Mr. Toye. Thank you very much."

"Glad to help. I told you, I don't want to get dirt on you."

I reached out and took his mitt in a firm grasp. "That's okay, sir. It's been a while since I've felt oil on my skin. I kinda miss it."

* * *

I met up with Melvin and gave him the low down on my conversation with Mr. Toye.

Melvin's eyes bugged out. "Just like that, he gabbed to you?"

I shrugged like it was nothin'. "He said I had a sweet face. I guess I'm just more likable than you are."

"I'm takin' you on my next interview." He straightened his collar. "What's next?"

"It'll be hours before Mr. Riker gets home. Tell you what. You go on over to the East Side. Put those acting skills to work and see what you can dig up in the neighborhood about Mr. Lovelace. You know, talk to the neighbors, see if there's a local grocery, stuff like that. We'll meet back here at five o'clock."

"I know how to investigate a target, Toots."

"Which is why I'm sendin' you."

"What'll you be up to?"

"A little of this, a little of that."

His gaze turned suspicious. "You're being awfully cagey."

"You're still on my list, pal. I can't have you around all the time." I held up my hands. "I intend to keep my word. You'll get the scoop first. You don't have to dog my every move to get it."

He held up a finger. "I told you. I'm not your killer. But fine. You go your way. If you welch on me, you'll regret it." He stalked toward the bus stop.

I watched as he boarded the next ride. Melvin had some rough edges. I'd told the truth. He was on my list of suspects. But for all that, he was kinda growin' on me.

Like mold.

Chapter Twenty-Six

I headed back to *The Daily* offices. Emma was there, platinum hair frozen in place. She was pecking away at her typewriter, as though she was afraid real typing would ruin her nails. "Hey, Emma. Remember me?"

She looked up at me and frowned. "You paid me to rat on Melvin the other day."

"I didn't do anything of the kind." Why were people so negative? "All you did was tell me he was here."

"So you could follow him home and get him into trouble."

"I followed him, yes. If he's in trouble, he did that himself." I paused. "Is he in hot water?"

"I'm not telling you anything. I don't want Mr. Carmichael to get mad at me, too."

"Melvin's on the outs with his editor?"

She lifted her chin. "I didn't say that."

It was almost amusing. "Well, we were talking about Melvin. And then you said you didn't want your boss to get mad at you as well. That kinda implies that he's mad at Melvin."

She clenched her fists. "Stop tricking me!"

I didn't point out that the trick was simple grammar. "What's Mr. Carmichael mad about?"

"I'm not saying."

"Okay." I examined my own ragged fingernails. "By the way, I'm working with Melvin now, did he tell you that?"

"Are you telling the truth?" Her voice betrayed her doubt.

"Yep. He's my partner for this investigation. In return, he gets a story. Which I s'pose would get his editor off his case. If you talk to me, you'll be helping him." I waited. "You want to do that, right? 'Cause you like Melvin, don't you?" It was a shot in the dark, but worth it.

"Of course I like him. Melvin's a sweetheart."

I schooled my expression. "You don't say?" It wasn't the word I'd have chosen.

"You gotta get to know him, that's all."

Maybe she had a point. After all, my own view of Melvin had softened as I got to know him. "I was thinkin' you wanted a little more than a workplace friendship. I saw you simpering at him when I was here the other day. Smiling, fluffing your hair, squaring your shoulders, so your bosom was front and center."

She flushed.

"Don't worry, I completely understand. Young men are in demand these days. Melvin's got a job, and he's not half-bad looking." He'd be even better if he'd iron his shirts and use better table manners. "I don't blame you for flirting a little."

She crossed her arms. "You better not be horning in on my turf."

I wiggled the fingers of my left hand. "I'm rationed, okay? I've already got my guy. Melvin is just a friend. He scratches my back, I scratch his."

Emma didn't look like she bought my line, but at least she didn't tell me to get out.

"Anyway, what's up with Mr. Carmichael?" I dragged over a chair and sat.

She tapped her fingernails. Finally, she said, "He really wanted that shipyard story. Melvin told him no dice. You've seen what his face looks like, right?"

I nodded.

"No story is worth getting punched over. Melvin told him to relax. He had a lead on a story that was a real humdinger." Her eyes widened. "It's the one he's workin' with you, right?"

"That's it. He's right, it's pretty juicy. A murder. But here's the thing. I

CHAPTER TWENTY-SIX

need to know I can work with Melvin, that he's a standup guy. That's where you can help."

"I don't want to squeal on him or anything."

"You wouldn't be. In fact, you'd be helpin' him get the story that could launch his career. He's gonna write about the case I'm workin' on right now, a murder. It's a big story. Think of how grateful he'd be if you help him get it." I let her imagine how Melvin might repay his debt.

She leaned forward, any trace of suspicion gone. "What do you need?"

"Tell me about Monday night, just this week. Melvin said he came into the office to do some work. Is that true?"

She gave me a thousand-watt smile. "You bet. He was here most of the afternoon. He left around four, maybe four-thirty. He told me he was going out to meet a source for a story over dinner."

"Right. And then he came back here."

The light dimmed. "I…I think so. At least I figured that was his plan."

"You didn't actually see him?"

"No." She frowned. "I left at five." For a moment, she looked like she was gonna turn on the waterworks, but then she brightened again. "But Tuesday morning, his story was done and all ready for printing. Doesn't that prove he was here?"

It didn't, but I wasn't gonna break her heart by tellin' her that. "It helps, sure. Was anybody else here on Monday night?"

She thought. "Our typesetter, maybe. Charlie."

"Is he here now? Can I talk to him?"

"Yeah, hold on." She got up and went to the back. She returned a couple of minutes later with an old man in tow. His fingers were stained with ink and his hair, what was left of it, was white as paper, but the blue eyes were sharp. "This is Charlie."

I introduced myself. "Monday night this week, was Melvin Schlingmann here in the evening, working?"

"Yep. Helped me set up his story for the next edition. Stayed late that night."

"How late?"

"I was here until almost eleven."

Which meant it would've been hard for Melvin to kill Edward, at least when the cops thought he'd died. I didn't think it likely someone at the boarding house wouldn't notice a visitor arriving close to midnight. I stood. "Thank you."

"He didn't stay that long, though. Just me."

I froze. "I'm sorry?"

"Melvin left around nine or so. I told him to skedaddle, he'd done enough."

Just like that, Melvin was back in the picture. "Thanks again." I turned to Emma. "You want to help me again?"

She gave me a blank look. "What more do you need?"

I took out my notepad and pencil. "Do you know the name of Melvin's source?"

* * *

Emma had not known who Melvin was meetin'. She didn't think he'd tell her, but she said she try and weasel it outta him. In the meantime, I went to his home.

Melvin's apartment on Girard was definitely not the swanky part of town. The buildings were packed tight and looked a little worn at the edges. Most of 'em coulda used a fresh coat of paint. Here and there, someone had tried brightening things up with a flowerpot, but even those were chipped. A couple of windows boasted blue stars, but not many. The whole neighborhood had an air of having been abandoned. I wondered how many of these places had belonged to single guys who shipped out.

I knocked on the door of Melvin's building, a house converted into apartments, upper and lower. His name was on a black iron mailbox fastened to the front. There was only a single front door and no other exterior entry point. I guessed it was a common entrance with the individual doors inside.

A second rap brought an older woman in a blue housedress and white apron to the front. She wore dirty carpet slippers, and her brown hair, streaked with gray, was scraped into an untidy bun. "I don't got any money

CHAPTER TWENTY-SIX

for war bonds," she said. "And I don't got free rooms."

"I'm not selling anything and I'm not interested in renting."

She blew a wisp of hair off her forehead. "Then what do you want?"

I gave her my name and occupation. "Does Melvin Shlingmann live here?"

"That louse." She clicked her tongue. "For the time being, he does."

"What do you mean by that?"

"He's behind on his rent. I'm not gonna wait forever."

"He has a job. Has he told you why he can't pay you?" Surely if Melvin had been fired, Emma would have said something.

"If you call working for a ratty little paper a job. 'I gotta pay my sources, but I'm workin' on something, and I'll be flush soon.'" Her mimicry of Melvin's voice was spot-on. "Sources my foot. I told him if he doesn't pay up, he'd better hope those folks have a spare bed 'cause I'm done waiting."

Melvin's clothes weren't flash, but he didn't look like a guy barely scraping by either. Where was his cash goin'? Drink? No, that didn't seem in character.

The woman interrupted my thoughts. "You said you were a detective? What do you want with him?"

"He's a person of interest in a case I'm working on." I checked my notes. "Did anyone ever come and visit him here? Do you know if he had a girlfriend?"

"Him? What self-respecting girl would want to be saddled with a man who doesn't pay his bills? No, he didn't bring visitors to this house. He ate at the cafe across the street a lot. You could ask over there."

I was sure she wouldn't hesitate to give Melvin a lecture even if he had guests. That had to explain a lot of why he didn't bring 'em around. "Did he come home Monday night?"

"Don't know, don't care. I'm not interested in seein' him unless he's got my money."

The woman's abrasive attitude set me back on my heels. I understood being unhappy at being out the dough, but her reaction seemed excessive. On impulse, I checked her left hand. There was a dull gold band on her ring finger. If she was a woman whose man was overseas, barely able to make ends meet, she wouldn't appreciate her boarder stiffing her for months at a time. "You didn't even hear him?"

"I don't think so. I was listening to the radio like I always do. I keep the darn thing on all the time, ever since they delivered that blasted telegram." Her face was stony.

I looked at the window. I hadn't missed it. There wasn't a gold star. "I'm sorry for your loss, ma'am. Was it your son?"

"My husband." Her eyes were dead. "Another six months, and he'd have been too old to be drafted. Now I got nothing. We never had kids. Never thought I'd end up on my own relying on a deadbeat tenant just to keep a roof over my head."

I revised my estimate of this woman's age. She couldn't be more than fifty, although she looked fifteen years older. Grief must have aged her. "I understand why you'd feel that way. Are you sure you didn't hear or see Melvin on Monday night?"

She heaved a sigh and rubbed her cheek. "I didn't see him, that's for sure. I didn't speak to him either. He knows not to show his ugly face unless he's got greenbacks in his hand. However, the stairs in this place creak something awful. I don't think a cat could go up and down them without making a ruckus. I didn't hear anything."

"When did you go to sleep?"

"Not until one in the morning, maybe even two. I have insomnia these days." Her hollow voice matched her eyes.

I wanted to say somethin' but words failed me. "Thank you. Again, I'm so sorry about your husband."

She shut the door.

* * *

I checked for traffic and crossed to the tiny cafe. It was much smaller than a diner, with only half a dozen or so tables and no counter. Each one had a red-and-white checked tablecloth. The walls were covered with old pictures showing various buildings in Buffalo over the years. Some of the photos had

CHAPTER TWENTY-SIX

people in 'em. I recognized Mayor Kelly and a couple of city councilmen. Those I didn't know must be politicians from earlier times. The inside of the place was homey, a joint that made its money serving locals.

A lady who looked a little older than Mom, with her black hair twisted into a bun at the nape of her neck, came over. She wore a plain black dress and white apron. Her thick ankles showed above worn black shoes. She grabbed a laminated menu without looking at me. "Table for one, or are you expecting someone?"

"Thanks, but I'm not here to eat."

She stuffed the menu back in its cubby and said, "We don't have a public restroom."

"I don't need one." I introduced myself. "Do you know a man named Melvin Schlingmann? I've been told he eats here often."

"The name doesn't sound familiar." She frowned. "Oh, do you mean Mel? Skinny guy, might be better looking if he put on a few pounds?"

"Could be." I glanced at her name tag. "Hettie, is it? He's a writer for a tabloid newspaper. He lives across the street."

"Yeah, that's Mel. What about him?"

"I just spoke to his landlady. She, uh, didn't seem too keen on him."

Hettie clucked her tongue. "I'm not surprised. Agnes has had a rough time of it since her husband died. Crying shame, it was. He bought it at Kassarine Pass, early on. Anyway, Mel doesn't make things easy on her, that's for sure. I've told her a dozen times if I've told her once, she should kick him to the curb and get a new tenant. One that'll pay her on time."

"I'm confused. She told me he eats here all the time. He must have the cabbage."

"Oh, he does. We don't feed people for free. He always has plenty of scratch to spread around for those stories of his. Brings people in here for interviews. You'd think he'd pay for his lodging first."

My ears perked up. "He brings people in here?"

"Quite often. He said once it's a better place to get people to talk."

"When was the last time?"

"Oh gosh, I don't remember." She called over to another waitress. "Agnes,

177

when was the last time Mel was in here?"

Agnes paused in her work. "This past Sunday? I think that was it."

"Was he alone, or did he have company?" I asked.

"Alone. No, wait." Agnes set a hand on her ample hips. "He came in alone. Then a man joined him."

Eureka! I grabbed my pencil and notebook. "What did this man look like?"

"Tall, not fat, not thin, light brown or dark blond hair. A working stiff, judging by his clothes."

The description was vague, but it coulda been Edward Kettle. I wished I had a photograph. I should have borrowed one from Genevieve Zellwig. "Was it a friendly meeting?"

Agnes laughed. "Not in my book. The man didn't even stay for dinner. He busted in here, saw Mel, and sat down. They talked a bit, then the man stood. 'I told you to back off. Keep it up, and you'll find yourself in more than hot water,' he said. Pretty close to that. Then he stormed out. Old Mel didn't look too happy."

"Was that typical of what happened when Melvin had company?"

Hettie shook her head. "Naw. It was usually more like the other person ate while Mel took notes. No wonder he's as thin as a rail."

"Did Melvin ever bring a girl in here?" I asked.

"Rarely." She shook her head. "Although there was that one from Saturday. Remember her, Agnes?"

"Oh yes." Agnes laughed. "She was a pretty little thing. Quite honestly, I don't know what she saw in him. Of course, beggars can't be choosers these days. A flat foot like Mel is better than nothing."

I looked at her. "Flat-foot?"

"That's what kept him out of the service. He wanted to be a correspondent for the War Department, but he has flat feet, so they wouldn't take him." Hettie shrugged. "He wasn't happy. Got big ideas, Mel does. The way he was bragging to this girl was shameful. I've seen that newspaper he writes for, and it barely deserves the name."

I looked between the two women. "Did you hear what he was bragging about?"

CHAPTER TWENTY-SIX

"Not in detail. All he kept saying was that he was hot on the trail of a big story, and he only needed one guy to be able to write it. He went on about how this guy was sure to crack and give him the scoop. To be honest, I think he was pulling her leg."

"This girl, did she have blonde hair? You didn't catch her name, did you? It didn't happen to be Emma?

"Oh, no, she was a brunette," Hettie said. "Mel called her Irene at one point, but that's all I caught."

I thanked the women for their time and left. Had the man they described been Edward Kettle? And who in the world was Irene?

Chapter Twenty-Seven

I had a name. But I didn't think it was gonna be very helpful. There were prob'ly dozens of Irenes in the city. It would take forever to track down all of 'em, and I didn't have the time. I did the only thing I could do. I walked to the corner store, found the pay phone, and dropped a nickel to call Emma.

After I soothed her ruffled feathers, she told me Melvin had never brought a girl to the office. "Who are his friends?" I asked. "He must go out for a beer with someone after the paper is put to bed. Doesn't he?"

"I don't think I should talk to you anymore. Sooner or later, you're gonna get him in trouble." Her voice was prim, yet hurt at the same time. "Maybe you should ask his landlady."

"I did. She's got a beef with him, and until it's over, she's not sayin' much that's useful." I stared at the dial on the phone. "He's never said anything?"

"Not to me."

I'd have to squeeze Melvin for some more names to bolster his alibi when I saw him later. "Listen, I'm gonna give you my telephone number. If anyone, and I do mean *anyone*, calls or comes in to talk to him, call me." I rattled off our number.

"It'll cost you fifty cents every time I have to do it."

Her rates were highway robbery, but I didn't have a choice. I agreed and hung up the phone.

Now what? I wasn't gonna meet Melvin until four o'clock. I left the store and lit up. I blew out a cloud of smoke and watched it dissolve in the rain. If only I could get into Melvin's digs. He had to have somethin' there that

CHAPTER TWENTY-SEVEN

would give my investigation a jolt.

Wait, why can't I? I wasn't a cop. I didn't need warrants or anything complicated. I only needed the landlady's permission.

But when I returned to the house, no one answered my knock. What would Sam Spade do? Break in. Could I do that? If I got caught, I'd be in a world of trouble. Maybe. The woman I spoke to earlier didn't seem all that concerned about her tenant. Would Melvin come home while she was out? I doubted it. He was hot on the trail of other leads. Unless, of course, he was the killer, he'd sold me a bill of goods, and was off havin' some fun with Irene. If he came back and found me inside his place, it wouldn't be pretty. But the man was a safe I needed to crack. A quick trip into his place would either incriminate him or clear him. That was my idea.

I stepped back and studied the house. The front door was heavy, and since it led outside, it might even have a chain or deadbolt. I wouldn't get in that way. I circled the property. There was a side door on the left of the house, but when I peeked in the windows, I figured it only led to the downstairs 'cause I didn't see any access to the second floor.

The backside of the building, however, had a fire escape. I jumped up and pulled the stairs down, then took them up to the second floor. They ended at a plain white door. A couple of empty Coke bottles were on the landing. Did Melvin come out here to think or work on his writing?

I knelt and examined the lock. The paint peeled off the wood of the door and the brass was tarnished by the weather. It looked pretty standard, at least from the outside. Did it have a deadbolt? It was a second-floor entrance, after all. And even if it did, Melvin might not bother to engage it.

When I announced my intention to become a detective, the girls at Bell had thrown me a little going away party and had chipped in for a set of lock picks. "I've seen enough movies to know Sam Spade needs to get into places," Florence said with a wink when I unwrapped them. "Make sure you get real good with 'em."

I'd practiced on our back door for weeks, and I thought I was at least as good as a movie detective. The set was small enough to fit in my purse. I slipped it out and looked around. Nobody was in sight, and if anybody walked down the street, they'd never see me. I hesitated. Breaking and entering was illegal. But I'd done everything I could. No one had given me any dope on Melvin's activities outside work. Sam wouldn't be impressed if I got caught, but hadn't he encouraged me to become a gumshoe? Wasn't this part of the job?

Enough. If you're gonna do it, just do it. The idea is to be in and out without anyone knowing. Besides, what if this proves Melvin is innocent? You'll be able to stop worryin' about him and focus on the others. I took a deep breath.

My practice paid off. It took less than two minutes for me to unlock the door, which opened into Melvin's kitchen. It was a lot neater than I figured. 'Course, that might mean he didn't eat at home much. The linoleum was dingy, but clean. The counters were bare, the cupboards almost the same. He only had two plates, two sets of flatware, one coffee mug, and one glass. The percolator in the corner was dusty and made me think he got his coffee at diners. It would definitely be better quality.

I moved to the front room. A wooden-cased wireless and a slightly battered couch covered most of the threadbare carpet. A scratched table with a lamp took up the corner. A pile of mail, most of it bills marked as second notices, covered the top. There weren't any books or magazines, but newspapers were stacked in the corner. Most were the *Courier-Express*. Melvin had written notes on almost every local news story, his cramped handwriting filling the margins. As I read his comments, I was surprised. He didn't write complaints. Every one was ideas on how the story coulda been better, or notes when he thought the writer had done a particularly good job. Maybe he had some talent after all.

The bathroom was stark. A clawfoot tub surrounded by a shower curtain overwhelmed the tiny space. The toilet was jammed into the corner next to the smallest sink I'd ever seen. The medicine cabinet held only shaving supplies, aspirin, and a bottle labeled "liver pills."

I was beginning to think the guy didn't have a life at all. I'd not seen any pictures or personal items besides toiletries. Did he do anything here except sleep? I hadn't even seen a telephone. Then I went into the bedroom.

It was the first room that betrayed any sense of personality. The bed

CHAPTER TWENTY-SEVEN

was made with military precision. The wardrobe in the corner held suit coats and shirts, and it looked like he organized everything by color. An old-fashioned chest of drawers held underwear and socks, again, all folded and rolled as if Melvin expected an inspection at any moment. If he kept his clothes so neat, why did he always look rumpled? It was as though he didn't care what happened to his appearance after he walked out the door in the morning.

There were two picture frames on the top of the chest. One was a sepia-toned photo of a couple dressed in finery. The other was a portrait of the woman. His parents, maybe. He'd tucked a snapshot in the corner of the picture of his mother. The photo showed Melvin with a pretty young girl, her dark hair in finger curls. They were in bathing dress on the sand. I recognized Crystal Beach, a popular amusement park in Canada, in the background. I pulled it out and flipped it over. *Me and Irene, summer 1941* was written on the back.

So this was Irene. I walked over to the window so I could get better light. She was cute, with a pert nose, heart-shaped face, and rounded chin. In the picture, her head came to about his shoulder. If I squinted, I thought I could see freckles on her cheeks. Melvin was still slender, but his frame was more filled out, although he'd never be a heavyweight. He was obviously happy, and it did wonders for him. This was a joe a girl would flirt with.

I replaced the picture and turned around. Besides a narrow bed, the only other piece of furniture was a small secretary's desk. It was dark wood and had two drawers with a set of cubby holes on top. I rifled the drawers. More old mail, a few pens and pencils, a couple of notebooks, and some loose paper. The one notebook was blank, but the other contained scribbles. I sat on the wobbly chair and read. Most of 'em were story ideas. The last two pages seemed to be the most recent. *Navy, ships, secret? Why guards? Find source.*

"Bingo," I whispered. At the bottom of the page, Melvin had written "Edward Kettle" and circled the name heavily. Why? The most logical reason was that Edward was key to whatever story Melvin hoped to write. I wanted to take the notebook with me. But it was too big to fit in my purse. Plus, if

Melvin came home and noticed it missing, he'd know someone had broken in. The whole idea was to go unnoticed. But now I was sure Melvin knew more about Edward than he'd said. I made a note to buy a small camera, but I was outta luck this time.

The cubby holes were full of envelopes. Some were letters from his folks. Three were from the *Courier*. I slipped out the most recent. "Dear Mr. Schlingmann," I read. "Thank you for applying for the position of staff reporter for our News department. Unfortunately, the sample pieces you sent did not meet our standards. Regretfully, we must reject your application at this time. Should you wish to submit stories from a higher-quality publication and reapply in the future, please send to…." An address followed.

"Poor sap," I said. I knew how it felt to have an ambition in life. It looked like I was a lot closer to mine.

The last letter was personal. I almost didn't read it until I noticed the name in the return address. Irene Smithers. This had to be the same girl, the one I was lookin' for. But this was a private letter. How would I feel if some stranger read my letters to Tom? On the other hand, it could contain important information. I opened the envelope and pinched the letter.

I stopped. No, I couldn't. I had some principles. Yes, I had busted in to Melvin's apartment, gone through all his stuff, what little of it there was, and read his rejections from the paper he obviously wanted to work at more than anything, if he'd applied three times. But I had to draw a line. I would *not* read a love letter from his girl. I made a note of Irene's address and put the letter back.

"Melvin! You in there? I can hear you moving around, you louse," a woman said from the hallway.

I froze. The landlady. She'd said the steps creaked. The floors couldn't be much better. Obviously, she'd come home, heard me movin' around, and thought I was Melvin. If I stayed still, hopefully, she'd leave.

The doorknob rattled. "You aren't foolin' me, you know. I heard your footsteps, stomping around up here like an elephant."

I bristled. I had not stomped.

CHAPTER TWENTY-SEVEN

"I'm warning you. I need your rent. If I don't get it, you'll be out on your backside. You hear me?" She tugged on the door again.

Did she have a key? I looked at the bedroom door, which was wide open. If I closed it, would she come in here? She wouldn't risk seeing Melvin in his skivvies, right? She sounded pretty mad, though. Maybe she would. If she found me instead of Melvin, would she call the cops? It was very likely. I closed my eyes and muttered a prayer to the Virgin Mary. What was I thinkin'? The Holy Mother would not help a sneak. But St. Nicholas was the patron saint of repentant thieves, wasn't he? At that moment, I was very sorry I'd broken in.

I heard a scuffling at the lock, and after what seemed like an hour, the landlady's steps faded as she went down the stairs. *Thank you, St. Nicholas. I'll never do it again.* Creeping like a mouse, I went to the back door. It was time to get out of Dodge.

* * *

As soon as I'd snuck out of the apartment, taking care to lock the door behind me, I checked the time. It was three o'clock. I expected Mr. Riker to be home between four and five. I studied the bus schedule. I had time to see Irene and meet Melvin with plenty of breathing room.

Irene's address was in Lackawanna on Melroy Avenue, near Our Lady of Victory hospital. I could see the green-topped roofs of the church easily over the houses. I'd never been inside, but as a good Catholic, I'd heard it was one of the grandest churches in the area.

I walked the two blocks from the bus stop to her house, which turned out to be an apartment building. I couldn't see how she'd be living with her whole family. Maybe she shared the place with a friend or a close relative, like a sister or cousin. The building was brick, with wide concrete stairs leading to a set of wooden doors. The exterior was as neat as a pin. Bethlehem Steel was a good ways away, west toward the lake, but I could smell the smoke and see the billowing gray clouds from Irene's front step. What a wonderful thing to wake up to.

The front doors were not locked, and steel-fronted mailboxes lined the wall in the entryway. A little white strip with "I. Smithers" was on the front of box 1C. I walked down the hallway and knocked. No answer. I waited a moment and tried again. Still nothing. I crossed the hall to apartment 1D. A young woman, maybe five years older than me, answered. She was dressed in a white nurse's uniform, clean as snow. A small watch was pinned to her breast. The stiff white cap nestled in a crop of dark red curls. "Can I help you?"

"I'm looking for Irene. D'you know if she's home?"

She gave me a suspicious once over. "Who are you, and what do you want with her? And don't tell me you're a friend because I've never seen you before."

I gave her my spiel. "I've never met Irene before, but I understand she knows a joe who is an acquaintance of mine."

She said nothing.

"His name is Melvin Schlingmann. He's a reporter, of sorts."

"I know him." Her tone of voice told me she'd rather not. "What does it have to do with Irene? They split ages ago."

"Then you knew they were together." I'd suspected as much, but it was nice to get confirmation.

"Yes. We all knew he was bad for her, but she kept hoping things would work out." She clicked her tongue. "Some men, though. You just can't change them."

"Don't I know it." I thought a moment. "Do you know why things ended? Did Irene get jilted, or was it her choice?"

"She called it quits. He kept promising he'd get a better job with a reputable paper, and it never happened." She checked the watch. "I have to get ready to go to the hospital."

"Sure thing. One more question?"

"Only if you make it quick."

"Do you know when Irene and Melvin saw each other last?"

She shrugged. "No. Months ago, I think. I have to leave. If you wait, Irene may be back soon, unless she went somewhere after work."

CHAPTER TWENTY-SEVEN

I thanked her, and she closed her door. Irene's friend didn't know Irene and Melvin had been together this past weekend. The postmark on the letter I'd found was from last fall. If the couple had split, what had convinced Irene to see him again?

Chapter Twenty-Eight

I took the neighbor's advice and settled myself on the porch steps. While I waited, I lit a cigarette. I thought it likely that Irene had kept her meeting with Melvin a secret from her friend. Considering the reaction his name had gotten, I could understand why. 'Course, that made me wonder how come they'd been together in the first place. I wasn't sure I'd be able to date a guy Dot disapproved of so strongly. That wasn't true. I *wouldn't* be able to do it. Either Irene saw something in the scruffy reporter that her friend hadn't, or she and the girl across the hall weren't as close as I thought.

At about quarter to four, I spotted a white-clad figure approaching from the direction of the hospital. As she got closer, I was sure I recognized the brown hair and face of the girl in the picture at Melvin's place. "Excuse me, Irene Smithers?" I stood and brushed off my backside.

She slowed. "Do I know you?"

"No. But we have a friend in common. Melvin Schlingmann." Yes, it was a stretch to call Melvin my friend. But I needed to get her on my side quickly.

"How do you know Melvin?"

Now that she was closer, I could make out her soft brown eyes and smooth skin. I'd been right about the freckles. She was a little shorter than me and wore a nurse's uniform, much like the girl I'd spoken to, but not as crisp. If she'd just finished a shift at the hospital, that made sense. But even given the bland uniform, white stockings, and work-like shoes, I could see Irene was a looker. In addition to the sweet face and doe-like eyes, she had a slender build, narrow hips and filled out the uniform nicely. Her voice, even though it was tinged with suspicion, was soft and musical. I had a fleeting thought

CHAPTER TWENTY-EIGHT

that I agreed with her nurse friend. What had a girl like this seen in a sad sack like Melvin? Then I remembered the picture at the beach. There'd been happier times in their past. A pang of regret shot through me.

I flicked ash from my cigarette. "I met him through an investigation." I told her who I was.

"What on earth could a person like you have to do with him? He's, well, he has his problems, but he's not in trouble, is he?"

"I hope not." I exhaled. "Melvin knows, or I should say knew, a client of mine. I'm tryin' to find out more about that."

Irene waved her hand in front of her face. "Your client is dead?" She noted my expression and smiled. "Please, Miss Ahern. I'm a nurse. You went from present to past tense. There's only one logical reason for that. The person is deceased." She coughed.

She must not be a smoker. I carefully ground out my Lucky on the wall and replaced it in the pack. "Sorry about that. Anyway, yeah, Edward—that's my client—was murdered earlier this week."

"And you think Melvin did it? I refuse to believe that. He's made some bad decisions, but he's a good person at heart."

"I hope you'll understand why I can't take your word on it." I glanced around. "Is there somewhere we can go that's more comfortable and talk? I hate to keep you standing out on the street. I used to work on my feet for eight or more hours. I know how bad you want to take a load off at the end of the day."

She pointed at the door. "Would you like to come in? We can have a cup of tea or a Coke. I suppose it's irresponsible of me to invite a stranger into my home, but you don't strike me as the dangerous type."

"I'd like that. I promise, I don't bite." I followed her up the steps and into the building. She unlocked her door, and we entered. I immediately took stock of my surroundings. I hadn't been wrong, the place was tiny. She either lived by herself or maybe with one other person. The kitchen and living room were all one space. The furnishings were sparse, but immaculate. Mom would have approved. You coulda eaten off the shiny linoleum floors and not a crumb marred the countertops. A refrigerator hummed against the far wall. I didn't see a coffee pot, but a tea kettle occupied one of the spots on the stove, and a glass jar of teabags was positioned right next to it. Two chairs with lace doilies flanked a low wooden table. Through the half-opened door, I could see a narrow bed. The other door, which was closed, must lead to the bathroom.

Irene crossed to the stove, filled the kettle, and put it on to heat. "Make yourself comfortable. Would you like tea or Coke?"

"Tea is fine, thanks." I sat. The chair's cushion felt soft, as though it had held up a lot of people over the years. Up close, I could see tiny fuzz balls on the fabric.

She took down two mugs and put a tea bag in each of them. "It'll just be a moment while the water boils."

She was gonna talk to me in her uniform. "If you wanna go change, I'll watch the kettle."

"I don't think I should leave a stranger alone in my apartment."

"If I'd wanted to rob you, I woulda broken in before you got home. If I intended to mug you, I coulda done it already." I glanced around. "You say Melvin is a good person. Do you trust him?"

She paused. "Yes, I believe I do. In the important things."

"He trusts me. Go change. I promise everything will be right where you left it when you get back."

She hesitated. "You gave me your name. I can find you," she said in a wary voice.

I held up my hands. "I wouldn't expect otherwise."

She went to the bedroom and closed the door.

I got up and crept over to the small desk in the corner. There weren't any pictures on it. I eased open the drawers and found envelopes, stamps, and plain stationery. The middle drawer held an assortment of pens, paperclips, and rubber bands. It wasn't until I opened the bottom drawer on the right that I found anything interesting. There was the same picture of her and Melvin at Crystal Beach that I'd found at his place. It was at the bottom of a stack of paper. Obviously, she'd put it out of sight, but couldn't bring herself to throw it away.

CHAPTER TWENTY-EIGHT

I heard the door open and scurried back to my seat. Hopefully, she hadn't seen me digging through her things.

"Water not boiling yet?" Irene had changed into a red cotton twinset and demure A-line skirt of navy blue. Her feet were bare.

"Haven't heard a thing," I replied.

She went to the fridge and opened the door. "I'm afraid I don't have much in the way of milk. I live on my own, so I don't get it delivered daily. But I do have a little sugar."

"I'll take it black." I watched as she took out the milk jug and a spoon. "You live by yourself, huh? What's that like?"

She laughed. "Sometimes it's wonderful, and other times it's lonely. It's nice to be able to relax after work and not worry about making a big dinner, but a girl can only listen to the radio by herself for so long before she feels depressed. I'm thinking of getting a cat. At least there'd be something else with a heartbeat around."

"I wouldn't know about that, bein' lonely, I mean. My older brother is in the Pacific, but I still got a sister and two brothers at home, all younger. But the cat's a good idea. There's a stray in my neighborhood who adopted me. 'Course, he might only be hanging around 'cause I feed him."

"Cupboard love." The kettle whistled. She took it off, poured water in both mugs, and brought them over to me. "Where's that, your neighborhood?" She handed me a cup.

"I live in the First Ward."

"Right in the city? It must be nice having your family around." She added sugar to her tea and stirred.

"Most of the time. Other times, I wish I had enough dough to get my own space, like this."

Irene had more education than I did, that was clear from the way she talked. Besides bein' a nurse and all. She was at least five or six years older than me, too. But she was easy to talk to, open and friendly. It was a good attitude to have with sick people.

I blew on my tea. "You work at Our Lady of Victory, isn't that right? I talked to your neighbor across the hall."

191

"Lenore. Yes, we both do. We thought about sharing an apartment, you know to keep the costs down, but I work mornings and she works evenings, sometimes nights. We didn't think our schedules would go well together." She sipped. "Enough chitchat, Miss Ahern. How do you know Melvin?"

The question was straightforward, but it didn't sound like she was accusing me of anything. "I told you, he knew my client." I looked for somewhere to set my tea, but I didn't want to mark the wood, and I didn't see a coaster or anything, so I held it.

"The one who was killed."

"Yes. I've learned Melvin talked to him before his death. Melvin told me he was writin' a story for his...newspaper."

She laughed softly. "You can call it what it is, Miss Ahern. It's a tabloid rag."

"Please, call me Betty." Irene didn't pull her punches despite her china doll looks. "I'm pretty certain Edward told Melvin to buzz off. See, whatever Melvin was writin' about, it had to do with the work down at American Shipbuilding."

"Which is most likely something to do with the war and not public knowledge." She sighed. "Yes, that sounds like Melvin. He wanted to make a name for himself."

"Do you know why?" I had a good idea after talkin' to him and seein' those rejection letters, but I wanted to hear it from her.

"Melvin desperately wants to be a reporter for a big newspaper. It's been his goal for ages and he hasn't been able to catch a break." She paused. "It's why we broke up."

"Oh?" I waited, hoping she'd take me into her confidence. After a moment, my patience paid off.

"You have to understand, he was a different person when I met him. He was funny, charming, and he wanted to change the world with his reporting. But without a college degree, big newspapers wouldn't give him a look. I didn't mind him writing for something like *The Daily*, not really. Yes, I would have preferred if he'd been able to get a post with the *Courier-Express* or a local magazine, but I understood the difficulty. What I didn't like was the

CHAPTER TWENTY-EIGHT

way he was going about it."

Again, I waited and took another drink.

"He thought he needed to make a splash. That if he had one big story, the *Courier* wouldn't be able to say no. I'm ashamed to say he had another motive."

"What was that?"

"Me." Irene held her mug in her hands, eyes thoughtful. "He couldn't believe I'd want to date him unless he was a big-name reporter. I told him over and over that wasn't true, but he wouldn't let it go. Then the draft happened. When they wouldn't take him, he became even more convinced he needed to do something to win me. Boys."

"I hear ya," I replied in a show of feminine unity.

She continued. "Melvin wasn't focused on the *quality* of the story, just the sensationalism. At first, it was just silly things. Rumors about the Buffalo City Council, puffed up pieces about Buffalo's social elite that hinted at impropriety, things like that."

"But..."

She sighed. "After Pearl Harbor and when Buffalo's industry went into high gear to support the war effort, he changed. He spent more time snooping around places like GM, the Ford plant, and Bethlehem Steel. He said he was only doing what every other reporter out there was doing, making sure the public knew what was going on. At least there weren't any secrets there, thank goodness. But I didn't like it. I told him that he wasn't helping matters by making things up when he couldn't get facts. We were at war, for heaven's sake. He tried to get into the Army as a war correspondent. Did you know that?"

"Someone told me he's a 4F 'cause of his feet."

"I think that was the last straw. No, I take that back. Right before I broke things off, he applied at the *Courier* again. Another rejection. Coming so close to the Army decision, well, I think it was too much. He became bitter and negative. I told him I didn't want to be with someone like that and if he couldn't change, we were through."

"Let me guess. He didn't take it well." I took another drink of my now lukewarm tea.

"He didn't." She took two circles of cork out of a drawer in the table, handed one to me, and put her mug down on the other. "It wasn't pretty. We were both shouting about how the other didn't understand. He wound up storming out, and I didn't see him for months." She got up and went to the desk. When she came back, she was holding the photograph. "This was one of our last good times. I can't bear to throw it away."

"You two look pretty happy. I've never been to Crystal Beach, is it nice?"

"Yes. The water is as clear as crystal. That's how it got its name." She sighed, a wistful expression in her eyes. "I love him, Betty. But that doesn't make me ignorant that what he's doing is wrong." She held my gaze. "He's better than what he's doing. He could be a good journalist. Really good. If only he'd stop trying to take shortcuts."

I set down my cup and pulled out my notebook. "You met him recently, didn't you?"

"I did." She looked at her clasped hands. "He called and told me he was on track to write the story that would get him in at a big paper. He wanted to tell me about it. I agreed to meet him at a little café near his house, hoping something was different. But when I got there, nothing had changed."

"How do you mean?"

"He told me about what he was writing, and I said it was just like the others. It wasn't any good. Not only would it be damaging, it was almost definitely illegal and wouldn't impress the editors at the *Courier*. They wouldn't want to hire a guy who reported war secrets. Yes, American Shipbuilding can't hide all the activity, but there wouldn't be guards if we weren't supposed to stay out of it."

I paused in my writing. "What did he say?"

"He told me I didn't know what I was talking about. We only *thought* what was going on would benefit the war. He'd been told to talk to a guy who would, quote, spill the beans about what was really happening on the lakefront. Needless to say, I ended the conversation and said if this was the path he was determined to walk, I didn't want to be any part of it." She brushed tears from her eyelashes.

CHAPTER TWENTY-EIGHT

"When was this?"

She looked up. "Last Saturday. You didn't say what your client did for a living."

"He worked for American Shipbuilding."

The silence was heavy. Finally, Irene said, "You think he was the man Melvin was told to talk to, don't you? *Is* there something going on?"

"I do, and I don't know. To the best of my knowledge, what's happening down at the shipyard is exactly what we all think. Work to support the Navy."

She sipped her tea, then asked, "But why would Melvin kill this man? I mean, even if he refused to talk, is that worth committing murder over?"

"It is if my client threatened to turn Melvin in to the cops, or worse, the feds. Melvin could get convicted of treason or something."

Once again, the quiet stretched between us. "When was this?"

"Edward was killed Monday night. And Melvin doesn't have a good alibi. He said he was at work, but he left in plenty of time to be able to go to Allentown, slit Edward's throat, and get home. No one saw him."

She blinked. "What do you mean slit his throat?"

"That's how he died. Someone nearly cut his windpipe in half, just like butchering a pig."

Irene shook her head. "No, I won't believe it. Melvin is no saint. He might get into a fight and accidentally kill someone. But cold-blooded murder, especially as violent as that? I've seen a lot at the hospital, Betty. Melvin told me once he didn't know how I could stand it, all the mess. He'd faint dead away." A determined light came into her eyes. "Besides, I still love him, and I refuse to believe I could care for a man who'd be that callous."

I absolutely believed she didn't think Melvin was guilty. Unfortunately, an investigation didn't work that way. It wasn't enough to *believe* something was true.

I had to prove it.

Chapter Thirty-Nine

I left my telephone number with Irene and told her to call if she remembered anything or if Melvin got in touch again. Then I wandered to the bus station. It was not yet four-thirty, but I wanted to get back to Mr. Riker's place, so I was sure to see him when he got home. I hoped to beat Melvin there, too. I wanted to ask him about Irene and what she'd said. Too bad I couldn't arrange to test whether he was really that squeamish about blood. Not conveniently, anyway.

I arrived on Fargo and grabbed a spot across the street from Mr. Riker's apartment building. I leaned against the light post and re-lit my cigarette from earlier. Around me, people went about their business. Children pulled wagons of paper and cans, askin' folks for more. A few girls, who I guessed were students at D'Youville, walked down the street, arms full of books and chattering with each other. Housewives came out to sweep their front steps. The lake wasn't far to the west, so seagulls scavenged for food along the sidewalks. Just another late afternoon in a working-class Buffalo neighborhood.

I'd gone through my smoke and was thinkin' about another when I caught sight of a man coming toward me. He was too far away for me to see his face clearly, but he wore the heavy clothes of a working man, and he looked familiar. *What is William Townes doin' down here?* As far as I knew, he didn't know Albert Riker from Cain. And Mr. Townes was not the college type, never mind that D'Youville didn't admit men. I stepped behind a tree so he wouldn't see me.

As he approached, I realized my mistake. It wasn't Mr. Townes. Mr. Riker

CHAPTER THIRTY-NINE

whistled while he walked, the brim of a cap pulled low to protect his eyes from the setting sun. He carried a lunch pail in one hand, the other was stuffed in his pants pocket. He said hello to a woman who was outside her home. Then he paused to give a boy pulling a wagon what looked like a newspaper.

There were enough people around that I thought I'd be safe confronting him. "Mr. Riker. I've been waitin' for you to get home. I'm Betty Ahern. We talked on the phone."

He scowled. "Don't you got better things to do than harass honest working people? Go play your detective games somewhere else. I'm busy." He tried to push past me.

I jumped to the side to block him. "I only need a couple minutes."

"Scram, girlie." This time, he got around me.

I trotted to catch up. "Why'd you tell Melvin Schlingmann to talk to Edward Kettle about the shipyard?"

He turned. "I didn't do no such thing."

I stopped and made sure to stay outta his reach. "That's not what Melvin tells me. His line is that you said Edward would give him a great story if Melvin threatened to tell everyone he was a homosexual."

"If you knew what was good for ya, you'd keep your nose outta my business."

"You also offered to sell Melvin the goods, but he couldn't afford it. What I don't understand is why you'd give up Edward? I mean, if Melvin got the scoop from someone else, wouldn't that make your information worthless?"

He smirked. "You're assuming I told that skinny reporter the truth."

I batted his words around in my head. "You mean you didn't think Edward knew anything?"

"Oh, I'm sure Kettle knew enough to make that little jerk happy. But Kettle wasn't gonna give it up. Or so he said."

"Then why?"

"Can't you put it together? A faggot like Kettle ain't got no place in America. He calls himself a patriot? Bah. A real American don't act like him. A real man has normal relationships."

I wasn't gonna change his mind, so I decided to let the comment slide by. "You knew Edward wouldn't talk. You were counting on Melvin writin' a story that would expose Edward's secret and get him fired. Or worse." My respect for Albert Riker, which hadn't been high to start, dropped lower. I might not agree with or understand Edward's choice of who to love. But if word had gotten out, he'd have been ruined. He woulda been beaten up or worse. I couldn't stomach that. Whatever a man was, he didn't deserve such treatment. Mr. Riker, it seemed, didn't care about anybody but himself.

He shrugged. "Kettle'd get what was comin' to him. That's all. He thought he was so much better'n the rest of us. He shoulda kept his nose out of other people's business. That's all I'm sayin'. You keep outta my way, I'll keep outta yours. Mostly."

It mighta been my imagination, but Mr. Riker was bein' too cagey. There were a ton of easy ways to get Edward canned. Heck, just tellin' management about him woulda been enough. Why all the complications? "Then what were you sellin'?"

"'Scuse me?"

"Melvin said you wanted to give him some information, but he couldn't afford it. You said Edward woulda been a dead end. You were just tryin' to make his private life public knowledge. I want to know what information you had that you thought was valuable enough to give to the highest bidder."

He didn't respond.

"While we're at it, where were you Monday night into Tuesday morning?"

"Why?"

"That's when Edward was killed. You didn't like him. You set him up and didn't agree with his personal life. Some folks might say that's motive. I see you carry a work knife." I pointed at his belt.

"Any man with my kind of job might need a good knife at any time. Maybe you gotta open a box or cut rope or whatever."

"You're pretty beefy. I bet you could cut a guy's throat, too."

Mr. Riker's face darkened, and he took a step toward me.

There were still plenty of people on the street. My instinct told me it didn't matter. I skipped back to stay away from him.

CHAPTER THIRTY-NINE

"You're gettin' awfully close to meddlin', girlie. You think Edward Kettle's death was a tragedy? Better people die all the time." His voice was low, almost a snarl.

I didn't ask who he considered "better people."

"Where I was is none of your business. Go play detective somewhere else 'cause you're barkin' up the wrong tree here. Remember what I said. I don't like folks standin' in my way. Some men wouldn't hit a dame. I'm not one of them." He stalked away.

Despite the warm afternoon sun, I shivered. That had been too close for comfort. I shoulda brought Lee with me. He couldn't match Mr. Riker for size, but Lee knew his way around with a knife.

As I watched him walk away, an idea tickled the back of my brain. But every time I tried to pull it out to examine it, it slipped through my fingers.

Nearby, a bell tolled five o'clock. I might as well call it a day, go grab some dinner, and maybe hash things out with Dot and Lee. I'd leave out what just happened, though. I didn't feel like gettin' a lecture.

It wasn't until I was on the bus and halfway home that another thought struck me. Melvin hadn't shown up. What had happened to him?

* * *

Mary Kate met me at the door when I got home. "I took a message for you." She held out a scrap of paper. "It's from that skinny guy who you don't like."

I took it. "The reporter?"

"Yeah, him." She bounced on her toes, hand out.

I flipped her a dime. "Here. Go get yourself something sweet."

She clasped the coin in her fist. "Hot diggity dog! Wait'll I tell Michael and Jimmy!" She scampered off before I could say anything.

Great. Now my brothers'd be harassing me for somethin' to do. I'd have to come up with an idea so I'd be prepared. I smoothed out the note and read.

Hey, Toots. Sorry I blew you off with Riker this afternoon, but I'm chasing a hot tip. I think it'll be the one that breaks this thing wide open. Meet me for breakfast at Moe's tomorrow. Same time. You're buying.

It was written in Mary Kate's neat script, and Melvin had most likely dictated it word for word. What could be more important than talkin' to Mr. Riker this afternoon? Luckily, I still had a good bit of the dough Edward had paid me at the beginning of the week. But if I had to keep buyin' Melvin's meals, I wondered what kind of profit I'd make on this case, even if Edward's sister chipped in.

After dinner, I wandered down to the Tillotson house. Sure enough, Dot and Lee were in his backyard. "Hey," I said and lit a cigarette. "What are you lovebirds up to?"

"Nothin' much." Dot blushed.

Yeah, right.

Lee ruffled her hair. "What's buzzin', Betty?"

Cat had followed me down the street. He ran over to Dot and pawed at her leg. She picked him up and stroked his back. "You find out who killed Mr. Kettle yet?"

"Seems the more I learn, the less I know." I told them most of what had occurred during the day.

Lee tapped ash from his smoke. "You're telling us you partnered up with that no-good reporter?"

"I didn't have a lot of options." I sat in an old kitchen chair. Cat left Dot and leaped onto my lap. I scratched his chin. "I wouldn't admit it to Melvin, but I need the help."

"If I didn't have to be at Bell, you know I'd give you a hand, right?" Dot asked.

I waved my hand. "Gosh, I'm not criticizin' you. I'm not sure you'd be able to help. Melvin's not much of a reporter, but he does have some contacts." I told them about the message he'd left. "I just wish he wasn't such a...."

Dot nodded. "Hack."

"Right." I blew out a cloud of smoke. I didn't think much of his table manners or his willingness to do anything, including ruin a man, for a story. On the other hand, Irene struck me as a nice girl, and she clearly had a higher opinion of him. Maybe he really was a diamond in the rough. Very, very

CHAPTER THIRTY-NINE

rough.

Lee leaned against the garage. "Run that by me again."

"What part?" I asked.

"Melvin's conversation with Albert Riker."

I wound Cat's tail gently around my fingers. "Mr. Riker offered to sell him a story, but Melvin couldn't afford it. Mr. Riker told him to see Edward and threaten to tell everyone Edward was a homosexual unless he talked."

Dot squeaked.

"Oh, come on." I ashed my gasper. "You can't still be hung up on that, can you?"

"You aren't?" Her gaze was faintly accusatory.

Was I? "Not really." I held up my hand. "I'm not sayin' I'm completely okay with it, and I don't understand it, not by a long shot. But the man is dead, Dot. Murdered. That's not right, no matter what he was or who he loved. Besides, Jesus ate dinner with a lot of folks who were considered outcasts. It didn't bother him. Shouldn't we be the same?"

She didn't respond, but her expression became troubled.

"Anyway." I inhaled and stroked Cat. "That's one of the things tripping me up. What Mr. Riker said."

"It doesn't make sense, that's for sure." Lee pointed his smoke at me. "Why not negotiate with Melvin? Why send him to another source and make your information less valuable?"

"Exactly."

"Also, that's what Riker thinks is a big story? Some guy's private life?" Lee scoffed. "Edward was a line worker, not the CEO or a major political figure. I mean, yeah, it'd be embarrassing for him, but it's not like Riker was gonna out Mayor Kelly. Now *that* would be a scandal."

Dot plopped herself down on the grass and sat cross-legged. "He'd lose his job, wouldn't he? Mr. Kettle?"

"Maybe, but who cares?" I asked. "Besides Edward, of course. Lee's right. Outing Edward isn't worth the hassle."

She pulled up a tuft of grass. "Are you sure that was the point? Sounds to me maybe it wasn't. But I can't think of what it would be."

Which brought me back to what had been buggin' me in the first place.

My cigarette had burned down, and I ground it out. "No, that's why he turned Melvin on to Edward. If Edward was outed as a homosexual, he'd be discredited. No one would believe anything he said. As for exactly what, well, I dunno. Yet." I stared into the distance. Why? Then it hit me. "I got it."

"Got what?" Dot asked.

"Edward was a patsy. Or that's what he was s'posed to be. The leak is Mr. Riker. Edward found out, and Mr. Riker tried to set him up with Melvin. And it worked. Edward was fired."

Lee mashed out his own smoke. "But if Riker eliminated the threat, why kill Edward?"

"I don't know that he did," I said. "Get rid of the risk, that is. If Edward didn't back down, maybe Mr. Riker decided to shut him up permanently. But it makes more sense than shootin' himself in the foot over whatever the big story he wanted to sell was." I stretched out my legs. Cat slid down and jumped onto the yard. He glanced at me and gave an indignant *meow*.

Dot patted her knee to try and get his attention. "Mr. Riker is the killer?"

"I think so. I do wonder why he'd get into leaking Navy secrets in the first place, though." I watched as Cat groomed his paws. "Nobody saw him at Edward's boarding house, but he hasn't given me an alibi."

"And the rest of your suspects?"

"Mr. Townes was at his bar, like he said, but he disappeared for a bit, so he coulda gone home. Mrs. Finch saw him that night, too. Melvin's alibi is shaky. And I don't know squat about this Raymond Lovelace."

"Then what are you gonna do?" Lee asked.

I thought it over. I looked at him and said, "I guess I'm gonna try and get a bank loan."

Chapter Thirty

The next morning, I arrived at Moe's promptly at eight. The joint was hoppin'. Almost every table was full, and there were only one or two open spots at the counter. I stood inside the door and scanned the crowd. No Melvin.

Gert came over. "Can I getcha something, hon'?"

"I'm lookin' for Melvin. Is he here?"

"Haven't seen him."

"He said to meet him for breakfast."

She tipped her head. "Who's buyin'?"

I rolled my eyes. "Who do you think?"

Gert chuckled. "Then he'll be here. Why don't you take a seat at the counter? When he comes in, I'll send him over."

I pulled a sheet from my notebook and scrawled my plan with Raymond Lovelace. "Just in case he doesn't, would you give him this message?" I handed it to her.

"Sure thing." She tucked it in her pocket.

I moseyed through the crowd to one of the empty stools. I wasn't particularly hungry, since I'd eaten at home, but I ordered coffee and buttered toast since sittin' there without food would not be appreciated by the staff.

A man settled in on a stool, leaving an empty space between us. "Good morning."

I turned my head. "Sam, what're you doin' here?"

"Don't look straight at me." He sat and pushed back his fedora. "When I have time, I like to stop for breakfast." He glanced up at the waitress. "The usual."

"Two eggs over easy, bacon, toast, and coffee," she said. "Coming right up." My own java arrived, and I blew on it. "Any leads in the Kettle case?"

"Some." He unfolded a napkin and laid it in his lap.

I took stock of the other people in the diner. Two uniformed cops sat in the far corner, but they weren't close enough to hear us, especially over the din of the other patrons. "Are you gonna make me beg? And why am I not s'posed to look at you?"

He gave me a lopsided grin. "Check the front window. Be casual."

I followed his instructions and shook back my hair so I could peek over my shoulder. A man in a suit stood outside, staring at us. "Friend of yours?"

"Fellow detective. One of them follows me every day, off and on, to make sure I'm toeing the line." Sam's coffee arrived, and he added cream. "He'll watch me for a minute or two. When he leaves, we can talk."

I gave a low whistle and turned my attention to my plate, which had just arrived. "You really aren't popular, are you?"

"Nope." He stared straight ahead. "Doing the right thing isn't always easy."

Sure enough, the snoop left after he was sure Sam's intentions were nothing more sinister than filling his stomach. "He's gone," I said, licking butter from my fingers. "How long do you think you'll be in the dog house over tellin' the truth about a fellow cop?"

"At least until they're sure I won't rat the new guy out. Maybe longer." His shoulders twitched. "You go first. What have you learned?"

I brought him up to speed on my investigation. Another private dick might have played it cagey with Sam, him being a homicide detective and everything, but we'd built up a good relationship. I knew he wouldn't take advantage of me and that he'd share in return. As much as he was allowed to, that is. "When was Edward killed?"

"Based on the forensic evidence, they think it was Monday night. Maybe as late as midnight, but not much after that. The fact that no one noticed anything until the morning affirms that. My reasoning is that everyone was asleep. Any earlier, and the smell of all that blood would have tipped someone off."

CHAPTER THIRTY

"Has anyone admitted to seein' one of our suspects?"

"The only one who was definitely there was William Townes, which you knew. But that's hardly surprising. He lives there."

I'd have to go back to the house and see how easy it would be to get in and out without bein' noticed. "Next question. Have you ever been to Cosmo's?"

"No, but I've heard of it." He laughed. "Don't look like that, Betty. It's my job to know things. Quite honestly, Cosmo runs one of the quietest social clubs in the city. Which makes sense, considering the nature of his clientele."

"Yeah, I guess they don't want everybody knowing their business, do they?"

"Nope." His breakfast arrived. "Given that, I'm surprised he talked to you at all. Do you know anything more about Lovelace?"

"Only what I told you. Melvin is s'posed to be finding out before I pay him a visit. I'm waitin' for him. Actually, we were gonna meet yesterday, but he never showed." I toyed with a crust of bread. "Does Mr. Riker or Mr. Townes have a record? Does anyone?"

"Both Riker and Townes have been in bar brawls, but nothing major. We have nothing on Lovelace or Schlingmann."

He'd left a name out. "Frank Hicks?"

"He's a puzzle." Sam dragged a piece of bread through his eggs. "His parents are very respectable, as is he. Aside from the stories out of Philly. But not a whiff of anything since they opened up the store in Orchard Park. Frank has some interesting friends, though. He's been seen in the company of an enforcer named Lester Jankowski. He works for one of Buffalo's lower-level crime bosses."

I thought of the incident I'd seen the previous day. "Heavy guy, fighter, wears a pinkie ring?"

"That's him."

"I saw Frank talkin' to him yesterday. Frank's workin' on a problem for him."

"Did he say what?"

"No, only that Mr. Jankowski needed to be patient."

Sam broke off a piece of bacon. "Keep your eyes peeled. You see Hicks and Jankowski together, you let me know. Do not approach them, you got it?"

"I'm not stupid, Sam."

"No, but you can be reckless." He grinned. "Looks like the reporter stiffed you again."

"It does. I got his address. I'll stop by and see if his landlady has seen him. Otherwise, I just gotta wait." I finished my coffee.

"Good luck." He paused. "Did you make an appointment with Lovelace?"

"No, my plan was to just drop in." I stood. "I figured he'd have a hard time ignoring me if I was a prospective customer."

He nodded to the pay phone. "But he could pass you off to an underling. Call and make him see you. When you get in his office, hit him with what you know." Another hesitation. "And don't trust Schlingmann. He may say he'll cooperate, but even if he's innocent of Kettle's murder, he'll sell you out in a New York second for a story."

"I wasn't born yesterday, Sam."

He winked. "That's my girl."

Chapter Thirty-One

Makin' an appointment with Raymond Lovelace turned out to be easy. I half-expected him to say he was too busy and I'd need to meet with another loan officer, but I guess maybe the war had left him short-staffed 'cause his secretary barely asked for any details beyond my name and reason for meeting. I said I'd be there by ten, which gave me plenty of time to check on Melvin.

But when I got to his apartment on Girard, he wasn't there. "I haven't seen him since yesterday," the surly landlady said.

"When was that?" I asked.

"Early. I was still eating breakfast. He tried to sneak down the stairs and left. Like those stairs don't squeak, and I couldn't see his face as he passed the front of the house. I heard him stomping around up there early in the afternoon, too. I went up there, and he didn't open the door, but I knew he was in there."

I stayed mum and hoped my expression didn't betray me. She was already sore at Melvin. I didn't wanna think how she'd react if she knew it was me she'd heard in his apartment.

She growled. "I swear, if he doesn't pay me by the end of next week, he'll be out of here, and I'll have a fire sale of his things to pay his bill." She slammed the door.

Where was he? I took the message out of my purse. He'd definitely planned on meeting me to talk to Mr. Riker yesterday. Mary Kate's message from him was clear. Unless both had been a ruse. Had he run into trouble? Or was I wrong, and he'd skipped town before I could pin the murder on him?

THE TRUTH WE HIDE

Either way, I couldn't do anything about it now. Maybe Mr. Lovelace would have some info for me. I headed to the bank.

The branch Mr. Lovelace worked at was on Bailey Avenue. The houses were modest, and the people of Italian descent. It was bordered by a primarily Polish neighborhood, which meant there were a lot of big, fancy Catholic churches around. Most of the patrons in the bank were working class, either men cashing checks from one of Buffalo's factories or Italian grandmas and housewives. I spied a couple of Polish women with *babushka* head coverings as well.

I walked up to a woman sitting at a desk at the front of the bank. "Excuse me. I have an appointment with Mr. Lovelace at ten."

"Betty Ahern? About a loan application?"

I nodded.

"Have a seat over there." She got up and went to the office in the back corner. A minute or two later, she returned. "Mr. Lovelace will see you now."

I followed her. Raymond Lovelace sat behind a large mahogany desk. A lamp with a green-glass shade took up one corner. His chair was covered in leather. The chairs for customers were nice, but not nearly as fancy. He wore a slate gray suit, white shirt, and dark-red tie, with a matching pocket square. His dark wavy hair was touched with white at the temples. His face was lined, but he looked distinguished, not old.

He stood when I entered. "Miss Ahern, please, have a seat." His voice was deep and mellow. It would be good for radio. He looked powerful, but at the same time, he gave off a gentle air. I could see older women bein' attracted to him. Younger women, too.

And middle-aged men.

I took my seat, and the secretary left.

"Now, I understand you wanted to inquire about a loan." He sat down and pulled some forms out of a drawer. "Do you have income and collateral?"

He seemed like a nice man, and very professional, so I squirmed a little as I responded. "To be honest, sir, I'm not here about a loan."

"Then why did you make an appointment?"

CHAPTER THIRTY-ONE

"I wanted to talk to you about a man named Edward Kettle."

His reaction was so small, a casual observer woulda missed it. Just a tiny tightening of the skin around his eyes. "I'm sorry, that name doesn't sound familiar. If you don't have business to discuss, I'm afraid I can't help you."

"But I do, have business, I mean. Just not about money." I removed my notepad and pencil from my purse. "I don't know any other way to put this, but I've been told you and Mr. Kettle were lovers."

His face purpled. "How dare you?"

"Please, I know this is a delicate subject. You're married and have kids. I understand you don't want 'em to know." I paused. "Mr. Kettle is dead. Murdered, in fact. But I'm sure you read about that in the paper."

"I didn't read any such thing." His voice was as cold as a winter gust off the lake. "Please leave."

I sat tight. "Mr. Lovelace, look. I understand. Well, I don't really, and I didn't know Edward real well, but he struck me as a good guy. You do, too." I gripped my pencil. He hadn't called for someone, but I'd seen the guard out in the lobby. I figured I was a minute away from bein' thrown out. "I have no plans to tell anyone about your relationship. But the cops are gonna come visit you, if they haven't already. You want to keep this under wraps? Talk to me now. Help me find Edward's killer. A quick end is the best way to prevent the wrong ears hearing a truth I know you'd rather keep hidden."

Mr. Lovelace coulda been frozen in place. His gaze was one of the most hostile things I'd seen in a long time.

"I gotta assume you cared about Edward, right?"

Again, no motion.

Yet he hadn't tossed me out on the street, either. I looked over my shoulder. His office door was heavy, the glass panel thick and wavy. I lowered my voice. "I get it. I ambushed you. I'm sorry about that. I didn't want to come to your home. I s'pose I coulda nabbed you while you were out of the office, but I figured it'd be too easy for you to give me the brush-off in public. And we might be overheard. Here, I had a perfectly legit reason to see you, your staff wouldn't eavesdrop, and you'd have the excuse of tellin' your secretary I left 'cause you couldn't help me."

His posture relaxed a smidge.

"My lips are zipped. Edward hired me to look into why he was fired from American Shipbuilding. I'm not interested in anything else."

"He wasn't a traitor like they claimed," Mr. Lovelace said, voice soft.

"I didn't think so then, and I'm sure of it now. He's dead, and I owe it to him to clear his name, find his killer, and his sister wants answers. Will you help me?"

He ran his hands over his desk blotter. "Let's pretend I did know Edward Kettle the way you say. What kinds of things would you ask?"

I could play along with this. "How long had you been together?"

"Six months."

"Where did you meet?"

"At a lounge."

"Cosmo's?" I ignored his look of surprise and took it as confirmation. "Did the two of you get along?"

"For the most part, yes. Edward may have worked as a manual laborer, but he was educated, gentle, and had a wonderful sense of humor. If we had been acquainted, as you claim, we wouldn't have seen each other often. At first, that wasn't an issue." He paused.

I looked up. "At first?"

Mr. Lovelace fussed with the papers on the desk. "Edward knew I was married. It would have been important to keep this hypothetical relationship hidden from my wife. But it could be things had changed. As in any situation, one partner could have grown more demanding."

"Could he want you to leave your family or somethin'? We're still pretendin', of course."

His face betrayed his dismay. "Heavens, no. In a situation like this, one partner would never insist that the other meet him or suggest a divorce. I see you wear an engagement ring, Miss Ahern, so you obviously have some experience with situations of a…romantic kind. How one person can start wanting more than the other."

"Except in my case, he's overseas."

Mr. Lovelace inclined his head. "But surely you've seen this happen with

CHAPTER THIRTY-ONE

your friends. One person wants more time from the other. Time it isn't possible to give." He closed his eyes briefly. "To continue this supposition, one person might say it was possible to meet more often, at various places in the city. After all, at first glance, there is nothing unusual about two men having drinks at a bar, is there? They could be business associates."

This story broke my heart. I couldn't imagine having to hide the fact that Tom and I were together, sneaking around Buffalo to see each other. "I guess. But both people would be takin' a risk, wouldn't they?"

"That's quite true. And if one of them didn't want to, well, it would bring tension to the relationship. Maybe the person would become demanding. It might make the second man give an ultimatum to accept things or leave.'"

I read the discomfort on Mr. Lovelace's face. "I can't imagine that would go over well, huh?"

He looked at the desk top. "Not if the one asking was stubborn. He might make a bold statement of his own, such as the only way he'd leave is if he died."

I sat back. Did he realize what he'd just said?

A second later, I knew he had because he looked at me, eyes wide. "I didn't mean murder. No reasonable person would do that. If you'll allow me to continue my supposition, I think it would be better to let it go. After all, relationships do run their courses But I can't imagine anyone killing over it. Not the way the papers said."

"So you did read about it."

He flushed. "This is all speculation, yes?"

"Just two people talkin' about something that might have happened."

He breathed a sigh of relief.

I tilted my head. "Where were you last Monday night?"

"I was in Rochester, on a business trip."

"Do you have any proof of that? Anyone who can back you up?"

He passed his tongue over his lips and dropped his gaze. "Unfortunately, no. I turned in all my receipts when I filed my expense report. There was no one else from Buffalo at the meeting. But my secretary can confirm my itinerary."

"And you can get the receipts back, right? Just ask your secretary for 'em."

Again, his face reddened. "I believe she's sent the report to the main office for payment."

Why did my instincts tell me he was lyin'? "How did you get to Rochester?"

"I took the train."

"Which one?"

He hesitated. "The 20th Century Limited."

I leaned forward. "That train runs from New York to Chicago through Buffalo, but it doesn't stop in Rochester."

He licked his lips. "I…I made a mistake. Yes. That's not the train—"

"Mr. Lovelace, please. You either weren't in Rochester, or you didn't take the Limited. Which is it?"

He deflated like a balloon. "I was in Niagara Falls with a…friend. I had my wife drop me at the train station. Then I walked across the street and took the bus to Niagara Falls." He mopped his face. "To continue our pretense, let's say I did love Edward. He may have asked too much of me. Wanted too much of me. I couldn't be with him any longer."

I almost felt sorry for the guy. "What's your new friend's name?"

"I can't tell you that. He's married as well."

"Then we're in a pickle. 'Cause if you lied and said you went to Rochester, who's to say you aren't lying now? You coulda stayed in Buffalo, killed Edward, hid out for a day, and then come home."

He clenched his hands. "You have to believe me."

"Give me the name of the man you were with. I've been discrete with you. I promise the same for him."

"I can't."

I stood. "Then I can't believe you." I scribbled my number on his notepad. "If you change your mind, this is where you can call and leave a message."

"I shouldn't have done it," Mr. Lovelace said.

His words stopped me at the door. I turned. "Did what?"

"Not what you think." He held up his hands. "I shouldn't have gone to Niagara Falls. The fact is, Edward understood me in a way no one else did."

I raised my eyebrows.

CHAPTER THIRTY-ONE

"Not that." Mr. Lovelace waved a hand. "It was more. We talked books. He loved jazz music and the theater. We discussed politics and the war. It was a meeting of the minds. I don't get very much of that in my life." He sagged. "My wife is very caught up in the social aspect of being a bank manager's wife. She isn't a reader, and trying to get her interested in current events, beyond organizing women's association drives, is almost useless. Edward rounded out my life. I will miss him."

I studied his face, suddenly showin' every one of his years. I didn't doubt his genuine sorrow. But it could also be regret for a poor decision. "I'm sorry for your loss. Please, if you change your mind, call me."

I left his office and closed the door behind me. I didn't think he'd want his secretary to see him all upset. If he was innocent, there was no use in destroyin' his life. If he wasn't, well, I'd find out eventually.

The secretary looked up. "Was Mr. Lovelace able to help you?"

"No. I guess I'm not a good candidate for a loan." I shouldered my purse. I hadn't gotten what I was really after, either.

Chapter Thirty-Two

I left the bank, found the nearest payphone, and called home. "Mom, has that reporter, Melvin, left me any more messages?"

"I haven't talked to him this morning. Are you expecting a call?"

"No. But he was s'posed to meet me this morning, and he didn't show."

"Are you worried?"

I was pretty sure Melvin could take care of himself. At least, I was confident he could talk his way out of just about anything. If it came to blows, he was in trouble. "Yes and no. I'll call Detective MacKinnon."

But Sam hadn't heard from or seen Melvin either. "We went around to his place, but the woman there wasn't terribly helpful."

"He's behind on his rent." I stared across the street.

"Hmm," Sam mumbled to himself. "He's still only a person of interest to us. But I'm going to put out some feelers and see if he's popped up anywhere in the city. If you find him, let me know."

I agreed and hung up the receiver. I didn't know what to make of Melvin's disappearance, so I did the only thing I could do.

I went back to Edward's boarding house on North Pearl to check the outside. There was some shrubbery along the front of the building. A tall maple tree shaded one corner. I circled the property. Edward's window was at the back of the first floor. Someone coulda killed him and snuck out that way.

But no. If that had happened, the killer would have had to walk through the blood. There'd have been footprints. There wasn't any blood or fingerprints on the windowsill, either. The killer had to have left through the front door.

CHAPTER THIRTY-TWO

As I stood there, staring, Mrs. Finch came outside. "Can I help you? Oh, Miss Ahern. Why are you back?"

"Good morning. Mrs. Finch, are you sure you didn't see anyone who didn't belong at the house the night Edward Kettle was murdered?"

She frowned and brushed a strand of hair from her face. "No, can't say as I did. I'm sorry."

"Would it be hard for someone to avoid bein' seen? I mean, if a stranger did come in, would someone absolutely see him?"

"It would be possible to avoid notice, but not likely. At least not earlier in the evening." She pointed. "Those windows belong to the front sitting room. If you go in the door here, you'd have to pass that room. That's where the men go to smoke or read the paper or listen to the radio at night. I would think it would be very hard to slip by without being seen."

Darn it. "What about later? You said some of your boarders work swing shifts or nights. Do you hear 'em come and go?"

"Very rarely." She chuckled. "My room is in the back corner, and I'm a very deep sleeper. Unless I'm having trouble falling asleep, I don't hear a thing. Of course, most of the men are also very courteous if they are coming or going late at night. They keep the noise to a minimum."

"Did you have problems sleepin' that night?"

"I nodded off at ten and didn't wake up until five the next morning." She sounded regretful.

Double darn it. "And you're absolutely sure you didn't see a stranger around."

"Yes. The only person I saw was Mr. Townes. He did walk down the hallway past Mr. Kettle's room, but he lives down there."

I perked up. "When was this?"

"Right before I went to bed, so around nine-thirty or ten?" She hesitated. "I'm so sorry I can't be more helpful." She did sound truly regretful.

"Thanks, ma'am, but you've helped me more than you know." William Townes claimed he'd been at Chauncey's, but the bartender said he lost sight of him. That would have been right around the time he'd been spotted at home. "I don't s'pose Mr. Townes is here right now, is he?"

"No, he's working. Shall I give him a message?"

"I'll come back." I turned to go, but stopped and faced her again. "Could I use your telephone?"

"Of course, dear." She led me inside to a black telephone in the front hall. I picked up the handset and dialed. "Hey, Sam. Can you meet me at Edward's boarding house this afternoon around four?"

"Of course. Why?"

I looked down the hallway toward Edward's room. "I need to shake down a witness."

* * *

From the boarding house, I went back to Forest Avenue, where I'd seen Frank and Lester talking. The street was just as busy as it had been yesterday. Old ladies and young mothers did their shopping while grocers and stores showed off colorful displays. I stopped at a newsstand and bought a copy of the *Courier-Express*. "You work here every day, right?" I asked the balding man who took my money.

"Seven days a week, rain or shine," he replied.

"Have you ever seen a man who looks like a real bruiser?" I described Lester to him. "I think his name is Lester Jankowski."

The man shifted his gaze to the ground. "Never heard of him." He stepped away.

I caught his sleeve. "You know him, don't you? Or you've seen him at least."

The man looked at me. "I don't know anyone named Lester Jankowski. If you know what's good for you, you don't either." He turned to another customer.

What was Frank Hicks doin' hanging around with a mob boss's enforcer? I wandered down the street. Every so often, I stopped at a shop and asked inside about Lester. Every time, I got a hurried denial, and the person left me alone. Lester obviously had a reputation in the neighborhood.

I was about to give up when I spotted the man I was after. He stood in the

CHAPTER THIRTY-TWO

middle of the sidewalk, takin' up space and forcing others to walk around him. It looked like he was talkin' to one of the store owners. Not that the man was sayin' much. Lester was jabbing a meaty finger in the guy's chest, and the poor guy was doin' his best to sink into the pavement.

I sped up. "Lester Jankowski! I've been lookin' for you."

Before I went another five feet, someone pulled me out of foot traffic and into a display of fruit. Frank grabbed my shoulders. "What do you think you're doing?"

My heart gave a hitch. "I'm gonna talk to a witness. What are you doin'? Shouldn't you be at work?" My skin tingled from his grip, but I fought to keep my face calm.

"I'm on the evening shift. What could you possibly have to talk about with that man?" Frank nodded over his shoulder toward Lester. "He doesn't have anything to do with Edward Kettle."

"But you do. I saw you talkin' to Mr. Jankowski yesterday. That's a connection in my book."

Frank paled. "It's none of your concern."

I pulled away and crossed my arms. "I'm makin' it my business. What are you workin' on for him? What's the obstacle that was removed? Was it Edward?"

Frank's handsome features smoothed. There was no trace of the dimple now. But his eyes were as deep and soulful as ever. "I'm telling you. It has nothing to do with Kettle. Trust me."

"Why should I?"

"Betty, you seem like a pretty street-smart young lady. I know you've probably had a much rougher life than I have, growing up in the city." He looked around, then back at me. "I don't want to see you get hurt. I think I've been pretty clear. I like you. I want to get to know you better. For your own safety, stay away from Lester."

"Not unless you tell me what's up."

His gaze was somber, eyes dark. But it was a look of concern, not hostility. "I can't. On my honor, it has nothing to do with your investigation. It's not even really illegal. You have to believe me. You say you're engaged? Let me keep you safe. Please."

God knew I wanted to. Everybody told me what a great person Frank was. Peaceful, helpful. He worked with the insane for no money because he couldn't betray his conscience. He was one of the few men I'd met who didn't think the idea of a female detective was something to laugh at. And he was a heartthrob.

But I couldn't. "Not unless you tell me why you and Edward were fighting."

The regret in those deep brown eyes nearly broke my heart. "I can't, Betty," Frank said. "That's between Lester, Edward, and I. It's my problem to solve. Please leave. I won't let you hurt yourself." He walked away.

I started forward, then stopped. During my talk with Frank, Lester had disappeared. I turned around, but Frank was also gone. Coincidence? Or had he planned it that way?

Chapter Thirty-Three

After Frank walked away, I interviewed some of the other shop owners. None of 'em were particularly talkative about Lester. "He's an enforcer for one of the crime bosses," said one man. "If you're smart, you'll stay away from him." No one could even guess at what he'd want with the Quaker son of a furniture salesman, much less one who worked at a hospital for the insane. Not that anyone expressed any interest.

Stumped, I glanced at a nearby clock. It was almost noon. I found a payphone and called home. "Mom, any messages for me?"

"None," she said. "You sound like you expect to have some."

"I do." I told her about Melvin standing me up at Moe's earlier.

"Perhaps you got lucky, and he's not interested in you any longer."

Maybe, but I doubted it. Melvin had too much ridin' on this story if he wanted a job with the *Courier-Express*. "If he calls, tell him I'm over on Forest, between Claremont and Richmond, and I expect to be here for a bit if he can meet me."

I tried the offices of *The Daily*, but no luck. I wondered about callin' his landlady again, but the way she'd sounded the last time we spoke, I figured Melvin would be avoidin' her. Where else would he be? On a long shot, I phoned the bank where Mr. Lovelace worked. Melvin hadn't been there. I was down to my last two nickels.

A thought crossed my mind. I called *The Daily* again. "Emma, it's me again."

"He's not here," she said in a bored voice. "Same as I told you three minutes ago."

"Yeah, I know. I have another question. Did you see Melvin at all today?"

"Uh, lemme think. Yes, he was here when I got in this morning. I remember, because I thought it was strange. He's not usually in the office so early."

"Did he tell you anything about what he planned today?" There was a long silence. I could almost imagine her playing with her hair, lost in thought. "Emma, did he?"

"Hold your horses," she said. "Yes. He said he'd be out all day tailing a couple of guys and not to expect him back before evening, if he came back at all."

"Did he leave any messages for me?"

"No. I gotta get the other line."

I remembered seeing two telephones on her desk. "You really have two numbers?"

"We only list the one, but if it's busy, the incoming call rolls to the second. Hold on."

I waited and heard her speak.

"Betty? It's Melvin. He called in to ask if I'd heard from you, and I said I had you on the phone."

"Great. Where is he?"

She spoke, voice muffled. "Oh, for pete's sake."

I heard a click, like she'd set down the handset. Then Melvin's voice, very faint. "Toots? Can you hear me?"

"Barely," I said. "What is goin' on?"

"I had Emma hold the receivers together. Look. Meet me at St. Luke's on Richmond. I've got him pinned in a diner up there. We might have thirty minutes, tops."

St. Luke's was about halfway between Buffalo State Hospital and D'Youville, not far from the circle at West Ferry. "Who?"

"I've been tracking down Riker and Townes." He swore. "He just came out. I gotta go. I'm headed north on Richmond. If you go in that direction once you get here, and walk fast, you'll catch up to me sooner or later."

"Melvin? Melvin! Who's 'he'? Who are you after?"

CHAPTER THIRTY-THREE

Emma answered. "I think he hung up. I could hear the dial tone. That was pretty creative, don't you think? I don't know how well you could hear him, though. Did you get what you need?"

I heard some thumps, like she was moving things around on her desk. I looked at the clock. "Sort of." I had a direction, but not much more. Although, if I moved fast, maybe my questions would get answers.

* * *

The trolley dropped me off at around ten minutes after noon on Richmond near St. Luke's, an impressive gray stone church for some Protestant faith. The arched windows were dark and the trees lining the street were just putting out their leaves. It was a quiet, pretty place. I only saw one problem.

I walked up and down the sidewalk, but I didn't see hide nor hair of the skinny reporter. I spotted a neat diner across the street from a payphone and reasoned that's where Melvin had made his last call. He'd said go north, so I headed off. "When I find him, I'll smack him," I muttered. I stopped a heavyset grandmotherly lady. "Excuse me, have you seen a young guy lately? He's shorter than me, thin, brown hair, and might have been holding a notebook."

The woman pointed. "He went that way. He nearly knocked me over, he was walking so fast. Young people have no consideration for their elders."

I wasn't sure if she was includin' me in that statement, but I wasn't gonna stick around to find out. "Thank you." I continued north toward West Ferry Street. As I walked, I mulled over his words. He'd been on the trail of both Mr. Riker and Mr. Townes. But only one had been in the diner, or that's what I was assuming. Which one? He coulda taken five seconds to tell me.

But the further I walked, the less likely it seemed I'd catch the elusive reporter. The houses on Richmond were all Victorians, well kept with neat yards. The people on the sidewalk were a mix of older folks and very young children, too little to be in school, in the care of their mothers. There weren't any hiding places, and it didn't look like the sort of neighborhood any of my suspects had any business bein' in. But I was sure the phone I'd passed was Melvin's last known location. The woman I'd spoken to a minute ago supported that. I kept walkin'.

As I neared the intersection with West Ferry, I saw a group of people clustered on the sidewalk. A man was lyin' on the pavement. "What's goin' on?" I asked a bystander.

"That man there." He nodded toward the figure. "I saw him bump into another man. Then he took a few steps and fell down. I think he's injured."

I got closer and sucked in my breath.

It was Melvin. His eyes were closed, and he was on his side, clutching his stomach. His face was pale. I rushed over, knelt, and shook him. "Melvin, what's wrong?" I glanced at his hand, and that's when I saw a wet, red gleam.

It was blood. Melvin had been stabbed.

I carefully rolled him over to expose his shirt, which was soaked with blood. Nearby, a woman screamed. "Somebody call for an ambulance," I said. "And the cops. Find the nearest payphone. Or bang on a door and ask to use a telephone. Quick!" I looked up at the man I'd talked to. "You. You said you saw him bump into a guy. When? Which way did the other man go?"

"Maybe two minutes ago? Not long." He gulped, face as pale as a fish belly.

"And you didn't think to ask if this guy was okay?"

"Well, he kinda was walking, like I said. Then all of a sudden, he slumped down. I asked him if he was all right. He didn't answer, and I turned to ask again, but then you showed up."

I cursed. Under the circumstances, I figured God would forgive my choice of words. I also said a quick prayer to the Virgin Mary. "What did the other person look like?"

"Uh, tall, I think. And heavyset. I think he had dark hair. Older guy."

A small crowd grew as people stopped to gawk. "No, he had light hair," another man said. "He went off that way." He pointed north toward the circle.

"You ninny," an old woman said. "He went back toward the church. And he wasn't old, he couldn't have been much more than thirty."

Another man piped up. "You're the ninny. If he was that young, he'd have

CHAPTER THIRTY-THREE

been drafted. He was much older. But he wasn't tall. My cousin, he's tall. He's at least six-foot-six, and this guy was much shorter than that. Not even six foot or I'll eat my hat. He turned east up at the corner."

"I think he was tall, but he wasn't heavy," one of the young mothers said, clutching her child. "He was a beanpole if I ever saw one. He nearly bowled little Thomas here right over. He turned left. I saw it clear as day."

I shoved down a scream. Talk about useless. Every one of these people described a different man who'd gone in every direction. *It's not possible. Why can't two of 'em agree?* If Melvin snuffed it, I'd never find out what he'd been up to. Not unless he took notes. I yanked a bandanna outta my pocket, folded it, and pressed it to Melvin's belly. "Where's the ambulance?"

His notebook. Where was it? I patted Melvin's pockets. He was out cold, his face paler than I'd ever seen human skin.

A man knelt beside me. For a moment, I didn't recognize him. But when I did, my jaw dropped.

It was Frank.

He looked at Melvin's wound. "He's bleeding, but the knife may have missed anything vital. I can carry him to the hospital."

It took me a moment to understand him. "The State Hospital? That's more than six blocks away! And it's a mental hospital."

"Do you want to wait here while he bleeds out? We may not be Our Lady of Victory, but we have facilities. Patients do occasionally hurt themselves." He took a moment to push Melvin's hands to his gut. "Melvin, can you hear me? I need to you press right here as firmly as you can." He lifted the patient. "When the police arrive, send them to the hospital," he said.

Melvin didn't make a peep.

I stood. "I'm not waitin' here."

"Fine. One of you others." Frank nodded at the bystanders. "Tell the police we've taken the victim to the State Hospital." He took off at a quick pace, and I was forced to follow. I prayed he was right and we could get Melvin to the hospital in time. It wasn't until we'd covered three blocks that I recovered enough to think of another important question.

What was Frank Hicks doin' at the intersection of Richmond and West

Ferry?

Chapter Thirty-Four

I paced the hallway outside Melvin's room. A doctor and a couple of nurses had gone inside. Shortly after that, a uniformed Buffalo police officer showed up and followed them inside. I wondered if they had the ability to help him here, if he'd wind up gettin' sent to another hospital. Frank stood beside me in the hall. "They'll take good care of him."

"What if he needs surgery?" I asked as I stared at the closed door.

"If so, they'll send him somewhere else. But I'm quite certain they're making sure he's stable before they transport him anywhere." He reached out and touched my shoulder. "Are you okay?"

I jumped like he'd stuck a live electric line on me. "Don't touch me."

"Does it bother you?" He took a step closer. "You didn't answer me."

"I'm fine. Don't I look it?"

"Not exactly."

I stepped away. Frank's gaze followed me. "How come you were right there? Did *you* stab Melvin?"

"Of course, I didn't." It was a simple statement, no hint of frustration. "As for why I was there, I was on my way to work. I do live around here, remember." He stepped closer. "Are you sure you're okay?"

"I'm fine," I said again. Frank walked to work. It made sense. But not quite. My mind was too caught up with Melvin to think clearly. "But you were there. You coulda stabbed him."

"None of those people described anybody who looked like me."

My laughter sounded harsh to my ears. "Are you pulling my leg? Not a single description matched. Heck. Maybe it *was* you, and they hadn't gotten around to sayin' so yet."

He took another step. "What must I do to convince you I'm not a killer?"

"What's up with you and Lester Jankowski?" I edged away. "Did Edward know about it, and you got him out of the way?"

His dark eyed-gaze held me. "I can tell you are a decent person. Stay away from Jankowski, please. I don't want you to get hurt, and he wouldn't hesitate to do so. He has nothing to do with Edward Kettle."

Fortunately, I was spared the need to respond. At that moment, the doctor and the cop came out. "Are you the two who brought him in?" the officer asked.

I pulled away from Frank. "Yes. Is Melvin gonna be okay?"

"He's stable, and we're making arrangements to transport him to Our Lady of Victory," the doctor said.

"Can I talk to him?" I took a step toward the door.

The doc stopped me. "We have him pretty doped up. I doubt he'll say anything. This officer would like to speak to you first." He nodded to the cop and left.

The officer, paunchy with thinning red hair, took out his pad. "What's your name? How do you know the victim?"

I gave him my name and explained how I'd spent my morning attempting to track down Melvin and how he'd been on the tail of one of my suspects. "When I caught up to him, he was lyin' on the sidewalk."

"You didn't speak to him?"

"No, he was completely out of it." I stared at the door.

"And you don't know which of these two men, Riker or Townes, he was following?"

"No." I wished I did. "Did you find his notebook?"

The cop held out a soggy red rectangle. "This was in his jacket pocket."

The notebook was soaked in blood. Even without touching it, I could tell the pages were practically glued together. "I don't s'pose it's readable."

"I can't even get the sheets apart. Mr. Schlingmann is lucky you were on the scene."

Darn it. Melvin mighta made notes about his latest findings, but they were

CHAPTER THIRTY-FOUR

useless now. I turned to Frank. "Luck or something else."

The cop looked at him. "What's your name?"

Frank gave his name, occupation, and address. "As I said, I was on my way to work. I'm an orderly here. It was fortunate I saw Mr. Schlingmann and was able to get him here for care."

I studied Frank's neat slacks and shirt. "You aren't dressed for it. Your job, I mean."

"I was doing business for my father. I planned to change once I was here. I always keep a spare uniform in my locker for just these kinds of situations."

"Like after you stab a guy and you need to change clothes?" I glared at him.

He stayed calm. "For when I'm running late and can't stop at home before I go on duty."

The cop's gaze bounced between us. Finally, he said, "I think I have everything. One of my fellow officers reported to the scene and got witness statements. If I need anything else, I'll be in touch." He left.

Frank and I stared at each other for a long minute. His look was calm and concerned. "I have some time before I go on duty. Why don't you let me take you out for lunch?"

"I gotta check on my friend." I opened the door.

Melvin lay on the bed, as pale as he'd been on the sidewalk. A nurse adjusted a bottle of blood hanging by the bedside. "He's barely conscious. There's no point talking to him."

"That's what you say." I moved to the bedside. "Melvin, hey. I'm here."

The nurse made a note on her clipboard, hung it on the foot of the bed, and left.

Melvin's eyelids fluttered open. "Hey, Toots." His voice was low and a little slurred. Maybe from the drugs. "You found me."

"And thank goodness I did." I took his hand. "You know, you didn't have to get yourself stabbed to prove you weren't the murderer." I left out the fact that doing so hadn't eliminated him, but it had moved him down my list.

"Not my best move, huh?" His eyelids drifted shut.

"Melvin, who was in the diner?" No answer. "You said you were followin' up on Mr. Riker and Mr. Townes. Which of 'em were you after when you got stabbed?"

The nurse bustled in. "You have to leave, miss. We need to get him ready for transport."

"Just a sec." I leaned closer. "Melvin, what did you learn about Mr. Riker and Mr. Townes?"

He'd slipped into unconsciousness.

The nurse pushed me away. "I'm sorry, but you have to go." She flapped her hands and hustled me out of the room.

Outside, Frank was nowhere to be seen. The nurse closed the door on me. Was Frank's presence a coincidence?

Or had Melvin been followin' the wrong guys?

Chapter Thirty-Five

Melvin's stabbing raised the urgency I'd felt. On the phone, he'd mentioned Mr. Townes and Mr. Riker. But Frank had been right there when it happened. If he'd been walking to work, why hadn't he been dressed for it? And why was he so far south of both the hospital and his apartment? His turning up was awfully timely.

I decided to pick off the easiest suspect first, although "easy" was not exactly the word I'd have used. I didn't need the name of Mr. Lovelace's new lover to clear Mr. Lovelace as a murderer. I only had to put him in Niagara Falls on the night Edward died. I couldn't picture the straitlaced banker slitting a throat. Then again, I hadn't seen him as a homosexual, either.

I needed a Niagara Falls telephone book. The city was a hot spot for honeymooners and vacationers, but two men tryin' to pass unnoticed wouldn't stay at fancy digs. They'd opt for one of the smaller, seedier motels in the city. I walked down Elmwood until I found a corner store. "'Scuse me," I said to the cashier. "You wouldn't have a telephone directory for Niagara Falls, would you?"

"You're whistlin' dixie for that, doll." He laughed. "Does it look like I get a lot of customers in here who wanna call Niagara Falls?"

I ignored his mocking tone. "Do you know where I could find one?"

"I dunno. Library?" Another customer walked up to the counter, and he turned from me without another word.

Since I preferred films, I rarely borrowed a book. Nevertheless, the silent, cool interior of the main branch of the Buffalo Public Library impressed me, much as it had when I was lookin' into some family history for one of my prior cases. I went up to the main desk. "Pardon me. Where would I find a Niagara Falls telephone book?"

"Over here." The librarian led me to a shelf with a collection of directories from Buffalo and the surrounding towns. "But you can't check it out."

"That's okay. I just need to look up some numbers." I took the thick volume to a table. I'd been to Niagara Falls a few times, just enough to be sorta familiar with the city. I flipped to the listing of motels. Based on the addresses, I rejected any of 'em close to the Falls, or with a view, as too flash. Any place with a box ad was out. Even narrowing my search, I came up with a list of six places where those lookin' to avoid notice might hole up for a night or even a couple of hours.

After I returned the telephone book, I went to a nearby delicatessen that had a payphone. I changed a dollar for a bunch of nickels. But when I went to the telephone booth, it was occupied by a young woman with red hair who was yakkin' away. I knocked on the glass. "Hey, I gotta make some calls. How long are you gonna be?"

She turned her back on me.

I walked to the other side. I didn't have the time or the patience to find another phone and I didn't want to wait, even a few minutes. "This is really important. Are you gonna hang up soon?"

Again, she turned, and this time, raised her voice. "So I said to Alice, 'Alice, you need to listen to me.'"

If this girl thought I was gonna take a powder, she was wrong. I dug some bills out of my purse and waved them in front of her face. "I'll give you two bucks to hang up, right now, and let me use the phone."

"I'll call you back." She dropped the receiver in the cradle, left the booth, and snatched the cash outta my hand. "It's all yours." She headed for the door.

I dropped a coin and called my first mark. "Hello. My name is Mrs. Imogene Branch. I just found out that my no-good louse of a husband is cheating on me. But I need proof. Did a man rent a room last Monday night? He would have been alone."

"What did he look like?"

CHAPTER THIRTY-FIVE

The question made me realize a huge problem with my plan. What if Mr. Lovelace hadn't rented the room? I'd have to roll the dice. I gave the woman Mr. Lovelace's description. "But in case his new hussy got the room, did you get any single check-ins Monday night?"

"Hold on." The sound of snapping gum came over the line. "I was working Monday, and the description doesn't sound familiar. I just checked our registers, and there were no single rentals on Monday. Sorry. I wish I could help you find the cheater."

I thanked her and hung up. I called the next four motels, repeating my story of a wife who'd flipped her wig over her faithless husband. The men who I talked to sounded bored, but the women were all supportive. I hung up, proud of my acting skills. I'd have to tell Melvin. I hoped he was doin' better after the move to Our Lady of Victory.

I hit pay dirt on the last number on my list. "Oh, him. Yes, I remember." The woman's voice held a clear note of disapproval. "Meeting a woman, was he? He swore he was a traveling salesman who needed a room for the night, but I knew he was up to no good. Did he hire a hooker for a party or something?"

"What do you mean?"

"I saw another man go to the same room a little while later." Her voice turned prim. "We get all kinds, I tell you. But this takes the cake."

I could picture her, sounding prissy but eager for dirt. "No, I'm pretty sure it was just him and the woman. Isn't that enough?" Before she could continue, I thanked her and hung up.

Mr. Lovelace had been off with a new lover. I could take him out of the frame. I was relieved. Uncovering a murderer didn't bother me. But having to tell a woman that her husband of whoever-knew how many years wasn't who she thought he was? No, sir. *That* was somethin' I'd rather not do.

I dropped my last coin and called Sam. "Hey," I said when he got on the line. "Can you take a late lunch? We need to meet earlier than I said."

He paused. "Lafayette Park. Fifteen minutes." He hung up.

Chapter Thirty-Six

My question to Sam about lunch was not just an excuse. My stomach rumbled, and my feet were killing me. I hadn't eaten since breakfast. Before I left the deli, I went to the counter and ordered a corned beef on rye to take with me. I stared out of the front window while my sandwich was being made. People passed by, and most of 'em didn't even look around. But then I thought I spotted a familiar face.

It was Frank Hicks.

I ran to the front door, but by the time I got outside, he was gone. I went back.

"I thought you'd left without your grub," the man behind the counter said.

"Nah, thought I saw a friend." I took my food. I tried to sound casual. "Say, you ever seen a guy in here, little taller than me, dark hair and eyes, looks like he belongs in the pictures? His first name is Frank."

The man paused, then shrugged meaty shoulders. "Don't sound familiar. Should it?"

"Not particularly." I thanked him, grabbed a Coke from the cooler and a bag of chips. I paid for my lunch and went outside. I unwrapped the waxed paper and took a huge bite. What was Frank Hicks followin' me for? He had no business bein' downtown, at least that I knew of. If that had been Frank, that is. I'd only seen a flash of a face. I was so caught up in my case, it could be my imagination was playin' games with me. Besides, Frank said he was goin' to work. Which meant he'd lied if he was followin' me.

That shouldn't have surprised me. As Sam would say, everybody lies.

Sam told me to meet him in Lafayette Square, so I strolled down to the park

CHAPTER THIRTY-SIX

and plopped down on the grass. I felt like a rat trapped in a maze. Melvin was outta the runnin' for Edward's murder on account of bein' stabbed. Okay, that didn't necessarily take him out of the picture. But it was too much to think his attack had been unrelated to his questions about Edward. Too bad he'd been doped up and unable to tell me anything. I'd called while I waited for my lunch, but there was no change in his condition.

Someone sat down next to me.

I looked over to see Sam MacKinnon. "Why are we having a picnic?"

"I like to eat in the park when the weather is nice, and it's not uncommon for me to take a late lunch when I'm working an investigation. If we talk here, we're less likely to be overheard." He held a brown paper bag. He took out a rectangle of waxed paper and unwrapped it. "You know, I ought to swear off roast beef sandwiches until after the war. The quality of beef just hasn't been the same." He took a bite. A little dark yellow mustard leaked out of the side.

I complied and opened my chips. "Still bein' followed?"

"Not right now, but you never know."

"I know what you mean." I crunched a chip. I turned slightly, so I could watch him out of the corner of my eye.

He lowered his sandwich. "How so?"

I told him about seein' Frank, or someone I thought was Frank. "But I dunno. The more I think about it, the more I doubt it was him."

"He had no reason to be where your friend Melvin was, either." Sam gave me a look.

"Well, that was near Buffalo State Hospital." I shook my bag. "Any news on that?"

"It's not a homicide, so it's not my department. Schlingmann is still a person of interest for me, though, so I did follow up." He took a bite and chewed. "Witnesses on the scene gave a variety of descriptions and reported the suspect going in several different directions after the incident."

"I know." I stared into the chip bag. "That doesn't help much."

"No, but it's also not uncommon. In the heat of the moment, witnesses are often unreliable. They're following up so if there's anything to learn, we'll find it."

I ran my memory of earlier that day through my brain. The hospital was north of Ferry Circle and the church where Melvin had been set upon. Several blocks north. Frank's apartment was practically across the street from it. "Do you think Frank Hicks was tailin' Melvin?"

"It's possible. It could be that Melvin was on to something Hicks didn't want him to know, or...."

"He hoped Melvin would lead him to me." I crunched another chip. "Frank is a Quaker. He's s'posed to be non-violent."

"And yet he's a suspect in a murder. Hicks *says* he's a Quaker. His mother says it. He goes to their meetings. But it doesn't mean a thing."

No, it didn't. "But he's so handsome." I hated the whiny tone in my voice, but it just didn't seem fair a good-lookin' guy could be such a low-life.

Sam laughed. "There's no requirement that murderers be ugly." He licked mustard off his fingers. "Besides, aren't you engaged? That doesn't mean you can't notice another man, but you strike me as a little more attracted than you should be."

He was right. "Have you been able to find out what he's doin' with Lester Jankowski?"

"Not the details, but enough that I know Jankowski's got him involved with something to do with the State Hospital."

"Which doesn't have a thing to do with Edward."

"Not directly. But knowing what you do of your client, what do you think he'd do if he found out about an illegal arrangement?"

I didn't have to think long. "He'd say somethin'. Edward had flaws, but from everything I know, he was honest." Which meant he hadn't gone to the furniture store about some long-past accusation against the elder Mr. Hicks. He mighta been using that as a cover to learn more about Frank. "I guess that makes sense, except no one saw him the night Edward was murdered. In fact, the only person I can prove was there is William Townes. Big deal. He lives there."

"True. But he had no love for Kettle. He admits he'd been drinking earlier. Could one of his friends have riled him up and sent him home on a mission?"

CHAPTER THIRTY-SIX

I was running out of chips. "To get rid of someone he considered a moral degenerate?" It was possible, even though everything I'd learned about Edward made me believe he'd been a pretty good guy.

The thought caught me off guard. When had I changed my thinkin'? I wasn't sure, but I knew Edward Kettle was a guy I'd be glad to have a beer with. He was a patriot, an honorable friend, a good tenant, and a loving brother. And maybe those things were more important than who he loved behind his closed bedroom door.

I dragged myself back to the problem of Mr. Townes. "The bartender at Chauncey's admitted he'd lost sight of Mr. Townes for a while. But that doesn't make sense, either. He came back to the bar. He wasn't covered in blood. How likely was it that the killer avoided gettin' sprayed? In your professional opinion?"

"It would be hard, but not impossible. Besides, Townes was at home. He could have changed before heading back to Chauncey's. And yes, I know, the bartender claims he was wearing the same clothes. You learned earlier today how reliable eyewitness testimony is." Sam finished off his sandwich. "I'm still trying to track down all the men he was drinking with."

"Oh hey, it nearly slipped my mind. Get a load of what I learned about Mr. Riker." I filled Sam in on my suspicion that Mr. Riker was the real leak at American Shipbuilding. "I wish I knew what they were up to. It has to be somethin' about that ship in particular. The Coast Guard seaman at the gate goofed when he told me there'd been more metal shipments received than the last time, although that could be 'cause of a different ship size."

Sam wiped his hands on the grass. "Good luck ferreting that out. And staying out of jail while you're at it." He stood. "Here's something I have for you. Riker is in a money hole and by quite a bit."

"No way. His landlord says he's always on time with his rent."

"That may be, but he's late with everything else. Our sources say he took out a loan from one of Buffalo's biggest sharks last year. The note was due last January."

I crumpled my empty chip bag and leaned back on my hands. "Really? Has he paid any of it?"

"Not a red cent. Word on the street is Riker has put the shark off a couple of times already. Could be why Riker needed a big payoff from selling military information."

I'd been wonderin' why Mr. Riker was so keen to run his mouth. "That means I have one guy with a motive who wasn't there. Another who hated the victim and was there, but was s'posed to be, and a third who might have a beef with the victim and who keeps turnin' up where he shouldn't be."

Sam tugged his fedora into place. "That's about the size of it."

I squinted at him. "You're not bein' very helpful, Sam. I have all this information, but I can't tell what parts of it are useful."

He stood and held out a hand to help me up. "Welcome to detective work. Now. Isn't there someone you want me to talk to?"

Chapter Thirty-Seven

We left the park separately, to confuse anyone who might be watchin' Sam. He met me at Edward's boarding house on North Pearl. "Exactly who am I supposed to intimidate?" he asked.

"William Townes. I want to know where he was on the night Edward was killed. Besides Chauncey's, 'cause I'm pretty sure he left. You'll be helpin' yourself, too. If he comes clean, it won't matter if you can't find all of his drinking buddies." I started to walk up to the door, but then I stopped. Mr. Riker was walkin' down the street.

No, not Mr. Riker. It was Mr. Townes. *That's important*, I thought. But I couldn't immediately put my finger on why and in a matter of moments, Mr. Townes arrived.

He looked from Sam, who showed his badge, to me and back again. "What is this, a welcome committee? I know it ain't a bust. There'd be a uniform here, and you wouldn't bring a girl."

Sam's face didn't move. "We want to talk."

"About what?" Mr. Townes jutted out his chin.

I matched his stance. "Where were you Monday night between nine and ten o'clock?"

"I told you, at Chauncey's, having a beer."

"The bartender said he lost track of you."

"He's a busy guy and his job is to sell booze, not keep tabs on the drinkers." He pushed me aside.

In a flash, Sam had him by the collar. "You're not being helpful."

"I answered her question," Mr. Townes said in a croaky voice.

"Not in a useful way." Sam glanced at me. "Let's try this again. We know you were in the bar. You left at some point around nine and were back by ten. Where did you go?"

I nudged Sam. "He's turnin' a little purple."

Sam eased his grip, but only a smidge.

"All right, all right!" Mr. Townes gasped to get the words out.

Sam let go.

Mr. Townes cleared his throat and rubbed it. He tugged his shirt down. "I left the bar when you said. I met with a woman."

"What's her name?" I asked.

"Belinda."

"Last name?"

He grinned. "Don't know. We weren't together long enough for us to become that familiar, if you know what I mean."

It took a moment, but I got the message. Belinda was a prostitute.

Sam broke in. "Where'd you go?"

"Behind the bar, there's an alley. I ain't got the dough for a lot of romance. I'm more of a get it done kinda guy." He leered. It didn't help his looks.

Ugh. "I thought you went home with the waitress?"

"That was later."

What a charmer.

"Is Belinda there often?" Sam asked.

"Why? You got an itch, Detective?" Mr. Townes took one look at Sam's face and stepped back. "Yeah, she works the bar regular. In fact, go there tonight and you'll find her."

"We'll do that," I said. "You'd better hope her story matches yours."

"It will. Is that all?" Mr. Townes looked at us. When we didn't move, he walked away.

I watched him go. "What a jerk."

"Yes, but it's the kind of story that would be true." Sam dusted off his hands. "I presume you're heading home. You leave Townes's alibi to me. I'll let you know if it doesn't check out."

CHAPTER THIRTY-SEVEN

"Thanks." I gave him a nudge. "You're pretty good at the muscle act. Too bad you're a cop. Say, have you noticed that Mr. Townes and Mr. Riker kinda look alike?"

"Not particularly. Why?"

"Never mind." I couldn't be the only person who noticed. For the life of me, I didn't know why it mattered. But it did.

* * *

Instead of spinning my wheels, I went home.

Mom called out as soon as she heard the front door. "Betty, is that you?"

"Yes. Do you need somethin'?"

"No, but you have V-mail. It's on the table."

I walked over to the little desk where we left the mail that came for others in the house. I checked the calendar. It was too early for Tom to reply to the letter I'd sent him in March. Yet there it was, plain as day. A red-and-blue striped envelope with my name on it. It was postmarked early April. I slit open the envelope and read the short note inside.

Dear Betty,

I won't be able to write for a while. I can't say where I'm going or what I'll be doing, but I expect I'll be pretty busy. This note is just to tell you I love you, I miss you, and I can't wait until I get back so we can start our home life together.

Love,

Tom

I stared at it. Elation at having a letter from Tom and knowing he'd been okay a month ago warred with a sense of dread. I folded it and slipped it in my pants pocket.

Mom came out of the kitchen. "I assume it's from Tom. What does he say?"

"Not a lot. He won't be able to write for a while. He didn't spell it out, but I think he's got orders to go somewhere. He wanted to tell me he loved me."

"That's sweet." She studied my face. "What's wrong? I would have expected you to be happier."

"Oh, nothin'. Just the case." I forced a smile. "Do you need help with dinner?"

"Not right now. Did you have plans to see Dot or Lee?"

"It'll be a bit before they get home. I guess I'll play with Cat. If you need me, holler."

While I waited for my friends to come, I sat on my front step and lit a Lucky. I took Tom's letter out and read it again. "I don't know, Cat," I said when he sauntered into view. "I'm glad to hear from Tom, don't get me wrong. But what does he mean by *home life*?"

Cat blinked.

"I didn't think you'd be able to tell me. Anyway, I got a case to solve, right?" I told him everything I knew. "What do you think, huh? Which one of these yo-yos is my killer?"

Cat blinked at me again and *meowed*.

"You're as much help as Sam."

Lee and Dot walked up, arm in arm. "It's a bad sign, talkin' to your cat," Lee said.

I tickled Cat under the chin. "I almost understand him these days." I tapped ash from my cigarette.

Dot spotted the striped envelope by my side. "Is that from Tom?"

"Yep. He sent it a month ago."

"He tell you anything important?"

"Not really." I hesitated. "He can't wait to start our *home life*." I looked at her.

She chewed her lip, eyes somber.

"What's wrong with that?" Lee said. He took a cigarette out of his pocket. "Gimme a light."

I held out my smoke so he could light his. "He didn't say what he meant."

Lee half-grinned. "How many meanings could it have?"

"He didn't say anything about me workin' once he comes home. 'Specially about me bein' a detective."

"But he only knows you're solving puzzles, right? If he wrote in April, it was before he got your letter tellin' him you'd decided to be a detective

CHAPTER THIRTY-SEVEN

as a job. So he can't mean anything about that because he doesn't know. " Lee was clearly tryin' to sound reasonable. "And it doesn't necessarily mean he wants you to give up work and stay home. I don't know why you're so upset."

Lee would stand up for his best friend. Yet he made sense, too. "Are you sure?" I asked. "What if that's exactly what he means?"

"Does it make a difference? You love him. Don't you want to be a good wife?"

I gave him a flat stare. "You're sayin' good wives stay at home? Hasn't this war taught you women can work and keep a house at the same time?"

His face reddened. "That's not what I meant. Don't twist my words."

I puffed on my Lucky. "Tell me this. Let's pretend you and Dot get hitched."

She blushed.

I ignored her. "When the war ends, what if she tells you she wants to work outside the house? What would you say?"

"I'd want to talk about it, of course," he said.

Dot stepped away and crossed her arms. "Let's talk now, mister. I'm s'posed to be the little housewife while you earn the bacon, is that it?"

He threw up his hands. "Holy smokes. I didn't mean it like that."

"What *did* you mean?" she asked.

He blew out a cloud of smoke. "There's no way you're gonna get me to say women can't or shouldn't work outside the home. Be reasonable. I've seen you two in action, and you're darn good at what you do, whether you're buildin' planes or findin' killers. I wouldn't want to take that away from you, and I'm pretty sure Tom won't either."

I ashed my gasper. "I sense a *but* coming."

"But." He grinned. "Marriage is a partnership, right? You gotta talk to each other. I'd want to have a conversation about what Dot wants, what I want, what we need as a family, stuff like that. And then we'd make a decision, together, about what was best for us. Same as you and Tom."

I didn't say anything.

"Right?" he asked, a challenging note comin' into his voice.

"That would be logical." I studied my cigarette. "I guess I'm just wound up about Edward. It's got me seein' things right and left. Heck, I thought I saw Frank Hicks followin' me earlier."

Dot's head swung in my direction. "He was? Whatever for?"

"That's just it. I'm not sure it was him." I told them about my day. "For all I know, it coulda been a guy who just looked...."

They waited for me, then Dot said, "Looked what?"

I blinked and focused on her. "That's what was botherin' me earlier."

"Huh?"

"About Mr. Riker and Mr. Townes."

Dot and Lee exchanged a look. "Do you know what she's talkin' about?" Dot asked him. "I'm lost. How did we get from Tom, to Frank Hicks, to those two?"

"When Sam and I went to talk to Mr. Townes, I thought, just for a second, I saw Mr. Riker. It's happened before today, too." I stood up, Tom all but forgotten in my excitement. "Don't you see?"

"See what?" Lee asked, the exasperation in his voice clear.

I was gonna have to slow down for my friends. "Mr. Riker and Mr. Townes look like each other."

They spoke at the same time. "They do?"

"Well, not really. If you see them close up, you know it's two different people. But if you just catch a glimpse of 'em, or see one of 'em at a distance, you might confuse one for the other." I told them about mistaking Mr. Riker for Mr. Townes when Melvin and I were waiting outside the apartment near D'Youville.

Dot spoke slowly. "Okay. But I don't get it. Why is that important?"

"Because." I threw my cigarette butt in the gutter. "When I talked to Mrs. Finch, that's Edward's landlady, she said the only person she'd seen the night Edward was killed was Mr. Townes. What if she really saw Mr. Riker?"

Dot scoffed. "I think she would know her own tenants."

"I'm sure she does. But what if she only glimpsed him?" I waited, but Dot frowned. "She might assume it was Mr. Townes. She mighta even talked to him." I swung my gaze to Lee. "You see what I'm gettin' at, right?"

His forehead showed the wrinkle it did when he was thinkin'. "I guess so.

CHAPTER THIRTY-SEVEN

But Betty, if she talked to him, she'd *know* it wasn't Mr. Townes. If that's so, why does she insist it was?"

It was a puzzle, but I was too excited to worry about it. "I'll figure that out later." I picked up Cat and spun him around, which earned me a yowl and a hiss. I dropped him and he stalked off with a swish of his tail.

"Okay, now I *don't* understand," Lee said. "Don't you have to know right now?"

"Relax. I'll talk to Mrs. Finch tomorrow, and it'll work out." I hugged him and then squeezed Dot. "You guys are the best."

Dot looked at her boyfriend, her expression blank. "Do you know what we did?"

Lee seemed equally as confused. "Haven't got a clue."

"It doesn't matter." I chucked both of 'em on the shoulder. "The important part is you did it."

Chapter Thirty-Eight

I went to Mrs. Finch's boarding house early Saturday morning. She was sweepin' her front sidewalk. "You again? I thought I'd answered all of your questions."

"You did, but I have one more," I said. "When I was here last time, you told me the only person you saw on the night Edward Kettle was murdered was William Townes. Is that right?"

"Yes. He was in the hallway," Mrs. Finch said.

"How did you know it was him?"

She puffed up. "Didn't you hear me? I *saw* him."

"Did you speak to him?"

"I sort of waved." She clutched her broom.

That struck me as odd. Why wouldn't she say good night or somethin'? "Did he respond?"

She shook her head, a quick, nervous gesture.

"Would you say that in a trial? When you're a witness in court, you have to tell the truth, or you'll get in trouble."

She paled, eyes wide.

I'd expected a stronger answer. That she'd be quite sure it was her boarder. Instead, she struck me as frightened. "Mrs. Finch, you can trust me. Did Mr. Townes look funny? Was he covered in blood?"

"No, *he* wasn't," she said in a squeaky voice.

I was dead sure she was scared. I heard the emphasis on *he*. "It wasn't Mr. Townes, was it?"

She stared at me. "I...I can't say."

CHAPTER THIRTY-EIGHT

"Can't or won't?" I stepped closer. "It's okay. I'm pals with the detective who was here when they found Edward. Anything you tell me, I'll tell him."

Mrs. Finch seemed to shrink in on herself. "Will he know?"

"Who?"

"The man in the hallway."

It hadn't been Mr. Townes. "Tell me what happened."

She shot a frightened look around, but we were the only two in sight. "I was on my way to bed. I passed the hallway, and I saw a man. I thought he was Mr. Townes, so I said goodnight and asked if he needed anything before I turned in. He didn't move, so I took a couple steps toward him. That's when I realized it *wasn't* Mr. Townes."

I hadn't been the only person to be fooled. "Did you know him?"

"No, it was a stranger. He...he had blood on his hands and the front of his shirt. He was standing outside Mr. Kettle's door. He said...he said to be quiet and not to tell anyone or else he'd come back to take care of me." She whimpered. "I really did think it was Mr. Townes at first. When the police came, I told them that's who I'd seen. I knew Mr. Townes was out. I knew the police would learn that, so he wouldn't get in any trouble. And I could always say I must have made a mistake or something."

"It's okay. I don't blame you for bein' scared." I hugged her.

"I lied to the police. I'll be arrested, won't I? And even if I'm not, what if this man learns I told the truth? She sobbed against my chest.

I patted her back. "You aren't gonna be arrested. I told you, I'm friends with the detective. You were threatened. It'll be okay."

She pulled back. "He killed Mr. Kettle, didn't he?"

"Yes, ma'am. I'm quite sure he did."

She pressed her hands to her mouth. "He'll come back and murder me in my sleep!"

"No, he won't." I handed her my handkerchief.

She blew her nose. "How can you be sure?" Her eyes were wide and red-rimmed.

"Because he's gonna be in jail." Just as soon as I could tell Sam I'd found his murderer.

Chapter Thirty-Nine

I left Mrs. Finch at her door and walked to the street. Melvin musta found out about Mr. Riker, or at least enough to make Mr. Riker nervous. He'd taken a big risk knifing Melvin in plain sight. Then again, I'd gotten fifteen different descriptions from witnesses. Maybe the risk wasn't as big as I thought.

I flicked my Zippo and lit a cigarette while I considered my next move. Should I call Sam? I could ask Mrs. Finch to use her telephone. But I'd learned in the past that Sam had his own sources. I doubted I'd find him in the office.

I was right. I left a message for him to call Mrs. Finch.

I could go home and wait for Sam to make the collar. But how long would that take? What if Mr. Riker sold whatever information he had from the shipyard and skipped town? Not only would he get away with murder, but with treason. I didn't know what the information was, but if I could protect our boys, my conscience told me to act, even if all I did was make sure Mr. Riker was around to be arrested.

My mind made up, I headed off. But when I got to the apartments on Fargo, Mr. Riker was gone. "Did he leave for good?" I asked the building super. "Or just out for a bit?"

He chuckled. "All his stuff is still up there, so I'm thinkin' he'll be back."

"Tell me. Did Mr. Riker ever mention owing money to anyone?"

"Never. We didn't talk much, but I told you before, he paid his rent. Albert was a little close-mouthed, come to think of it. Oh, he'd say hello and things, but he wasn't one for long conversation."

CHAPTER THIRTY-NINE

"Then he could have. Owed dough."

"I suppose. What are you getting at?"

I wasn't sure. "Can I take a peek at his place?"

He *tsked* at me. "I don't think I should do that."

"You think he'll be home soon?"

"No."

I craned my neck to look up the stairs. "It'd be real helpful if you'd let me in. Just to look around, and I won't be long. I promise I won't take anything."

He gave me a long, hard look. "It's the principle of the thing. The man hasn't said one way or t'other. How do I know you won't get Albert in trouble?"

"Or he could be in a bind, and what I find could help him," I said. "All I want to do is poke around. But if you don't wanna let me, that's okay."

He squinted at me, like he was thinkin' over his options. "I'm not lettin' you in by yourself."

I held up my hands. "You can watch me like a hawk."

He fumbled with a large ring of keys at his waist. "This way. God help me if Albert *does* come back and finds you here."

I had a feeling that wasn't gonna happen, but I kept my yap shut.

He led me up the stairs and unlocked the door to 2B. "This is Albert's place. I'll stand right here by the door."

I went inside. I had no idea what I was lookin' for, so I started with the overflowing desk in the corner. I picked up a stack of envelopes and flipped through what were mostly bills. Almost all of 'em were marked *Past due*. Whatever Mr. Riker had borrowed dough for, it had not gone to payin' his utilities. But I didn't find anything else, no personal letters or notes.

I sat down in the chair. The thing squeaked in protest as it tilted back. I turned my attention to the pile of newspapers on the floor. It was so high it was leaning to one side. There were old copies of the *Courier-Express*, some of which went back to summer of '42. He'd circled stories about American Shipbuilding and the project on the lake, but no details.

I tossed aside the newspaper. On the desk were copies of a magazine, *Seapower*. I skimmed the pages. "Was Mr. Riker ever in the Navy?"

"Not that he ever told me," the super said. "Why?"

"He's got copies of a Navy magazine." I held up an issue.

The super left his post by the door. "Oh, that. *Seapower* isn't for service members. It's information for civilians."

The issues jumped around in months, but they all had stories about aircraft carriers. In the margins, Mr. Riker had written "old." Old what? Had he been watchin' what was written and lookin' for something? Perhaps related to the work he was doin' here in Buffalo?

I took a quick look through the rest of the apartment, but there was nothing of value. A few chipped plates and a dented percolator in the kitchen. A hard, narrow bed in the bedroom with a battered wood dresser. All of the clothes had been taken out of it.

Mr. Riker had definitely left town. I faced the super. "You're absolutely positive Mr. Riker never talked about his work at the shipyard or needing dough, or any of his friends?"

He rubbed his chin. "No, I can't say that he did."

Darn it.

"We did talk about the Navy, though. I served in the Great War, hunting U-boats in the Atlantic. I mentioned how the Navy was fine, but how at least the boys in the trenches didn't have to worry about the deck catching fire under your feet."

I perked up. "What did Mr. Riker say?"

"Now, let me think." He rubbed his chin. "Something about how that was the last war and they'd have to find different problems to worry about, how it was more likely a boat would go down from being opened like a can of sardines than fire. I laughed and said as long as the decks were wood, fire would always be a problem. It didn't matter what the hull was made of."

Steel decking? Maybe. It'd go along with what Seaman Barnhard had said about metal shipments from Bethlehem. Sure, there'd still be fires, but metal decks would be a lot more immune than wood. If the concept worked on whatever they were buildin' down at the lake, it could be rolled out Navy-wide. How much would that information be worth to our enemies?

It was an idea.

CHAPTER THIRTY-NINE

My attention was caught by the contents of a metal trash can next to the desk. There was a pile of charred paper someone, most likely Mr. Riker, had tried to burn. I picked it out, careful not to smear ash all over my clothes. The top sheets were unreadable, but the flames must've gone out before the entire pile was consumed 'cause I could make out the writing on the last sheet. At least enough of it to recognize what it was.

Edward's address.

I leaned back in the chair, my mind churning furiously. "Albert Riker is a welder, right?"

"I think he mentioned that once," the super said.

"I know he was. He arranged to get assigned to this project. What if they're playin' with steel decks for ships?"

"That's crazy."

"Humor me. He'd be workin' on this new decking design, right? I don't know why he borrowed it in the first place, but I know he needs money. What if he sold the dope on the ship's new feature?"

"Albert would never do that," the super said. But the wobble in his voice betrayed his doubt.

I drummed my fingers on the arm of the chair. "But he's got a problem. His co-worker, my client, finds out and says he's gonna turn Mr. Riker in to the bosses at American Shipbuilding, if not the Coast Guard. Edward was an upstanding, patriotic guy. It's what he'd do."

"But you said your client was dead, murdered. You think Albert saw an opportunity to get this Edward fella out of the way and killed him?"

I shook my head. "Not at first. He told a reporter who was snoopin' around to talk to Edward. That got him, Edward, fired for suspicion of sellin' secrets, but nothin' was proved. Dollars to doughnuts, Edward went to Mr. Riker and doubled down on his threat." I stood. "Thank you, sir, you've been very helpful." I started toward the door. It all fit with what I'd talked to Lee and Dot about earlier. It was a good story. I thought Sam would find it very believable. Did he know? Was he on Mr. Riker's trail already?

The super's voice stopped me. "Are you gonna call the cops on Albert?

I turned. "I was just about to do that. Can I use your telephone?"

Chapter Forty

Outside, I looked at my pack of Luckys, but I only had a couple of smokes left, so I put them back in my purse. Sam had not been at the office. I left a message for him on the chance he'd call and could hot-foot it over to Fargo Avenue. It was likely he was out pounding the pavement, hot on the tail of Edward's killer. But was it the right one?

As I stood pondering my next move, I blinked.

Frank Hicks was across the street, staring at me.

I rubbed my eyes and looked again, but he was gone. I turned to the super, who'd followed me out. "Did you see a joe across the street? Young, dark hair, good looking."

The super followed my finger. "I don't see anyone. My vision at a distance isn't what it used to be, I'm afraid. The wife says I should get glasses, but who can afford them?"

I'd seen him, I knew I had. This was the second time Frank had shown up behind me. Three if you counted him bein' there when Melvin was stabbed. Was I wrong about Mr. Riker? I was quite sure I'd figured out his scheme at the shipyard. But what if he hadn't gone to Edward's that night to kill him? Or what if Mr. Riker had gone to Edward's house intending to off him and found Frank had beaten him to the punch? Would Frank decide to keep followin' me until he was sure I wasn't a threat? I nibbled my thumbnail.

I was bein' silly. Mr. Riker was my culprit, I was sure of it. Whatever Frank was involved in, and he definitely was up to something, it didn't have anything to do with Edward.

That didn't mean Frank wouldn't hurt me to keep me from exposing the truth about his activities with Mr. Jankowski.

I focused on the super. "One more question."

"What is it?"

"If you were gonna meet someone, and you didn't want to be seen, where would you go? It would be close to here." I couldn't explain it, but I was convinced Mr. Riker wouldn't leave his neighborhood for the meeting with his contact. He'd stay close to home and make sure he was on familiar turf, in case something went wrong and he had to scram, quick.

The super shrugged. "That's easy, Front Park." He pointed. "There was a military hospital there, but the land was sold in the 20s for the Peace Bridge. They demolished the buildings, but there's some good out-of-the-way meeting places. Because of the bridge noise, it's not real popular, so it'll be mostly deserted."

"Will you do me a favor?"

He scowled. "What now?"

"A homicide detective may come here lookin' for me. If I don't come back and tell you otherwise, would you send him to the park? Please?"

He threw up his hands. "Fine. Anything else you'd like?"

"No, sir, that's enough." I dug a fiver out of my purse. "Thanks again."

He took it and stomped inside.

I headed off toward the park. I had no intention of confronting Albert Riker. If he'd killed Edward, he'd shown he was capable of anything. But neither did I intend to sit back while a murderer, and possibly a traitor, got away scot-free.

* * *

I made my way over to Front Park. The grounds were scattered with tree limbs from an earlier spring storm. It must not be that popular a place if no one had cleaned it up yet. If Lee had been with me, he'd have recited chapter and verse on the fort's history. All I knew is that it was old. I could still see faint traces of the buildings that were knocked down when they built the approaches to the Peace Bridge. Even on a weekend, traffic, mostly trucks,

CHAPTER FORTY

made their way to and from Canada. It was an important crossing point between the two countries. I didn't remember the bridge opening. I'd only been three at the time. But Pop told me it was a big party. Even the Prince of Wales came to it.

I immediately saw why someone would come here for a secret meeting. It looked deserted. The truck traffic on the bridge muffled conversation, and between the building remains and a few clumps of trees, there was plenty of cover.

Looks could be deceiving, though. I transferred Sean's switchblade, which I'd taken to carryin', from my purse to my coat pocket. My knife wasn't nearly as big as the one Mr. Riker carried, but it was better than nothing. Not better than a gun, but I wasn't ready to take that step in my new career.

As I prowled around the park, I felt, more than saw, someone behind me. Each time I whipped around, ready to sock whoever was there, only to see empty space. "You're losin' your grip, Betty." I returned to my task.

Just as I was about to give it up as a lost cause, a man entered the park. A day ago, I might have been fooled by the similarity, but now I recognized Mr. Riker.

He kept to the shadows and headed for a stand of young oaks at the far corner of the park. I wiped my sweaty palms on my slacks, gripped my knife, and followed, stayin' quiet as Cat when he was on the prowl for mice. I got close enough to see Mr. Riker stop and flick a lighter twice. Then he put it away. It had to be a signal of some kind.

Another man came outta the trees. "You got the pictures?" he asked in the raspy voice of a man who'd spent a lotta years on a bar stool.

Mr. Riker didn't flinch. "You got the dough?"

"Show me the goods."

"You first."

Holy heck. The deal was goin' down right this minute. I shoulda tried harder to find Sam. When the two men parted, who was I gonna follow? On the one hand was a murderer. On the other was a man who could damage the U.S. military by sellin' secrets to the Axis. I immediately thought of Sean serving in the Pacific, facing the Japanese. Would his ship get these new decks? I knew then what I had to do. *Sorry, Edward. But we can nab Albert Riker later.* Somehow, I thought Edward would agree with me.

The unknown man held out a bag like the kind doctors carried, but it was dark, maybe leather, and even at a distance, I could tell it was a bit beat up. He opened it. "Five large, all in twenties, like you asked."

Mr. Riker pulled out a stack of bills and fanned them. "Do I have to count it?"

"You can if you want, but I'm gonna get outta here." The man shot a furtive look around the grounds.

I sidled around a tree. My foot came down on a fallen branch. The *crack* sounded louder than it prob'ly was. I froze.

The man's head whipped around. "What was that?"

"I dunno. Wait here." Mr. Riker pulled his knife from his pocket and headed toward me.

Mother Mary, help me. What could I do? The tree would be easy to climb, but I'd make a racket, and that would definitely tip the men off to my presence. Why couldn't Sam miraculously show up, like he had before?

I wasn't gonna count on a white knight. I tip-toed to another tree, keepin' outta sight of the buyer. Mr. Riker had disappeared. Where had he gone?

"Gotcha, you little sneak." His hot breath hissed in my ear, and arms like iron bands grabbed me.

I yelped, and instinct made me jab backward with my switchblade. It bit muscle, and Mr. Riker howled in pain. He let go of me, and I ran for it. I risked a glance behind me. The buyer had disappeared, along with the bag of cash. Mr. Riker was hot on my tail, blood darkening the leg of his trousers where I'd stabbed him, but the wound didn't slow him down much. I veered to my right in the direction of Porter Avenue, which I figured offered better cover than Busti Avenue, even though Busti was the closer street.

As fast as I was, Mr. Riker had longer legs. He ate up the ground between us. I wasn't gonna make it to safety. I yelled at the top of my lungs. I hadn't seen anyone, but maybe someone who lived nearby had decided to take a stroll. The sound of trucks on the Peace Bridge swallowed up my voice. I had to make it to the street, or I was a goner.

CHAPTER FORTY

A shape hurtled out of nowhere and crashed into Mr. Riker. He rolled and leapt to his feet with a feline grace I hadn't expected. I looked at my savior, expecting to see Sam.

It was Frank Hicks. "I'd leave the lady alone if I was you," he said, voice calm.

Mr. Riker spat. "What're you gonna do about it, boy? I don't see you holdin' a weapon."

"I'm a Quaker. We don't believe in violence."

"Then how're you gonna stop me?" Mr. Riker sneered.

I thought it was a pretty good question.

Frank remained calm. "You're going to stop yourself."

I couldn't help but look at him. Was he nuts?

Mr. Riker gave a short, ugly laugh. "Right. Boy, I've already slit one throat. What makes you think I'll hesitate one second to do the same to you?"

Also a good question.

I hadn't come to the park expecting a confession. Now all I had to do was survive long enough for the cops to show and make the collar. Did Frank think he was gonna talk Mr. Riker into giving up? I had my doubts, but at least his attention was focused somewhere other than me. I cast my gaze around the ground, looking for a better weapon than my little switchblade.

Frank continued to patter on in a soft, reasonable voice. Was this how he talked to violent patients? Could I trust him? *That's not important right now.* I would grill Frank on that later. After the man threatening to carve us into pieces was taken care of.

I spied a fallen branch on the ground, one that looked to be a good size, a few feet away. I inched toward it.

Mr. Riker swung around. "Don't move, sweetheart. I planned to take care of Quaker-boy here first, but I'm not picky."

Frank took a step forward. "You really don't want to do this."

"Shut your trap!" Mr. Riker switched his focus. "Girls might fall for those pretty-boy looks of yours, but they won't work on me."

I met Frank's eyes. *Keep him occupied*, I thought. With any luck, he'd read the message in my eyes.

It seemed he did, 'cause he resumed his soothing speech, while I crept toward the limb. I reached down and curled my fingers around the nice, thick branch. Not quite as good as a Louisville Slugger, but close.

Frank took a step backward. "I'm sure that if you examine your heart, you'll see that what you're doing is wrong."

"Maybe I'll examine yours instead, you chicken-hearted wimp." Mr. Riker lunged.

I swung with all my might.

CRACK!

Mr. Riker crumpled like a puppet that'd had its strings cut.

Frank looked at me. "I hope you understand. I couldn't hit him."

I threw aside the branch. "Yeah, well, good thing I could."

Chapter Forty-One

I stood over Mr. Riker's body while Frank crouched down and thumbed back his eyelids. "Did I kill him?"

Frank checked for a pulse and held his hand under Mr. Riker's nose. "No, but he'll have quite the headache when he wakes up." He stood. "I don't know whether to congratulate you or scold you."

"Seein' as how he'd have gutted both of us like fish without a second thought, a simple *thank you* is enough." I kicked away the wicked work knife that lay near Mr. Riker's outstretched hand. *Is this guy for real?* "Explain something to me. You wouldn't hit him, but you'd tackle him like a football linebacker?"

"I saw you in danger, and I reacted. I didn't give it much thought. I'll have to speak about this in meeting this week." Frank's dimple flashed, and he gave a little bow. "You have my gratitude. Although I had hoped neither of us would need to resort to violence."

Yeah, he had to be jokin'.

He must have read my disbelief in my expression, because he sobered and continued. "I meant it, Betty. Quakers don't believe violence is an answer. Ever." He glanced down. "Even smashing someone's head with a branch. You're right. You could have killed him."

"You heard him. He murdered Edward. Five'll get you ten he stabbed Melvin Schlingmann, too."

"I don't doubt you. Your reporter friend must have learned something that threatened Mr. Riker here."

I mused about the last call I'd had from Melvin. "He'd figured out that

257

Mr. Townes could be mistaken for Mr. Riker. He might even have learned Mr. Riker was the one at Edward's boarding house the night Edward was killed and was followin' that lead, maybe even the man himself. Mr. Riker cottoned on, and Melvin paid for it." Despite the warmth of the spring sunshine, I shivered.

"But why?"

Frank didn't know about the ships. I told him the whole story. "What are you doin' here? Lester Jankowski is nowhere in sight."

"After your friend was hurt, I was even more concerned for you. I knew you were after the same person." He gave me a solemn look. "When I said I wanted to keep you safe, I wasn't limiting myself to Lester."

I wanted to tell him I was the one who knocked Mr. Riker out, but I figured that would sound ungrateful. "Thanks. I wish Sam would show up and take this mook away."

Mr. Riker moaned.

"We need to tie his hands, quick. I shoulda thought of that before," I said. "You got any rope?"

"It's not something I carry around."

"What about twine or even string?"

"Fresh out."

"You're no help." I looked around, but there was nothing. "Grab his belt. We need to tie up his hands." I snapped my fingers. "The belt. Now." Frank tugged it loose and I used it to secure Mr. Riker's hands behind his back. Hopefully, that would do until Sam showed up. To be extra careful, I took a few steps so I'd be out of Mr. Riker's reach if he woke up.

Frank followed. "You said Albert Riker needed money." He ran a hand through his hair. "I wonder why he chose to betray his country instead of working off the debt."

"Guys who loan money like that aren't patient. Besides, he was taking a powder. I bet he wanted dough to skip town, not pay off a loan shark." I thought about my next words. "You ought to know a little bit about that, seein' as how you're workin' for Lester Jankowski. I bet whoever held the paper for Mr. Riker is the same."

CHAPTER FORTY-ONE

Frank looked away, but he didn't deny anythin.'

I pushed on. "What's up? If he's got you doin' somethin' illegal, maybe I can help."

The dimple reappeared. "That's very sweet of you, Betty. But it's not truly illegal." Frank exhaled. "Unethical, perhaps, but not illegal." He paused, perhaps thinkin' about what he wanted to say. "You know about my father, why he had to leave Philadelphia. The story is untrue. At least the part where my father had a role in the racketeering ring. He had no idea those men were using his store as a distribution center. The federal investigators realized that and dropped the charges."

"Why wasn't that the end of it?"

"Because people like to talk." A bitter twist touched Frank's smile. "Not long ago, one of my father's competitors from Philly expanded into the Buffalo market. He resurrected the rumors, hoping to put my father out of business. That was the first reason Edward Kettle came into my life. He didn't want his sister buying from a traitor."

"And Lester Jankowski was the second?"

Frank nodded. "Jankowski told me he could...solve my father's problems."

I crossed my arms over my chest.

He waved a hand. "Not that way. Not killing, I don't believe so. He said he could *encourage* my father's competitor to leave. I'm ashamed to say I didn't ask what he meant, and I didn't want to know." He hung his head.

I let him be quiet. He wanted what was best for his family. I could sympathize with that. I wasn't sure how far I'd go to protect Pop, but I didn't want to find out.

After a moment, he lifted his face to mine. "The help came at a price. Jankowski has a daughter. The girl is disturbed, has hallucinations, perhaps is in the beginning stages of schizophrenia. You may not know, but treatment for mental disease can be brutal." He exhaled. "Buffalo State Hospital takes a different approach. They try to be kinder. But it's expensive, and we don't have unlimited space."

The pieces snapped together. "Mr. Jankowski wanted you to pull some strings and get his daughter into the hospital."

"Correct." Frank gazed away at the passing trucks. "I'm not a doctor. I can't simply admit the girl into the facility. I was trying to use what little influence I had to get her preferred treatment from one of our physicians. I had finally found one willing to help, when Edward showed up again. He'd seen me with Jankowski and wanted to know what I was doing with a criminal. Of course, I couldn't tell him."

"Which meant Edward figured you were up to no good and threatened to go to the cops. Or at least get you fired."

"You are a smart woman, aren't you?" He didn't look at me. "Being a conscientious objector, my choices are limited. I have to work, but I can't take any old job. It's true I could do something in war manufacturing, like so many others. But I don't want to build materials for killing."

"You could be a field medic. I bet the Army'd take you for that in a heartbeat."

He faced me, his smile a little sad. "Perhaps. But I fear I'm not brave enough for the battlefield. How can I do any good when I'm cowering in a foxhole for myself?"

The note of reproach in his voice surprised me. This guy really thought he'd muff it and couldn't bear the thought of letting his fellow soldiers down. I didn't bother to point out that many of those men would be searching for cover themselves, that no one would blame him for bein' scared. "If you're so chicken, what brought you here today?"

"I've been following you since yesterday."

I smacked my hands together. "I *knew* I wasn't seein' things. Whatever for?"

"Your friend, Melvin, came to the hospital near the end of my shift. The way he acted, the questions he asked, I knew you were pursuing the murderer of Edward Kettle and getting close. That was bad enough. I didn't want you getting tangled up with Lester Jankowski, even a little bit. Especially if I could protect you. That's why I was there when Melvin was stabbed. I wasn't following him, but you." He waved at the semi-conscious Mr. Riker. "Good thing I did."

I didn't know whether to be flattered or insulted. A bit of both. "I can take

CHAPTER FORTY-ONE

care of myself."

"I don't doubt it. But you see, my beliefs don't just require me to renounce violence. I'm supposed to help people." He stepped closer to me. "And despite how difficult you can be, I do like you, Betty."

I fought the urge to lose myself in his warm brown eyes. Frank's smile suddenly seemed more than simple friendship. I swallowed hard.

"You're more than a pretty face," he continued, voice soft. "You're smart, a little impetuous maybe, but strong-willed. You aren't a detective because you think it's fun, you believe you can help people, and you want to. I admire that. I'd like to get to know you better. As a friend only, of course."

The air thickened. Frank's face came close to mine, his eyes half-closed. *He's gonna kiss me.* The thought panicked and thrilled me at the same time. Now that I knew he wasn't a killer, I wanted to see what kind of kisser he was. One little smacker couldn't hurt, could it?

I pulled away and stepped back. "I can't." Frank said now that he wanted to be friends. I was no dope. I knew the type of friendship I had with Lee was rare. I didn't want to break Frank's heart.

I didn't want to break Tom's, either.

Frank didn't look away from me for a good long moment. Then he let out a long breath, and his gaze dropped to the ground. He stuffed his hands in his pockets and half-turned away.

The sound of police sirens split the air. I stared at Frank as Sam pounded across the grass.

"Betty! Are you okay? I got your message. Is Riker here?" Sam asked. He stopped abruptly, and his gaze flicked between Frank and I.

I came back to myself. "He's over there. He confessed before I hit him on the head." I pointed at the branch.

"Is he dead?" Sam holstered his gun and crouched on the ground.

"No, but he might wish he was when he wakes up."

Frank cleared his throat. "Is there anything you need from me, Detective?"

Sam stood and studied the pair of us. "Yes. If you'd give a statement to one of the uniformed officers over there, that would be helpful."

Frank nodded. "I'll see you, Betty. Or not." He walked away in the direction

261

Sam indicated.

Sam turned to me. "What did he mean by that?"

"Just take care of your prisoner and leave me alone."

* * *

Frank and I gave our statements to the police, him to a uniformed cop, and me to Sam. Frank must have talked fast, because he was done way before I was. "You showed up only minutes after the action stopped."

Sam's gaze was too knowing.

I knew I had to be blushing. "What about the buyer?" I asked. "He got away."

"No, he didn't. My officers caught him running out of the park. He tripped, fell, and bundles of cash spilled out of his bag. So they held on to him. He'll be turned over to the feds."

"Good. I'd hate it if he got clean away. Do you need anything else?"

He paused. "You can go. If I need you, I know where to find you." He rubbed my shoulder. "Nice work on this one."

I thought about goin' home and waitin' for Lee and Dot to get back. But I owed a report to Genevieve Zellwig. I hopped the trolley to Hamburg. This time, I didn't dawdle as I strode through the village to her home and knocked on the door.

She opened it, perfectly dressed and made up as always. "Betty. Is there something you need? Do you have any news?"

"I found your brother's killer."

Her hand flew to her mouth. "Please, come in. Can I get you anything to drink?"

"No, thank you." I couldn't even pretend to want refreshment to be polite. I shoulda been flyin' high with another success under my belt. What was wrong with me?

We went to the same sitting room we'd used last time and sat in the same chairs. "Please, start at the beginning," she said.

I did. I talked for at least fifteen minutes. "Not only was Edward innocent

CHAPTER FORTY-ONE

of the accusations, he got killed 'cause he knew who really was guilty and wouldn't let it go. I guess he thought doin' the right thing was more important than keeping the facts about his private life hidden."

Mrs. Zellwig's smile was sad. "That is so like Edward. His dedication to the truth was impressive."

"Except when it came to himself."

"You have a point." She folded her hands in her lap. After a moment, she stood. "I'll get my checkbook." She left before I could object. She returned, sat, and opened it on her knee. "I believe you were going to charge Edward fifteen dollars per day. I said I'd double your fee."

"But I solved it by the end of the week. Edward paid in full. You don't owe me anything."

"I wouldn't be comfortable with that arrangement. He hired you to clear his name. I wanted you to find a murderer. It's quite different, and you've been working that all week." She uncapped a silver fountain pen. "That's thirty dollars times five days, which is one hundred and fifty dollars, correct? Math never was my strong subject."

I goggled at her. "Uh, your arithmetic is fine, but that's way too much dough."

"Nonsense. Oh wait, do you have any expenses to add?"

"Mrs. Zellwig, I can't take that. If you insist on payin' me, just gimme the same as Edward and we'll call it square."

She fixed me with a steely-eyed gaze. "I'm a woman who pays her debts, Miss Ahern. You found my brother's killer. You restored his honor by proving he didn't commit treason." Her eyes shimmered. "You don't understand how much that means to me. I loved Edward. I wish he could have reconciled with his family, but it's an imperfect world. One can't have everything." She detached the check from the book and handed it to me.

My hand trembled a little as I took it. I'd never held so much cabbage in my life. "You're welcome. I'm glad I could set your mind at ease."

She cocked her head, studyin' me much like a bird sizes up a worm. "If you don't mind my saying so, you look as though your own is a little troubled. Can I do anything?"

I stood. "No, ma'am, but thanks for askin.'"

Chapter Forty-Two

From Hamburg, I went to Our Lady of Victory Hospital to check on Melvin. I found him sittin' up, although his face was still pale. He was tryin' his best pickup lines on the nurse. She was ignorin' him. When he spied me, he said, "Hey, Toots! Aren't you a sight for sore eyes?"

I nodded at the nurse. "I see your powers of persuasion are as keen as ever."

"Nurse Fields is resisting my charms, but I can tell she's gonna crumble any second now." He winked outrageously.

She gave him a faint smile and left.

"You're breakin' my heart, doll," he called after her.

"You might wanna lay off," I said. "After you write this story and get a job at the *Courier-Express*, Irene'll get mad."

He sobered. "You've talked to Irene? How'd you find out about her?"

"Um, now, don't snap your cap. I kinda broke into your apartment." I told him the story. "I called her on my way over here. She said she'll be by to see you. Heck, she mighta stopped in while you were asleep."

He leaned back. "I don't know whether to be angry or impressed. I think I'm a little of both."

"Good."

"I told you I didn't kill Edward Kettle." He sat up straight. "Wait, after I write the story? You nailed him? Albert Riker?"

"This morning."

"I wasn't dreamin'. You *did* come to see me. I was so doped up, I didn't know whether it had happened or not."

"It did, and you helped me crack the case, too." I held out a bag. "Your old notepad was ruined, so I bought you a new one. And a pack of new pencils." He yelped in glee. "Holy mackerel! You gotta tell me everything. Wait." He pointed to the table across the room. "Get me a glass of water first."

I poured and handed it to him.

He gulped and gave it back. "Okay, shoot."

I flopped into the visitor's chair and told him the whole story. I didn't skimp on the details. After all, I had promised him juicy. "By the time the cops turned up, Mr. Riker was out cold."

Melvin calmed down enough to give me a solemn look. "You shouldn't have put yourself in such danger, Betty. What if Hicks hadn't turned up? Or your detective friend had been delayed?"

"I've gotten outta jams before. Besides, I was pretty well hidden until I stepped on that stupid twig. If that hadn't happened, Mr. Riker never woulda seen me, and I coulda gone to Sam without bein' in a lick of trouble." I shrugged. "But you wouldn't have such a good story. That reminds me." I stretched my legs. "What put you on to Mr. Riker in the first place?"

Melvin set aside his pad. "I was thinkin', and I realized Riker was too keen for me to finger Edward as the leak at American Shipbuilding. Why? Obviously, he didn't like Edward's, ah, lifestyle. Then I realized, who better to make a patsy for your crime than a joe who knew what you were up to? But that led me to wonder why Riker would turn traitor in the first place. Then I realized Riker and Townes look kinda the same. I wondered if the landlady had actually seen Riker when she claimed to have seen Townes."

"She did, she told me. As for motive, Mr. Riker wanted the money 'cause he was in debt."

"Yep. There are people who will pay a lotta dough to learn what new developments the military has. I don't know what it was, but Riker had to have had somethin' to sell." Melvin licked dry lips.

I poured another glass of water from the pitcher and handed it to him. "My guess is steel decking for ships." I told him my idea.

He drank and sighed with relief. "Good thinking. Anyway, my guess, and I'm sure your Detective MacKinnon will confirm, is that Edward found

CHAPTER FORTY-TWO

out about Riker. Shining the light on a traitor was more important than anything else, so he told Riker he was gonna squeal. Riker had to shut him up." He made a face. "In fact, I think I put my foot in it. I talked to Riker the day I was stabbed. I mighta told him too much, tryin' to make him mad enough to spill the beans. It didn't work, so I took off to follow a lead on Hicks. Riker followed me and tried to do the same to me as Edward." He looked at me. "I'm impressed you got me to the hospital."

"I didn't," I said. "Frank Hicks did. Turns out *he* was followin' *me* to keep me outta trouble since I wouldn't let the meeting with Lester Jankowski alone."

"What was up with that, anyway?"

"It's nothing to do with Edward." I told Melvin Frank's tale. "Edward saw Frank and Lester together. That's what led to their argument."

"Hmm." Melvin eyed me. "You want to say somethin' I can tell. Spit it out."

"I know I told you not to write anythin' until after the case was over, and then you could write whatever you wanted. But I got two requests."

He waited.

"Please don't write that Edward was a homosexual. Leave that truth hidden. The man died exposing treason, let him be a hero and let his family live in peace."

"That's one, what's the other?"

"Don't mention Frank Hicks. That whole arrangement has nothin' to do with Edward's death. Frank's only tryin' to help his family. If it comes out that he's makin' deals with criminals, he'll lose his job. There aren't many he's allowed to have, I guess."

I expected him to immediately say that as a member of the press, he was honor-bound to write everything. Instead, he stared at me for a long minute.

"Deal," he said.

I couldn't believe my ears. "You won't?"

"I'm a reporter, Betty. Not a lowlife. You're right. Those truths have nothing to do with the story and won't help anyone."

"Well, gosh, Melvin. Thanks."

His eyes twinkled. "Besides, this piece is gonna go a long way toward winning Irene back. I wouldn't wanna put that at risk."

Self-interest wins the day. Now *that* was the Melvin I knew.

* * *

I found Lee and Dot sittin' on his back porch. "Betty!" Dot said, crushing me in a hug. "We heard about Albert Riker's arrest on the radio. Are you okay?"

"You're gonna get burned." I held my cigarette away to avoid settin' her curls on fire. "I'm okay. At least I will be, as long as you don't bust one of my ribs."

She released me and stepped back. "Are you sure? You look kinda funny."

"There's nothing wrong with me. At least not physically."

Lee stretched his bum leg. "What happened? The radio only said Riker had been apprehended at Front Park, and two unnamed civilians on the scene were unharmed. But we knew it was you. Who else was there?"

I talked. And talked. And talked some more. Even thought it was at least the third time that day I'd told the story. I included everything about confronting Mr. Riker, Frank's intervention, my visit to Genevieve Zellwig, and my chat with Melvin. "And that, as they say, is that." I did not tell them about the almost-kiss between Frank and me. I didn't think either of my friends could handle that.

Lee whistled. "One hundred fifty bucks? Are you serious?"

"Yep."

"Sellin' out the Navy and murder. What a rat. He deserves to fry." Lee lit his cigarette and shook his head.

Dot's attention, however, snagged on another detail. "Frank Hicks was followin' you?"

I knew that's what would grab her. "That's what he said. He didn't want me gettin' in trouble with Lester Jankowski."

She folded her arms. "Would you have?"

I puffed. "I think so, yes. If I'd continued, which I'm not sure I would have

CHAPTER FORTY-TWO

done, once I learned Frank wasn't the killer. What Jankowski wants Frank to do, it's not exactly against the law. But it isn't right, either. They'd be puttin' a fix on the admissions system at the hospital and jumpin' the line."

"And he said he just wants to be friends?"

"Yup."

"Do you believe him?"

Lee's head jerked up. "Dot, drop it. It's none of our beeswax." But from the look he gave me, he was askin' himself the same question.

* * *

At dinner, my family was appropriately amazed at the dough my latest investigation had brought in. Mary Kate and the boys made me promise to take them to the candy store. I offered to give Mom some for the house budget, but she waved me off, sayin' I'd be better off putting the money in my trousseau.

"I'm gonna write to Tom," I said after we finished eating. "After I help clear up, of course."

"Nonsense," my mother said in a brisk voice. "Mary Kate can help me. You go do what you have to. I'm sure wherever Tom is, he'll appreciate a letter from his sweetheart."

I shut the door to the room I shared with Mary Kate and sat at the desk, took out a sheet of paper, and began to write.

Dear Tom,

I got your last letter. You said you'd be out of touch for a while. I hope wherever you are, you're safe. Well, as safe as you can be in the middle of a war. Lee, Dot and I were talking about you earlier. We all miss you. Lee and Dot send their love.

I finished up a new case today. This one was a real humdinger.

I stopped. Would he want to know? His last V-mail sat on my desk. *I can't wait to start our home life.* I knew what my folks had, what Lee's had before his father crawled inside a bottle. I wasn't sure I wanted to stay at home like Mom or Mrs. Flannery, but I wanted a good life. Tom didn't want to hear about his fiancée puttin' herself in danger.

I crumpled up my letter and tossed it in the trash. After I rewrote the first paragraph on a fresh sheet, I continued.

My life is very different without you. I don't know how long this war is going to go on or how much I'll be changed when you come home. Honestly, I expect you'll change, too. I guess that'll be up to us to figure out.

Until then, stay safe. I think of you every day and light a candle every week at church. I'm looking forward to you being home. It'll be like you never left.

All my love and still your girl,

Betty

A Note from the Author

The Corn Belt Fleet was a real thing. When the idea of training naval pilots on the Great Lakes was first proposed by Commander Richard F. Whitehead, then an aviation aide at the Great Lakes Training center, it was dismissed. However, after the attack on Pearl Harbor, it was resurrected, this time with more enthusiasm.

Two luxury steamships, the SS *Seeandbee* and the *Greater Buffalo*, were sent to the American Shipbuilding Company in Buffalo. There, they were converted into faux aircraft carriers, which were christened the USS *Wolverine* and USS *Sable*, respectively. The USS *Sable* was outfitted with experimental steel decking to replace the wood commonly in use. After work was complete, they were sailed to Chicago, where they were used for training.

Pilots had to complete ten successful takeoffs and landings (later reduced to eight) before they were assigned to duty in the Pacific to fight the Japanese. More than 17,000 Navy pilots qualified on these ships and as many as 40,000 sailors were trained as flight crews, leading one Naval historian to dub them "the top guns of 1943." One of the graduates was George H.W. Bush, who would later become the 41st President of the United States.

To say the 1940s was not a good time for the LGBTQIA+ community would be an understatement. Homosexuality was illegal and most gays went to excessive lengths to conceal their private lives, resorting to codes and secret gathering spaces. When I decided to write about this time period, I consulted with fellow author John Copenhaver. Very little written history exists, leaving much to the imagination, but he did direct me to James Lord's *My Queer War*, Robert Peter's *For You, Lili Marlene: A Memoir of World War II*, and Jeb Alexander's *Jeb and Dash: A Diary of Gay Life, 1918 – 1945* as resources. The rest is my imagination, but my instincts tell me it's not too far off the mark.

I have used language I believe is accurate for the times and many thanks go to both John and Edwin Hill for supporting me. While these words may make people uncomfortable, it is crucial that we not whitewash the sins of the past. As the saying goes, "those who forget history are doomed to repeat it." Since straight, cis-gendered people continue to use this language and perpetuate horrible acts, it is important to note that while we have come far since the 1940s, there is still so much work to be done.

Acknowledgements

This was a particularly challenging book to write, and I have many people to thank for getting me to the finish line.

As always, thanks to my critique group—Annette Dashofy, Peter W.J. Hayes, and Jeff Boarts—for keeping me on point, pushing me when needed, and pulling me back when I've gone a little too far. You guys are the best.

Much love and gratitude to the staff at Level Best Books and the Historia imprint—Harriette Sackler, Shawn Reilly Simmons, and Verena Rose—for allowing me to continue Betty's story.

Many thanks to John Copenhaver and Edwin Hill for encouraging me when I said, "I'm thinking of writing this book." John was generous in sharing resources for research, and both were supportive of my language decisions. I am honored to call them friends. Go buy their books.

I could not be a published author without the support, wisdom, education, and resources from both Sisters in Crime and Pennwriters.

A big shout-out to my father, Gary Lederman, for always answering my frantic texts about Buffalo's history. It's like having a research librarian on call.

And last, but never least, my love and gratitude to my family, especially my husband, Paul. I love you.

About the Author

Liz Milliron is the author of The Laurel Highlands Mysteries, set in the scenic Laurel highalnds and The Homefront Mysteries, set in Buffalo NY during the early years of World War II. She is a member of Pennwriters, Sisters in Crime, International Thriller Writers and The Historical Novel Society. She is the current vice-president of the Pittsburgh chapter of Sisters in Crime and is on the National Board as the Education Liaison.Liz splits her time between Pittsburgh and the Laurel Highlands, where she lives with her husband and a very spoiled retired-racer greyhound.

Also by Liz Milliron

THE LAUREL HIGHLANDS MYSTERIES
Lie Down with Dogs
Harm Not the Earth
Broken Trust
Heaven Has No Rage
Root of All Evil

THE HOMEFRONT MYSTERIES
The Lessons We Learn
The Stories We Tell
The Enemy We Know